THE
EVER
KING

TITLES BY LJ ANDREWS

Broken Souls and Bones

THE EVER SEAS SERIES

The Ever King
The Ever Queen
The Mist Thief

THE
EVER
KING

BOOK ONE IN THE EVER SEAS SERIES

LJ ANDREWS

ACE
NEW YORK

ACE
Published by Berkley
An imprint of Penguin Random House LLC
1745 Broadway, New York, NY 10019
penguinrandomhouse.com

Copyright © 2023 by LJ Andrews
"The Ever King Bonus Scene" by LJ Andrews copyright © 2025 by
Victorious Publishing, LLC
Excerpt from *The Ever Queen* copyright © 2024 by LJ Andrews
Excerpt from *Broken Souls and Bones* by LJ Andrews copyright © 2025 by
Victorious Publishing, LLC
Penguin Random House values and supports copyright. Copyright fuels creativity, encourages diverse voices, promotes free speech, and creates a vibrant culture. Thank you for buying an authorized edition of this book and for complying with copyright laws by not reproducing, scanning, or distributing any part of it in any form without permission. You are supporting writers and allowing Penguin Random House to continue to publish books for every reader. Please note that no part of this book may be used or reproduced in any manner for the purpose of training artificial intelligence technologies or systems.

ACE is a registered trademark and the A colophon is a trademark of
Penguin Random House LLC.

Title page art: Crown © tomertu / Shutterstock
Book design by Alison Cnockaert
Map by Eric Bunnell

Export edition ISBN: 9798217190188

Library of Congress Cataloging-in-Publication Data
Names: Andrews, L J, author.
Title: The Ever King / LJ Andrews.
Description: First Ace edition. | New York: Ace, 2025. | Series: Ever Seas series; book 1
Identifiers: LCCN 2024050610 (print) | LCCN 2024050611 (ebook) |
ISBN 9780593955024 (hardcover) | ISBN 9780593955048 (ebook)
Subjects: LCGFT: Fantasy fiction. | Novels.
Classification: LCC PS3601.N55268 E94 2025 (print) |
LCC PS3601.N55268 (ebook) | DDC 813/.6—dc23/eng/20241031
LC record available at https://lccn.loc.gov/2024050610
LC ebook record available at https://lccn.loc.gov/2024050611

The Ever King was originally self-published, in different form, in 2023.

First Ace Edition: August 2025

Printed in the United States of America
1st Printing

The authorized representative in the EU for product safety and compliance is
Penguin Random House Ireland, Morrison Chambers, 32 Nassau Street,
Dublin D02 YH68, Ireland, https://eu-contact.penguin.ie.

A man he's not, we work we rot,
No sleep until it's through.
A sailor's grave is all we crave.
We are the Ever King's crew.

To the queens who love the beautiful black heart of the villain.
Face it, they're hotter than the hero.

AUTHOR'S NOTE

Welcome to the dark world of the Ever. I hope you enjoy the book and the deep, possessive romance between Livia and Erik. That is the reason for this note—some might find early actions of our morally gray Ever King the kind that blur the lines of right and, well, brutal.

He's not snuggly (at least not until we peel back some layers), so know that some of his actions are dark and vicious.

The world of the Ever is set in the same world as my Broken Kingdoms series, bringing the fae Vikings of that series some sly pirates, bone ships, and sea shanties. Please note, my nautical friends, that although I did research on the swashbuckling lifestyle, this is a fantasy book, and I have taken liberties with my *Ever Ship* that might differ from historical accuracy of the vessels sailing the Caribbean seas.

Without further ado, welcome to the Ever.

CONTENT WARNINGS

Descriptive scenes of torture
Family abandonment
Explicit sexual content
Gore
Violence
Mutilation
Bullying
Panic attacks
PTSD
Dark themes
Murder
Anxiety
Kidnapping
Traumatic brain injury from torture

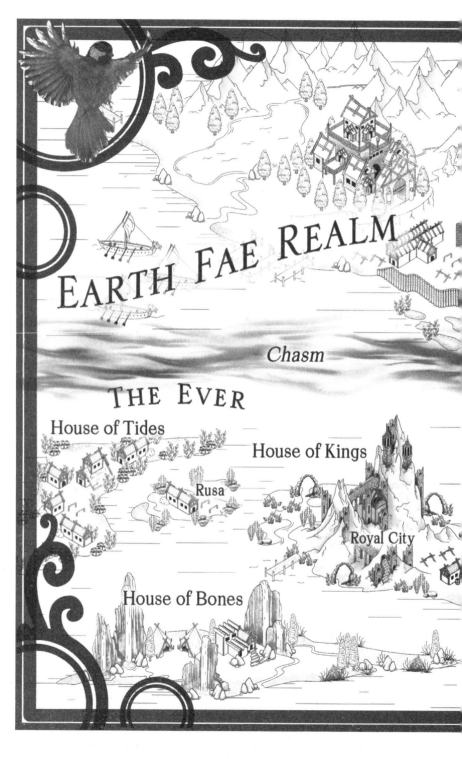

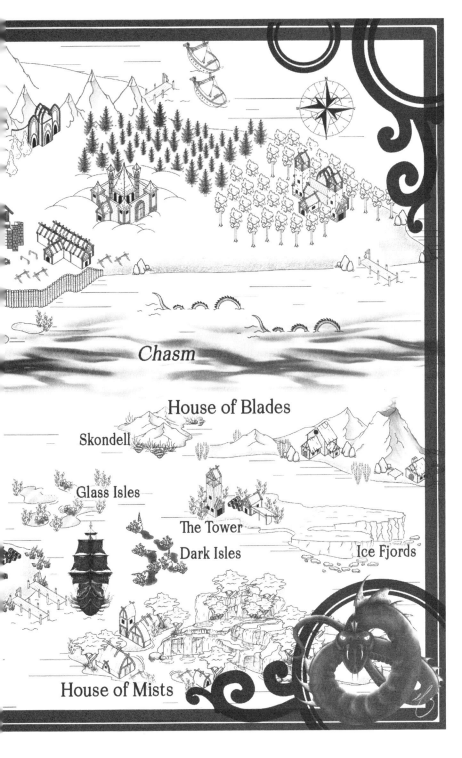

THE
EVER
KING

PROLOGUE

That Night

THE ENDING NEEDED to be altered.

The girl spent the whole of the afternoon crossing out lines with her raven feather quill, then adding new, better words to read to the boy in the dark. A tale of a serpent who befriended a songbird. A tale where they lived happily ever after, for in the girl's version, the snake never devoured the bird.

Long after the moon found its highest perch in the night sky, the girl slipped from the loft in the battle fort near the shore. Crouched low, she used the tall snake grass as a shield until she found her way to the old stone tower. The top had caved in, and it wasn't much of a tower anymore, but the walls were as thick as two men standing side by side.

Along the foundation, iron bars covered a few openings. In her head, the girl counted six barred windows before she crouched at the final cell.

"Bloodsinger," she whispered. Since the end of the battle, she'd practiced the breathy pitch to be loud enough that the boy inside would hear, but the guards stomping along the borders would think it nothing more than the hiss of a forest creature.

Five breaths, ten, then red eyes like a stormy sunset appeared from the shadows.

He was a frightening boy. A few turns older than her, but he'd fought in the war. He'd raised a sword against her people's warriors. A boy who still had dried blood on his skin.

Her heart squeezed with a strange dread she didn't understand. This was the last night she might see the boy; she needed to make it count.

"Trials come with the sun," the boy said, his voice as dry as brittle straw. "Better leave, little princess."

"But I have something for you, and I've got to finish the story." From the pouch slung over her shoulder, the girl took out a small book bound in tattered leather. Inked over the cover was a black silhouette of a bird and a coiled snake. "Want to hear the end?"

The boy didn't blink for a long pause. Then, slowly, he sat on the damp earth and crossed his legs under his lanky body.

The girl read the final pages marked in her new, palatable ending. The songbird and serpent grew to be friends despite their differences. No lies, no cunning, no tricks. Each word drew her closer to the bars until her head rested against the cold iron and one hand drooped between the gaps, as though reaching for the boy inside.

"'They played from sunup to sundown,'" she read, squinting at her messy writing. "'And lived happily ever after.'" A smile crossed her features when she closed the bindings and glanced at the boy.

He'd reclined back onto his palms now, legs out, bare ankles crossed. "Is that what we are, princess? A serpent and a songbird?"

Her smile widened. He understood the whole point. "I think so, and they were still friends. That's why tomorrow at the trials you can, well, you can say we won't fight no more. My folk will let you stay."

No more blood. No more nightmares. The girl couldn't stomach any more blood from hate and war.

When the boy kept quiet, she dug back into her pouch and took out the twine. On the end was a silver charm she'd used her last copper to buy. A silver charm of a swallow in flight.

"Here." She held out the handmade necklace through the bars and let it fall. "I thought it could remind you of the story."

All at once, the distance between them was a blessing. Any closer and the boy might see the flush of pink in her cheeks. He might see that her hope in the charm was less about recalling the tale and more about remembering *her*.

With slow movements, the boy took hold of the charm. His dirty thumb brushed over the wings. "Tomorrow, I'll be sent away, or I'll greet the gods, Songbird."

Her stomach dipped, and something warm, like spilled tea, flooded her insides. Songbird. She liked the name.

"That's what happens when you lose a war." The boy's lips twitched when he placed the twine around his neck. "There's no stopping it."

The race of her heart dimmed. She dropped her chin. Hopeful as she was, the girl wasn't a fool. She knew the only thing saving the boy's neck was that he *was* a boy. Should he be a man, he'd lose his head. He had fought against her people; he hated them.

Like the serpent from the story hated the birds in the trees for their freedom in the skies.

She didn't care. A feeling deep in her bones drew her to the boy. She'd hoped he might be drawn to her too.

Hope failed. True, he was young, but he'd always be marked as an enemy. Banished and forbidden.

She blinked and reached once more into the fur-lined pouch. "I know this is important to your folk. Thought maybe you'd want to see it once more."

The girl cupped the gold talisman shaped like a thin disk with care. It was weathered and aged and delicate. A faint hum of strange remnants of magic lived in the gritty edges. If her father ever learned she'd snatched the piece from the lockbox, he'd probably banish her to her room for a week.

The moonlight gleamed over the strange rune in the center of the coin. The boy in the shadows let out a gasp. She didn't think he'd meant to do it.

For the first time since she'd started reading to him, the boy climbed up the stone wall and curled his hands around the bars. The red in his eyes deepened like blood. His smile was different. Wide enough she could see the slight point to his side tooth, almost like the fang of a wolf, only not as long.

This smile sent a shiver up her arms.

"Will you do something for me, Songbird?"

"What?"

The boy nodded at the disk. "That was a gift from my father. Watch over it for me, will you? I'll come back to get it one day, and you can tell me more stories. Promise?"

The girl ignored the wave of gooseflesh up her arms and whispered, "Promise."

When the sound of heavy boots scraped over the dirt nearby, the girl gave one final look at the boy in the darkness. He held up the silver bird charm and grinned that wolfish grin once more before she sprinted into the grass.

The speed of her pulse ached as she hurried back to the longhouse. Her gaze was locked on the disk in her hands; she never saw the root bursting from the soil. The thick arch snagged the tip of her toe and sprawled the girl face down in the soil.

She coughed and scrambled back to her knees. When she looked down, her insides twisted up like knotted ropes. "Oh no."

The disk she'd promised to protect mere moments before had fallen beneath her body. Now the shimmer of gold lay in three jagged pieces in the soil. Tears blurred her vision as she gathered them, sobbing promises to the night that she'd fix it, that she'd repair what was broken.

Perhaps it was the despair that kept her from noticing the strange rune that once marked the surface of the disk was now branded on the smooth skin below the crook of her elbow.

In time, the more she learned of the viciousness of the sea fae who attacked her people, the more the girl looked back on that night like a shameful secret. She made up tales about the scar on her arm, a clumsy stumble down the cobbled steps in the gardens. She'd forget the boy's promise to come for her.

The girl would start to think of him as everyone else did—as the enemy.

If only the girl had kept away from those cells that night, perhaps she would not have unraveled her entire world.

1

THE SONGBIRD

BLOOD WAS IN the air. Pale sunlight had barely clawed through ashy sea mists around the shore, but the hot tang of blood filled my lungs with each breath.

I pulled back the thick woven shades to see if some gory death had taken place at the base of my family's tower. The dirt roads carving through the wood-and-stone fortress we called home for two weeks every summer were filled with loud merchants and courtiers preparing for the festival.

No bones. No flesh. No blood.

I let the shade fall back into place, my thumb tracing the roses and ravens embroidered in the threads—symbols for our Night Folk clans in the kingdom of the North. The kingdoms of the East, South, and West had their own unique markings.

I was losing my damn mind. Brutal nightmares of snakes devouring little birds took up my sleep. Now I was bringing the blood and death from dreams into reality. Maybe it was because the Crimson Festival marked the end of the war. Or maybe it was because this festival was the tenth since our enemies, the sea fae, were locked beneath the tides.

With every fading summer, the haunting dreams grew more vivid, like a waking nightmare. A distant promise from a lanky boy locked in a cell had become a poison in my mind, an endless image of monstrous serpents rising from the sea night after night.

I was a fool. There hadn't been a single whisper of Sea Folk since the Great War ended. This summer would be no different.

To soothe the tension in my blood, I opened a drawer in a table beside my bed. Inside were three lumps of what once was the rune talisman. Since the disk shattered, the pieces had grown more brittle, as though returning to nothing but sand on the shore. They were hardly shapes anymore.

I slammed the drawer closed, climbed back into the wide bed, and pulled the heavy fur quilt over my head. Alone, I could succumb to the race of my uneasy pulse, the damp sweat on my palms, and the nervous tremble in my veins.

The fortress was designed to house all four royal families of the fae realms. To the Sea Folk we were all earth fae, but in truth, we were made of clans with different magics and talents.

All the clans fought together to win peace during the Great War against dark fury—what my clan called magic—and the folk of the Ever Kingdom—the sea fae. *His* people. The festival was an excuse to celebrate the victory and gave me a reason to see everyone I loved through days of field games, archery, lively balls, and too much sweet ale. I couldn't puzzle through why this summer felt so . . . different.

"Livia!" A heavy pound on the thick oakwood door rattled the rafters overhead. "You're needed and yet are nowhere to be found. I noticed your absence first, in case you ever wondered who cares for you most."

It must be terribly late in the morning if Jonas was the one sent to fetch me this time.

A strategic move. Well played. That vulgar tongue of his was equal parts charm and weapon. He knew how to use it well.

"Woman troubles!" I shouted, muffling my voice into the pillow. "Best to move along."

"I'm up for the challenge." A pause, then a few clicks came from the latch, and the door swung open.

I shot up in the bed, frowning. "Jonas Eriksson, I warned you about picking my locks."

Jonas flashed the roguish grin that won too many hearts in his home court in the East. "I do recall you once said I was forbidden to do so, and I simply forgot to care."

Bastard.

Jonas filled the doorway with his height and width. One of two princes of the Eastern Kingdom, he'd been busy as a child, and even more active as a man. Jonas's body was made for battle while still being lithe enough to slip between shadows like a thief in the night.

His agility around locks and small spaces would be unsettling if he was sinister. The truth was, Jonas and his twin, Sander, couldn't help their proclivity to sneak. They'd been raised by a rather cunning king and queen who'd both thieved themselves a time or two.

Jonas strode to the tall window and tossed open the heavy curtains. I blinked when the sunlight burst through the room, and a gust of wind followed, carrying with it more imagined blood, more hints of the sea.

Jonas spun around to face me, his hands on his hips as he smirked.

"Pleased with yourself?" I scratched my scalp through wild tangles of my dark braids.

"Immensely." As the eldest of the Eastern princes, Jonas's bright verdant eyes and the devious grin beneath the dark scruff on his jaw kept more than one lady slipping into his rooms. If they knew the goodness of his loyal heart under all his schemes and wit, they'd never leave him in peace. "Get up. The coaches are about to leave."

Gods, how late did I sleep?

"Hurry, Liv. I mean this with love. It's going to take some time for you to get presentable. You look like a goat swallowed you, then shat you out."

"Have I told you that you're *not* charming?"

"Many times. You're still wrong." Jonas dropped one knee on the foot of my bed. "You seem distressed, Livie. Tell me what's troubling you."

"Nothing is troubling me except you."

"You wound me." He pressed a hand to the emblem of a sword encircled in shadows stitched to his dark tunic. His court's seal. Jonas's face sobered a bit as he studied me until I wanted to sink under my quilt from his scrutiny. "No teasing. Are you all right?"

My shoulders slumped. A downside to having friendships built from infancy was knowing every tell and every flinch of each other's faces. We knew the other's weaknesses and strengths. Their fears.

I fell back against my pillows, eyes locked on the rafters. "I had the dream again last night."

"Well, dammit." Jonas tossed aside the three knives sheathed to his belt, kicked off his boots, and crept over my bed. "Why didn't you say so?"

The idiot positioned himself against the wooden headboard, crossed his ankles, and opened an arm, beckoning me to his side.

I didn't move.

Jonas raised his brows and flicked his fingers. "I'll wait all damn morning, Livie. You know I will."

"You're wonderfully wretched."

Jonas chuckled. I gave in and nestled against his side. He kept his arm tight and protective around my shoulders.

For a moment, we were silent. Then, his deep voice rumbled from his chest against my cheek. "I know the festival brings a lot of memories, I know those sea sods left with a lot of threats toward your daj and family, but they're never coming back. And if they did, it'd be my honor to cut old Bloodsinger's head clean off."

I smiled and hugged his waist. Only my friends knew about the dreams I'd had since the end of the war. When the serpent in my dream came for me, when its jaw unhinged and swallowed me whole, somehow even in my dream, I knew it was sent by Erik Bloodsinger.

The Ever King.

He blamed Valen Ferus, the Night Folk king, for the death of his father.

It was true, my father had killed King Thorvald of the Ever a turn before I was even born. But he'd had damn good reason to do it.

Erik had been a boy during the wars, with nothing but threats and unattainable promises.

I knew all this and still couldn't shake the heavy weight of something dreadful on the horizon. As if peace were some fragile bit of ice, and it was only a matter of time before it all cracked.

"Now"—Jonas wrapped his other arm around me, sank a little against the headboard, and rested his stubbled cheek against my forehead—"let's get your mind off things, shall we? You know Lady Freydis—"

"Jonas, I swear to the gods, if you keep talking—"

"No, listen. Something happened, and I can't quite wrap my mind around it."

I sighed. "Fine, what happened?"

"Last night we arrived at the fort, and everything was going as usual. Sander hurried away to be strange and stick his nose in books. I had delightful plans with Freydis arranged from last turn's festival, so it wasn't a surprise to find her in my room."

I rolled my eyes but grinned. Jonas genuinely seemed befuddled by something. If he had any sense, he'd realize Freydis had an interest in his title, much like his interest was in her body, not her heart.

"What happened?" I asked, pinching his side. "Did she demand a crown yet?"

"Not at all," he said. "You see, she wasn't alone. There with her was Ingrid Nilsdotter."

My eyes widened. "You're not serious."

"Oh, I'm very serious. Now my question comes, because at one point there was a position where we—"

"Gods. Stop!" I shoved him away, scrambling out of the bed.

"What?" Jonas gaped at me. "I thought you'd want to help. Freydis did this thing with her legs, then Ingrid—"

"Jonas, don't say another word, or I will cut out your tongue." I rushed to the corner of my room and ripped open the painted wardrobe door. Frantically, I rummaged through gowns, tunics, trousers—anything to get me away from this fool and his salacious trysts with courtiers. Behind the dressing shade, I hopped on one foot as I slid into a pair of black trousers. "Go speak to Sander about all this. I mean, truly, what possessed you to think I'd ever want to know about . . . ?"

My words died off when his laughter drew me to peek around the shade.

Jonas, hands laced behind his head, reclined back with a smug kind of grin on his handsome face. "No, don't stop getting dressed. You're doing so well."

Jaw tight, I threw one of my ankle boots at his head. "You said all that to get me out of bed."

"I deliver on what I say, and I promised you'd be down there with us. Don't question my methods when they work. Especially on important days like this." Jonas slid off the bed and picked up my dainty silver circlet shaped like a vine of blossoms. "Did you forget the new Rave officers arrived this morning to see our parents off to council? Meaning, Alek. Remember him? Last I knew, you were beloved cousins, but perhaps it has changed these six months he's been gone."

The grin couldn't be helped. Aleksi was more like a second brother. He'd earned his officer rank in the Rave Army and had been stationed in the Northern frosted peaks for training the last half turn.

"I haven't forgotten, you snob." I'd looked forward to this moment when we could all be together again, and one dream had tossed me into unease, distracting me from the Rave caravan that arrived to escort the kings and queens to their annual council.

I scrambled to finish dressing, rinsed my mouth, and resorted to Jonas's help in smoothing my braids.

A quarter of a clock toll was all it took before I abandoned my bedchamber, my blacksteel dagger sheathed at my waist and an arm laced through Jonas's.

"I bow to you, my friend," I told him once we reached the winding staircase to the great hall of the fort. "That was one of your better lies to get me moving."

He pressed a kiss to my knuckles, grinning. "Ah, Livie. Who said it was a lie?"

2

THE SONGBIRD

THE FORT WAS abuzz with tailors and seamstresses fitting courtiers and nobles for gowns, fine jackets, and doublets for tomorrow's masque. Servants and warriors trekked the steps up to the four corner towers to ensure the rulers of every realm were well tended.

While the Night Folk clan tower was quiet and docile, the second tower, belonging to the Eastern realms, always had a great deal more noise heard throughout the fort.

"Is Sander tormenting your people?" I asked Jonas when we crossed through the open great hall. As beautiful as his brother and equally as sly, Jonas's twin brother brought out the solemn side of the pair. Where Jonas reveled, Sander observed. When Jonas fell into bed with a new lover every gathering, Sander remained with us—his friends, his family, his familiars.

Jonas peered toward his family's tower and laughed. "No, I think someone called my daj 'Highness' or some other royal term of endearment; now the hells are breaking loose."

I laughed, but in reality, it could be true. Like my parents, all the kings and queens of our realms fought wars for their titles. Not all were born into the life of a royal, and the twins' father much preferred being remembered for his life as a schemer and thief than a king.

"There they are. Looks like Alek is being swarmed. Gods, look at that sod." Jonas pinched his mouth in disapproval. "He's returned to us all proper and stiff."

Outside the open gates, our families were gathered near a caravan of black coaches surrounded by our Rave warriors. Aleksi, dressed in his dark, silver-trimmed Rave uniform, was enveloped in embraces, croons, and praise from the royals of the Night Folk clans.

I chuckled when my cousin offered polite grins but shook out his hands in unease. His soft brown skin was clean-shaven, and his thick chestnut hair was braided down the center of his head. Kohl lined his golden eyes and his lips.

"He's stiff because you know how he feels being the center of attention."

Jonas snorted. "You can't tell me Alek isn't secretly dreaming of becoming a grand hero. He's just quiet about it."

We quickened our pace, carving through the preparations, my gaze on my cousin and family. Alek's fae ears were sharper than mine, but only because I was half fae. I grinned when my mother's icy, pale braids came into sight when she wrapped her slender arms around Alek's shoulders, holding him close.

Elise Ferus was a fae queen, but mortal by birth. Her life was extended like the fae folk's after she underwent a fury spell once she took vows with my father.

Jonas strained his neck. "Dammit. Look at the sky. We'll hit storms if we don't get to the cove soon."

The doors to the wooden gates were tied back, letting in the shimmer of sunlight on the dark water. I followed his gaze to the jagged edges of the shore. Angry clouds still rolled over the horizon. Almost like they were waiting for some catalyst to bring the storm's rage to our doors. Fear wanted to take hold, wanted to convince me the dread I felt earlier was some dark premonition of something to come.

Not far from the shore, a dark streak carved over the surface of the sea. A current where the water was different, where the sea frothed like stagnant waves that never crashed onto shore. The Chasm, a barrier between my people and the fae of the sea.

Most folk hardly paid it any mind during the festival, but I could never look away. Almost as though the tension in my chest was simply waiting for the warded barriers of the Chasm to peel back and a rush of sea fae to burst through.

Another poisonous thought left to fester from promises made by a boy in a prison cell.

The Chasm was sealed. Undisturbed as always.

Breathe. Focus. Nothing was different. The fortress was well guarded, with Rave guards trudging the watchtowers and outer gates. Laughter still filled the corridors, be it from a servant or noble. The Chasm was there, a mark of a different world, but one locked away between the tides.

Nothing had changed. It wouldn't change.

"We have plenty of time to watch you get drunk on the shore. Come on, there are the others." I led us to a canvas canopy, where the heirs of every realm hid from the morning heat.

Sander Eriksson lifted his dark green eyes from the yellowed pages of a leather-bound book. The same eyes as his brother, but with even more cunning. "Livie. What story did Jonas tell to get you down here?"

"You don't want to know." I released Jonas's arm and went to stand beside Mira, the princess of the Southern Kingdom.

She adjusted the circlet in the shape of spread raven wings braided into her auburn hair and gave me an exasperated look. "Take this beast from me."

Rorik, my younger brother, kept flinging a wooden sword and catching Mira's hips or thighs as though a fierce enemy stood in his sights. Only nine, and small for his age, Rorik made graphic battle sounds as invisible invaders died gruesome deaths.

Sander slapped his book closed, tucked it into the back of his trousers, then scooped Rorik onto his shoulders. "You want to be a Rave, Ror?"

Rorik grinned. "Hells yes."

I reached up and flicked the tapered point of his ear. "What did Maj say about language?"

"Don't be snitchin', Livie, and she won't know."

Jonas barked a laugh and clapped hands with the small prince. "Ror, when did you become a smartass?"

I gave Jonas a strained look when my brother went on to repeat the word "ass" at least three times. Rorik was small but had a ferocious spirit and idolized the Rave, Aleksi most of all. My brother had the same dark eyes as our father but lighter hair, as if the paleness of our mother were trying to break through.

"Alek looks like he's going to toss his insides." Jonas jabbed his elbow into his brother's ribs. "Ten gold penge he vomits from whatever trauma the higher ranks put him through in the peaks."

Sander held Rorik's legs and mutely assessed my cousin as he approached his commanding warriors. "I'll take that bet."

Mira rolled her eyes and muttered, "Always the same with you two."

I bit my cheek. There could be no stopping the twin princes from scheming and making sly deals. Ploys and tricks were in their blood.

"He's going to go." Jonas gripped Sander's forearm, studying Aleksi without blinking. "There he . . . dammit."

Aleksi strode with unmatched confidence as he bid farewell to the commanders in each Rave unit. Jonas had reason to make the gamble. Regal as he appeared, Alek despised the attention his rank engendered in the courts. As a prince, now a Rave officer, doubtless he could feel the prickle of every eye as he clasped forearms with his fellow warriors.

Jonas pressed a fist to his mouth when Aleksi turned without a misstep to greet his fathers—my uncles, Sol and Tor.

Sander held out a hand once Aleksi successfully embraced both his fathers without a stumble. Jonas cursed and slammed ten coins into his brother's palm.

A horn blew from one of the watchtowers.

"Finally," Jonas muttered.

"Your mother would be heartbroken if she knew how desperately you wanted her gone," I whispered.

"How dare you," he said, affronted. "My mother is the light of my heart. But I have plans for this festival, and there are some things a mother should not be privy to when it comes to her son."

"He's never been the same since Maj walked in on him with one of his sparring partners a few months ago," Sander said, voice low.

Jonas blanched. "It was awful. Couldn't look her in the eye for weeks."

Rave gathered around the coaches. Sander removed Rorik from his shoulders and joined Jonas as they left us to bid farewell to their family. Mira went to hers. I took my brother's hand despite his protests and dragged him toward our clan.

Our people—the Night Folk fae—had the gods-gift of controlling the earth, while the Eastern realms with Jonas and Sander used tricky magic of the mind and body. Mira's people took the Southern and Western edges, where fae could twist fate, shape-shift, or compel the mind with cantrips and illusions.

My gaze drifted to my mother and father.

The waves of my father's ink-black hair were tamed, and the

sides were braided off his face, revealing the points of his ears. He whispered something to my mother, a contrast to him with her ice-pale hair and crystalline eyes. She covered her mouth to hide a laugh at whatever he had said.

Both were brutal warriors but tender and loving to each other to the point of nausea. If ever I found a love, I'd always secretly prayed it would be like theirs.

"Alek!" Rorik called out even before shouting for our parents.

Aleksi grinned and shoved through the crowd, aimed straight for us.

A little shriek of excitement scraped from my throat when I practically choked my arms around his neck. He caught me around the waist and squeezed tightly.

"You're not allowed to leave me with Jonas's short attention span for six months ever again."

Alek laughed and gestured to his new uniform, complete with a new seax blade. "Well, what do you think?"

I trapped his strong face in my hands. "You look snobbish, pretentious, and dull."

Aleksi's laugh rumbled deep in his chest before he smashed me against his side, suffocating my face in the pit of his arm. "What was it you said? Formidable? Incomprehensibly powerful? Cousin, I can't hear you. What did you say?"

Winter brought my twentieth turn and, with it, Aleksi's twenty-first. We still managed to bring out the childishness in each other.

"Bleeding hells, Alek!" Rorik's lips parted. "You've got a captain's blade!"

Aleksi kneeled in front of the boy to show him the new seax. I was half worried my younger brother was going to swoon, and the other half was concerned he might burst into tears, the way he stroked the steel of the blade.

"Livie." My mother's soft touch fell on my arm. She studied me for a breath, as though she knew my night had been turbulent. She always did. "All right, little love?"

"Fine." I hugged her waist and let my head fall to her shoulder even though she stood shorter than me. "All gone with the dawn."

My mother stroked my arm, gentle and safe. She'd done all that could be done to ease the nightmares that had plagued her daughter for turns. Sleeping draughts, letting me curl between her and my father, lullabies, assurances. Now she simply held me like this, letting me know she was always there.

With a sigh, she tilted her face to the sky. "I hope tomorrow's games aren't wet for you."

"Better not be 'cause I'm gonna kick Alva in her stupid legs," Rorik said, abandoning Aleksi and slashing his wooden sword again. Alva was the daughter of my father's first knight and had somehow become the prince's ultimate rival. "They're so long, like twigs. I bet I'll snap 'em in two."

I snorted. Rorik slashed his sword again in sloppy strikes to his invisible villain. He had a long way to go before he donned the black gambeson like Aleksi.

"Gods save me from this boy," my mother muttered under her breath, then closed her eyes. My mother was no weak thing, but I had a feeling a son like Rorik would be the undoing of any mother.

All at once, Rorik stopped his imaginary battle and beamed when another Rave approached. "Stieg!"

Stieg was my father's captain and had been beside my parents before they even took vows, turns before the war of the sea. He was as steady as the sun and as firm as granite, and I was certain Rorik dreamed not of the crown he'd been born into, but the day he served beside Stieg.

The captain stepped next to Rorik, a smirk on his battle-gnarled lips. "Practicing, young prince?"

"Always."

Stieg chuckled, ruffling Rorik's hair. Scars, inked runes on the captain's cheeks, and the bone hoop pierced through his nose added a touch of ferociousness, but one look at the playful gleam in the steel of his eyes gave away his true temperament.

"The coaches are ready, My Queen," Stieg said, tipping his chin in respect.

My mother sighed, and when she looked at me, her brow furrowed in concern.

I linked my arm through hers. "Maj, I'm fine. Go. Be free of us for a few sunrises."

She covered my hand on her arm with her palm. "Ten turns. Hard to think you were not much older than Rorik when all the fighting ended. This turn's festival is a landmark in how far we've come, so it *feels* different."

My skin prickled. Did she feel the unease as I did? I swallowed, refusing to spiral into thoughts of what it could all mean if everyone had a bit of disquiet this turn. Odds were I felt strange for the same reasons as my mother. A great deal had changed, and these significant turns caused us to think back on everything that had happened.

That was all.

Rose thorns wrapped around a dagger and a battle-ax were painted on the doors of the Night Folk coaches that would take my uncles and parents to the annual royal council.

Councils were always held at the palace of the last king and queen to be crowned. Both were rather keen to avoid large gatherings like the Crimson Festival and welcomed the different clans to their palace in the knolls, a two-day's distance.

There, they oversaw any troubles in the realms, likely reminisced about the wars they had all fought together, and kept our world locked in continued peace.

My mother drew both Rorik and me into another embrace and kissed my cheek and the top of his head. "Liv, swear to me you'll be wise, safe, and will keep Jonas from making ten new Eastern heirs while we're gone."

"How would he do that?" Rorik asked.

Maj and I shared a look and laughed, pulling him close a little longer.

While she fussed over Rorik and the ways he would be expected to abide by Stieg's orders in their absence, I slowed my steps as I approached my father's back. No one ever surprised the man, but he was distracted by conversation with my uncles enough that I just might—

"Hello, little love." My father turned around when I had two paces left.

"Gods, Daj. I think your fury accentuates your ears." I rolled my eyes and waited for him to open his arms before dipping around him and embracing my uncle Sol first.

To stir the brotherly rivalry between the two was wholly worth it when my father frowned and glared at his brother.

"Uncle," I said, "I feel as though I've not been able to speak to you since we arrived."

Sol was handsome like my father, but instead of dark Night Folk eyes, his were deep blue like mine. He pressed a gentle kiss to my forehead. "Because my king is an ass and demands all my time."

A choking noise from my mother drew our eyes. She glared at Sol and jabbed a finger toward Rorik, who, again, muttered "ass" under his breath.

Sol mouthed a quick apology, then winked at me. "Girl, you look more like your lovely mother every day. Fortunate for you."

The praise was welcome, but a stretch of the truth, and utterly meant as a jab at my father.

True, my mother was beautiful, but eyes were the only thing we shared. Even then, the sea blue of my eyes matched Sol's more than hers. My skin was a soft, roasted brown like my father's, and my hair was a shade of night with hints of red and a touch of blackened blue.

I batted my lashes, then stepped to embrace my uncle Tor. Serious and thoughtful, Tor was a beautiful balance to his royal consort. I had fond memories of learning the patience of battle from Torsten. He was firm, decisive, powerful, and cunning with every strike.

By the time I met my father's gaze, he'd clasped forearms with Aleksi, shooting me a glance over my cousin's shoulder. "Oh, is it my turn now?"

I wrapped my arms around my father's waist. We had a bond, and ever since I was young, he'd been the safest place I could think to fall.

He pulled back, a smile on his face as he cupped my cheeks in his rough palms. "I've decided to take you with us to the council."

I smirked. He said the same thing every turn.

"Valen, you will not," my mother called from beside the coach. "You will let her out of your sight and let her be free."

"Free to be scooped up by fools who only think with their cocks," he called back.

"All gods." My mother closed her eyes, then kissed Rorik's cheeks with a look of pity. "It is no wonder he says the things he does with such a family."

"Liv." My father let an arm drape around my shoulders as he pulled me to one side. "I wanted to warn you, I've had more than one request from"—he swallowed like he'd tasted something sour—"our noblemen for your *time*."

My heart stopped. "Time, as in . . ."

He frowned. "They're interested in a match, little love."

All gods. Foolish to be taken off guard by such a thing; I was the heir of the Night Folk clans, the whole of the region in the north. I would be expected to claim a consort or husband eventually. The truth throttled me from behind. Of age, yet I'd hardly experienced . . . *anything*. A few stolen kisses from gentry boys across the kingdoms, usually on dares to show Jonas I wasn't a prude.

I wasn't bold with men, but Mira was the only one who knew how inexperienced I was in the facets of love.

A match. It sounded so . . . dull.

I didn't want a match just because that was expected. I wanted passion, the burn that if my love didn't touch me soon, I'd burst. I wanted heat and mess and obsession.

What if I selected a match only to discover we bored each other after five turns, and I never experienced another's hands?

"Livie." My father tilted his head, voice low while the others chatted around us. "You know I'd never agree to anything against your will."

"I know." I forced a smile and gripped one of his hands.

He kissed my knuckles. "It does leave me unsettled to know a slew of unworthy bastards will be here with you while I am not."

"I wouldn't worry, Daj. I'm surrounded by overprotective men. One wrong move and there will be missing fingers."

He scoffed and tugged me against his side. "Forgive me, but putting your safety under the watch of Jonas Eriksson does not put my mind at ease."

"I heard that! Now I feel I must prove you wrong by stirring something on purpose." Jonas's voice rose over the bustle from his family's coach.

"See? No worries," I said through an embrace. "Stieg and much of the Rave are with us."

My father pressed a kiss to my forehead. I bid farewell to my mother and uncles once more, then watched as every ruler over the fae realms loaded their coaches and left the fort, Rave guards following on foot or on horseback.

While leaders of the realms toiled over duties, on the morrow their heirs, nobles of the gentry, warriors, and courtiers would celebrate with games, archery, ax-throwing, sailing trips around the coves of the isles, then the masquerade with more feasting and debauchery when the sun faded.

Guards were always nearby. Even Jonas and Sander had appointed guards, but they were rarely seen, forced to be as sly as their royal charges, who sought to lose them every turn. It was safe here. We could roll our eyes, taunt our parents, but they would never leave us completely unprotected.

When Rorik was taken in by Stieg and three more Rave guards assigned to the youngest prince, Jonas approached with arms open.

"Let the festival begin." He clasped Alek's forearm. "Welcome back. Now that you're trained to cause violence, may I place a request to have you as my personal guard at the masque tomorrow? I have a feeling I will need doors protected from any snooping. Don't be alarmed by any noises you may hear."

"No," Alek said. "And maybe, just once, you might actually dance on your feet."

"Gods, how boring. I'll keep my way of dancing, thank you." Jonas twisted his grin into one of his devious smirks, the kind that added an attractive dimple to his cheek. Tonight, Jonas's schemes must've fallen to me, for he turned his dark gaze to mine. "May we finally begin celebrating *our* way."

"Is it wise to go so near the Chasm with a storm on the horizon?" Mira was the one who asked, and I was glad for it. My heart was restless, a constant thrum of trepidation, and for the first time in turns, I didn't want to think of that day the sea fae were locked behind the wards of the Chasm.

"Yes," Jonas insisted. "More so since Livie is nightmaring again, and from this moment on, there is no more fretting during the Crimson Festival. Now, come on. Let's see if we find any of those sea singers."

3

THE SONGBIRD

WHEN WE WERE littles, Aleksi and I would spend nights in sprawling forts we'd build out in the gardens. My fury connected to the earth, as for most Northern fae. I was able to thicken shrubs, brighten blossoms, even heal deadened soil.

Our forts used to look like something out of a storybook forest.

There we'd huddle around a lantern, and Aleksi would tell me scary stories about the sea singers and their proclivity to hunt the land folk for our strong bones. He had a knack for description, and I was still a little convinced every blade and necklace owned by a fae of the deep was made from the bones of their enemies.

If Jonas and Sander were visiting, the tales grew even darker. Their magic was different than my bright fury—they worked in nightmares and darkness.

Anyone who did not know the twin princes would never guess they could create such fearsome images, then force it into one's mind. A fear that had not existed before, and after they were through, would never be forgotten.

Once we all matured into our abilities, we didn't use them against each other like we had as children. So the fear clinging to my heart like a leech didn't come from a trick of the twins. It was nothing more than my own cowardice.

I sat stiff on the bench of the longboat, one knee bouncing. Mira untied her thick auburn hair and let the sea wind run through it like the fingers of a tender lover. Aleksi and Jonas rowed. No mistake, a subtle competition was underway with how they kept glancing at each other and digging deeper with every stroke.

I folded my fingers on my lap and kept a firm watch on the approaching shore of the jagged isles that marked the boundary of the Chasm of Seas—the divide between the waters of our folk and those of the Ever Kingdom.

Strange, sometimes, to think there was a world beneath the waves. I could read all the texts from poems to sagas to lore, and the truth was that none of us truly knew what lived in the Ever.

Was it nothing but wet all the time? Did eels and fatted whales enter sea cave homes?

Black currents thrashed against the skiff as Aleksi and Jonas carefully guided the boat into a cove. Fear was heady, like stones piled in my belly, but there was a pull to the water. A fascination I couldn't dull. The mightier I tried to turn from curiosity, the mightier came the pull to the sea. Like a thick rope around my belly, it yanked me back to the edges between two worlds.

"Out." Jonas waved his hands at us and reached into a black leather satchel shoved under one of the benches. From it, he removed a bottle with rich amber ale inside. "Tonight, we start the revelry off the way it should be done. Honey brän."

I used the scratchy rigging to heave myself out of the skiff and onto the sun-heated stones. "Only you would get sloshed so close to the Chasm."

"This is why we're here, Liv," he said. "Hells, I'm half convinced Bloodsinger's dead. Probably beheaded by his folk after we tossed him back into the sea."

I ignored the way the thought burrowed like a thorny bramble in my chest. It'd be best if the heir of the Ever was dead and gone. I laughed to prove to Jonas—and myself—I felt the same.

Sander built a fire on the shore. Mira handed out small sponge cakes with toffee syrup filling the center.

"Krasmira Sekundär." I sang out her full name and popped a small cake onto my tongue. "Did you take these from the cooking rooms *before* the festivities began? Against the rules, my friend."

She huffed; her stormy eyes narrowed. "Yes, I shall go down in the sagas as the vicious princess who stole some cake."

Sunlight bled across the horizon like a streak of blood as night came to swallow the day. Soon enough we'd all be pulled away by members of our unique courts vying for our attention. At the first festival, we'd missed each other and stolen away to hide and celebrate amongst ourselves for half a night. Only us.

Ever since, we always spent the first night together as friends, away from duties and propriety.

We danced, laughed, and taunted Jonas about his confusion over how to handle two women in his bed. The way he finished off the last of the brän, I was certain he took our taunts as a challenge to take no fewer than three at once.

"Jonas, I beg of you, don't do this." I laughed; my head spun a bit in a lightheaded ale haze. "You'll just get injured, and your father will have to get you un . . . unstuck."

Mira giggled, letting her head fall to Aleksi's shoulder.

Sander smirked. "Daj wouldn't save him. He'd shame him by bringing everyone around to gawk at him."

"This entire conversation is pointless." Jonas blew out his lips and rubbed the stubble on his chin. "First, Daj would never shame me; I'm his favorite. Second, there is no realm in any kingdom where I would get *stuck* or *injured* doing what I am skilled at doing."

"Oh?" I said. "And what is that?"

"I think you know, Liv, but I'd be happy to describe it in detail. You might learn a thing or two."

I snorted and rose to my feet. "Ah, Jonas, one day some fearsome creature is going to steal your heart, and you will not know what to do with yourself."

He reclined onto his elbows and crossed his ankles, a wicked kind of grin on his face. "One lover for the rest of my days? I think not."

"Speaking of lovers," Aleksi said, eyes on me. "What do you think of rumors that more than one noble sod has been talking to Uncle Valen, Liv?"

The brän all at once didn't sit right in my gut. I waved the thought away. "I think if the rumors are true, they are brave souls to approach my father instead of me."

"Well spoken, Livie! Make them kneel!" Mira shouted. She clapped a hand over her mouth, squeaking out a drunken laugh when it dawned on her she'd bellowed her declaration.

Sander lay back on the sand and closed his eyes. "They're fools if they think your father would hand you over for some political alliance."

A smile teased my lips. Talk of suitors had changed over the turns. In a different time, perhaps it would be common for a father to arrange his daughter's marital vows. Not my father.

When my parents met each other, it had been at my mother's dowry ball. The king had arranged for her to be bartered for a strategic match, and the highest bidder would be the winner. My father was not even in the running; now they were rulers over a realm. They of all people would never force a match on their children.

I supposed I'd always been waiting for the burn in my heart, a feeling of insatiable need and desire. I wanted the passion I saw amongst my own folk, and now, looking back, I'd likely passed opportunities to be daring, feckless, to be left breathless from a night meant solely for pleasure.

A Jonas way of thinking, but not such a silly idea. I had nothing but inexperience to offer anyone.

"Maybe you won't be forced to take a husband," Jonas said, voice heavy with drink. "But if drunken bastards start to hang all over either of you two, they'll wind up missing."

There was a bite to his tone. Even drunk, even nearly a turn younger than me, Jonas was like a protective brother who didn't take well to men looking at Mira and me for our rank alone.

Hazy with drink herself, Mira hooked one of her slender arms around his neck and pressed a loud, wet kiss to his cheek. "You know, as stupid as you are most days, you have one of my *favorite* hearts."

He sloughed her off and flopped back onto the sand, humming the eerie song of the sea—one that tantalized the hair on my arms like a frightening memory. "A man he's not, we work we rot . . ."

I turned away, their songs, laughter, and drunken insults to each other at my back. My steps were unsteady, so once I reached the water's edge, I carefully positioned myself on the ledge of a thick stone to watch the sun fade over the dark sea.

A moment later, Aleksi sat beside me. "Thoughts?"

With a sigh, I let my head fall to his shoulder. "Many."

"I have two ears."

"I don't know, Alek. Something feels different. Now all this chatter about vows and suitors. I feel like I'm spinning forward, yet not really living."

"What do you mean? You're the heir of the Night Folk."

"Yes, because I was born to it. I spar with you and Uncle Tor, but beyond knowing the blade, what have I done? I hardly use my fury. I haven't . . . well, I haven't even tried to know people outside of you four."

"You mean men?"

Heat flushed my face. "I mean everything. I look at you, all handsome in your new gambeson, and I realize I've not really strived to be more than comfortable. Even Rorik has a desire to be something more than his birthright, and he's nine and insane."

Aleksi grinned. "Then be reckless, Liv. This festival, forget propriety, forget the nerves. I know, I know, easy for me to say. But maybe this is your gut telling you to be daring. A little bold. Who knows what might happen?"

I nudged his side with my elbow. "Odd thing coming from you, honorable Rave."

Alek scoffed and reclined onto his elbows. "Spend months with First Knight Halvar and his men, and you realize even the most honorable of our warriors have been more than reckless."

I grinned. "Maybe you're right and I should do something bold. Something out of the ordinary for me."

My cousin hugged me to his side as the sun sank deeper, until it was hardly a sliver over the sea. The fading gilded light sliced through the dark water. It brought a calm, a strange peace, watching the water ebb and flow over the dangers of the Chasm.

"Alek," I asked. "Do you really think Bloodsinger is dead?"

He stiffened. Aleksi never liked to speak about the sea fae, and I didn't truly know why.

"I think he is nothing we need to think about. Dead or alive."

I didn't know why my mouth opened or why the words spilled out like vomit. Blame the drink, but I couldn't stop myself before I whispered, "I lied."

"About what?"

"I have been bold once before."

"Oh really? How is that?"

A sting gathered behind my eyes. Gods, not here. When I drank too much, tears flowed over the simplest things. Sander was a sleepy drunk. Jonas grew pensive and thoughtful. Aleksi held ale like a stone. Mira giggled. I bleeding cried.

My voice croaked and whimpered with ale-soaked words as I blurted out the truth at Aleksi's feet. The truth of the story I read to the boy in the dark, the token of friendship in the shape of a silver bird, the truth about the golden emblem of the Ever.

I left out the part about my scar. No doubt a critical part of the story, yet my brain was desperate for Aleksi to tell me I was overthinking. It didn't want confirmation of the fears, not really.

I swiped my hand under my nose. "I was going to convince Erik Bloodsinger we didn't have to be enemies. We could be friends. He even promised to return for his stupid golden disk someday."

"Is that what's been bothering you lately? His threat means nothing, Liv. Erik Bloodsinger cannot come through the barriers. Ever." Aleksi's jaw pulsed. "Did you not know this?"

I buried my teeth into my bottom lip. There were comments made through the turns that the Ever King would never see the land again, but I always took it for boastful talk amongst warriors.

"After the war, they used his blood to create the barriers. They guard against it. Nothing is strong enough to break those walls." He eyed the sea for a few breaths, then smacked my knee with the back of his hand and stood. "I'll prove it."

My cousin stripped his tunic.

"What the hells are you—"

"Care to go for a swim?" The gold in his eyes flashed with a touch of mischief so rare for dear, honorable Aleksi.

"Are you insane?"

"No. I promise I won't let your precious royal neck drown, but I want you to see what it means to cross the Chasm."

A few more breaths, a few more inner words about why this was a terrible idea, then the brän took hold, and I went to the water's edge, hardly caring that I remained fully clothed.

Hand in mine, Aleksi winked and began to count to three. He made it to two, then wrenched me into the waves in one great leap.

Cold stole my breath like dozens of stitching needles in my pores. I swallowed against the shock, then embraced the tug of the currents.

I'd always been drawn to the sea. Days spent fishing with my daj or swimming in the fjords in the Northern realms were some of my fondest memories. Slowly, I blinked my eyes open. The sting of seawater irritated my eyes until they adjusted. Whether it was fury or simply the magic of the sea, my vision cleared like looking into glass.

Aleksi tugged on my hand and pointed straight ahead. From the shore, the Chasm was nothing more than a dark stripe, a deep current that flowed in opposition to the rest of the sea. But here, beneath the waves, it was a bleeding cyclone.

Water thrashed and spun in a frenzy. The Chasm split the gentler currents of our barriers like a true wall. White frothy currents flowed from sky to sea floor, while the calmer sea stuck to the flow of the horizon.

I was enthralled, drawn forward like an insect captured by a web weaver. Somewhere in the chaos rose a sweet tune, a voice soft and gentle, one that blotted out any other sound. My pulse raced, like the song was calling to me.

Unbidden, my hand stretched forward. A tug somewhere deep in my belly drowned my muddled mind with nothing more than an insatiable need to draw closer. I flattened my hand against the roar of the Chasm wall. At once, I yanked it back. What felt like a hot barb jabbed my palm and scorched along my skin until it raised the ridges of the rune scar on my forearm.

Aleksi pulled me away, eyes narrowed, and used his head to gesture to the surface.

"What the hells, Livie? I wanted you to see it, not touch it." He wiped water from his eyes and swam closer. "You get sucked in there, I'd be going in after you, then I'd get our family's first mark of shame for being removed from the Rave the same day I was promoted."

My pulse pounded in my skull. I wasn't certain I heard much of his rant at all.

"Liv." Aleksi nudged my ribs. "You all right?"

I licked my lips free of the salty water and smiled. "Yes. I'm glad you showed me. You're right. How could anyone get through without emerging half dead?"

"Did you sods see that?" Jonas's slurred voice drew our attention. He pointed the bottle of brän toward the darkening horizon. "Lightning, but it looked like fire."

Aleksi pulled himself free of the water, then turned and offered a hand for me. "Lightning often looks like fire, so you're likely right on, Jo. Well done."

"No, you sod, it was red."

Mira whooped. "The gods are announcing the Crimson Festival!"

Jonas laughed and loudly agreed. Onshore, Alek faced me. "No more thinking he's coming, Liv. He's not."

I wrung my damp hair and nodded. "You've proved your point."

"Good, because we have greater worries right now."

"Like what?"

My cousin looked over his shoulder. "Like how we're going to get Jonas off his ass before this storm hits."

Aleksi jabbed a finger toward the sky.

"Better hurry," Mira called to us.

Mountains of ashy clouds rolled over the sea like a marching army. Aleksi hurried ahead, but a shudder rippled down my spine. The raised scar had grown red and irritated, almost scorched. I wasn't troubled by my skin, no more than I was troubled by what I'd seen when I touched the Chasm.

An omen was the only explanation. The instant the water of the barrier licked my skin, for a fleeting moment, a golden city had shaped in my mind's eye. Cheerful bells rang like a signal or a summons.

As if they were beckoning me to come home.

4

THE SERPENT

SCREAMS OF ANGUISH—of true agony—produced a twisted delight deep in my bones.

The kind that heated the blood, raced the heart, drew me back for more, again and again. No mistake, the sounds seemed to be the only way I could feel that euphoria, the thing folk called joy, anymore.

There was power that came when a village careened into a frenzy at the mere sight of black bone hulls, sharp spikes like the spines on a sea serpent, and bloody sails. The heady taste of panic and fear and pleading had become my purpose.

Tonight went differently, and it was damn aggravating.

Flames danced across the walls of the neatly aligned wood and wattle cottages. Heat burst out the windows, and smoke and ash soaked the alleyways of the dwellings all the way to the hills.

A winding cobbled road curved around the steepest hillside, where the lord of the Rusa township built his manor and all its sharp peaks.

I looked forward to watching it burn.

By now, the melodic tune of screams and terror ought to be shattering the silence of the night. There were a few sobs, a wail or two, but the folk of Rusa, when the black hull of the ship sliced through the sea surface, submitted as though they'd anticipated the attack.

From my position on the deck, I could make out the main square of the village, an open place made of dark polished stone like night trapped in glass. Countless villagers huddled with their pitiful families. Dressed in nightclothes, littles sniffled and clung to their mothers. Fathers had chins lifted, no doubt waiting for the knife to the throat when the threat hadn't even been made yet.

My grip on the rail tightened until each knuckle ached. I didn't know if I was more irritated that they did what I would've commanded before I commanded it, or that each man seemed so resigned, so at *peace*, with his fate.

There was nothing delightful about cutting a man down when he was already on his damn knees. The chase, the fight, the knowledge that you overpowered a foe was half the excitement.

On deck, two of my crew held a half-naked man between them. I dragged two fingers across the brim of the tricorn hat atop my head and pulled it off, revealing the black scarf that always covered my skull when I stood aboard the ship.

The scar cutting through my lip went taut when I curved one side of my mouth. "Lord Murdo."

Both points of the man's ears had been sliced. The slight blue-cream shade to his skin was darkened in blood. He lifted his head with effort and met my eyes. "My K-king."

I curled one hand under his bearded chin. "Your king? Is that what I am?"

"Yes," he said, breathless.

"Hmm." With care to hide the bite of pain in my left leg, I lowered to one knee until we were nose to nose. There it was. Gods, the fear flashed vibrantly in the dull gold of his eyes. Without care for the gashes on his scalp, I slammed the tricorn onto his head. "What I think is you wanted this for yourself."

Murdo's forehead wrinkled. "No, My Lord."

"Oh, I think you did. Why else would you be so foolish as to steal from your king?"

"I swear to you, I did no such thing."

From the back quarters of the ship, Larsson, my second mate, stepped onto the deck. He always seemed ready to laugh through the violence. This moment was no exception. A wry grin played on his mouth, and the slight glow of gold in his dark eyes was bright with excitement.

Beside Larsson stood a stoic man, hair like fire, and ears pierced in blue stones from lobe to the sharp tip. For a moment I reveled in Murdo's twisted glare from the betrayal.

"I don't believe you, since your bastard sold you out." I leaned forward, lips against his ear, and whispered, "Pity your son hates you."

"Athol, you traitorous—"

A closed fist slammed into Murdo's jaw, silencing him.

I glared over the man's head at a masked face, hidden beneath a hood. Celine gave me a one-shouldered shrug in return. She was dressed in a thick tunic, topped with a woolen coat that hit her thighs. No one at first glance would know a woman was beneath it all. She preferred it that way.

Folk of the Ever always underestimated females. Her twisted delight came in revealing herself before she drew her blade. To end a man with the look of stun still on his face kept Celine grinning for weeks.

"Athol has brains, unlike you, Murdo." I clenched my teeth as I stood, careful not to show the fire of pain in the bones of my weak leg. A glimpse of weakness, and I'd be dealing with nothing but assassins come to slaughter their pitiful king. "You took what did not belong to you, and it truly makes me dream of what my blade would look like sticking out of your eye socket."

Murdo blanched. "The witch . . . she needed a cherished possession of . . ."

"Of what?" I folded my arms over my chest. "Don't stop there, keep talking. Whose possession did you need?"

"The king's."

"That's right. The *king*." I gripped his hair and wrenched his head back until he met my gaze. "You were duped by a half-wit spell caster. You think the Lady of the House of Mists has not used her fiercest witches to heal this land? You think you will be the one to do it?"

"What choice do we have, *My King*? You might control the Ever Seas, but you don't know how to heal it either. Like you, we're all trapped in this dying land. Forgive me for not being willing to give up just yet."

I didn't need to look to know the rot was there. Deadened forests covered half the Rusa isles. Charred foliage, fruit trees, and crops were brittle and worthless. Even some of the springs and coves in the distant isles had darkened, spilling out decaying fish and eels unfit to eat.

Rusa was not the first to be claimed by the poison.

I wanted Murdo's tongue, but only because he spoke the truth. Turns after earth fae sealed off the Chasm, something had shifted in the Ever Kingdom. An imbalance grew between worlds, and a poison took root.

I'd hunted for answers, pillaged and thieved for lore and artifacts. The only hope for healing I had left was the power gifted to the former king by the most powerful of sea witches. A gift that strengthened the Ever King, and what I needed now was more damn power.

The lost mantle of my father was a talisman with power unmatched, meant to be used by the true Ever King.

The trouble was I could not reach it. A price was placed upon such a gift. Should it be lost, the mantle could not be taken back for ten turns. A punishment for being foolish enough to lose the gift of a sea witch, I suppose. The earth fae had now owned my father's power for twenty.

Ten turns ago, the opportunity to challenge had been there, and I let it slide through my fingers by making a different choice. A choice that now led to the destruction of my own kingdom.

Another tenth turn was about to fade away, and I still had no way to open the damn Chasm.

My people knew my father's mantle had been conquered by the earth bender king. It wouldn't take much to count the turns and realize the chance to take it back was ending. I wasn't surprised they'd gone to such lengths to find a way to heal what was dying.

Unsurprised, but it didn't mean I needed to be merciful at the betrayal.

Murdo spit blood at my feet. "When our king leaves us to destruction, the desperate will do anything. Perhaps a new king might finally return the Ever to its former glory."

"You could be right, Murdo. But we'll never know." I'd learned quickly how to fight with a weak limb and have a weapon in hand before an enemy even noticed. My knife rammed between two of his ribs. There were the screams I craved. Hand on the hilt of the bone knife, I leaned close. "We'll never know, for you cannot take what is mine by right, by blood, and by destiny."

I yanked the knife out of his ribs. The old lord spluttered and gasped. Close to his face, I dragged my tongue along the blade, letting the tang of his blood drip from my lips down my chin.

With the point of one slightly elongated canine, I pricked my finger until a bead of blood surfaced. Murdo's skin paled.

"Swear your fealty, Murdo, and you won't greet the Otherworld today."

The lord sucked in a sharp breath and nodded. He clutched his side and maneuvered to his knees again. A gasp of pain scraped from his throat when he bent forward and pressed a kiss to the toe of my boot.

I chuckled, low and harsh, then kicked my foot up, knocking

two of his teeth out. Blood slicked the top of my finger now. I crouched, failing to hide my own grimace, and hovered my palm near Murdo's wound.

"I accept your vow." Through the hole in his side, I jabbed my bloody finger. The bastard roared in pain when I twisted and scraped more than was needed. Convinced enough of my blood had tangled with his, I stood.

Murdo let out a few gasps, head on the deck.

When silence surrounded us, a groove gathered between his brows. "M-my King?" He stammered the words like a question, waiting. Already the veins of crimson snaked from his wound, coiling around his belly, up his rib cage, aimed at his heart. He convulsed. "King Erik . . . p-p-please."

"Did you expect me to sing?" I tilted his head. "I wonder why. I don't save traitors."

Spittle and blood foamed at Murdo's mouth. His eyes grew wet and glassy as his body twitched from the poison of my blood. I'd earned the name Bloodsinger at a tiny four turns when my father tested the magic of his heir.

In the worst of ways, I'd discovered exactly what my blood could do.

A simple song from me would save Murdo. But with silence, my blood would fester and destroy his insides until his heart gave out. I didn't utter a sound and returned my fallen tricorn to my head, adjusting it low on my brow. Like it was an insignificant piece of the deck, I stepped over Murdo's body and strode for the gangplank leading to the shore.

"You going on land?" Celine's twittery voice was muffled beneath her mask.

"You found it?"

"We did."

"Then I am going to retrieve it." With a jerk of my head, I gestured at Athol. "See to it he understands what happens if he follows in his father's footsteps."

Halfway down the plank, another form came to my side. I clenched my fists. "I don't need you to guard me, Cousin."

Tait, my obligated first mate, didn't move away. Half a head taller than me, Tait was built like a shield, broad and thick. We shared the same bronze-brown skin, but Tait's hair was as dark as shadows and fell over his shoulders. Mine was like the soil underfoot and shorter. The scarf on my head kept it free of my eyes, but the scars on the back of my neck reddened with irritation when my hair grew too long.

There was little love between the two of us. Harald, his father, had seen to it what affection we once had as small boys was slaughtered through harsh treatment and forced distance.

No doubt, Tait suspected I was the one behind the death of his father. He'd be right, and I was convinced he didn't press me on it out of fear I'd do the same to him.

Again, he'd likely be right.

"Where is it?" I snapped.

Tait lifted a beringed finger, pointing at a woman who clung to a girl no older than twelve. "Their alchemist was to make an herb poultice with it."

On our approach, the mother shifted in front of the child. Folk of Rusa all shared pale skin, a shade of ivory, some nearer to slate. The flames reflected off every tone like glass.

"You must be the alchemist of the isles?"

The woman's chin trembled. "Yes, My Lord."

I smirked, flashing the bloodied tooth in my mouth. One knuckle dragged down her cheek. She closed her eyes and whimpered when I gripped the back of her neck and drew her face close. "I hear you have something of mine, love."

"We d-didn't know, My King."

"I believe you. Hand it over."

"Halle," the alchemist woman said gently. "Yes, come here, my girl. Return it to the king."

The young girl fluttered her dark lashes. Bleary eyes locked on mine, but slowly she handed over the silver charm. She was terrified, so small. Somewhere, buried deep, there was a desire to sympathize with her fear. I'd been a frightened boy once. But turns of learning how dangerous the heart could be kept any tenderness for the child where it belonged—locked away where I couldn't reach it.

My instinct was to snatch the silver bird away and shove it into my belt, safe from anyone touching it again, but I kept my movements controlled. Calm.

My fingers curled around the old twine. Many times, it could've been replaced with gold or silver chains, but I'd kept it the same itchy string from that night so long ago. I bent a little lower and tucked the girl's hair behind one ear. "You have my thanks, my lady."

She bowed her head. "Please, d-don't punish my mam. We thought we had it as your gift to melt down for the poultice."

I hummed, inspecting the edges of the small bird's wings. "This little charm caused a great deal of strife, didn't it?" I pinched the charm between my fingers and held it close to her face. "Truth is, I'd give up half my palace to get this back."

Tears lined her lashes. "We didn't know, swear it. Please f-f-forgive us."

"Afraid it's not up to me, love." I took a long step away from the girl and lifted my voice over the crackle and snap of fire devouring homes. "You claim to be my people, yet you have been disloyal and untrusting. Have I not offered refuge in the royal city with me?"

I slammed a fist into my chest. "I have opened my gates to every realm, every land where the darkening is fiercest. Yet you stay, and seek out your own ways to take *my throne, my crown*, by thieving from your king. I think the worst part of this whole ordeal is that you thought I wouldn't *find out*. I always uncover disloyalty."

I snapped my fingers and one of the crewmen tossed a burlap sack. It landed at my feet. Without dropping my gaze from the girl, I reached for the sack.

The girl shrieked and buried her face in her mother's shoulder when I removed the dried, decaying head by the hair.

"I've come to return your false sea witch." I tossed the head into the crowd. Folk spluttered and hurried away when it dropped with a wet thud. "She lied to you and took your coin. Now your village is in ruins, and your lord is dead.

"But I'm not without mercy. There are some here still loyal to your king. Lord Athol is now your man. He shall decide who is loyal enough to join him on your upcoming journey to the royal city and who is not. I leave your fate in his hands."

Athol abandoned the ship and sneered at the people of the isle. They stared at Murdo's second son with trepidation. Tait remained behind to give Athol his instructions on bringing folk into the royal city by the next high tide.

They couldn't stay here, not with the darkening spoiling their land.

A cinch built in my chest, almost like guilt, at having failed another realm. The way to end this rot seemed like it was right there within my grasp, yet it always slipped through my fingers and tossed me back a hundred paces whenever another realm was abandoned.

Celine met me by the gangplank. She'd removed her mask, and her full lips cut into a smirk, showing off her white teeth against her brown skin. She dragged her fingers over a straight pink scar across the center of her throat, like it was a comfort through the tension. "You know," she began, "that Athol bastard has a vendetta against half the village."

I shrugged and rubbed my left thigh. "That will be their problem. They ought to learn how to plead for his mercy swiftly."

"Well, are you satisfied now that you have your precious bird back?"

Celine mocked me often about my charm. She was the only one who could and get away with it. She could taunt all she wanted; I'd still cling to the bird. An untamed obsession.

I dragged my nose along the silver wings, imagining the girl's scent buried in the metal. Someday, I vowed to destroy my enemy, but another, darker side wanted to destroy his heir in a different way. Devour her like the serpent from the story she once told.

I wanted nothing more than to tear through the walls, shatter her world, then take what was left of her.

As though my thoughts summoned my twisted desires, the tide slithered higher onto the shore, soaking my boot. Celine was chattering on about our journey home, words I couldn't take in any longer. My blood sparked with a jolt of something . . . familiar.

The rune mark on my arm prickled like flames licking across my skin. I tugged on my sleeve and had to bite my damn lip to choke back a shout of surprise. The ridges of the cursed mark had deepened to rich crimson, dark enough it almost looked black.

Not possible.

Without a thought for my anguished muscles and bones, I dropped to the water's edge, dipped two fingers into the sea, then lifted them to my tongue. Savory and salty, but beneath it all was . . .

"Celine, there is blood in the water."

"A few folk have died tonight." Celine arched a brow.

"No." I tasted the water again. A twist knotted my insides, an insatiable pull toward the shadows of the deeper Ever Seas, where currents led to the Chasm. "*My* blood."

"Yours?" Her eyes widened. "Your blood was used to . . . seal the barriers. If it's filling the sea, then . . ."

I hesitated and took another breath as if giving time for the sensation to die like a cruel trick. The pull never faded. "The Chasm has been opened. I feel it."

Celine drew in a sharp breath. "Erik, don't taunt me with this. Are you speaking true?"

I wheeled on her, teeth bared. "Would I lie about this? Gather the crew. We're leaving."

"By the damn gods." Celine fanned her face. "It's happening. Really happening. Okay. Okay. Tait, you swab, get back here!"

I stormed up the gangplank, shoved through a few crewmen cleaning the deck of Murdo's body, and took the five steps to the helm two at a time.

"Where to, My King?" Larsson leaned over the rail of the steps. Beneath the bloody red shade of the scarf over his skull, his dark hair blew about his face.

I touched the jagged handles on the helm and the ship shuddered beneath the connection. Gusts of cool wind picked up the sails.

The corner of my mouth twisted into a grin. "To the place songbirds sing."

5

THE SERPENT

OPEN. THERE FOR the taking, for destroying.

The maelstrom tides of the Chasm had always existed, a common border between the realms of the sea and land. A window to another world. Wilder below the surface than they looked above, the Chasm's tides thrashed and tumbled in a storm I wanted to embrace.

Powerful ships of the Ever could sail above or below the surface, but when speed was warranted, below was the only way to command the currents.

The bruising pace we'd kept brought us from the Rusa isles to the Chasm in less than half a day. Doubtless, the crew had been as curious as me to see if the wards preventing the king from entering had truly fallen. Here it was, open and unguarded.

Water on the side of the earth fae was like a night sea with white stones and silver fish. The Ever Seas shifted to cerulean tides and vibrant sea life of plants, endless caverns and cliffs, and sly creatures one would never see coming if they did not know the waters.

From the first teardrop of the gods that formed the Ever Seas, the kings held the strength and burden to ease their folk through the barriers between the different fae worlds. But under my father's rule, the lady of the sea witches gifted Thorvald his mantle to forever mark his bloodline as the rulers of the waters.

The talisman allowed the *Ever Ship* to carve through any sea, any ocean, any storm without straining the natural magic of the king's blood. It gave the Ever Folk access to all the fae worlds; it shielded ships during crossings into dangerous waters with sea singers and dark creatures.

When the Great War between the earth fae and the Ever ended, our enemies held my father's mantle. The earth bender Night Folk king won it turns before by murdering Thorvald, and I'd failed to win it back. I wouldn't fail my father again.

"After today, we'll finally take back our kingdom," Celine whispered at my side.

"No more waiting." My lip curled. "Now get to your post."

Celine never cowered under me. She rolled her finger off her forehead in a mocking kind of salute and bowed at the waist. "Yes, Highness."

Turns of hating, of fighting, of searching were all at once ended. A thought almost too overwhelming to comprehend.

Almost.

"At your word, My King," Larsson hummed from the stem.

Beneath the surface, words became a song. A sort of melodic current we felt more than heard.

I gripped the handles of the helm until the skin on my knuckles ached. At the rise of my fist, the ship jolted. Little by little, pressure from the sea gathered as the Chasm drew us into the center of its violence.

The earth fae had made me a prisoner within my own kingdom, but I was still the king of the sea. It bowed to me.

The serpent figurehead broke into the Chasm's thrashing currents.

Mutters and a few shouts of surprise rose from the crew as furious water battered the hull. A whirl of foam and sea devoured the sails. I kept my tune, and the ship was tossed swifter but straighter. Like sailing through a violent storm, the *Ever Ship* rocked and dipped but never lost course.

Delighted cries rose from the crew, a glimpse at the mania and depravity we all embraced to survive the seas of our kingdom. Closer and closer came the gleam of the surface, shifting to a dull light behind angry mists and clouds.

"Keep her steady!" I hissed at the crew.

Celine wrapped rough rope around her wrist a second time, pulling the sails taut as we rose toward new seas. Larsson widened his stance at the stempost as he shouted orders to secure flapping rigs. Tait was a specter, silent and morbid, at my back. Perhaps he had some of the same gruesome thoughts as me—last we saw the earth fae lands, we'd been boys on the losing side of a war.

We'd been prisoners. Wounded. We'd nearly been sent to the gods more than once.

I closed my eyes again and dragged my fingertips through the water as it began to calm the nearer we came to the other side of the wall. One command, and I angered the seas on the surface.

I wanted thick rolling clouds over the water. I wanted our ship to be a ghost in their world.

My desire was to rush and spill blood, to burn it all. I forced my hand to guide the currents around the ship to ease us upward, hidden in what would seem a natural sea storm. A damn lifetime of revenge hung in the balance. Impatience would not be my downfall.

Fire burned in my chest. I'd nearly forgotten what it felt like to surge through these waters, nearly forgotten the rush, the discomfort.

"Hold tight, you bastards!" Celine roared, laughing wildly when the tumult lessened. She gripped thick ropes of rigging and lifted onto the rail of the ship, leaning into the chaos.

Pressure from the water eased. A ripple of waves drew nearer.

I held my breath until the spray of the sea battered my face in a new way. The ship carved through the surface in a flurry of white-capped waves. Wind whipped against the red sails. The colors of the Ever Kingdom seal—a serpent skull and two crossed blades—flapped madly in the storm.

Once the ship settled on the surface again, the deck was silent but for the slap of rain and the hiss of wind.

Then, like the realization struck all at once, the crew roared against the rumble of thunder. They pounded fists into the air, flung curses at the shoreline visible through the storm clouds we brought with us.

I let out a rough breath. We were here. Earth fae walls and rooftops all sprawled out, not a care in their precious little world, ripe for the plucking.

"To the Ever King!" Celine cried, a fist above her head.

The crew followed suit. Tait met my gaze across the main deck. Even in my ruthless cousin's eyes, his repulsion of me was replaced with a dark thrill for vengeance.

Larsson tipped his chin before beginning a slow, dark song. "A man he's not, we work we rot, no sleep until it's through . . ."

I faced the shore, a grin on my mouth as the rest of the crew raised their voices.

A sailor's grave is all we crave.
We are the Ever King's crew!

6

THE SERPENT

ONE BOOT PROPPED on the rail, I leaned onto my elbow over my knee, waiting.

"How long?" I snapped.

Tait removed a watch made of gold and silver with cogs that ticked swifter if danger was near, a tell that our time was running short. "Three chimes."

Teeth clenched, I faced the empty sea again. Night had been thick when we arrived and hid the ship in a deep, empty cove near the Chasm border. Now a sliver of pale dawn was cresting over the horizon, and two of my crew had yet to return from their small reconnaissance of the shore.

They were sly. Patient. It would take time.

Still, the desire to act scorched a hole through my insides. The risk of losing my opportunity to impatience grew closer to a reality with every passing breath.

"Oi! There they be." A thick-necked man with bone rings in his ears pointed into the murk of clouds from the stern.

I didn't fight the limp in my leg, for the crew had seen it. I merely stepped with it to quicken my pace across the deck. The crewman handed over the black-and-gold spyglass. One eye closed, I peered through until I found the shadow of the rowboat breaking through the waves.

I slammed the spyglass shut. "Pull them aboard. Move your asses, you wretches!"

Boots pounded over the damp wood. Heaves and grunts raised the heavy bone grate over the lower deck. Half a dozen men slid down the ladder rungs through the hatch to meet them belowdecks.

Palms flat on the rail, I peered over the edge and waited for the hidden door to heave open from the fattest bulge in the hull.

Ships of the Sea Folk were masterpieces. Even the simplest fishing sloop was shaped from the rib cages of powerful whales or corpses of ancient sea snakes. The cracks and crevices were filled with sea oak, a soft wood that bent and gave with the violence of the tides and resisted damp for nigh a hundred turns before barnacles and rot needed to be careened away.

With a skeleton of bone and sea oak, ships carved through tides with speed, agility, and silence.

But the *Ever Ship* was a vessel made for gods.

A vessel powerful enough to sail through the Chasm without snapping a mast. The red sails were stitched with thick canvas, and petrified scales from deep-sea serpents were staked in the hull. Impenetrable.

The most convenient piece of the king's ship was the stowaway door in the hull. It opened to take on our hauls and rowboats without the delay of cranks and rigging. The door could open, swallow half a hull of water, then lock in place and spit out the tide it took on as we sailed away.

Larsson rowed, and Celine held a lantern through the dark, guiding him into the hull. They were the two members of the crew who blended best with the earth fae. Celine with her green eyes instead of the pale or red of most sea fae, and Larsson with his lack of a sea voice. The magic of the Ever lived in the voices of its people. Some, like Larsson, had no ability of the sea.

Celine emerged from the hatch and tossed the hood from her head. I dug my fingernails into the meat of my palm until crescents carved into my flesh, all to keep from rushing across the ship to greet them.

Celine crossed the distance over the main deck in long strides. Her dark curls whipped about the frustrated grimace on her face.

"What?" I gritted through my teeth before she even reached me. Patience wore thin, and I only had so much to give in the first place.

"When you cease looking at me like you will tear out my eyes, I will tell you what we found." Celine arched a brow. She was the only soul who could get away with speaking to me like that, yet she still had the brains to speak it under her breath.

My throat was thick, but I managed to speak without spitting the words. "What did you learn?"

"There are countless people here. The ship will be at risk of being overtaken by their warriors if we draw too close. We should take the skiffs to the docks on the north side of the isle. There seems to be a festival in full bloom, but with it is also an open trade market." Celine let out a quick breath. "We'll be able to dock there and enter as tradesmen."

If this day ever came, I'd always imagined screams and terror when the crimson sails broke through the mist. I wanted the earth fae to know their reckoning had come. I closed my eyes against the wind. What mattered more was finding my father's mantle and winning it back from the Night Folk king.

It called to me, and I wasn't leaving without it.

"Leave me at the helm, Erik," Tait said, voice low. "I'll keep her hidden."

My cheek flinched. I didn't look at my cousin, but I didn't need to.

He already knew the answer. I might not trust easily, but there was no denying Tait held a deep-rooted loyalty to the ship, to our kingdom.

Not to mention he was bound by blood, the way his father had been bound to mine, to see to it the Ever King never met his destruction.

Without turning around, I waved a hand and said, "Ready the boats."

THE DOCKS WERE one pace away. Already, Celine, Larsson, and a few more of the crew were shouting like freshly arrived traders. I was paralyzed.

"Erik." Larsson cocked his head. "Find a way to blend in before you're recognized."

Recognized. Because I'd been here too many bleeding times. Battled these people. Felt their blades on my skin.

My jaw pulsed. This weight in my blood was nothing more than weak, pathetic fear. The crew was blood-bound to serve the *Ever Ship*. Still, if my men saw me trembling like a boy about to piss in his trousers, no mistake, they'd find a way to mutiny.

"You've the right to be here." It wasn't Larsson. He'd melted into the crowd ten paces away. Celine had her hat pulled low on her brow, and she played the part of a boat hand tethering the already tethered skiff to the dock. "You have fought for this moment. Now claim what is yours before they get another chance to take you."

My eyes narrowed in a tight glare. Not out of anger for Celine. More that she was right, and I hated that she needed to say it at all.

With a tug, I used the rigging of the skiff to haul me onto the dock. For another breath, then two, I drew in the air of the land. Different than the Ever, yet the same in many ways. Sweet and fragrant. Not with the cool winds of my realm; there was more heat here. More savory herbs and cloyingly sweet scents.

I'd left my tricorn hat on the ship and covered the black scarf on my head with a knitted wool cap. The gold hoop I wore in my ear was tucked in my trousers, and the ruby-hilted cutlass was in the hands of Tait with a hefty threat he'd lose those hands if a scratch were to be found on the blade.

We'd armed ourselves through the pirated supplies from old battles with earth fae—seax swords, axes, daggers, and a few of the strangely captivating blacksteel weapons had been pillaged across the centuries before the Chasm closed.

"Here." Celine handed me a small glass vial with murky fluid inside. "For the eyes."

She motioned sprinkling a few drops of the vial over her eyes. Teeth hidden, dressed in simple clothes, without my blade, the most notable indication that I did not belong here were my eyes.

I blinked through a sting from the drops, then tossed the vial into the waves.

"Well?" I opened my arms, facing Celine.

"Nothing but a common earth fae." She adjusted her thick belt around a tattered dress. No mistake, she'd burn the thing the moment she could.

With a sack of stolen grain slung over my shoulder, I stepped into the flow of crowd.

Larsson drifted back to us, taking a place on my left. Head down, he had a bit of straw between his teeth, and a black strip of leather tied his dark hair off his neck. Celine took my other side. She played her role well. A woman overwhelmed by the vastness of a place. More than one man stopped to help her retrieve the linens she kept dropping.

They were so taken by her praise, they never took note of her hand swiping purses from belts or knives from sheaths.

"Gods, did every bleeding soul on land convene in one damn place?" Larsson frowned when we trekked a slope to the top of a wooden staircase that would lead us into the trade square. Bodies packed the space, haggling, chattering, and utterly unaware the sea had returned.

"Come on. We need to find where he sleeps."

"How do you know the earth bender will have it with him?"

"The call drew us here, didn't it? Means it's here." I spoke briskly, but my mouth twisted in a grin. The deeper reason was my little songbird wouldn't break a promise, and she had promised to look after it always.

Tall buildings shaded the square. Some made of wood, others of pale stone. Moss and a few shelled creatures dotted the crags. There were carts and tables lining the cobbled paths, stacked with all manners of trade. Pelts from their mammoth forest creatures, gutted eels and fish, bangles made of wood and jade, and bright masks with feathers and ribbons decorating the neutral features.

A wooden spear handle shot out in front of me. Without lifting my chin, I rolled my eyes to meet those of a girthy man in a black gambeson. Two swords hung at his waist, one a bronze blade with a raven hilt. By his side was another man dressed the same, with two scars like fingernail marks on either cheek.

"State your trade," the first said.

"Grains," Larsson muttered. His accent had shifted to something refined and strange. Aboard the ship, he spoke with a constant hum of revelry and a touch of darkness.

"At the festival?" The two guards glanced at each other.

"Folk need feed even at festivals, do they not?"

The guards scoffed. The first poked at the sacks in our hands. Little time went by before they gestured us forward.

"Welcome to the Crimson Festival, grain sellers."

The guards mocked our measly trade. No ribbons or gold to sell, true, but we'd pillaged long enough to know that it was always a better disguise to be unassuming. The dull and dreary commoner rarely earned a second glance.

Babbling excitement was everywhere. Even the most common of folk chattered on about games and feasts. What was the celebration?

The more we followed the roads that wrapped around the fort, the more my blood pounded in my head. A pull forward I couldn't sever. We were close.

As the latecomers of the festival trade, we were forced to set down our sacks near a woman who was chopping off the heads of strange, gangly birds with a bit too much force.

"Ah, thought I'd be alone this turn again." She used the bloody knife to point at one of her birds. "Not many like the smell of river pheasant. I find it has a nice tangy scent." She laughed and swiped her dark, sweaty hair off her brow.

"Not afraid of a little blood, lady," Larsson grumbled.

"Selling oats, are you?" She swung her knife, eyes on our sacks instead of the bird.

"Aye" was all I said before I turned my back on her.

Celine gave me a significant look. One meant to tell me something I couldn't read.

When I didn't move, she sighed, irritated, and smiled sweetly at the woman. "We've never come during the festival."

"Oh. You from the peaks in the Night Folk realm? Bleeding hard to get off those cliffs even once the frosts are gone."

"Aye," Celine said. "The peaks. Finally scrimped enough to make it this turn."

Another whack, the thud of a head, and the woman grinned. "As you should. Everyone deserves to celebrate. Can't believe the Great War ended ten turns ago. Feels like mere months."

My fists clenched. "It's felt longer to us."

"Ah, isolated in the peaks, are you?"

"You could say that." Every word seethed with bitterness.

"Seeing as we're new," Celine went on with a glare pointed at me, "what exactly goes on tonight? What's all the bustle?"

The woman began stripping feathers off her latest beheading. "Hells, girl. How isolated are you in them cliffs? Tonight's First Night, and that means a masquerade ball at the fort."

"Ah, yes. Now I recall hearing mention of it." Celine turned and offered me a wink.

There was our way in. I stepped beside Larsson and handed him a few copper coins from Celine's thievery.

"Find us something to wear so we might blend in," I told him. "While the front gates are occupied with people entering, we'll use that time to go around . . ."

My voice trailed off when laughter rose over the chatter. As though snared into some strange trance, I followed the sound over Larsson's shoulder in time to catch sight of a few discreet guards, three men with blades on their belts, then the source of the laughter—two women stepped onto the road from one of the shops.

Both lovely, but I was drawn to the taller of the two. Hair as dark as spilled ink was intricately braided over her slender shoulder. Soft skin the shade of damp sand. A slight tapered point to her ears, less pronounced than mine, but her eyes were what drew me in. I wouldn't forget those eyes. Blue, like the calmest lagoons of the Ever.

I was frozen. Captivated.

When she laughed, her head fell back in such a way that the sun brightened her cheeks until they looked bronze. Breath, thought, words, the lot escaped me.

A perplexing kind of darkness took hold in the deep sinews of my chest. It was cruel, wicked, and greedy. Never had I desired something so fiercely. I didn't understand it, and I didn't try. The draw to her was like a crawl for water after being lost in the blaze of the sun.

Such a beautiful little bird. What a pity it was that her serpent had come to ruin her.

"Ah, taken with the princesses, boy?" The woman and her half-plucked bird came to my side. "If you come from the high peaks, I'd expect you to know Livia at least."

Oh, I did. My mouth twisted into a sinister sort of grin.

"Out of us all, my brother leaves home the least," Celine said, no doubt trying to salvage my oddities.

"Ah, well. Take a good look," said the woman. "Likely won't get a chance once the masque begins. With the Night Folk king and queen gone, more than one cocksure boy will try to steal a chance with their daughter."

I whirled around. "The king, her father, he's gone?"

No. No, that wasn't possible. I was led here. The mantle would be with the king. I needed that damn talisman like I needed to destroy him.

"Left before yesterday's midday meal," she said, spitting out a feather that had landed on her tongue. "The rulers of the realms always meet at the Kunglig Palace for council during the festival."

Dammit. My breaths came in short, sharp jolts.

An idea formed. Lines would be crossed.

"Woman," I said sharply.

"Beeta," she returned.

"Why do the men wait for the king to leave before trying to touch his heir?"

Beeta snorted. "Because misplace a hair on lovely Livia's head, and her father will have yours. The man would go to war if she asked it of him. The king adores her."

Gods, how I hoped that was true. My next steps would depend on it. If I could not go to the king, I'd make him come to me.

Down the road, her laughter rolled through me again, like falling without knowing how it would end at the bottom. From here I could still make out the profile of her face, the slope of her nose, the sly way she bit that full lip.

A step away from Beeta, I gripped Larsson by the throat. "How well do you dance, Larsson?"

His sneer showed the glisten of his white teeth. "As well as you need, My King."

"Then take the coin I gave you and see to it we are suitable for a royal ball."

I stepped out into the road once more, watching her. Studying her.

She was never theirs anyway. Not really. From the moment the songbird tried to appeal to the serpent, she was mine.

7

THE SONGBIRD

THE GREAT HALL was blazing.

The feathers of my fan fought against the muggy air of too many bodies packed in one space. I scratched my damp cheek beneath the black mask over my upper face. A dainty thing made of black and silver lace with raven feathers splayed out over the brow.

"Do not let me drink like last night, Liv. It doesn't agree with me." Mira lifted the golden mask and tipped a flute of sweet cherry wine to her painted lips. She winced against the burn.

I chuckled and took the horn from her hands. "You sweet little thing. Shall I get you some milk instead?"

Lips pinched, fighting a grin, she elbowed me, then faced the ebb and flow of couples in the ballroom. Ladies of the various courts donned vibrant gowns of all colors—midnight blues, silver and gold, moss green trimmed in black, and rich burgundy like the sweetest plums.

Men wore groomed furs on their shoulders or tunics made of soft linens and wool. They boasted blades of all sizes on their polished belts. Some preferred axes, like my father, others a powerful seax, but most came prepared to dance the night away by keeping only simple daggers at the ready.

The festival was rife with sweetness. Pomes dipped in thick

sugar sauce. Glazes over honey rolls, cakes stuffed full of sweet berries or cream or tart syrups. Pheasants roasted over racks in the cooking rooms down the corridors. Savory hints of rosemary and sea salt perfumed the sweat in the great hall. Sweet wines, sharp liqueurs, and foamy drinks were kept on a constant flow.

Lanterns cast flickering light over the gray stone floor from tallow candles in silver cages, and a layer of glimmer powders over the floor made the entire hall appear to be made of gold.

Masks shielded faces, some more than others, but I could recognize the faces that mattered most.

Near a banquet table, Aleksi stood with more than one Rave and even more ladies seeking the warmth of a warrior for the night. Sander sat ten paces from us with a drinking horn and more than one written trade agreement from his realms in hand. His mask was askew on his face, and he hardly seemed to realize he was here to have fun.

Jonas, as expected, was nowhere to be found.

"Last I saw of the rake, he had a lady with a goat mask on his arm heading for the gardens," Mira told me when I pressed. She rolled her eyes and snatched the horn from my hand again.

We wouldn't see him until the noon sun, no doubt. The bridges of my feet ached from standing in place so long. I'd taken my turn about the dance floor, desperate to be carefree, desperate to hole away with a man for the night and discover, at last, what it felt like to be a little bold and risky.

The trouble was, for every man who'd asked for their dance, all I wondered was if they had spoken to my father.

Were they thinking of power, prestige, and nothing of me? Did they even care to know I painted windows across the whole of the castle back home in Night Folk territory?

I doubted any of the men who'd asked me to dance cared my paintings were done so when the dawn light struck, rooms burst into color, and they drew smiles from our staff and my family. Would they mind if I woke screaming from the mare demons placing cruel images of shadows and serpents in my head? If I chose to let them kiss me, touch me, to have all of me, would they know they were the first?

I shuddered and let out a breath. Too much thinking, not enough doing. I'd promised Alek—and myself—I would forget nerves and nightmares, and I'd live tonight.

A man with curled horns like a ram's on his mask approached. He bowed at the waist and held out a hand for Mira. "Princess—"

"Tobias," she said with a huff. "You're not supposed to know who I am."

"Impossible when you light up the room with your beauty."

She snorted and handed me her horn again. "Flattery of his daughter will not earn you a place on my father's council. If you believe so, you do not know your own king. You must flatter my mother first, then me, but most of all, you must *amuse* him."

"Hells, Mira, you think I don't know that? King Ari doesn't seem to find my jests amusing." Tobias finally broke. He'd attended lessons with Mira since they were children, and the man never hid his intentions to be on the right hand of Mira's father as a high-ranking noble.

"Such a shame." She tapped his nose under the ram mask. "Couldn't possibly be because he knows your game, could it? You keep trying to present like you're a suitor for me, Tobias, yet my father and *everyone* know you don't favor women."

"Simple solution: I'll pretend you were born a prince."

"Ah, so you think my only choice is to vow with you?"

"With your temperament," he said, nose in the air, "most likely."

"I take offense to that and will be sure to let my father know."

"You're impossible." Tobias closed his eyes and held out a hand. "I'll forgive you if you dance with me, my horrid princess. Put me at ease that we're still friends, right?"

She sighed and took his hand. "I suppose if we must."

I laughed when they strode arm in arm, bickering, until Mira turned around, voice low. "Liv, don't look now, but I think you might have another admirer."

She nodded to the far side of the room. There, a man stood in the shadows, one shoulder leaning against the wall. A simple black mask hid his features from brow to chin, and only the tousled waves of his dark hair were visible.

The hair on my arms lifted. From here I couldn't make out his eyes, but his masked face was aimed at me. Only me.

Knots tangled in the pit of my belly when the man shoved off the wall. He dragged gloved hands down his satin tunic, all black, the same as his mask. I took a step to the side. Across the hall, he mimicked my step in the same direction.

A dangerous air hovered around his shoulders. Darkness and mystery. My heart thudded fiercely enough I could hear it in my head. I stepped again. My stranger did the same. Again and again, like a wolf who'd found its prey.

I didn't recognize his stance, his stride. His aura left me wondering if he might hail from the dark corners of the Eastern realms. The thought of asking Sander faded when I took another step, putting his table in my wake.

Only a few paces away, my stranger maneuvered like an underwater dance through courtiers, never dropping his hidden gaze from me. Like my steps were chained to his, I couldn't stop. I couldn't turn back.

I lost my breath when all at once he was in front of me.

Tall enough I had to tilt my chin to meet his eyes. A flash of dark brown and almost... red, like the deepest sunset. For a long, drawn-out pause, he held my gaze, studying me, breaking me apart, then piecing me back together.

Without a word, he reached out a hand. I prayed he wouldn't see the way my fingers trembled, and placed my palm onto the warm leather of his gloves.

His voice was low, a rasp like a stormy wind, when he said, "Dance with me, little bird."

I tilted my head, confused. He chuckled softly and teased some of the raven feathers on my mask.

"Oh." Heat flooded my cheeks beneath the shield. There was something thrilling about not being addressed as "Princess" or "Lady." He could be playing coy, but I liked the idea my stranger truly did not recognize me.

I tightened my grip on his hand. "I'd be honored."

My shadow led me to the center of the hall. Once he determined we were at an appropriate place, he tugged me close. Not enough to be untoward, but enough I knew he was strong. Beneath his dark clothes, his body was hard, broad, and powerful. My hands slid over his shoulders. One of his large palms settled on the small of my back.

Lyres and panpipes played a cheery melody, and he fell into step with the tune. For several heartbeats, we said nothing, merely kept our gazes locked.

"What has changed?" he asked, sliding away from me, hand still clutching one of mine, before the music pulled us back together.

"What do you mean?"

I could not see his mouth, but his voice shifted pitch, like a smile had curved over his face. The stranger leaned close, voice soft. "I've watched you the entire evening. Not once have you seemed so . . . afraid of a partner."

"I'm not afraid of you."

"Glad to hear it. For I hope to dance with you again. Maybe another after that, and I would hate to make you uneasy, little bird."

Hells, he was intense. "You don't make me uneasy. I simply can't place you."

"I could say the same."

He didn't know me. I'd wanted to be bold, daring. With a stranger who bled power and mystery yet did not know what title burdened my blood, I could be anything.

With a deep swallow, I pressed my body a little closer. Breasts smashed against his chest. On the intake of breath beneath his mask, his fingers drifted lower to the slope of my backside.

"So, who are you, little bird?"

A rush of something dangerous hummed in my bones. "Yours, I suppose. For a little while."

My shadow made a noise, a sound deep and throaty like a growl. He leaned his masked face near mine; the heat in his strange eyes burned in desire. "Speak more words like that, and I will need to keep you longer than a little while."

He dragged the nose of his mask along the side of my throat. My skin prickled; my knees struggled to hold my weight. A pool of heat slid between my thighs, and I nearly gasped at the sensation. I'd felt an attraction to men since my girlish eyes found Stieg at age seven. Naturally, I was certain I'd take vows with the warrior someday. Until I met Hugo Nilsson in gentry lessons at the wise age of nine.

Then the secret pull to a boy forbidden to these lands. A pull I kept hidden even from Alek. But even more than my fleeting pull to Bloodsinger, my body craved the darkness of my new stranger.

I'd wanted a night to live in the throes of pleasure. A man with such an aura doubtless knew how to accomplish such a thing.

For a second, a fourth, then a fifth dance, I clung to my stranger. Time didn't seem to matter much. He spoke few words, mostly asked about me, but occasionally when we'd stumble, or my heel stepped on his toe, he'd try to keep in a laugh, until I tossed my head back and laughed for the both of us.

"You say you paint?" he said when the tune slowed again. "What do you paint?"

I was unaccustomed to anyone outside of my friends asking me about what interested me. My stranger had done that with every dance. In turn, I'd blurted out every light to my soul. Fishing with knives and spears instead of nets, blossoms and soft grass, and painting.

I cleared my throat. "It's strange, but I started the habit for my younger brother's entertainment when he was tiny and never stopped. I paint windows with a thin gloss. When it dries and the sun hits the pane just so, it's a little like stepping into a fairy tale."

His fingers splayed over my spine, touching every divot. "Perhaps you might show me these window paintings someday."

Gods, was I doing this? Mouth dry, blood racing, I pressed a clammy palm to his chest. "I . . . I've painted the fort windows in . . . in my chamber. If you'd like to see them."

His fingers curved, digging into my hip. "Lead the way, little bird."

Breathe. Focus. I took a step back. "Give me a moment to . . . to tell my friend where I've gone. She'll fret needlessly."

He dipped his chin. "I shall wait for you in the corridor."

I spun away. Another scorching look from him, and I might convince myself it was too much. A stranger? Could I do this? A few steps without his nearness, and my heart convinced my mind. Yes, I would never have a greater regret if I did not experience a bit more of that man's hands.

"Mira." I tapped her shoulder when I found her still arguing with Tobias over something frivolous only found amongst longtime childhood playmates.

"Livie." She gripped my arm and yanked me down. Half a head taller, I had to dip for her to whisper by my ear. "I cannot even see that man's face, but he, unmistakably, wants to take a bite out of you."

I grinned, taking her hand and squeezing. "Let us hope he does. I'm . . . I'm taking him to my chamber. Now."

Mira's lips parted. "Liv, are you certain? It's just, you haven't—"

"I know." I tightened my hold on her. "I want to do this, and if I don't, I will curse myself come morning."

She snorted. "Do this, and you might still be cursing come morning if he does not know how to conduct himself properly."

Mira was the best friend to keep around should you need a bolster of bravery. Never one to discourage us once our minds were made up, Mira simply stood back, ready to catch us if we fell.

"I wanted you to know in case you couldn't find me."

"Wise. A good first step. Should you go missing, I know whose cock to cut off."

"Gods, Mira." Tobias groaned. "How much wine have you had?"

She waved him away and gave me a devious grin. "Good luck, Liv. I expect every detail."

I gave her a quick embrace and whispered as I pulled back, "Never tell Jonas."

She snickered. "Afraid the man can smell when a woman has been bedded. He'll just know. Prepare yourself."

My body was ablaze in anticipation as I wove through couples until I slid into the shadows of the back corridor. I looked up and down twice. My shoulders slumped. He was gone.

"Did you think I would leave you, little bird?" Gloved fingers trailed down the back of my arm.

"For a moment I considered you thought better of doing this," I whispered.

His laugh came out in a low rumble as he wrapped an arm around my waist, aligning my back with his front. "I swear to you, I've waited a long time for a moment as perfect as this."

8

THE SONGBIRD

THE CLIMB TO my family's tower had never taken so long. Behind me, my stranger held my hand, still masked, and took in the stone stairwell as we went.

"A tower," he said once we reached the top. "You come from high ranks?"

If he knew I was a future queen, would all this change? I wasn't ready to find out. "My father is a nobleman, yes. Does it frighten you?"

I let out a shriek of surprise when he took hold of my waist and pressed my back to the cool stone of the wall two paces from my chamber door. Again, he slid his covered nose against my throat. My breaths came sharp and heavy as his hand skated up the side of my ribs. His thumb teased the underside of one breast.

Such a simple touch, and still my body arched for more.

"If I were a wise man, I might deal with your father first." His thumb slid over the mound of my breast and caressed the hardened peak of my nipple through my bodice. "But I'd rather deal with you."

I let out a ragged sigh when he drew the heel of his hand over the same places as his thumb, never palming my breast fully. This was more a tease, a glimpse at what he might intend to do behind closed doors.

I slapped my hand behind me until my grip found purchase on

the latch of my door. At the click, my stranger pulled back. He took my hand and, facing me, backed into the room.

The moment the door was closed, he had me against the wall again, only this time his body caged me there. I drew in a sharp gasp as his leg slid between my thighs. My gown had layers, but a whimper escaped my throat when he leaned in, the muscles of his leg rubbing wickedly against my throbbing center.

"Let me look at you." He hooked his thumbs under my mask.

I gripped his wrists. "You as well."

A low chuckle bobbed his throat. "Soon, but not yet."

From beneath his collar a few edges of white scars were visible. Maybe he was a Rave. Maybe he knew exactly who I was but believed the distance between our titles would never allow us to touch in such a way.

I cared little for ranks or classes, but I would play his game. Nothing so trivial as a mask would get me to stop this. Those gloves, now, those were another matter. I craved the touch of skin to skin, desired to know if his hands were firm or gentle, smooth or calloused.

With care, my shadow lifted my mask. I held my breath and waited for recognition, maybe a sudden change of heart. It never came.

His eyes shifted, hinting at a grin under his mask, and he lifted a palm to my cheek. "You're perfect."

He glided his fingers over the line of my jaw, the slope of my throat, until he reached the edge of my neckline and slid his fingertips beneath the bodice. Much lower, and the greater part of my chest would be bared to him.

He pressed his hips into mine, adding a touch of heated pressure at the apex of my thighs. I widened my stance, wanting more of him, wanting fewer layers between us.

He gathered bunches of my gown, tugging the skirt up my legs. "If you want more, little bird, all you must do is ask."

"I want . . ." I choked on my voice when his thumb brushed my inner thigh. Smooth leather roved dangerously close to my aching center.

"What do you want?"

"You," I breathed out.

"Certain?"

"Yes." I arched into him, seeking his touch.

In one swift motion, my stranger gripped both my wrists in one of his strong hands and pinned my arms over my head. A squeak of surprise melted to a moan when he arched his hips, slight enough the hard muscles of his leg nestled between my thighs, causing an unfamiliar rush of sensation.

My head spun; I hardly noticed my sleeves had slid up and his thumb gently rubbed the scorched scar near my elbow.

"What do we have here? A bind rune?" His eyes held firm to the mark.

Dammit. The fact he saw the straight lines of a rune amidst the bruising only heightened my unease that I'd done something horribly wrong by touching the edges of the Chasm. Most days, the mark was faded, but since returning from the shore last night, it was red and raised.

"It's nothing. A clumsy moment with a bruise to prove it."

By the hells, let that be the end of it. I didn't want overwrought fears about the Chasm and runes to bleed into my thoughts and take away from this moment and this man's hands on my body.

He dragged his thumb over the outline of the bruise for a few more heartbeats. I needed to steal his attention back. A slow roll of my hips brushed against his. The copper red of his gaze returned.

"Show me who you are."

For a moment he seemed to gnaw on the request. "Then you must play a game with me, little bird. I'll tell you two truths, and one lie. Guess the lie, and I'll do as you please. Get it wrong, and you do as I please. Agreed?"

All gods.

When I paused too long, he tilted his head. "Afraid?"

To my bones. I simply didn't know if it was fear that a stranger might harm me or that I'd be ruined for anyone else come morning. The precipice was there. I needed to decide if I would leap over the edge or remained unchanged. Comfortable.

"Agreed," I croaked at last.

"Good." He shifted so that his hips were fitted squarely against mine, glided his other palm up my thigh again, and hooked my leg around his waist. "You have family, but I am the last of my line."

My heart cinched. What a soft confession. His gloved hand kneaded the sensitive skin of my inner thigh. A gasp broke from my throat when he pinched my skin, a tease, but the bite of pain shocked my blood.

"Next one," he said, voice rough. Again, his hand began its torturous climb toward my center. "My magic frightens others, so I am careful where I use it."

"What is your fury?" I winced. He might not be Night Folk fae. "I mean, what is your magic?"

"Ah, I can't tell you yet, or that would ruin the game." He chuckled and released my wrists to hold me around the waist when the barest flick of his thumb found the wet slit of my core. I sucked in a breath and clung to his shoulders like a ballast in a maelstrom.

"Since boyhood," he went on, circling his thumb over my sensitive flesh. "I've had a favorite folktale. You might know it."

"What . . . what is it?"

"Have you ever heard the tale of the songbird and the sea serpent?"

My body stilled, frozen in place. He'd gone as still as me, and his fingers dug into my hip with an unforgiving grip.

"Do you know it?" he asked, voice rough.

"I . . . I think so." Hair prickled on the back of my neck.

"Do you know how it *truly* ends?"

I shook my head.

He laughed, not gently anymore, almost wicked. "You've now told me three lies, Songbird."

"What did you call me?"

"That was what you wanted to be, wasn't it? The songbird the serpent didn't destroy."

From the inside of his tunic, he produced a string of twine around his neck. On the end, a silver swallow. As bright and smooth as the day I'd tossed it into the cell.

Blood froze in my veins. I didn't blink when his thumb abandoned the horridly intimate place beneath my dress and tucked beneath the jaw of his mask. Time slowed when the stubbled jaw came into sight, the scar that puckered one part of his top lip, until those seductive eyes turned cruel and vicious.

The mask thudded onto the floor.

Not possible.

My mouth moved before my mind could convince it to keep quiet. "Bloodsinger."

His lips curved in a vicious snarl. The point of one of his slightly elongated teeth sent a shock of fear to my chest. "Hello, love. I promised I'd come for you. Have you figured my lie yet? For I have figured yours."

The way he had me balanced on one leg made it hardly an effort to kick my feet out from beneath me. I screamed as I fell. In the next moment, Bloodsinger had me on my back, his body forming a cage over the top of me.

"A bruise? Is that what's on your arm? No, I don't think so." He slid the sleeve of his tunic up his arm where a raised scar, nearly identical to mine, marked the place below the bend of his elbow. The same rune in beautiful filigreed designs. Bloodsinger leaned his face alongside my cheek. "Where is the mantle? You said you'd keep it safe."

He'd slaughter me if he ever found out. I thrashed, trying to squirm out of his grip. Erik merely tightened his hold and smashed my arms to my sides. "Why so afraid? Did you change your mind about seeing me again?"

"Go to the hells," I spat.

"That's not polite, love." A scream scraped from my throat when he gripped my jaw. "Now, I'll ask again. Where. Is. My mantle?"

"I don't know."

"You don't know." Bloodsinger clicked his tongue in disappointment. "No doubt your father does, right, Songbird?"

I pinched my lips. He was mad if he thought I'd put my mistake at the feet of my father. I'd never give up any of my family.

At my silence, he laughed. "That's answer enough. Up you go."

Long overdue, my damn instincts recalled I was the daughter of warriors. I clawed at his face. Again, he yanked my wrists over my head. I kicked at his legs. He pressed all his weight against me. My knee sought every bleeding man's weak spot, but before I could thrust my leg, Bloodsinger had a stiletto dagger leveled at my throat.

"That's enough. All these turns, I thought you wanted me to take you away from here."

Teeth bared, I lifted my forehead to his. "Touch me and my father will hunt you down to the depths of your hellish kingdom."

His laugh rattled against my body.

"Oh, love." Bloodsinger stroked his gloved knuckles over my cheek. "That is exactly my hope."

The bastard gripped my hair and dragged me to my feet. I screamed and thrashed, and in the next breath had a soft black scarf wrapped around my wrists. In and out, he wove the fabric like chains across my skin. When I fought, when I flailed my arms, he hummed and tightened his grip on my skin. The bastard enjoyed the fight.

Once my wrists were bound, Bloodsinger slammed me into his chest. "Let's take a walk."

I spit in his face.

Through a wretched sort of laugh, he gripped my chin, arching my neck. "Hear well your options. Walk with me, or I order my crew to slaughter everyone. I swear to you, those drunken fae downstairs will never see them coming. I'll be sure to point the loneliest men at that pretty friend of yours."

"You bastard."

He slammed my back to the wall. The force of it robbed me of my breath.

"I promise you something, my little songbird." Those eyes leered down his straight nose. This close I could make out the faintest freckles on his soft brown skin. Reluctantly, my lungs filled with the odd scent of him, salt and leather and something sweet, like the sugared glazes in the hall. Bloodsinger pressed his lips to the side of my cheek. My fists clenched as he whispered, "You will be a pleasure to break."

The next moments blurred. The sea king stole a tallow candle off a sconce and dragged me toward the window. My screams, at long last, drew pounding footsteps up the winding tower steps. Guards shouted commands. They called my name.

"It's Sea Fo—" My words cut off when Bloodsinger's rough palm covered my mouth.

"I could do with a bit more subtlety." He shook his head as though disappointed and paused at the window.

Moonlight shone through diaphanous paint on the glass. A painting from last turn when I'd stroked long brambles of red roses and tall green waves.

Almost tenderly, Bloodsinger undid the latch and nudged the window open. I'd half expected him to grin as he shattered the first part of my world.

He tipped the candle to the lower slats of the roof. Something glistened over the surface, but at the touch of the spark, a running flame spread over the top of the wooden slats.

"No!" I struggled until he shoved me through the window.

Erik Bloodsinger took hold of the scarf binding my wrists. A wink was all he gave before he took off across one of the thick beams in the opposite direction of the blaze devouring my entire world.

9

THE SONGBIRD

TEN PACES MORE and the hells shattered through our peace. The flames at our backs reached for the velvet night. The glow cast its cruel crimson dance across the courtyard. From the shadows, dozens and dozens of ghostly figures stepped into the light.

Sea fae charged into the fort.

Horns blasted from the watchtowers, and Rave warriors spilled out to meet them. Tears burned behind my eyes. I refused to let them fall. I needed to stay alert, stay clear, and snatch my chance to break Bloodsinger's fingers, take an eye, snap his wrist at the soonest possible moment.

I winced when screams from within the great hall took me from behind. Nearly everyone I loved was in there.

Bloodsinger heaved me forward at the edge of the tower roof. His strong arm curled around my waist. "Hold tight, love."

Without warning, he spilled us over the edge. My scream was muffled beneath the squall of shattered glass, the roar of casks bursting into flames. The ground struck, too soft, too scratchy. Bloodsinger had landed us into the back of a feed wagon that hadn't been there earlier. I choked on straw and stale oats, and had little time to catch my breath before the cart lurched forward.

A woman's holler of utter delight rose from the driver's bench.

Hooded, she clapped reins against an old, frail mule. The beast protested but quickened its pace.

"Damn creature! You be on land, so run!"

The cart bumbled through the courtyard. I tried to reach for the rail, ready to toss myself over it, but I was ripped back.

Bloodsinger gripped my ankle. "No foolish ideas, Songbird."

"No," I snapped. "Only wise ones."

With a grunt, I hiked up one knee, and slammed it into the side of his leg with every piece of might I could muster at this angle.

"Godsdammit!" He gripped his leg, jaw taut in pain, but righted swiftly. The red in his eyes flashed with violence. Bloodsinger scrambled over the straw, knowing what I planned before I'd even made a move to do it.

He was swift, but not swift enough.

I staggered to the rail of the cart, closed my eyes, and leapt off the edge. Sloppy and unskilled, all I could do was pray my head didn't catch beneath the wheels. I landed on the cobbled courtyard, face down, my bound wrists jabbed against my heart.

Move. Move. I scrambled to my feet, sprinting ahead without a look over my shoulder. Chaos had overtaken the fort. Banquet tables were overturned. Flames licked along the walls of the tower. Ladies stumbled amidst their full gowns. The glitter of masks sparkled like golden starlight in the hedges.

The crew of Bloodsinger was everywhere. Like locusts over crops, their blades sliced at our Rave. Hells, I needed a weapon. I was no warrior, but I could bleeding well hold my own. My thoughts turned to Rorik and the other littles. No mistake, they were guarded, but if the Rave were pulled out here to fight, the young ones needed to be led to safety.

I ducked my head and sprinted along the edges of the yard. As I ran, my gaze scanned faces, desperate to find Alek, Mira, or the twins. They *had* to be safe. I couldn't accept anything less.

The longhouse gates where Rorik and his playmates had feasted and reveled all evening were twenty paces away, untouched by flames, but I saw no Rave. No sign of anyone. Blood throbbed in my head. I hastened every step, ignoring the aches of muscles and joints.

"Rori—"

My voice tangled into a scream when two sturdy arms wrapped around my waist. I kicked and flung my bound hands around until a palm slapped over my mouth, and the jab of a knife met my ribs.

"Hush. There will be a place for you to scream later." His voice was death. Dark, cold, unfeeling. Bloodsinger drew a bit of blood from the pressure of his knife, barely splitting the skin, but if I kept thrashing, no mistake, my heart would meet the point.

His breath grew rough, almost haggard, as he dragged us between the wall of the fort and a stone smokehouse. Woodsy smells coated the sweat on my brow, the blood on his hands.

One arm wrapped possessively around my waist, Bloodsinger kept my body tight to his chest, his hand over my mouth and nose.

"Foolish games bring dangerous rewards," he hissed near my ear. "Remember that."

I stomped my foot on his toe, maneuvered out of his hold, and reached for the blade in his hand. Bloodsinger's face twisted in anger when I grabbed the hilt. With my hands bound, I was no match for him, and with a severe twist he yanked the knife away.

His palm surrounded my throat and squeezed. Not enough to cut off air but enough to threaten. "Listen to me, love. The sooner you follow my order, the sooner we leave your folk in our wake. Fewer lives lost. Your choice."

Each word crept from behind and throttled me. I go. The others live.

How was it even a choice when, if Bloodsinger spoke true, they were under attack because of me?

I didn't trust the man, but he shared the same mark as me. He'd appeared barely a full day after I touched the bleeding Chasm. This was my fault and my fault alone. I'd take my fate if it meant my people were safe.

I opened my mouth to agree to his twisted terms but was interrupted by a voice that cracked my heart.

"Livie!" Rorik's cry was strong, but beneath the bravado was a quiver of fear. "You let go of my sister."

Bloodsinger shifted forcefully, causing me to fall back onto my hip. My head whipped around, eyes wide. "No! Rorik, run!"

My brave, stupid brother bit his bottom lip. His skinny arms lifted an ax he must've found in the game yard. Though it was too heavy for him to properly swing, he gritted his teeth and lifted it against Bloodsinger.

The sea king tilted his head. "Little one looks just like him."

His hand choked the hilt of his dagger. The moment it flinched, I bolted to my feet.

"No!" I shoved myself between them, holding out my tethered hands like a supplicant. "Don't touch him. Please."

He held my gaze, a wild, manic fire in the strange red of his eyes, then he looked over me at Rorik, the boy still desperately trying to steady his ax.

I whimpered when Bloodsinger gripped the back of my neck and pulled me close. "Keep up, love, or I change my mind and scatter his bones."

The hilt of his dagger struck Rorik in the head. I screamed, and Bloodsinger caught me around the waist, hand over my mouth. Rorik crumbled to the ground, as still as death but for the soft rise and fall of his chest.

"Move." Bloodsinger gripped my wrists and led us into the storm.

Our pace was rapid, even with the painful lag of his leg. He was limping. In truth, I hadn't realized I'd kicked him so hard, but it gave me a single glimmer of light to cling to as he ripped me from my world. My folk.

We wove through battles and blades. Thoughts burned to a murky fog in my mind and tears skimmed along my lashes but never fell. Stun gathered like a shield over my body, guarding me away from the screams, the blood, the sharp slice of steel over steel.

A decade of peace had spun into a massacre in a single night.

I drew in shaky breaths, never entirely filling my lungs, and stumbled behind the sea king. Afraid to fight, afraid Bloodsinger would make good on his threat regarding Rorik.

"Livia!" Aleksi's voice rose over the battle. "He has the Night Folk princess. Go, move, move!"

A wet sob caught somewhere between my throat and my nose. I tried not to look, but one slight glance over my shoulder gave up Aleksi's frantic expression. My cousin and half a dozen Rave battled their way through the crowd, shouting my name.

Jonas and Sander were there, eyes black with their haunting magic, and both desperately fighting beside Alek. Both held black-steel blades and sliced through gambesons and chests as they battled like one mind.

"Livie!" Mira shrieked.

She was near the edge of the fort, surrounded by guards from her realms, and kept slicing a dagger, trying to break free of them. They wouldn't sacrifice their princess and caged her behind their round wooden shields.

A cloud of inky shadows coated their faces, but it faded swiftly when a guard took hold of Mira's wrists. As a powerful illusionist fae, no mistake, she was trying to break free with her magic.

"Livia!" she sobbed when the guard gave up and simply wrapped his arms around his princess's waist, dragging her clear of the fighting.

Bloodsinger watched it all, a vicious sort of grin on his face, as though we'd done exactly what he'd wanted all along.

Waves crashed against the edge of the gates. This far across the courtyard meant we'd reached the rocky foundation, where angry seas thrashed against white cobblestones at the base of the fort. My stomach lurched. A few tall gates and a cruel drop were all that was left between me and a watery grave.

"Look how many shall miss you, love." Bloodsinger laughed. "It's almost touching."

"Erik, stop this."

For the first time, the sea king went still. One hand gripped my throat. He spun me in front of him, using me as a shield.

On a staircase that led to one of the watchtowers on the gates, Stieg, blade out, looked nowhere but the Ever King. "Let her go, boy."

"Warrior." Bloodsinger gritted the word out as though it burned his tongue. "You look old."

What the hells?

"And you look lost." When Stieg stepped forward, Erik stepped back.

"You have a chance here, love," he whispered. "Do I call off my crew, or shall we have a bit more fun?"

I lifted my chin. "Stieg, stand down."

"Can't do that, Princess."

"They take me, they leave," I said, a croak in my voice. "Ror is near the smokehouse and—"

"I'm not letting you go." Stieg's jaw pulsed. "Erik, think hard about what you're doing."

Against my back, Bloodsinger's chest hummed with another laugh. "For turns I've had nothing else to think about, warrior."

"You're starting new wars."

"No. I'm finally ending them." He removed his hand from my neck and lifted it to his mouth. With a quick bite to his thumb, he drew a drop of blood on the tip.

"Erik, don't!" Stieg shouted with a new frenzy.

Bloodsinger painted my bottom lip with his own blood, then licked off the rest. "Best not to taste those beautiful lips, Songbird," he whispered. "Warrior, if you want to risk her neck, keep walking. If you want her to live to see another sunrise, then step back."

A wash of defeat painted Stieg's face. I didn't understand the connection between my father's captain and the Ever King, but his resignation at the sight of his blood brought truth to rumors. Erik Bloodsinger was made of poison.

Lost in the pause, I hadn't realized how near the cliff the sea king had guided us.

"Say goodbye, love." He didn't give me a chance before he waved his hand, and from the cove below us, the water swirled and we fell backward into the sea.

10

THE SERPENT

THE SEA HAD been a prison at dawn. Now moonlight revealed the truth of its beauty at long last. Its freedom.

For another fae, the fall might've shattered them on the rocks. For the Ever King, the sea rose to greet us.

My little songbird fought hard not to scream, but before the biting cold of the white foam took us, a shrill cry scraped from her throat. No doubt unwanted, she nuzzled closer, hiding her face against my neck.

A brief touch, but the sensitive flesh of the scars across my throat ached. I wasn't so certain it was a bad ache. As though the pain wanted to drag her in, seal her up, and leave her there to sweeten the rot left behind.

I sank into the tide. Eyes closed, the strength, the power, the rage of the sea brought the frantic beat of my pulse to a calm. Then the princess's damn heel struck me in the leg again.

She thrashed and kicked for the surface. Hands tied, it'd be slow going, and she was locked in a dead man's panic, the last frantic rush to cling to life. Sea fae grew sickly on land without submerging in water, but it wasn't as though I would die. Would I be miserable if I were left to dry in the sun for the rest of my days? Without a doubt.

To draw earth fae into the sea was much the same if left to the depths. The fae of the land were not like mortals, who could not hold air in their pathetic lungs for longer than a few counts. In the Ever Kingdom, they thrived within our realm better than Sea Folk could live in theirs. Many of the Ever Folk were descendants of kinder times between land and sea.

To travel the Chasm without the aid of a sea fae was another matter.

Earth fae might survive; drowning wasn't the worry, it was the violence they could not tame. The connection to the currents did not thrive in their blood, and the tides would do their best to shred them to pieces should they enter unaccompanied.

Right here, the princess had little reason to fear the tides, but she was gulping the sea in a frenzy.

This wouldn't do, and I had little patience or time to wait for her to realize the Otherworld was not beckoning her forward.

She'd hate me, maybe bite me—gods, I hoped so—for what had to be done.

I gripped a hand around one of her ankles and pulled her back to me. She gulped, released too much air, and stared at me with a hint of betrayal. Dreary thoughts must've been rummaging through her beautiful head. Would I choke her? Run her through?

I didn't have plans for all that. Yet. There was suffering to be had first.

Instead, I kissed her.

Once the stun of my mouth on hers faded, the princess kicked at me. As expected, she turned her fight against the pressure of the sea onto me. Those claws tried to dig at my face.

I pulled away only to grip her jaw. "You want to breathe, Songbird? Or shall I let the Chasm crush those lungs? Slowly."

Her eyes widened. To me, my voice beneath the waves was a low boom. What did it sound like to her?

I sneered and dragged my nose alongside her cheek. "I'll give you breath, but only if you behave."

Lore existed about the kiss of sea singers, one that gave endless breath to a land walker they loved more than the sea. No need to let on it wasn't true. She needed to believe some mystical spell from my mouth halted her panic, which in turn would make hauling her around simpler. In the meantime, I got to torment those sweet lips. I got to bring out the hate she buried beneath her cloak of innocence.

The princess was mine to ruin by right and destiny, and I planned to begin now.

My tongue slipped through my teeth and swiped over the salty damp of her mouth. She pinched her lips, face contorted in a bit of disgust. Stubborn little bird. This time there was no easing her into it, nothing gentle. I demanded her mouth and took it. She tasted like rain on the sea, fresh and wild. As expected, she resisted. Until I released a soft breath over her tongue. With my hands on the small of her back, the shudder rippled beneath my palms.

I offered another breath. She took it greedily.

The magic of transferring breath was myth, but . . . something was happening. A spark in the blood that shot to the rune on my skin. A heat that dug deep into my chest, drawing me closer, keeping me locked in her essence.

What was meant to be a moment of torment slipped into an obsession for more. More of her taste, more of her softness. More.

I wasn't alone.

Disgust faded from her features into something darker, almost feral. In another heartbeat, she clung to me like she craved the heat of my hands as much as I craved hers. The princess had her wrists bound, but her fingers curled around my tunic, holding me close. With a graceful slide through the current, she pressed her hips to mine.

Dammit. My body fought to react, to press back until she felt the hardness in my damn trousers building the longer I held her sweet mouth. Lust and need were weaknesses expected of others, but not— bleeding hells—not from the damn sea king.

I cursed and forced myself to pull back. With the connection severed, resentment was quick to return. She tried to pull away. I took hold of the scarf around her wrists and yanked her back.

Frustration, anger at my own weakness, came out in sharp, biting words. "Breathe now. Fight, and I give you to the crew. Comply, and you'll live to see the other side of the Chasm."

One hand wrapped around the scarf, I swam to the shadows of the water. When the darkness shifted upon our arrival, Livia gave a little shriek, releasing a cloud of bubbles. Crimson sails rose from the dark depths of the deeper sea. The gaping mouth of the serpent figurehead gleamed under the broken skeins of moonlight. On the hull, the armored door cranked open.

I took us in.

My songbird stopped fighting; she practically went boneless and allowed me to drag her into the stomach of the ship as though the ember of her fight was snuffed out. Pity.

Inside the hull, the door groaned and snapped as the heavy ironed chains clanked back into position. Swallowed water drained through the floor and was heaved back into the tides. We sank with it until my feet planted on the floor.

Though the whole of the ship remained underwater, inside the hull was little more than damp.

The princess, hunched and soaked, spluttered at my feet.

"Get up." I gripped under her arm. "You'll miss your chance to wave farewell."

"What, I—" Words cut off when I strode to a wide staircase.

The ship rocked. Livia slammed into the side wall. On instinct, I slipped an arm around her waist to keep her upright. She drew in a sharp breath when I opened the hatch to the main deck the same moment the ship carved through the surface.

The bow shot through the surf toward the moon, like a whale breaching the waves. I tugged her into my side and gripped the rail until the ship righted over the surface again. She slipped off a stair, forced to cling to me to keep from tumbling belowdecks. I laughed, reveling in her disquiet. The look she returned was wholly worth it—dark and hateful.

"What ways are you thinking of slitting my throat, Songbird?"

"It'd be foolish of me to give up my plans," she hissed. "I swear to you, it will be a show worth the wait."

"Such venom." With one knuckle, I stroked her cheek. "Careful with your threats of my untimely death, love, or you might end up stealing my heart."

On deck, crewmen tugged on the rigging, while some still clambered over the rails on their return from the land. At the sight of me and my songbird, voices rose in a chorus of chants and jeers. Most were aimed at the fae locked in the burning fort, but some were bolder and tossed their taunts at the princess.

Livia kept her eyes schooled on the deck, even on the steps leading to the helm.

Tait gripped the jagged handles, jaw tight, with a narrowed look I could see even buried in the shadows from the brim of his hat. "The mantle?"

I guided Livia in front of me, my palm open on her stomach. "Soon enough, but we now have something to barter."

Tait kept his frown, but a gleam of the thrill he never showed lit the ribbons of red in his eyes. Behind him, Celine had perched on one of the rails, Larsson beside her, blood splattered across the edge of his jaw.

Celine smacked her lips, licked grease off her sharpened fingernails, then threw the bone of whatever fowl she'd taken from the masque into the sea. "What a lovely haul you've brought us, My King."

Celine snapped her teeth, laughing when Livia flinched.

Larsson tossed a skin of coins between his hands. "The bastards are aiming to set sail behind us."

Celine took a spyglass from a pouch on her belt and handed it to me. Longships were being loaded. The glow of the burning fort revealed the endless warriors on the docks.

"They seek a chase, let's give them one." I folded the spyglass again and took the helm from Tait's hold.

One hand on the helm, one on my songbird, I faced the crew. "What d'you say, men? Ready to show these bastards what it means to chase the *Ever Ship*?"

The crew pounded their fists and began the eerie chant.

We work we rot . . .

I pulled Livia close to my side. "Hang on to me. I'd hate to lose you along the way."

She scoffed, teeth bared. "I'd rather drown in the depths than touch you."

"Suit yourself, love." I released the scarf between her hands and returned to the helm. "Hoist the banner, you bastards! The sea calls."

Hums and grunts and chants came from the deck as the crew scrambled to their positions. Four bulky men gathered near the mainmast and tugged on the black rigs, drawing the frayed banner of the Ever to the top of the sails.

Horns and battle cries echoed in the distance.

I glanced over my shoulder, just enough to witness a few of her people begin the hopeless pursuit. Those oars in their odd longships were no match for the sleek hull of the *Ever Ship*.

I met Livia's gaze. "Say goodbye, Songbird."

With a wave of my hand, a gust of wind caught the sails, they billowed out, and the ship lurched forward.

11

THE SONGBIRD

*S*AY GOODBYE.

Such a final statement, one my mind refused to believe even as Bloodsinger turned away, his strong hands locked on the ghastly spokes of the . . . wheel? I didn't understand this vessel. So large, so gaudy. There was nothing honed and smooth about Bloodsinger's ship. Nothing like our warships with their slender, serpentlike frames, with the square sails to catch the right amount of wind.

This vessel had black spikes like broken bones jutting off the sides, and the edges curved in such a way that a great frothy wake surrounded the hull.

Rave warships, well crafted as they were, would have a challenge even getting close.

I clung to the hope that this monstrosity would be dreadfully slow and the Rave would catch us before the Chasm. Until Bloodsinger raised a hand and an unnatural breath of wind captured those bloody sails. They whipped and cracked and careened the dark ship forward.

I stumbled, my hip striking the banister that surrounded the top level. A level seemingly designed to hold the odd wheel. The woman behind me laughed and offered a cruel wink and gripped the rigging.

My stomach tightened into a harsh coil, like briars and jagged points. The nearer the ship drew, the more the shadows of the Chasm shifted into something else. Like the eye of a storm, water spun and thrashed. It reminded me of a kettle boiling over a flame.

We were caught in the tug, a fish on a hook, being reeled into the center of the coil. The Chasm was truly devouring us.

A quick scan of the deck revealed no one but me seemed bothered in the least.

Bloodsinger hummed at his horrid wheel, a tune as low and terrible as a dark omen. His voice was almost lovely, like a ballad honoring a fallen lover.

But amidst the frightening beauty of the man was a sinister light in those horrid eyes, a cruel curl to the scar sliced through his lip. He was despicable, wretched, and I couldn't look away.

He balanced the wheel. Where the ship rocked to one side, he'd ease the handles to the opposite. A dance of give-and-take with the monstrous vessel.

"Hold tight, me boys! She be bringing us home!" A bony man laughed a bit maniacally against the spray of the sea and waved the tattered leather of his hat against the wind.

"Last chance, Songbird." Bloodsinger opened one arm, a gesture to hold to him. "You've my word, I won't let you go."

I turned my back to him, taking my chances with the Chasm. Hells, it might spit me back out if I fell overboard.

Or . . . it might snap my bones.

Surrounded by damp and I could not wet the back of my throat. The scarf tied between my wrists ached against my skin. If I fell overboard, how would I swim bound in such a way?

"Hold steady!" Bloodsinger shouted to his crew.

Gods, even the bleeding king braced, grip tighter on the sharp handles, knees slightly bent.

The roar of the Chasm drew closer. The bow of the ship tilted.

I hit the rail, heart racing. Dammit. We were diving. Water spilled over the deck, then to the first mast, then the center. Like an undersea creature lapping us up.

Perhaps come dawn I'd despise myself, but before I could think twice, I had my body pressed against Bloodsinger's side, my hands curled around his tunic. He didn't shove me aside (part of me suspected he might in the final moments) and in a graceful shift, he positioned me between his body and his jagged wheel. Both of his arms caged me as he kept his grip on the spokes.

"Face me, Songbird," he said, almost gently, against my ear.

The water was creeping up the stairs. He pulled me between his arms and aligned our chests in such a way my nose struck his. Gods, his eyes . . . I could tell myself they were awful, but in truth, they stole my breath.

I hated him for it.

As if he could read the contradictions of my thoughts, he grinned. "Wrap those arms around my neck. Like you did so well before."

"My greatest shame," I spat back, but complied. I lifted my bound wrists over his head, hooking them around his neck.

Water circled around my ankles. Damp as I was, the chill was still a shock. Unbidden, I tightened my hold on Bloodsinger's neck, clinging to him as though he were not the future cause of my death. As though he would keep me from destruction.

His body tensed, not from my touch—he'd simply stopped maneuvering the spokes. He froze until the Chasm took us under. Until the beauty and wonder of my world faded.

12

THE SONGBIRD

I'D ANTICIPATED THE waves tossing us about, but it was more like a fierce wind. My hair whipped around my face; pressure collided around us at all sides. Bloodsinger's muscles tightened in his shoulders, his arms. He wrenched the handles of his wheel to one side abruptly, and I had to throttle his neck to keep upright.

A good plan if I wanted to strangle the man, but the rumble of his laugh danced through my belly. He took pleasure in my fear.

I hated him a little more.

A muffled scream ripped from my chest when the ship tilted. By the hells, we were rolling, tipping, going to be plunged into the deepest parts of the Chasm. Was this his bleeding plan all along? Secure his crew to the deck, then let me go?

I never fell. My head knew we had tipped, yet my feet remained planted on the deck. I cracked my eyes, peering over Bloodsinger's shoulder.

Not possible. The sea was as clear as thin ice, and through ripples above us, soft golden sunlight brightened the shadows.

Faster than we dived, the bow surged to the surface. I lost my breath when a cool gust of clean sea air replaced the murky pressure of the undercurrent. My footing slipped when the bow slammed back onto the sea, swaying the deck wildly for a few heartbeats.

One of Bloodsinger's arms wrapped around my waist and hoisted me back upright. Locked in our horrid embrace, I was forced to press firmly against him and rest my chin atop his shoulder for my fingers to swipe the brine from my eyes. I blinked against a sun that had not been there moments ago.

"By the gods," I breathed out before I could stop myself.

Bloodsinger scoffed. "Welcome to the Ever."

The Ever Kingdom.

We were on a new sea, one made of cerulean glass and distant cliffs, and coves, and fjords. The dark storm that had surrounded the hull of the ship when it ventured to my side of the Chasm had faded. Now the laths and boards and spikes of the deck glistened like polished onyx.

Overhead was a rising sun, pale and brilliant. Not gold but soft ivory. To one side of the sea were distant shadows of land. The other way, the direction Bloodsinger led his ship, was nothing but open water.

The woman tilted her head back, absorbing the sun into her brown skin. "Do we make the call?"

Bloodsinger peered to the sea, tension in his jaw, but nodded. With a wink to me, the woman held out a vial. Bloodsinger didn't shove me aside. He made his movements with me as a fixture around his body. The glint of light on his teeth brought me to pause. Much the same as he'd done when he faced Stieg, the king dragged his thumb across the sharp point of his canine tooth until a bead of blood rolled over the tip.

Poison blood. He had poisonous blood, and I was pressed to him like moss to a tree. I stiffened, drawing Erik's gaze.

"No worries, love. Needs to mix with your blood before it boils your insides. Best not to swallow it though."

"Maybe I have a taste for blood." *Gods.* Nerves had a way of drawing out nonsensical, ill-timed words.

Erik did the unexpected. He gawked at me for five breaths, the blood on his thumb dripping down the curve of his hand, then he laughed. Not forced, not cruel, a true laugh that rumbled through his chest into mine.

He was a fiend, a tyrant, and his smile should fill my head with hate and bitterness. I could not look away. The man had a dimple in his cheek when he smiled, and it did something to his eyes. They burned like fire in the brush, wild and free.

He was a wretch, and hate for him burned with every pump of blood in my veins. The trouble was, hate was passionate and walked a fine line beside other passions—desire, lust, obsession.

When his laugh died off, Erik scraped his bloody thumb over the top of the woman's vial. The swirl of red tangled with the shade of blue in the water like a whimsical dance.

"Wait." Erik gripped the woman's shoulders and leaned toward her ear. He whispered something, so low I couldn't make out the sound above a rough rasp.

The woman arched one brow. "What is all that?"

"Just see that the supplies are there."

"Will Alistair even know what it is?"

Bloodsinger frowned. "That old fool knows everything from every realm. See that he has it waiting for our return."

"Aye, My King." She leaned over the rail of the ship, whispered words I couldn't hear against the glass of the vial, then tossed it into the current below. A shudder dipped the ship, and a ripple flowed over the surface of the sea. What did they do?

"Larsson!" Bloodsinger shouted. "Man the helm. I have a guest to see to."

The crew laughed in such a way my blood chilled in my veins. Bloodsinger took hold of my arms and lifted them over his head. Once again, he had the scarf gripped and tugged me toward the stairs.

My breaths came sharp and desperate. No mistake, he'd slaughter me in front of his crew and send pieces of me back to my family, or he'd rape me, batter me, then do the first two things.

"You don't need to do this," I whispered.

"Ah, but I do."

"Please." Gods, I sounded pathetic, a fool to show how terrified I truly was. I clenched my teeth until they nearly cracked and straightened my bent spine. If I died, I would die with a blade in hand and a great deal of Bloodsinger's deadly blood beneath my fingernails.

The crew moved aside for their king. I refused to meet any stares, refused to give them the satisfaction of my distress. His pace was swift, but he had a pronounced limp. The corner of my mouth twitched. In the cart, I'd kicked him hard enough that he'd reeled back, and I took a bit of pleasure knowing it had done damage.

Beneath the deck with his wheel—or helm, as he called it—was an arched door. He shoved me inside a small chamber. Modest, with a narrow table covered in maps and quills, and a cot. No quilts or furs, only a stretched piece of canvas tied with thick twine to heavy logs spiked into the floor.

Erik had to crouch to avoid striking his head on the doorframe. There he paused, and faced a few curious eyes of his crew. "Anyone enters without my say so, they lose their tongue."

With that he slammed the door behind us. He removed the hat from his head and tossed it onto the cot.

I took a step away from him. Night Folk fae were not small in stature, but Bloodsinger was a force. Broad, formidable. The scars peeking out from his black tunic brought a thousand questions I was certain would never be answered. Scarred and battered, he still moved like a man capable of lunging and striking without hesitation. A true serpent hiding in the surf.

I flinched when his hands went to the scarf. With an unexpected gentle touch, he unbound my wrists as he spoke. "Do you know why I took you, Songbird?"

"You lost the war and can't accept it?"

He sighed and tossed the scarf aside. "I figured you were naive, but I did not know you had no brains at all."

The insult cut like a lash. I didn't let it show. "Pity I can't find a way to please you."

The bloody sunset shade of his eyes shifted to something like a fiery night. "I'm sure you'll find a way. May I suggest watching your tongue around the one who controls how long you live?"

"Then you shall be disappointed." I regretted the words straightaway.

Bloodsinger moved like a spark catching fire. His firm grip found my throat. I let out a breathless gasp when he touched the tip of his straight nose to mine. "Why fight me? You called to me." He ripped my sleeve apart and traced the mark on my arm with his thumb. "It's no coincidence that I find my emblem imprinted on you. Like you belong to me."

"Don't flatter yourself. An accidental touch of—"

"Touch of what?" He grinned, the rough callus on the tip of his thumb tracing the side of my throat. "Did you call to me through the Chasm? The only way I could sail through was if the wards were gone. I think you had something to do with that." From under his tunic, Bloodsinger removed the silver swallow. "We're bonded, you and I. From the moment you began your little tale."

Acid burned in sick waves in my gut. "That was nothing but a foolish girl's attempt to protect her folk. There is no magic to it, there is no bond. I feel nothing for you but hate."

He shrugged one shoulder as if utterly unbothered. "Admittedly, I don't understand how you have the rune, but it led me back to you. Face the truth, love, you fastened your own chain around your throat."

I lifted my chin, heat flushing in my face. "I know you believe you must take vengeance on my family. I will not deny my father killed yours; we all know the story."

"You know the story?" His voice rose to a near bellow. "The death of the Ever King is not some tale you read in your little books."

"You despise us for the war, when it was your people who attacked first."

"Only because your people slaughtered a king of the Ever."

"Twenty turns ago, and only after Thorvald attacked one of our own." Anger heated my blood. Thorvald had attacked an innocent woman, a cousin of mine, to be exact. I'd seen the scar left behind. Thorvald's act of unprovoked violence spurred my father's ax to find the sea king's heart.

"I know well what my father did." New shadows darkened Erik's eyes. "I also know it was done after your folk spent weeks torturing his heir."

My retort dried like ash on my tongue. The scars on his neck, his lip, the ones clearly hidden beneath his shirt. Thorvald was killed before I was even born, ten turns before the Great War. If what Erik said was true, then as a tiny child, he'd been tortured.

It couldn't be true. The kings and queens, my family, they'd never do such a thing to a little.

"You're lying," I said through my teeth.

"What would be the point?"

Bloodsinger strode past me to a small cupboard. He reached inside and returned with a glass cruet filled with burgundy wine, then kicked out a wooden stool tucked beneath the table. The drink filled a smooth horn, dark and thick enough I considered it might be blood.

He licked his lips after a drink, drawing my gaze to the swipe of his tongue. How could a man be distasteful and desirable all at once?

"You want to think I am lying," he went on, "because otherwise it means those who love you with such tenderness might be as monstrous as me."

I slammed my open palm on the table. "You are a liar who seeks justice for a king who attacked my people unprovoked. Now you continue the legacy. I hope you burn in the hells for it."

"Believe what you will, but consider this—don't you find it strange your cherished warrior knew me?"

"Stieg." My heart jolted. "He called you by name."

"Yes." His mouth twisted into a snarl. "Who do you suppose guarded me during my first capture? The capture where my father rose through the Chasm to council with warring earth fae, only to be duped and have his heir used in a desperate attempt to heal the dying."

All gods.

Stieg was ferocious with a blade; he was Rorik's idol. Adored by many. If he guarded a cell with a child, it would've been done at the word of . . . my father.

I shook my head. "No. What would be the point of taking a sea child? They wouldn't do it."

"Fae clans battled for turns before the Great War between our worlds, Songbird. Don't you know your history? The desperate will do anything to survive." Erik tugged back the collar of his shirt. I winced. Across the side of his neck, tangled down his throat, across his shoulders were raised white scars. Some long, others short. Most formed over spots where the body bled most. His voice shifted to something cold. "Won't they?"

Sick tossed in my belly. I closed my eyes.

"Look at me!" he shouted. I jolted and snapped my eyes open. Bloodsinger rose and pinched my chin between his thumb and finger. "You think your people are innocent, and I do not blame you. How could you know any different when all your life they have painted us as the villains?"

"They wouldn't do the things you say." I hated how my voice cracked.

Erik's thumb brushed over my cheek. "Ah, love. You think your peace was won with gentle morals? We all have a darkness within us, and desperation to survive can reveal the cruelest pieces."

Breathe. Focus. I wanted to crumble. I wanted to flee to my folk and demand to know the truth. I knew of the land wars that united the realms and led us to the war with the sea. I knew of the bloodlust and the pain every kingdom had suffered.

Was it possible they'd grown desperate enough to keep each other alive that they leeched from an innocent?

Loath as I was to admit it, torturing a young sea prince, then killing his father seemed reason aplenty for the sea to rise against the land for an even greater war.

But he was lying. He had to be. My mother and father would never condone the torture of a child. Unless—dread hardened in my veins—unless harm were to befall one of them. Bonds went deep amongst our people. My father could be brutal and beastly if my mother were ever threatened. She could be the same. No life stood before her family.

I didn't pull away from his touch. I merely held his gaze. "No matter what I say, you believe your words, so what penance am I to pay, Bloodsinger?"

"For now, I'll take pleasure in their suffering and desperation to reclaim you." One corner of his lip curled. "I'll sleep better knowing they are imagining all the horrors you must be enduring."

"Horrors you plan to bestow soon enough, true?"

"I'd hate to spoil the surprise." Erik leaned into me; his mouth hovered over mine. "Let's just say you've become my most prized possession."

A thousand different ways he could use his blood to torture me rattled through my skull. I jerked my chin from his hold and schooled my gaze on the floorboards.

Erik clicked his tongue. "I've upset you. I do hate when you're upset."

"You did not upset me." I didn't look at him. "You disappoint me."

He went silent for a long pause. Long enough that curiosity begged me to look. His lips were set, a slight furrow of bemusement between his brows. Horrid and beautiful all at once.

"Disappoint you? Strange response. How might I better meet your expectations as your captor?"

The cruelness of his grin drove a spike through my chest.

I clasped my hands behind my back to hide the tremble in my fingers. "Call me foolish to even care, but I was kind to you as a child. Now you have twisted that kindness into something ugly." I scoffed. "Perhaps it is not you who disappoints me. Perhaps it is disappointment in myself for ever thinking a creature like you could have a shred of a heart."

My voice came out hushed, small even. A man like Bloodsinger was beyond feeling, yet I couldn't stop. "Do your worst, Bloodsinger. The heart I once showed you as a stupid girl is gone away where you cannot touch it again."

Erik pulled me against him. Chest to chest, hip to hip, his vicious eyes bounced back and forth between mine.

"You took pity on a boy because you knew I'd always be a threat. You wanted that threat tamed, so do not pretend you were kind out of the goodness of your heart. Kindness is not free, love. There is always something expected in return."

I didn't shrink under his scrutiny, and lifted my chin, our noses touching. "What sort of sad existence have you known to not understand genuine concern?"

"Save your pity and worry a bit more about your own life."

I yanked my arm out of his grip. He allowed it, but hot rage burned in his eyes. Somewhere, my words had lashed at him. I hoped he bled out from them.

I could not change what was done, but bringing Erik Bloodsinger back into our world was my fault. Whether my people were villains once mattered little in the now. I would pay the price to keep them safe, for I had brought the danger by believing there was something deeper in the heart of a villain.

Bloodsinger believed I'd visited him out of fear of what he would do. I'd never tell him the truth.

I'd been drawn to him like the flow of the sea; even when I'd been a girl he'd sparked some twisted curiosity, some tug to see him. I should've resisted, the same way I should've had the strength to resist the pull to the sea now.

I flinched when his hand rose. The strike I expected never came. Bloodsinger slammed his palms against the wooden hull, forcing my back to the wall. This close, I could make out the blood pulsing in his throat; I could taste the sourness of his rage.

"Take your vengeance, Bloodsinger," I said, voice rough. "Your mind is set, so do what you must, but I will never turn on them. I will never be your pawn to hurt them. I'll slit my own throat first."

He hesitated, then lifted the tips of his fingers to the heated ridge of my cheek. I turned my head away. The bastard only traced my jaw, almost like he was lost to the dark pits of his own thoughts.

When he spoke, his voice was cold, dead; it burrowed into my bones. "If only it were so simple, Songbird. You are the perfect, unexpected blade that will cut out the hearts of your folk. They'll suffer. You'll watch. Only when they're on their knees, pleading, will I give them the death they crave."

He was a lunatic. I didn't fight the tears anymore and let them fall. Not tears of sadness. No, my people had slaughtered the Ever Folk before. They would again. If my death was a price for their continued safety and peace, I'd happily pay it. These were tears of disgust.

"I will never help you hurt anyone I love."

"You're mine to use as I wish." He stepped back and opened his arms. "Face the truth. You belong to the Ever King."

Bloodsinger turned for the door. My lips parted. He was . . . leaving me? A man tainted by evil such as him surely played with his food before he tore it to pieces.

The stun must've muddled my brain and had the question spilling off my tongue before he left the room. "What do you plan to do with me?"

He paused at the door, hand on the latch. "For now, let you sleep. I don't want you stumbling on your feet like a fool. I hope you love your father as much as it seems. For you are about to stand in his place at the rack."

"You're the fool, Erik Bloodsinger," I whispered. "You think it will only be my father who comes for me? You've begun a war with an entire world. They will tear you apart and pike your pieces along every border of every realm."

"Well, take that thought and give yourself sweet dreams. For that is all they are—dreams." He gestured to the small window overlooking the brilliant water. "Try to escape, and I give you to my crew to do with you whatever they please. Try to toss yourself into the Otherworld, I'll keep you chained to me at all times. You understand? Now, sleep, scream, beg—I care little—but accept that you're mine and you always were."

The moment he slipped through the door and locked it behind him, I slid down the door until I met the floor, face in my palms.

Alone, where no one could see my failure, I broke into sobs.

13

THE SONGBIRD

THE DOOR POUNDED into my back. A huff of annoyance followed. "If you've gone and bled out on me, I'll be damn put out."

A woman's voice. I lifted my head from the cold floorboards. Somewhere during my tears, I must've fallen asleep exactly where Bloodsinger left me. My damp hair had dried in crusty waves. The back of my skull felt as though a molten knife dug deep, scrambling my brains about.

The corner of the door jabbed my hip again. I hurried out of the way, facing the entrance, ready to kick or claw until I could get my hands on a weapon.

The woman who'd sneered at me near the helm tripped over the lip after the door opened too quickly.

"Damn you," she grumbled.

Once her stance was righted, she adjusted a black leather hat over a single braid in her stormy hair. A strange color, like the silver of mist with dark wisps of thunderclouds woven throughout. Her skin was rich brown with a splatter of darker freckles over her nose and a pink scar across the center of her throat. One silver hoop pierced an ear. More than one sea fae only had one hoop or spike through one ear. In the case of this woman, she didn't have a choice.

Her second ear was rolled inward, as though it had never formed.

She narrowed her eyes, both flecked in brilliant gold and green, like a forest after rain. "Did you not see the bed? Or are earth fae just that stupid?"

"Think your words will wound me?"

"No, I was asking." She pointed to the cot. "Did you not see the damn bed?"

I paused. Strange, but she seemed to speak in earnest. Like I was nothing but an empty-headed fae for not accepting the generosity of a stiff cot in my captor's bedchamber. For a fleeting moment her logic and straightforward tongue reminded me of Mira.

I pressed a hand to my heart, missing her. Missing them all.

"By the seas," the woman said, gawking with a bit of horror when my chin trembled. "Don't tell me you're going to cry over not taking the cot. There's always tonight."

I clenched my fists, using the bite of my fingernails in the meat of my palm to dull the anguish of not knowing. "I was thinking you . . . you remind me of my friend. She was taken away during the fighting, but I still don't know if she's alive."

The woman arched a brow, perhaps stunned at the honesty instead of a snide remark.

What was the point in tossing insults back and forth? She was the one armed. I didn't want to risk one of the knives on her belt flying at me before I got my hands on one.

When the stun subsided, the woman shrugged and kicked the door closed at her back. She strode across the space, humming, and wrenched open two doors in the wall, revealing a built-in wardrobe. The space was stuffed with mostly black attire with a few crimson scarves and one green coat trimmed in silver.

The woman ignored the clothes and returned with a clay basin and wooden ewer.

"You're going to wash." She set the basin down with a nod as if her word was final and there'd be no arguing.

"Hard to do so without a drop of water."

"Ah, you do have brains." She smiled. A true smile of amusement. It was more unnerving than a sneer.

I did not want to witness humanity, not a shred of decency, amongst the Sea Folk. I wanted to see them for what I'd made them in my mind—cold, cruel, and monstrous.

The woman turned back to the wardrobe and removed a plain dark top with sleeves that billowed more than I was accustomed to and reached inside a satchel over her shoulder, tossing a bundle of deep purple fabric onto the tabletop.

"That's mine, and I'll expect you to care for it." The woman's mouth pinched. "Don't like trading my things. I knew the second I saw you I'd be the one tending to your every bleeding whim, seeing how no one else here has breasts."

I arched a brow. "We're the only women?"

"Not many women in the Ever set sail. Certainly not with the king." She paused, a slow grin on her mouth. "Except me."

I considered asking more, then stomped any curiosity down, buried under heavy layers of disdain and mistrust.

"Get washed," she went on. "Get dressed. You'll start to stink locked up in here."

"Then don't keep me locked in here."

"Oh, you'll see the ship," she scoffed. "I've been assigned to show you about as we go."

I swallowed through a scratch. "And where exactly are we going?"

"We'll be making our way back to the royal city," she said. "Wallow in here the entire time and you'll start talking to the walls. Small quarters with nothing but sea around you start to play tricks on the mind if you don't keep busy."

I'd take her word for it. My fingers trembled as I worked the numerous buttons on the masquerade gown. "Keep me from the king and I'll be your loyal shadow."

She snorted and shook her head like I was an utter fool. "Hard to do when it's his ship, earth fae. Now wash, and maybe I'll take you to the king so you can thank him for allowing you to live this long."

A bit of defiance bled to the surface. I thought of Jonas, of Alek. I even thought of tales I'd heard of my mother's sharp tongue against enemies.

I added my own step to the distance between us. "You must not have heard correctly. I will not be going to the king."

"You will." A booming voice made both me and the woman startle.

"Tait." She crossed her arms over her chest. "I've told you not to be slinking up on me like that."

The man was more than a little intimidating. Broad and strong, muscles on his shoulders, his chest, and the bulge of veins on his forearms hinted he'd swung more than a few iron blades.

His hair was tied off his neck, and like Bloodsinger, he kept the front out of his eyes with a black scarf. Two silver hoops pierced his ears, and gold rings lined his fingers. A black ink tattoo of a skull and crossed daggers over his chest was visible through the laces of his shirt, but it was the soft glow of red in his eyes that sent a chill down my spine. Harsher than the king's, more flames against a night sky, and the flecks of red were twisted with a rage that marked the man as one never to be with alone.

He crossed the room, hateful eyes pinned to me. "Get dressed. You'll be meeting Sewell today. King's giving you galley duties."

I didn't know what "galley duties" meant or who this Sewell was, but anger and bitterness from the night rampaged through my body.

"I must refuse *your king*." My voice trembled, slight enough I wasn't certain he noticed, but I did. It would be impossible to hide fear. In truth, no one on this ship would believe it if I tried. But strength did not mean there was no fear. I could stand tall, I could defy my enemies, and I could still be afraid.

"You'll dress yourself, or I'll do it for you. I won't be soft." He leaned in and lowered his voice. "And I'll let the crew watch. They'd be glad to gawk at this particular piece of plunder. That is what you are, Princess. Plunder. Treasure. Goods we split amongst ourselves. The choice is yours. I know my cousin well—"

"Bloodsinger is—"

"My king and my blood," he told me. "I assure you, if you insult him, he will insult you in turn by granting our desires. Who knows, you might find the crew chambers more . . . diverting than the king's."

Acid burned my stomach. "You're all wretched."

"Yes, we are." He didn't even attempt to argue the point and pulled out an odd device that ticked like one of the large bell towers with clock faces back home. I'd never seen such a miniature clock before. Outside city walls, my folk used the sun and instinct to tell the time of day. One more quick glance, and Tait closed his tiny clock. "You have half a chime."

"A chime? What the hells is a chime? A toll? A clock toll?"

He shrugged. "A chime is a chime."

I looked to the woman. She held up the skirt as though she'd missed the venom in Tait's voice.

"Fine." I blew out a long breath. "Go, and I will dress."

Seemingly satisfied, Tait dipped his head and abandoned the room.

Once he was gone, the woman chuckled. "Don't think Tait was lying to frighten you. It's our law aboard the king's ship. Whatever we acquire while sailing is split amongst the crew. Only the king himself may take precedence in a claim." Near the clay basin, she laid out a linen cloth from the wardrobe. "You have no control here, so why do you keep spouting off those harsh words?"

"Tell me this," I said. "Would you move swiftly if you knew only your own death awaits? Bloodsinger told me I am to suffer. I have no desire to run toward it."

She considered my words for a pause, then dipped her chin, a pensive expression to her countenance. "I suppose you have a point."

Ridiculous, but there was a moment where I hoped she might negate my claim that her king planned to torture me.

Hells, it was time to release the girlish fantasy that I was anything other than a foe to the Ever King. The look in his eyes when I'd read to him through the bars of his cell, the vulnerability I thought I saw, never existed. He was nothing but a monster in the tides.

"I cannot wash without water," I said again.

The woman waved the words away and placed her hand in the clay bowl. Eyes closed, she began to sing.

A soft, melancholy song with words I did not understand. "*Vatn till mín, safna saman.*"

My mouth parted when beneath her hand a trickle of water spilled into the basin, as if the clay were shedding a wash of tears. Three times she sang her song, until the water reached the rim of the bowl.

The woman lifted her gaze and shook the droplets off her fingers. "Satisfied now?"

"That . . . you . . . Can you all call upon water?"

"If you're a Tidecaller." She bowed at the waist. "That is what I am, Celine Tidecaller. Had a stronger voice once, for other things." Unbidden, her fingertips touched the pink scar across her throat.

Bloodsinger, Tidecaller. "Your names, are they hints to your magic or something?"

"Again, you've proven you do have brains." She lounged over the cot. "We don't do family names in the Ever. We are named by the talents of our voices. Most Sea Folk blessed with a bit of magic have some gift of their voice, some ability it can do. I've honed mine to travel through water, so I earned the name Tidecaller."

"So, that vial you spoke to yesterday . . ."

"An announcement to the royal house that we were returning from the Chasm." She gestured to the window. "A journey through the Chasm after so long will be made known across the kingdom. I'd expect a great crowd when we return."

Cold danced down my spine. Not only did I face the vengeance of the Ever King, no mistake, I would be the interest of the whole of his kingdom.

"Water's getting cold," she said, and pointed to the basin.

If sea fae were not horrid, I might think Celine caused the water to be a bit more comfortable on purpose.

The masquerade gown clung to my skin in crusty layers, and not that I cared if my scent offended the *Ever Ship*—frankly, a great many aboard reeked like rotted breath and dried sweat—but nerves left my underarms heady with mildew.

With Celine's eyes on the cliffs, I stripped from the gown, and a moan slid free once the damp weight of the skirt was gone.

"Soap." Celine crossed the room and rummaged through her pouch. She tossed a felt purse at me. Inside were pearls of fragrant soap—lavender, honey, and dewy moss.

I returned a clipped thanks. The part of me longing to find some light to cling to within this storm wanted to make Celine Tidecaller out to be kind. She wasn't. She was acting on orders from a tyrant king. She'd probably killed some of my people.

Still, she might be the only one I'd met so far who spoke without a guard up. If anyone could give me information, or a glimpse of how I might find a way out of here, it was her. "Tidecaller, Bloodsinger. What other names sail this vessel?"

"Wouldn't you like to know?"

"That's why I asked."

She snorted, then frowned as if she hadn't meant to be amused. The woman had a slyness to her features, like she might always be ready to share a salacious secret, but under the mistrust was something almost playful.

"The first mate, you already met. Tait is called Heartwalker. Larsson, the second mate, has no sea voice, but we call him Bonekeeper. You'll want to get a glance at the chain around his neck. Don't mistake a lack of magic as weakness. I assure you, he kills well enough."

Acid churned in my stomach. "What does Tait's voice do?"

"Ask him. Tait is the son of Lord Harald, brother of King Thorvald. Harald was killed in the Great War." She sneered. "If you think Erik Bloodsinger is the only one with a vengeance against your people, you're wrong. Now quit speaking and dress. You're clean enough."

Celine's patience seemed to have run its course. I stroked my hair with water to smooth the rogue pieces, then dressed in the clothes she'd offered. The top was thin and left little to the imagination on the shape of my breasts. The skirt was ruffled and hugged my waist too snugly. I let out a seam or two and used one of Bloodsinger's scarves as a makeshift belt.

Celine inspected me from brow to foot and offered a curt nod. "Good enough. I suppose we ought to get you to your post."

14

THE SONGBIRD

THE CREW WATCHED me with a collision of curiosity and disdain as Celine led me toward the hatch. Conversation cut off, men smoking wooden pipes stopped to gawk, and some hissed or studied me with a bit of disbelief.

"A lot of the men fought in the war," Celine said, holding the hatch to the lower decks open. "Meaning they've faced that earth bender daj of yours, and you sort of look like him."

I ought to be uneasy, but a second glance burned a new rush of pride in my veins. There was violence in their eyes, but when I saw it another way, there was fear. Sea fae feared my people; they feared my father.

I knew better than most the pain from the blood spilled during the war, but for the first time, memories of the gore didn't send my heart racing or my head spinning. It curled my lip and drew out a dark sense of pride that these folk knew the brutality of my people.

Until Celine led me down the staircase and I was faced with the Ever King again.

Erik leaned against a post, arms folded over his strong body, a smirk on his scarred lip. The scars he insisted were put there by the people I loved.

My folk were brutal, to be sure, but I prayed their viciousness had not truly maimed an innocent. If it was true, then part of me could not entirely blame Bloodsinger or his wretched father for all that had happened.

"Sleep well, love?" His eyes roved over my figure, halting on his shirt. A flash of heat—or rage—filled his gaze.

"I slept horribly, thank you. I'm told I begin my servitude today."

Erik chuckled. "The way you speak, it's as if you cannot wait until I put a chain around your neck."

"I never was one for patience." Backed into a corner, unarmed, surrounded by endless seas, the only thing I seemed unable to do was cease talking. As though my tongue yearned to antagonize the man who held my damn life in his hands.

Bloodsinger didn't seem ready to gut me for it. He even looked amused. "When you sail on the *Ever Ship*, you're given a duty, be it king or crew. We work as one, or we don't live long. There are two positions open, and I thought you'd take to a galley hand with Sewell better than the other option."

Bloodsinger shouldered his way through a door on loud hinges into a narrow cooking room. Near an odd iron box with a few pieces of hot charcoal placed inside, a man with a strong face and distant eyes spun around. He grinned, revealing white teeth but for the one made of gold in the front. "Little eel. Taste me cod?"

"Haven't had the pleasure today." Erik tugged me against his side. "Sewell, I've brought you company until we reach home, and—"

"Taste me cod, little eel?" His nose wrinkled, his teeth bared.

"Gods, I said not yet."

Sewell's eyes flashed, but he turned around, started muttering about ungrateful eels, and wiped down the stove with a dirty towel. He'd yet to even look at me.

Bloodsinger nudged me forward. "Do as Sewell says, love."

"I'm to be alone with him?"

"Frightened?"

"If you must know"—I paused to swallow and lowered my voice—"he doesn't exactly seem pleased to have a companion. What was the other option?"

"Ah, one of the men reminded me of the honorable tradition of a shipwife."

"A what?"

Bloodsinger's grin widened until I caught sight of the sharp point of his canines. "The lady of the ship. It can be lonely on these longer voyages, Songbird."

Bile burned my throat.

"I'm going to wager you choose to stay with Sewell, yes?"

"Yes. I choose Sewell over your damn bed."

"I suppose there is always time to change your mind." Bloodsinger stepped toward the door. "Sewell has sailed the Ever since the reign of Thorvald. He once knew his way around a sword better than any man I know until a rock smashed his head. Compliment his cooking, do as he says, and he'll take to you fine. Don't upset him; the crew values his feelings more than yours."

In a moment of desperation, I snatched Erik's hand. A faint glimmer of the strange spark I'd felt when he kissed me scorched through my palm. "Where are you going?"

"To the helm." He brushed a knuckle over my cheekbone, an irritating grin on his face. To Sewell, he tacked on, "Keep her breathing."

"Did ye try me cod, little eel?" Sewell asked.

The king was already gone.

The bastard left me without another bleeding word of . . . guidance, I suppose. How twisted my world had become when my heart reeled into a panic at the absence of Erik Bloodsinger.

The galley was a narrow space but oddly tidy. Iron pots and pans hung over a chopping block. Clay bowls, wooden plates, horns for drinking, and tin cups were arranged in orderly crates.

I cared most about the array of blades hooked on the back wall.

Pronged knives, ones that curved, a thick blade as wide as my palm. The Ever King could lick my damn ass if he thought I would stay unarmed a moment longer.

From the corner of my eye, I took note of the cook. A man who clearly once bore the weight of heavy blades. His shoulders were broad and powerful, but his eyes were soft against his brown skin. I couldn't guess how ancient or young the man was, but his beard was untamed, a few bone beads decorating thin braids throughout.

He kept looking at me like I was an invader.

Hands behind my back, I crept toward the wall of knives. The man muttered a bit more about princely eels. I didn't understand half of what he said, but with his back turned to me, I snatched a small straight blade knife from its hook.

"Little fox, that's what she is. Thinks she be sly." Sewell cackled and scrubbed a stain on the rim of the stove.

Damn. I clutched the knife behind my back, throat tight.

When the old man glanced over his shoulder, his eyes sparkled in something playful. "Tricky paws, little fox." He wiggled his fingers, cackling again until his lungs descended into a rough cough.

My shoulders slumped. "It's dangerous to be unarmed, you understand."

"We work we rot." He hummed, then spun around, eyes narrowed. "Did ye try me cod, little fox?"

I licked my lips. "Um, I . . . I haven't, but I'm sure it's delicious."

Sewell blew out his lips. "Eels and foxes cut their losses."

His words made little sense. I strode for the door, knife in hand, and gently pushed.

"Wouldn't be sticking me nose in the dark. Strange tides be upon us." Sewell clicked his tongue once, twice, then reached into a crate and dropped a handful of roots on the block. "The blade. Slice."

He made a gesture of chopping and pointed to the blade I pretended he hadn't seen me snatch off the wall.

Erik said Sewell was once formidable. I believed it. The man still seemed brusque but also tender. I loosened my crushing grip on the knife and took a cautious step to the chopping block.

Sewell beamed as if I'd accomplished some grand feat and, once more, made the motion of slicing.

My mouth twitched, nearly grinning, and I took up one of the roots. The cook observed three strokes, then turned back to his charcoal box and added raw strips of fish to the heat, humming the shanty of the ship.

Slowly, unease lifted, and I fell into a dance with the man, as though it had always been this way. Sewell spoke in riddles, with occasional clarity, but there were words I could puzzle through. "Shuffle" meant he wanted me to move, "muglet" was a drinking horn or tin, and for the plates and spoon he'd interchange "meat-eat" or "scoop."

I took it I was his fox. A fae from lands where foxes roamed. Eels and tidelings were his folk. Or so I assumed.

Sweat dripped over my brow by the time I'd helped Sewell ladle a watery fish soup into bowls. Three gruff crewmen, who said nothing to me and nodded to him, drifted in and out, taking the bowls to the crew. Through the thin walls, their laughter grew louder the more cherry rum they drank.

Sewell tapped my arm and held out a bowl. "Fill a fox's belly before the eel calls."

My eyes flicked to a wooden tray with a bit of hardtack and a covered bowl of stew. The king's meal was not served alongside his crew's.

In the presence of Bloodsinger, my stomach knotted too fiercely to even imagine eating. With Sewell, tension was gone, and my stomach writhed in protest for leaving it empty too long. I took the bowl greedily and slurped the salty broth, unbothered by the dribble on my chin.

"Thank you." Muggy heat warmed the galley, and through our new waltz of preparing meals, I'd slid the sleeves of Bloodsinger's shirt over my elbows to get a bit of cool air on the clammy skin. When I handed Sewell the bowl, his gaze locked on the rune on my arm.

The bowl clattered over the floorboards, and a small yelp slipped over my tongue when Sewell yanked me forward, holding my forearm close.

"No, no, no. Foxes take the tides."

"Sewell." My breath caught. "It's . . . it's just a scar."

The man ignored me and rubbed a thumb over the lines of the rune. "Called you back home with him. Not the usual way of things, but strange seas toss us now. Don't let them see."

Sewell scrambled for the small charcoal box. He hissed and cursed under his breath when fading embers struck his skin as he scooped some of the soot from the corner. He rushed back to me and painted my rune in the soot.

"Sewell?" Every muscle tensed when the cook rolled my sleeve over the mark.

His eyes were like wet glass. "Don't let them see, or they'll take you from him. Might even take your eel like they took two little eels, but what could I do? Had to do it, little fox."

"What did you do?" I whispered.

"Broke the way of things." Desperation filled his gaze, and my heart snapped in two. The man wanted to tell me what was in his head, but his tongue simply wouldn't allow it. "Like a fox amongst tides."

"Are you saying I've broken the way things are because of this mark?"

He patted my cheek, nodding. "Reasons we can't know, but be at ease, the heart of the young is not the same as the sire."

Sewell closed his eyes. His jaw tightened. For a long moment he seemed to gather his words, knowing he was making little sense, but in the end, he merely spoke whatever words came. "Marks of eels—" Sewell patted my arm. "Heal it all."

"Heal what?" My voice was hardly above a whisper.

"She called you back."

I clung to his hands. "Who, Sewell? Tell me who?"

"The Ever." His voice was clear, sharp. It was powerful.

It only lasted a moment before he hung his head, pleading in riddles. "Bring it back, little fox." Sewell blinked and a tear dripped over his lashes. "Don't let them take it away."

Once more he patted my arm. I blinked through a blur of my own tears and forced a smile. "I understand, Sewell. I . . . I won't let anyone see it. I'll be careful."

The man let out a heavy sigh. He pressed a kiss to my curled fingers, then smiled at me as he patted the top of my fist. Soon enough, Sewell was back to his humming and shanties. When Celine stepped into the room to take Bloodsinger's food, she studied the cook for a few breaths. He glanced at her over his shoulder, gave her a smile she returned, then they both turned away as though they'd never paused to look at each other. *Odd.*

I kept scrubbing, tilting away to hide the true tension in my face. As Sewell dried a few bowls and restacked them in their crates, I rubbed my thumb over the rune scar.

The Chasm had called to me. There was more to this mark. I needed to understand it. If it was as powerful as Sewell thought, then I might've found the one way to survive.

Or the way to kill me faster.

15

THE SONGBIRD

FOR THREE SUNRISES I rarely left the galley. I found a bit of peace with Sewell and his riddles. He had a laugh that built from somewhere deep in his belly, and when he rambled on with his nonsensical tales and struck a particularly humorous part, I forgot I was aboard the *Ever Ship*.

I forgot I wasn't free.

I'd drift to somewhere safe. Nights on the shores with my friends around fires, laughing at whatever woman Jonas had chasing him, or Aleksi's proclivity to follow rules only to break them when he wanted.

I'd let myself feel safe in the galley, like my family stood right outside the door.

On the third day, angry clouds mottled the sunlight, and the boisterous songs of the crew lowered to eerie hums and chants.

"Feed for an eel," Sewell muttered after we'd worked side by side serving the crew a meager midday meal of flatbread and salted herring. He pointed to the tray with an added splatter of berry jelly the cook saved for his eel king.

Sewell winced and slumped against the wall.

"All right?" I asked, stacking the last wooden plate in the crate.

He waved me away with a hand. "Cracks and aches from tussles with wolves."

Three days in, "wolves" I likened to my folk. I wasn't certain if I took offense or if I liked that Sewell viewed us as a bit ferocious. "Cracks and aches," the way he rubbed one shoulder, I could guess he had old wounds from the war.

"Save a stroll?" He gestured at Erik's tray, then gave me one of his slow, sly smirks barely visible under his wiry beard.

I frowned. "You want me to take it? Sewell, I told you, I find the king's manners appalling and would rather never experience them again."

Sewell tsked. "Feed the eel and warm the heart, little fox."

I chuckled. "I assure you, feeding Bloodsinger will not warm my fox heart. But for you? Fine."

I added a layer of charcoal soot over my rune to ease his concern about the mark, then nudged him gently with an elbow to his belly as I took the tray. Sewell pressed his fingers to his lips, then blew a kiss.

"You play unfair," I told him. "You and your puzzle words, but I think that was your plan to get me to do your tasks all along."

He turned away, humming and grinning, without a word.

I'd been locked away belowdecks long enough, a gasp escaped when I stepped from the hatch. Open seas no longer surrounded the ship. The dark laths maneuvered between serpentine cliffs, hundreds of lengths above us. White stone with mottled gray gave the illusion of frost and snow packed onto the ledges.

The water was gentle, but rows of hanging bones in omens and wardings left a heavy sense of dread in my belly.

"Finally braved the crew again?"

I startled, nearly spilling the plate over the rail.

Celine sat on top of an old cask. She pointed to the food. Her lips curled into a cruel grin. "I was starting to think Sewell either cooked you up in a stew or we'd scared you into madness."

"You think too much of yourself." I spun away from the rail. "You're not that frightening."

Celine let her face point toward the dreary sky and sighed. "Sure, earth fae. Better steady your hands, then. With all that rattling, Bloodsinger won't believe your lies."

Dammit. Each step farther from the galley, my skin prickled with discontent and clinked the silver spoon against the tin of the cup. Fear was a constant companion, but if I was to survive this, then I needed to be sly, needed to learn all I could about the Ever, or I'd be better off pitching overboard and taking a chance on the creatures below the surface.

I knocked once, then shoved my way into Erik's private chambers. In the days apart, I'd painted loathsome images of him eating bones or drinking blood. A way to keep him as a fiend in my head.

Erik disappointed me. Again.

He wasn't eating bones or drinking blood. He leaned over the small table, a yellowed map sprawled out in front of him. Laces were parted on his shirt, and it gave me a clear view of the silver swallow dangling off his neck and the tips of a black line tattoo on his chest.

The cuffs of his shirt were rolled, baring his forearms, giving up the hard lines of his lean muscle and taut scars carefully placed over his veins.

Bloodsinger was a wretch. A horribly beautiful wretch. Was it possible to want someone dead while taking too much pleasure in the sight of them?

Erik lifted his gaze without lifting his head. The rich satin red in his eyes deepened. "Songbird."

"Serpent." I placed the platter on the cot without looking at him. "Sewell said you needed to eat."

I was halfway back to the door when his soft laugh drew me back.

"I told you Sewell would take to you."

"Sewell is the only one who has shown me kindness, and he's much more entertaining than the rest of you, so I take that as the highest compliment."

Half of Erik's mouth curved. "You will not get an argument from me, except about the kindness. The way I see it, I've been quite kind."

"Really?" I scoffed. "Your insight to your own actions is concerning, King."

He chuckled and turned back to the map.

"Where are we?" Through the window, another cliff drew close.

"We're entering the Ice Fjords. Many smaller isles populate the area." He didn't lift his eyes. "We should arrive at the royal city in two days."

"That long? I've always been told the *Ever Ship* traveled impossible distances swiftly."

Erik chuckled. "That we can, love. Under the surface. As I understand it, the fae not of the sea—you—find that way of travel . . . discomfiting. We'll take the longer route."

I went still. He was keeping me more comfortable?

"I don't understand you, Bloodsinger."

His only reply was a deeper frown and shrug before he went back to his map. Anxious to be free of the cataclysm of conflicting emotions, I faced the door but paused. The soot still shadowed the rune on my arm, but the pink edges were beginning to bleed through.

I shouldn't. Fewer moments around this man was wisest. It was stupid, he wouldn't even care . . .

"Bloodsinger."

"Love?"

"I have a question to ask of you, and if you feel any hint of gratitude for the girl who tried to keep your spirits alive in that cell, I ask you not to mock me or lie to me."

My back to the king, I clenched my fists by my sides, waiting for a taunt, a rant for speaking to him so brusquely. All he did was clear his throat. The slide of his heavy steps sent a shudder down my spine.

I drew in a sharp breath when his grip curled around my arm and turned me into him.

"Consider this my opportunity to repay a girl for her folktales." He leaned one shoulder against the wall. "What is it you want to ask?"

Slowly, I brushed the soot off the rune. "Sewell saw this, and . . . it upset him. He, well, in his way, told me to hide it. To not let them take it."

"Them?" Bloodsinger's calloused hand slid beneath my elbow, cupping it in his palm. With his other thumb, he traced the mark.

"I don't know who he means."

"But you're here discussing it with me?"

"You have already seen it. I don't imagine he's speaking about you."

His mouth tightened. "You haven't asked a question."

"Do you know what it means or why it would be a worry for Sewell?"

Bloodsinger gently released my arm and rolled one of his sleeves over his elbow, giving up his own rune. "That mark is from the House of Kings. I'm sure it unsettled Sewell because the mark has never been on a woman."

My lips parted. "Never?"

"Never. To be seen not just on a woman but an earth fae? I assure you, Songbird, if there had been time, I would have asked a great many questions in your chamber."

He rounded the table again and pulled out two chairs. Taking one, Bloodsinger gestured at the other. I hesitated but gave in to the curiosity to know more.

"The rune is a symbol of the royal line of the Ever. What we call the mark of the king. It is the mark on the mantle you showed to me that night." He practically spat the last word. "The only possibility I've considered for it to be on your skin is that you touched it when you brought it to me."

What would become of me when he discovered the brittle golden disk was destroyed? I swallowed the knot in the back of my throat. I needed to admit the truth. Bloodsinger wanted my father's head when the blame belonged to me. "There is—"

"The mantle—" Erik began at the same time. He paused. "What were you saying?"

My blood chilled. "Nothing. What were you saying?"

"The mantle is why I came to you," he told me. "I have need of it, and perhaps, when it is mine again, we might put all this . . . tension between our worlds behind us at last."

I clacked my teeth together with such force I thought they might chip. If Bloodsinger spoke true, the one possibility of peace with the sea fae didn't exist. Because of me.

There had to be a way out of it. There had to be more I could learn, more I could use here to convince the king one shattered talisman did not need to end in bloodshed. My knee bounced as I stared at the map of the provinces. "How do your houses fit here? You mentioned the House of Kings. Are these provinces all related somehow?"

Erik dropped his gaze back to the map. "There are five noble houses of the Ever. Each controls a province and a gift of the sea. They all have strengths and talents that are utilized for the benefit of the kingdom. When sea fae develop a song, they are classed amongst the houses."

"A song?"

"Your magic lives in the earth. You likely know by now that ours is tangled with our voice."

"But if you're classed to the house," I asked, "how do so many different powers serve on the crew?"

For a moment he studied me, brow arched, like I might have ulterior motives. I did, in a way, but found I wanted to know. Some twisted part of me enjoyed learning about the Ever Kingdom.

After a drawn pause, he folded his arms. "Our magic doesn't force us to live within the origin house. Celine serves the House of Kings, though her ability to speak through the sea would be a voice from the House of Tides. The houses are kinship as much as they are power. Taxes and offerings are paid to the house of your voice. Folk without a power of the sea pay and honor the House of Kings."

"So, blood families might be made of different magic?"

"Our voices are unique," Erik said. "It is no different than the color of our hair or eyes. Every house is valuable, but the House of Kings rules all." He rolled up his sleeve to the rune mark on his arm. "The royal blood is the one that is branded—a mark of a king. As I said, to see it on a woman who is not born of the sea is bewildering."

"That mark was branded into you?"

He gave me a quizzical glance. "At birth."

"That's barbaric. Wear a damn crown to mark you as king."

"It's heavy and uncomfortable." Erik chuckled. "I find it amusing you think a simple burn is barbaric when you've threatened much gorier things."

"Don't make it out like I wallow in brutality. I'm not you, Bloodsinger."

"But you could be." Erik leaned over the table. My lashes fluttered when his lips drew near to my ear. "When I look at you, I do not see a whimpering captive. I see the schemes in that beautiful head that have not stopped spinning since you were brought here—"

"Use better words. I was *taken*."

"I'm convinced you live to antagonize me."

Under the table, my knee bounced. "Words are hardly a weapon against your blade and crew."

I drew in a sharp breath when he pinched my chin between his thumb and finger. "Do not sell yourself short and think you are not the most formidable of foes. I've no doubt you have the power to destroy me."

"I suppose time will tell." I tilted back to be free of his hands. Any longer, and I might lose the strength to pull away. "So, these lords, are they part of a council, or do you ignore them?"

"Only in my dreams." Annoyance pinched his mouth. "An unfortunate effect of crossing the Chasm is the lords would have felt it. I'll likely need to meet with those pious bastards soon enough."

"About me." I held his gaze. I didn't blink. "To discuss what they plan to do with me."

Erik leaned over the table. "What *I* plan to do with you, Songbird. Not them."

His voice was as dark as a violent storm. Threats wove through every word, and there was something horridly wrong with me. He was the most dangerous, he was the one with my life in his hands, and still I found some kind of wretched comfort in the possessiveness lining his voice.

"The way you're staring at your hands, either they've done something to offend you, or your thoughts are telling you not to believe me." Erik's mouth curved into a grin when I peeled my gaze from my lap.

"It's just what Sewell said. I'm already surrounded by fae who fought in the Great War and despise my people. Now I bear a mark that belongs to their king."

"You're not wrong, love. Many folk, including the lords of the houses, all fought for the Ever. They're powerful and have loyalty to their purses and themselves. If I can help it, you won't face them since they'll see you as a ransom, not . . ."

I tilted my head when his voice trailed off. "Not as what?"

"Not as you."

Erik Bloodsinger was a dangerous man. I'd expected it. But he was unexpected in moments such as this. I kept anticipating his brutality to fall over my head. Yes, he'd taken me, but there was almost something desperate when he looked at me, like he didn't truly want to bring me to harm, but he had schemes turning in his head and I was the key to them all.

"What are you thinking, love?" Erik shot one leg out and subtly rubbed the place near his hip. "I can't tell if you're going to war or tears are about to be shed. I'd prefer the first. I do love it when you fight me."

The pressure in my chest felt like I might be doing both. "Sometimes I wish I'd listened to my people and never snuck out to those prison cells."

He hesitated. "We share the same wish, no doubt for different reasons."

The sudden ice in his voice fueled the fire in mine. "Want to know what I really think, Bloodsinger?"

"I'm sure you're about to tell me."

"You're all bloodthirsty and power mad."

"Agreed." He grinned, but it twisted into more of a sneer.

"All you want is that damn gold disk of yours. Who cares who dies, right? Who cares if it begins a war?" I shook my head. "And me, I'm a fool for all the moments I've wondered about you, about this world. I even felt sympathy for the barriers of the Chasm being placed against you. Now I realize I'm nothing but a godsdamned fool."

Bloodsinger let me speak, he studied me as though he listened to each word, and the weight of his focus turned my stomach backward.

"Are you done?" The king spoke, not with malice, more like he truly asked.

I blinked my gaze to my hands and nodded.

"You're right. Partly." Erik flipped the map around in front of me. "The mantle does hold the power of the Ever. If it is won by another, a king cannot challenge the victor for ten turns. It's true, your father is the one I must challenge. Before I saw it on you, I was the only one with the mark of the House of Kings."

He pointed to a spot on the map. It was more a map of territories. Each position had a banner with runes and titles. Bloodsinger pointed to the largest of the territories.

"Why must you challenge him at all?" I slouched, exhausted. "Why can't you come to some agreement? He is not a fiend and would want peace."

"Would you let the man who killed your father go unchallenged?"

My stomach clenched. "I suppose if you ever succeed in your plan, then you will find out."

His face sobered for a breath. Like Bloodsinger was only now realizing if he slaughtered my father like he planned, it would ultimately position us as eternal enemies.

The door opened abruptly and banged against the wall. Tait, dressed and armed with the strange curved swords the crew used, hurried into the room. "We've received a distress call from Skondell."

Erik was on his feet in the next breath. "Has it spread?"

Tait shook his head. "They're being raided. It's Lucien again."

A low rumbling laugh broke from deep in the king's chest. He held out a hand for me.

"You want to paint me as bloodthirsty, Songbird," he said, voice rough. "Today, I'll give you the opportunity."

16

THE SERPENT

L UCIEN SKURK WAS nothing more than a damn pirate. A crook who'd been raised in the royal city, even convinced me as boys we were of like minds with our love of the sea. My fault rested in that I'd believed him. A mistake that led to a portion of the royal treasury being robbed and a swift vessel commandeered into the deep seas.

I'd warned the bastard. Touch another isle, batter another woman, gut another man unprovoked, and it would be his head under my blade.

By the time I reached the helm, my leg burned in a bite of pain, but a giddy delight sparked in my chest. Lucien duped a boy king once, but his lives were up.

Larsson leaned over the rail of the quarterdeck. "Cel got word it's a simple raid. Think it's worth the time and blood to divert? Lucien's a pest, but he's hardly a threat to you."

My grip tightened on the handles of the helm. "The bastard was given a warning, and it was one too many. He's to be a corpse by sundown."

"As you say." Larsson flashed his teeth, tipped the brim of his hat, and ducked away onto the main deck.

"What's going on?"

Dammit. In all my anger, I'd dropped Livia's hand and left her to weave her way through the bustle of the crew. Cheeks flushed pink from the chill of the breeze, Livia clung to a rope and lifted her gaze to the horizon.

She looked . . . like she belonged here, beside me, an open sea before us.

I tore my gaze away. "We're off to make a man much deader than he is."

"Gods." She grimaced. "The way you speak, it's as if killing is nothing. Does it not change you?"

I'd never forget my first kill. "Better to do the killing than be killed."

Commands ran down the ranks of the crew, every position sounding off, until I waved one palm and a thick damp breeze rose from the surf, filling the sails with a loud snap.

The ship hardly made a groan as it yielded to my hold and aimed the bow out of the walls of the white cliffs, reeling back toward the small island village of Skondell. It wasn't a great distance, and with the seas under my command, it would be a swift arrival.

Folk there kept to themselves, lived humble, nearly primitive lives, and sold the rare tide lotus throughout the kingdom. The black satin petals were rife with pain-relieving properties, often used during childbirth.

But mishandled, the lotus was vicious.

Stripped of the petals, the lotus stem and leaves became a powerful hallucinogen. One that left the victim wallowing in nightmarish madness for a full day and night with the smallest dose. Traded to the right ill-intentioned buyers, the lotuses became a weapon.

The people of Skondell had harvested the lotus blossom for centuries, a contribution made for the benefit of the kingdom in exchange for the freedom to live apart, unbothered.

To pick Skondell as a raiding point and breach royal amnesty proclamations was Lucien's way of cock measuring. A sort of twisted test to see if the king might act against him. He would know soon enough.

With both hands on the helm, I closed my eyes. The hum was low, a bare whisper on the wind, but it was enough to beckon the tides to serve in our favor.

Poison or health lived in my veins, but so did the sea. The honor of each king who sat atop the throne of the Ever came with the command of the tides. The bond was warm, like the swallow of bitter teas, and a bloom of power spread from the centermost place in my chest to my limbs. Thick mists wrapped around the hull. Wind crept from the south and kept our sails taut. The keel, jagged and sharp, sliced through the tides gently.

"Celine," I called down to the deck. "You and Stormbringer take her in covered."

Celine gave a lazy salute and went to the rail beside a brutish man with a patch covering an empty eye socket.

Stormbringer churned the seas and thickened the air with his voice. For turns, Celine practiced summoning water to the sky with heavy rains. It took time to develop the talent, long enough that folk started to notice how her voice didn't seem natural, but she managed to connect with Stormbringer's song, making the task simpler. Together, they could draw out fierce fogs and sheets of rain.

In moments, black clouds rolled in over the horizon and swallowed us in the dampness. Violent flashes of light snaked across the sky. When a grumble sounded overhead, the floorboards rattled beneath my feet.

Livia blinked to the sky at the same moment fat drops of rain splattered over her smooth cheeks.

She didn't duck away. Didn't shriek. For a wretched moment, I was lost in my songbird. The harder the rain fell, the more she tilted her face, reaching for the storm. My world intrigued her more than it brought disgust. The more she was near, the less of her presence I ignored.

A boom of thunder sounded, and I barked my commands. "Ready the spears! Move, you bastards!"

No sleep until it's through.
A sailor's grave is all we crave . . .

Hums of shanties were the response.

The crew didn't dally; they rushed to the rails on either side of the deck. With heavy iron hooks, one man snagged a loop staked to a particular floorboard and heaved open a compartment hidden in the deck. A second reached inside and raised thin iron barrels tucked belowdecks. On the top of each barrel was a hatch for loading; at the end was a gaping mouth.

"What are those?" Livia breathed out the question.

"Called ember spears. Steer clear of them." I called to Tait to take the helm. The moment he took the handle, I gripped Livia's elbow. "You can't be up here, Songbird."

"Wait, why?"

I led her to the hatch.

"Erik," she protested.

"I do enjoy my name said with such passion from your tongue," I said. "But I'm afraid it won't be enough for this."

"You're not trapping me down here if you're going to fight. I have no way to defend myself and—"

"You're right." I shouldered the loose hinges of the galley door open. "Sewell!"

The cook didn't startle, even had a knife in hand. With a hooded glare, Sewell spun the blade in his hand. "Going for a swim?"

I grinned. "Sounds that way. Keep a watch on her."

Sewell's eyes brightened at the sight of Livia. "Get lost, little fox?"

"I didn't." She lifted her chin and went to Sewell's side. "The king is under the belief I need to be holed away."

Sewell nodded. "Into the den, let the eels swim."

"Well, foxes can swim too." She leveled me with a glare but hugged her middle as if shielding herself. Whether from me or the racket on the upper deck, I wasn't certain.

"Don't leave the galley," I said. "No matter what you hear."

"No promises, Bloodsinger," she whispered.

"Make it a promise." I slammed the door before she could argue.

Lucien was a sick bastard. He'd take Livia, possibly Celine too, for a prize, ravish them, brutalize them, and the thought of it added one or two clever ideas for how I'd make him suffer today.

Tait turned over the helm when I returned.

"What's the word, King?" shouted a man who went by the simple name of Bones beside one of the ember spears.

Against the distant horizon, black smoke burned against the sky. Lucien was a delay, but one I'd gladly take.

I drew a long breath into my lungs. Wind whipped through the sails. The sea thrashed around the keel. "All hands, man your bleeding posts! Take her down!"

Roars of agreement boomed on the deck. The bow dipped, a diving creature in the tides, and water crashed over the deck, swallowing us whole.

17

THE SONGBIRD

A GRUMBLE OF THUNDER rattled overhead, an unnatural rumbling summoned by Celine and the man missing an eye. I'd heard the eerie hum of their voices, then seen the violent skies that followed. Air fae existed back home. Hells, Stieg was one and had the power to pull sharp gusts of wind, but not like the sea fae.

Their songs brought violence.

"Sewell, do you know what's going on?"

The cook stopped humming. He halted his scrubbing and came to a frightening standstill. For a moment, I thought I might've offended him, but a rush of blood jolted through my veins when his eyes went wide. "Down, little fox!"

I didn't have time to think, didn't have time to breathe before the thunder rumbled again, but it wasn't alone. A boom sounded somewhere overhead. The walls shuddered. Clay ewers and tin plates tangled in chaos. Pots and knives fell off hooks and clanged against the floorboards.

I covered my head as two heavy bowls fell over my back. A bite of pain carved into my shoulder when the rim of one bowl dug into my flesh before it clattered onto the floor.

"Keep her down. Keep her down!" Sewell shouted above me.

Only once his brawny arms wrapped around my shoulders did

I realize he was shielding me. The man was built strong but seemed weaker in a way, too gentle for a ship as this. It made me want to shield him. I tried to shift Sewell off my body, but another blast swallowed the cooking room in deafening booms.

Wood splintered in painful cracks as the ship lurched and pitched in the rough sea. The knife fell from my grip. I tried to scramble for it but was thrown back when the ship swung in the opposite direction.

"Dark tides, me boys!" Sewell shouted at the madness.

We were tossed about like we'd been trapped in a rolling rum cask. On a third blast, Sewell flung toward the back wall, me right behind. His body cushioned my fall, and on the impact, he moaned painfully.

I hurried off him and let out a garbled scream. One of the chopping knives had lodged into his side. A stark bloom of blood stained his dingy tunic. Sweat already lined his brow as he panted, gripping the hilt of the knife.

"No!" I pitched to my knees and grabbed his wrist. "Don't pull it." The ship rolled. I had to brace on the wall to keep from falling into him and lodging the blade deeper. "Dammit! Sewell, breathe with me."

He chuckled. "Shallow bite, little fox."

Not as shallow as he likely hoped. *Gods.* I didn't know this fae. No doubt he'd slaughtered my people by the dozens if he'd fought in the war, but he'd protected me. He was kind to me.

"Sewell," I said, breathless. "Hold here." I took his hand and secured his grip around a post marking the stove nook. "I'll be back."

"Dark tides, little fox. Best stay in the burrow."

"Well, I'm rather averse to blood and death in my burrow."

"Aye." He nodded as if our conversation made a great deal of sense.

"I'll be back for you." There was only one place on the ship I knew had clean supplies. "Don't move, and bleeding hells, don't pull out that knife."

I snatched the blade I'd dropped and scrambled to my feet, heart racing. Sewell hummed, but his skin was layered in sweat, and too much blood spilled from the wound.

All across the lower deck were cloth hammocks dangling from the ceiling. A few rooms near the back I took as wash areas or the rooms where the crew dined. Sweat, leather, and the burn of piss perfumed the space. Another cruel dip of the hull, and I used one of the hanging cots to steady myself.

Damn Bloodsinger. Always called for keeping the ship steady, and he was working mightily hard to toss the lot of us overboard.

I clamped the dull edge of the knife blade in my teeth and used both hands to steady my feet up the stairwell. Two more wild plunges over the storm-tossed waves, and I managed to crack the hatch wide enough for my hand to slip through.

"Dammit." A rope kept the hatch secured to the deck floorboards, trapping Sewell and me below.

I sawed at it with the knife until it snapped, then tossed the hatch and stepped into the chaos of the main deck.

Shards of wood and the black spikes flung over the deck in a cloud of smoke and ash. Crewmen scrambled up rope ladders to the high points of the mast. Most laughed wildly, much like Sewell, and swung from the rigging across a gap between the *Ever Ship* and a smaller ship with only one mast in the center.

Dozens of men manned the odd iron barrels pressed through openings in the hull I'd never noticed. One man opened a lid on the top, while the other dropped in a type of amber fluid. Together the men then braced the barrel.

My heart battered my ribs when the end of the barrel burst with a furious blast of flame and smoke, firing a glossy orb the size of a man's skull across the gap between ships.

What the hells was this?

"What are you doing?" Bloodsinger held on to the handles of his helm in an unforgiving grip. His hat was gone; only the black scarf on his head was left behind. Through the thin fabric of his billowy tunic, his muscles throbbed with the exertion of steering his ship.

"Get belowdecks." He glared down at me, teeth clenched.

"Sewell is hurt." I didn't give him a chance to protest before I sprinted into his chamber and flung open the wardrobe. "Linens. Linens. Oils. Where are they?"

I tossed quilts off the cot. Flung boots, tunics, and the fine green coat. Celine had taken out oils and linens when she'd forced me to wash before leaving the chamber. I spun around to where the washbasin remained. Spilled beneath the table was the overturned basket.

The ship lurched and caused my forehead to slam against the edge of the table. Dazed, I rubbed the spot, ignoring the heat of blood on my fingers, and grabbed the ball of linen wraps and the cleansing soaps.

Doubtless the wound needed to be stitched, but if Bloodsinger couldn't steady his bleeding ship, pressure would have to do for Sewell. When I shoved through the door, the edge slammed into Celine. Her teeth were jagged points, and blood spilled from her eyes.

She tilted her head to one side. "King says get your ass belowdecks."

"What happened to you?"

"Nothing." Celine patted her cheeks and lips, then chuckled and tugged on the points of the teeth, pulling them away. They were false, used to fit over her true teeth. "Terrifies stupid men. Now, get down there or end up in there."

She gestured over the rail of the ship. Gods! A swirling hole was punctured deep into the sea. Across the whirlpool was another ship.

Smaller, but with the same dark laths and thick sails. There was no end to the abyss between the *Ever Ship* and the smaller vessel, yet the crew was lining up along the rails, snatching thick ropes of rigging.

"Take her in." Larsson's voice rose over the maelstrom.

He couldn't be serious. I swung my gaze to the helm. Erik's jaw was set. His stance wide. He spun the helm rapidly until it caught, rotated as far as it would go.

I grasped for the rail of the stairs leading to the king's deck and watched in a bit of horror as the ship swerved abruptly off its course and dove bow-first into the torrent of the whirlpool. Before I had a chance to consider rushing back through the hatch, water spilled over my head. My lungs burned against the sea, and angry currents of the watery vortex pulled and shoved against me, threatening to rip me down into the depths.

The ship lurched as though tumbling down a rocky underwater hillside. A violent tilt and sway of the hull churned my gut, then in the next breath, the bow angled toward the surface again. With a violent jolt, the *Ever Ship* burst through the whitecapped waves on the opposite side of the whirlpool.

Bloodsinger worked with the whole of his body to control the tension of the helm. His voice was strained but furious as he barked orders for his crew to make ready. For what, I didn't know.

"Hold tight, earth fae!" Celine's high voice rose over the cries of the crew.

I didn't look behind, didn't question, and tightened my hold on the railing. The ship skidded through the waves, twisting until it carved through the sea at a new angle. In the next breath, a deafening crack rattled through the storm when the jagged hull of the *Ever Ship* slammed into the weaker rails of the enemy's vessel.

The bony spikes rammed into the wooden sides, skewering the second ship. There was no pause, no waiting, before the crewmen used the rigging and leapt from one deck to the next.

A hand curled around the back of my head. Erik, eyes dark with rage, pulled my brow to his. "Get below. Now!"

"Sewell is injured!" I snapped. "I'm not going to let him bleed out, you bastard."

For the first time, Erik noticed the supplies in my hands. He offered me a pointed look, then bared his teeth briefly. "Go, and seal that damn hatch behind you."

Without another word, the king wrapped a rope twice around his wrist and swung over the torrential sea to meet his enemy.

There was a pinch of worry that tightened in my belly, like an annoyance, a bit of unsettled meat. No reason to fret over Erik Bloodsinger's well-being. Truth be told, it'd be better if the gods took him to the Otherworld.

I spun on my heel, buried the disquiet, and raced down the steps belowdecks.

18

THE SONGBIRD

"SEWELL." I MANAGED to keep steady in the doorway without floundering about. My father always called it gaining sea legs. Even on our longships, when the tides awoke, it took a fair bit of balance to keep from spilling over the rails.

I lifted the supplies like a boon from battle, a triumphant grin on my face when I found the man still breathing.

"Tricky, little fox," Sewell said weakly.

I knelt beside him, inspecting the wound. Shallow, as he said, but hells, there was a lot of blood. I placed a gentle hand on the hilt. "I think we'll be safe to pull out the blade without you bleeding out, but it's not going to be pleasant."

"Pull it straight, little fox." He winked in one of his bouts of clarity.

"No pressure." I chuckled nervously and padded some of the linens around the blade, ready to catch the blood that would come. Hand around the hilt, I grinned. "I'm starting to think you know—" I yanked the blade free.

Sewell howled his pain but blew out rough breaths when I stuffed the wound with linens.

"—exactly what you're saying."

"Think what you think, little fox" was all he said before the door clanged against the wall.

"Don't touch him!" Celine shrieked. Blood was twisted in her braids, matting her hair together in clumps, rain dripped down her cheeks, but she seemed more disturbed at the sight of Sewell on the ground. She crossed the space in three sure strides and rammed her elbow into my ribs, knocking me aside. "What did you do?"

Frustration gripped me like a vise. I swiped a lock of hair from my brow and shoved her back, returning my hand to the bloody linens on Sewell's side. "What I did was help after he fell on a knife with all that damn rocking."

I'd planned to reprimand her more, toss a few insults at their carelessness perhaps, but clamped my words off when I caught sight of the tremble in Celine's chin.

Mere moments ago, the woman had false shaved teeth in her mouth. Now, at the sight of a little flesh wound, she was... weeping?

"Thunder Fish," Sewell said, beaming at Celine. "Save your rain."

Celine swallowed. "I'm not raining. Maybe a little since I'm so damn mad at your stupid ass. What were you thinking going and getting stabbed? I ought to cut you off, old man."

"Cut him off?" A flare of protectiveness jumped in my chest.

"Yes, cut him off." Celine studied me with a bit of irritation. "Who do you think supplies the man with his favorite sour currants?"

Sewell smacked his lips and let his eyes roll back in his head. Even Celine snickered.

I set to work, wrapping one of the long linens around Sewell's waist while Celine helped secure the binding in a tight knot over his belly.

"He'll need stitching," I said.

"Aye." Celine stood, hands on her hips. "I'll tell the king, but we'll need to tend to it until we can get him to a boneweaver."

"What the hells is a boneweaver?"

"What do you call the folk who fix your ails?"

"A healer?"

Celine paused, confused, then shrugged. "I like 'boneweaver' better. Help me get him up. We're needed onshore."

My blood felt too thick for my veins, but I buried the unease and focused on Sewell. "I heard Bloodsinger could heal wounds. Why not heal his own crew?"

"Taxing, that blood healing, and he's detained at the moment." Celine scooped an arm under the cook's shoulder. "Now hurry. The king doesn't want you left alone on his ship. We're all headed ashore, except you, old man. We'll see to it you sleep in the king's bed."

"Sweet songs, Thunder Fish." Sewell grunted when he staggered to his feet. The movement soaked the bandages with a new fountain of blood, but he didn't do more than wince and wrap an arm around Celine's shoulders.

I followed behind, prepared to steady the man should he stumble on the stairs. Sewell pinched his lips and muttered something about eel tempers. Celine told him since he'd be sleeping in the king's bed, it made him the king of the ship for a day. She seemed at ease with talk of invading Erik's chambers, and I resented how it made me think that Bloodsinger might not be a tyrannical fiend.

Once the cook was settled in the king's chamber, Celine led us back to the lower deck. The door carved into the hull was lowered. Smoke choked the freshness of the breeze, and foam on the tides was tinged pink.

"Get in." Celine gestured at a rowboat. Much as with the main ship, nothing about the common boat was simple. It was shaped like a jagged arrowhead and the rails were spiked with bits and pieces of what looked like fanged teeth. Some were chipped and cracked from wear, but it only added to the viciousness, and the oars were like knives, ready to slice through the waves.

Sweat gathered under my arms, my palms, at the nape of my neck. I'd tried to embolden myself at the masque, until I froze when Bloodsinger made himself known. Then again in the feed cart at the fort when I'd smashed his leg, until Rorik came, and I went boneless. I was empowered to chastise the Ever King for his wretchedness, until now.

Why would Bloodsinger drag me off the ship? I'd disobeyed his command. He'd been furious. A dozen different ways he might make me pay took hold and choked the air from my lungs.

"I think someone ought to stay and keep watch over—"

"Get. In." Celine yanked a roughly made sword from a leather sheath. Only halfway, but the threat was clear. "I got no orders saying I can't take a finger or two. Maybe an eye. Patience is long gone. Now get in."

I clenched my fists but complied. Celine took one oar, I took the other, and with great digs into the bloody water, we heaved the boat into the open tides.

On the shore, walls of fire toppled sod huts, a tower made of thick beams, and what appeared to be a worship center made of posts carved in runes arranged in an intricate pattern.

Amidst the flames and tangle of smoke, the ship's crew kept tossing other men into a huddle near the water's edge. Drawn blades meant there was no question blood would taint the sand soon enough. I cursed myself for leaving my knife in the kitchen.

Once the boat struck a sandbank, Celine hopped over the side, knee-deep in the waves. "Out," she said, and secured the oars.

I followed her onto the sandy shore. A dozen paces away, a shadow materialized from the dust and haze. His gait was staggered, but when Bloodsinger stepped free of the smoke, I saw why.

One hand gripped firmly on a thick rope, he dragged a bloodied man by the ankles. The man had a similar build and an injured leg, and Erik limped as he heaved his prisoner.

The sharp tang of bile burned my throat at the state of the man: a gash from the corner of his mouth split his cheek halfway open, two fingers bled from the tips—I doubted they were still intact—and small knives were rammed into the backs of the man's arms.

With every tug, the hilts of the blades would shift and twist in the flesh, drawing out raspy, angry shouts of pain.

Brutal. Cruel. Mesmerizing.

I had a twisted captivation with Erik Bloodsinger. I despised him in one breath, and in the next, I couldn't turn away from his cold, beautiful face. What created such a creature as him? What motivated such brutal punishments?

I knew war. I knew execution. But Erik seemed to enjoy the bloody game more than the outcome.

Low sobs peeled my gaze away from the king for a moment. My chest squeezed. Men and women, children and elders were gathered to one side.

They wore simple clothes, most barely covering their bodies. Their hair was rolled in tight cords or shaved close to the scalp. Those who were grown wore piercings laced with slender gold chains from lip to nose to ear.

Wives wept against their husbands' bare chests. Some children whimpered, their glassy eyes locked on the burning huts, watching their village crumble.

I blinked back to the man in Bloodsinger's grip. He'd been the one to cause this devastation. A strange sensation took root low in my stomach. Heavy and coiled, like a barbed knot of thorns, it bloomed through my body until it reached my lips. The corner of my mouth twitched into a smile, into a cruel thrill that the man responsible for the tears of littles was paying his dues.

Never had I embraced gore, but a shiver danced down my spine. I wanted the man to suffer. For a moment, I wanted him to suffer more than I did Bloodsinger.

I didn't know this side of myself.

Truth be told, she frightened me.

The Ever King dropped the rope. His captive let out a haggard breath. One simple wave of the hand from the king, and two crewmen hooked their arms beneath the prisoner's and levered him into a rough stance on his knees.

"The seas," Erik said, dark and low, as he accepted a knife from Larsson. He glanced over his shoulder at the prisoner. "Lucien, whose voice commands the seas?"

The prisoner spat his blood. "Hard to tell these days, Erik."

"Is it, now?" Erik turned, a thoughtful pinch to his face. "It hardly boggles me. I wonder why it is such a struggle for you."

Lucien scoffed but said nothing.

Erik stalked in front of the man, a beast to a mouse. With every step, he tapped the blade against his palm. "What is your purpose in coming to Skondell? The only thing I can gather is you're here for the lotus, no doubt for nefarious reasons." The king came to a halt in front of the man. "Who financed your campaign?"

"Ah, king of the seas, you sail beneath your own dark banner. You know no privateer worth his weight gives up his financiers. Makes for bad business."

"Hmm." Erik inspected the blade in his hand. "This is a rather dull knife."

Odd thing to say. Odder still was the way Lucien's eyes widened in horror.

I startled when Erik lunged at his prisoner. He might've limped from whatever injury I'd caused, but I was right about my theories—Erik Bloodsinger was a snake, swift and deadly, always waiting to strike.

A guttural scream clawed through the air when the point of the knife, with horrifying precision, lodged into the corner of Lucien's left eye. The two crewmen gripped the man tighter. Both held one side of his face, forcing him to keep still as Erik... worked.

The king didn't blind the man, not right away. He tugged and teased at the eye. I covered my mouth, hot sick rising in the back of my throat. Erik slowly lifted the eye, causing a bulge in the socket, but never finished the job.

Lucien sobbed and pleaded.

"I might consider a bit of mercy," Erik said, calm as a summer's breeze, "should you tell me who financed your campaign."

"Finish it, gods, finish it," Lucien sobbed, truly pleading for the king to pluck out his eye.

"Financier." The king lifted the eye a little more.

I took a bit of pride that I wasn't the one to vomit. A man somewhere near the water's edge retched when bloody sinews bulged from behind the socket.

My nerves twitched; the desire to flee, to swim until I tried my fate with the Chasm took hold. *Don't look away.* This was the man I'd face. Perhaps I was gazing into what the future held for me. Better to learn what I could now.

It gave me focus and purpose. It gave me a desire to act, not crack at the seams.

"These... isles are damned... anyway," Lucien sobbed. "The lotus was a... new attempt at a spell cast to... heal it."

Erik steadied his hand and looked to the northern tip of the isle. Beyond the smoke and flame, dark hills made of scorched grass were all that remained. Clearly the fire had eaten away whatever greenery there'd been.

Or so I assumed. Until the slightest burn of fear flashed in the king's eyes.

The king blinked. "Who wanted the lotuses, Lucien? Lady Narza?"

"I . . . I . . . I don't know their name. Payments were made without meeting."

"What purpose did they have for the lotus?"

"Might p-p-poison the blight away." Lucien groaned. "I was going to use s-s-some to b-buy entrance through the sea witch's realms to the far seas."

Bloodsinger's lip curled, revealing the points of his canines. "Thank you, Lucien. You've been most helpful."

Erik tugged on the hilt of his knife and removed the tip. It was horrible. The eye was bulged, out of place, and bloody. It was completely useless and no doubt painful.

The king left it in such a state.

He wiped the blood and fluids on Lucien's shoulder and grinned. "But you've chosen for the final time to prove that you're certainly not loyal to your kingdom."

With a fierce thrust, Erik rammed the dull knife into the center of Lucien's belly.

The man roared his pain and doubled over. The king spun on his heel, speaking to Tait and Larsson as he stalked away. "Hang him with his innards by a stake in the cove. A reminder of what happens when you cross the king."

Blood stained Erik's hands, but he made no attempt to wipe it off, nor the splatter on the sharp edge of his jaw when he approached. I dug my heels deeper into the sand and straightened my neck. The red of his eyes pulsed like a flame behind the pupil. For too many crushing heartbeats, he merely drank me in, devoured me in a single glance.

Without a word to me, he stormed toward the crowd of villagers. "Where is the Daire?"

"Come on." Celine appeared at my back and shoved my shoulder. "We're to follow."

"Where?"

"He's going to speak to the Daire of the isle, the lord, or in this case, the lady." She used the tip of her sword to point forward.

People huddled around Erik and a woman. She was taller than the king, eyes like moonlight, and a headdress of bone and intricate fabrics was tied into her corded hair. Bands made of leather and beads adorned her wrists and upper arms, and a necklace made of jagged teeth covered the whole of her chest.

They spoke in hushed tones, their heads close. The woman hardly seemed unsettled by the Ever King. Strange as it was, there was almost a bit of respect. Not only from her. Upon his approach, Erik had dipped his head and pressed her palm to his lips.

Not as a lover would, more ritualistic. Like a greeting shaped from turns of traditions.

The woman gestured around her village. Her people listened intently. I stepped back, unable to hear, and desperate to find clearer air.

Celine and the crew were focused enough on their king and the Daire, no one noticed I'd broken free. Down the shore, Lucien's screams had died off. I didn't want to look. To me, it was like earning a glimpse of my own fate.

The sand thinned beneath me, making way for wetlands and bits of grass to peek through the sea soil. Or what should've been grass and blossoms. Darkened stems and shriveled remains snapped to dust beneath my steps.

A sniffle came at my back.

Five paces away, a small girl with her braided hair tied back in a knot on her head hugged a cloth doll. Heavy tears dripped onto her dirty cheeks. She looked at me, then down at the scorched land.

"Fires?" I asked.

The child tilted her head, studying me. Perhaps she could not understand me. I pointed to the smoldering rooftops, then back to the ground.

The girl followed my gestures but soon shook her head. Clearly, she didn't understand. Words could be spoken differently, but heartache was the same across worlds. The child mourned her home and the beauty I was certain had once been here.

I smiled and waved her closer. Thoughts of my own fury magic were stored far away. What good would it do me here? I brightened gardens and thickened vines. For blossoms, I could make them more vibrant, smell sweeter.

A rather pointless gift for my predicament.

But with enough focus, I had succeeded in healing deadened fields, or low-yielding crops even. Land destroyed by fire, I'd never tried. Still, I knelt and pressed my palm against the dark soil.

A bite of something sharp, almost as though a barb pricked my skin, welcomed my touch. Nothing so horrid I couldn't keep my hand in place. I held my breath and waited for the familiar warmth of fury in my blood. The peace was there, a calm flow to the magic, but there was something else, something dark. A gasp slid out when the memories of the land seemed to hook around my palm and draw me in deeper.

No, no, no. Not again.

I tried to pull away, but some power, some force, clung to me and filled my mind with tales only the earth knew. Cries and pain from the ground under my fingertips dug through my belly, churning it in sick until bile rose in my throat. I tried to catch a breath, tried to pull away before my fury dragged me deeper, but I was frozen in place.

Few people knew my fury could do this, reveal any horrors that had taken place in a particular site. A discovery made during the war with the sea. Deadly histories, pain, attacks, murder, suffering, anything done atop the soil, I could feel if I went deep enough.

Unwittingly, during the war, the land gave up its horrors and offered blood and terror a child ought never to see.

I'd kept my magic tamed ever since, never pushed too far, afraid it would drag me under again, but one touch to this soil and it was throttling me in agony.

This place wasn't burned by fire, that much I knew. In my mind, a swirl of shadows surrounded a once-vibrant isle. Next, a strange taste that bled onto my tongue. Not the smoke or ash I'd expect from a fire-ravaged land, but a bitter taste like herbs and elixirs, tangled with a unique flavor like rain on the wind.

I'd sensed magic in the earth before. Each power had a different emotion, a different taste to the soil.

There was magic here. Dark magic.

The child squealed beside me but sounded as though she were wading beneath water. Still, it was enough to help me claw my way out of the grasp of the broken earth.

I opened my eyes, hands trembling. While I'd been tossed into a clue that something wretched had gone on here, the girl beamed and clapped her hands in delight. All hells, where my hand had touched the shriveled stem, now a brilliant golden flower bloomed. I'd never seen a bloom like it. Angular petals that gleamed as if made of true gold, and leaves that were more cloverlike than anything.

I buried my disquiet over dark magic in the soil and forced a smile at the girl. She grinned in return, then bolted back to her folk, shouting something I didn't understand.

A bit of pride took hold in my chest. My fury frightened me, but at least today, it had made a child more at peace with what had happened here.

But contentment shattered soon enough.

"What have you done, Songbird?"

19

THE SERPENT

LIVIA ROSE FROM the sand, dusted off her knees, and looked at me with contempt.

"I made a child smile. If you find it so disgusting, then I wonder what that makes you?"

I was only half listening. My attention was on the brilliance of a bloom sprouting through land poisoned by the darkening. The Daire had sent word to the royal city nearly a month ago to report a new isle being touched by the plague. But she felt it was oddly placed, completely avoiding the lotus fields. Had Lucien attacked to take the flowers for his own use?

There was something that did not sit well about this spread, and it was made worse now.

Here, in cursed soil, my little songbird brought back life.

My gaze flicked back to hers. "What did you do? Explain it to me."

"Explain . . ." She faced the new growth. "I . . . I used my fury. My magic. You do realize you've taken a land fae from the Night Folk clans. That means our abilities involve the earth."

"I know this!" I snapped. The day the earth bender king slaughtered my father, he'd lifted a rocky wall from the sea floor to prove his power. "What did *you* do?"

"I healed it," she said, voice soft, but it seemed like she was holding back. "That is one ability I have, though I'm not incredibly powerful with it. My strengths lie in giving more life to growth already in place. Like an amplifier."

It didn't make sense. I rubbed the scars on the back of my neck, trying to puzzle out in my mind how it was possible. Nothing, no spell casts, no song, no magic in the Ever had summoned life from the darkening since it began, and the edges of Skondell were thick with it.

A single touch from the blood of an enemy and new life sprouted.

How? I narrowed my gaze. "Do it again."

Livia swallowed. She lowered to her knees, fingers trembling, and reached for the dark soil. She winced, a vein of effort gathered in the center of her forehead, but slowly, a verdant patch of grass shed the curse, even brighter than before.

"By the seas," Celine whispered.

She stood behind me. Tait and Larsson had returned, and blood soaked their clothes and skin, but just as Celine had done, both gawked at Livia's trick.

"What do you make of it?" Larsson asked under his breath.

Livia pulled her hand away. "This isn't normal soil, is it? It feels a little strange, and the way you all keep staring like I might burst into flames, I'd like to know what's going on."

No one spoke.

My mind reeled with thoughts yet never led anywhere. I turned away. "To the ship. We go to the Tower." I paused to take hold of Tait's tunic, drawing his face close. "See to it the folk of Skondell leave for the royal city as soon as possible."

"Where do we put them?" His voice darkened. "They are solitary clans; it goes against their vows with the old gods to associate too freely with outsiders."

"I know my people," I said with a snarl. "Your lack of faith in my preparation is truly telling. From the first report of the darkening in Skondell, space was saved for the clan in the river caverns."

Tait's face softened, and he had the bleeding decency to look sheepish. "It is a good place."

"Is it?" I released his bloody tunic and stepped back. "What a foolish king I might've been if I'd not recalled they needed darkness before sunset for their prayers. Continue to presume I am not worthy of this crown, and you will join Lucien."

"EARTH FAE CAN be illusionists." Celine paced behind me. "That must be what it is. A farce."

My grip tightened on the helm. I said nothing.

"Surprising she had the ability." Larsson shaved a piece of pear with his knife and lifted it to his mouth. "But not so far into the realm of disbelief. Her father is the earth bender; it's possible she is an earth healer. You're taking her to the Tower because that is where it began, aren't you?"

"Yes," I said stiffly. I had to see if the poison locked in the soil of the Ever the longest could be removed. But I needed to understand what had happened with Livia's magic, why it healed the land, why it frightened her.

I needed to meet *her*—the lady of the sea witches and sirens. Narza refused to set foot in the royal city. I hated her for it but understood her reasons in the same breath.

Truth be told, I wasn't certain if she'd agree to meet at the Tower, a neutral ground where every noble house of the Ever could meet for council without fear of mutinies or underhanded deals.

"Celine," I said. "Call for Lady Narza, tell her the fate of the Ever depends on her agreeing to meet."

Celine's eyes widened. "You want . . . to see her?"

"I don't have a choice. I have need of her particular talents."

To face Narza turned my insides backward. It was necessary, but if the fiercest sea witch in the Ever Kingdom had her way, she'd see to it Livia hated me more than she already did. She'd see to it Livia found a way to be free of me for good.

Celine followed Larsson up the staircase to the main deck and paused at the top. "She risked her skinny neck for Sewell. I'm not letting anything happen to her after that, Erik. You know I won't." Celine shook her head, grinning in a bit of disbelief. "Didn't even know him. She's either got no brains or bigger balls than you."

"KEEP YOUR HEAD down. Don't you be drawing any attention to us. I want to drink and forget I have to play nursemaid. Hear me?"

I didn't need Celine's sharp tone to know Livia had stepped onto the deck. There was a knot in my stomach that split, surging through my blood whenever my songbird drew near.

The way the mark of the House of Kings on my arm burned, the insatiable need to lay eyes on her now that I had her—all of it meant something, and I'd rather it didn't. Too much was at stake to see the princess as anything other than a pawn in an endless war.

I didn't need to look; I did anyway.

She'd dressed in a pair of Celine's trousers and, again, wore one of my damn shirts.

One fist clenched at my side. That skin, her scent, was pressed against my clothing. I was a fool. A simple thought of naked flesh had me reeling like a feckless boy who had discovered his cock for the first time.

Livia's eyes darkened at the sight of me. Every joint and limb tensed, and she appeared ready to bolt or swing a fist at my head.

One elbow on the rail, I grinned. "Songbird."

"Serpent." Livia tried to hold her gaze steady when I stepped close enough that her breasts brushed over my chest with each draw of air. She failed. Her eyes bounced between mine, fear heady and perfect.

With my center knuckle, I brushed a lock of her hair away. Not one to touch gently—ever—I took a bit of gratification at clawing my way under her skin by shattering the defenses she tried to build between us.

Hate me, curse me, I cared little, so long as I was the first thought of her day and the last of her night.

"Behave today, love," I whispered. "This is no place for a sudden burst of bravery."

Livia's mouth curled into an unexpected sneer, and she leaned into me.

All at once, I wanted nothing more than to step back. There was a vast difference with me breaking through her boundaries compared to when she broke through mine.

The princess added another slice of discomfort when she walked her fingers up the center of my chest. "I will tell you something, Bloodsinger." Her voice was soft and breathless. "When I claim that moment of bravery, it will not be sudden. It will be slow. It will be well-thought-out. I will wait until I have you in my grasp. You may not even realize it has happened. In that moment, I will strike and watch you bleed."

I couldn't help the grin that followed her beautifully violent speech. Innocent and gentle, yet when prodded enough, out came the vicious beauty within. And she was mine. In what capacity, I hadn't decided. To ruin, to manipulate, to claim. Each had its merit and appeal.

"I do love when you try to seduce me." I pinched a lock of her satin hair between my fingers, drawing the curl beneath my nose.

Livia's mouth tightened, but she said nothing more.

Larsson leaned his hip against the rail, his back to the princess, voice low. "Lady Narza surprised us all. She arrived before dawn and wishes to first speak with you alone."

"Of course she does." I tightened my hold on the hilt of my cutlass. "Stay with the women."

Larsson's mouth twitched. "Have I done something to offend you, My King?"

Bastard chuckled like he'd won some great victory when I failed to keep the amusement hidden behind a scowl.

Tait glowered and smoked sweet herbs, avoiding my gaze.

"With me" was all I said, and strode down the gangplank into a growing crowd of people who lived on the isle of the Tower, all awaiting their king.

Gods, I despised them all.

20

THE SERPENT

MY LEG ROARED in burning pain by the time we approached the upper room. The Tower was a mere five levels, but by the end, the pain scorched deep enough I wanted Tait to lift me onto his back.

I clenched my hands to keep from rubbing the knot.

Tait's scowl deepened. "Blister Poppy is here. She might have that peppercorn oil you—"

"Utter another word, and I will stitch your tongue to the top of your mouth."

Tait snorted his disdain but had the brains to shut up. Few people knew how much trouble the wounds from my childhood caused, and I didn't need reminders that to most of my people, the visible scars were marks of a broken king. A weak king.

On this level, the debauchery in the pub on the first floor was nothing but a muffled commotion. The Tower was made of chipped wood, a few crystal sea stones, grime, and dust. It suited us well enough. A window adorned each side of the upper floor, giving us the vantage of watching every horizon for threats.

A floor below was where lords from noble houses would take the finer rooms with furs and silks. The middle floors held the washrooms and simple bedchambers with straw mattresses and tattered quilts. Finery mattered little when the rooms were meant to serve for a quick thrust into a lover's hole, then move on back to the pub for more.

Tait knocked on the door once, then stood aside.

"Keep watch, but if time drones on, turn your sights to the princess. No one is to touch her." The need for answers regarding Livia Ferus was potent. As though my fight to save the Ever Kingdom had somehow shifted to a battle for her.

The room wasn't large, but there was space enough for a table with two chairs and a single cot against one wall.

Near a table lined in seed bread loaves, pungent herbs, and herring oil, a woman in a tattered black cloak devoured a corner of the bread. Her tongue made loud movements as it lapped and slurped at the dribble of oil.

"Hail to the king," she said, voice rough as though she'd been screaming for days.

She faced me. Milky eyes flicked wildly in her head, never seeing me, yet trapping me in her gaze all at once.

"No need for disguises, Lady Narza." I kept a distance, holding my place by the door. "It's only us here."

Little by little, the marred skin and tattered robes bled into a new form, until Narza stood upright, shoulders back, her skin blemish free and pale enough there was a touch of blue to the tone. Her gown hugged the slender shape of her figure, and on her waist was a silver dagger crusted in blue clamshells that glowed in darkness, giving off light.

A muscle in my jaw pulsed. "I didn't think you'd come."

"How can I refuse when my king insists he has discovered the answer to the Ever Kingdom's toils?"

"I saw the deadened land heal." With a stiff step, I sat at the table and brushed away a layer of what appeared to be centuries-thick dust.

Narza drew in a labored breath through her nose. "How?"

Under the table, my fist tightened, the skin on my knuckles pulled white. "The daughter of my father's killer."

"You fool." Narza's gold-glass eyes flashed. "You've started a new war when we are already broken."

"I've started nothing. There is no way the earth fae can come through the Chasm and live."

"So sure?"

Unease burned in my gut. No, I wasn't certain. I tossed the thought to the back of my head. When we returned to the royal city, I'd see to it Livia's folk would never find her.

Narza frowned when I kept quiet. "Why did you call me?"

"I assure you, Lady Narza, you are the last summons I'd want to make. I have need of your gift to better understand what power the princess is wielding so we might continue to heal the kingdom."

Narza was silent.

"Did you not hear me?" I asked after the pressure of her quiet seemed to cave in over my shoulders.

"I heard." Narza scooped the flatbread through her oils again without taking a bite. "I do not understand why you took the woman. You've believed for so long the only way to be the Ever King is by claiming the trinket your father left behind."

"Trinket?" I shot to my feet. "The mantle gave him the power of the Ever. A gift from you, yet you lessen its value when we need it more than ever."

"My question remains unanswered. You believe all this and returned not with the trinket of Thorvald but with a woman."

"She bears the mark of the House of Kings." I ground my teeth together. The words were said without thought, and I would do a great deal to snatch them back again. The fewer who knew of Livia's rune, the better. My temper had a grip on me, as it always did around

Narza, and now I'd informed the woman I didn't trust with the truth of my songbird.

"You've seen this for yourself?"

"I would not have said it if I hadn't," I grumbled.

Narza tapped one of her pointed fingernails against her chin. "When you went through the Chasm, tell me, why did you go to the shores you chose? Out of all the land of the earth fae, why did you go where you did?"

"That doesn't matter."

"You asked for my help!" she snapped. "I will decide what matters."

I glared at the wall for a dozen breaths. "I was drawn there."

Through the frustration pounding in my skull, I nearly missed her sharp draw of breath. Before I could press her on the stun, Narza's flat expression returned. "Drawn? To the woman?"

"To the mantle. The earth bender had been there but had only just left. I took his heir as ransom."

"You took his heir, a woman with the mark of the House of Kings?" Narza's brow arched. "You feel nothing for her?"

What did I feel for Livia Ferus? Anger, aggravation, lust, passion—a tangle of conflicting emotions always swelled in my chest whenever the princess came too close. As though she'd unlocked some hidden cavern in the scorched edges of my heart and released the sunlight, shattering a prism of light in endless directions, in endless thoughts and feelings.

"She is a pawn," I lied. "A means to an end until my birthright is restored."

Narza chuckled bitterly. "You kings are all the same. Always looking for more power, more strength, when you do not see what you already have at your fingertips."

"I am the king," I agreed. "I have the power of the Ever Seas, but it is not enough. You know the power of the king is not limitless, or you would never have given Thorvald an amplifier like the mantle."

"You think you know things about the gift I offered King Thorvald? I assure you, there are pieces you do not understand." Narza looked out the window. Unspoken burdens shadowed her features. "I will meet the earth fae so you can know her magic, but only if you're certain it was not a trick of the eye. See that she does it again."

"I plan to," I said. "It's the reason we're here."

Narza hummed softly in her throat. "Good. Then I will remain. Do not make my presence known."

I was hardly listening. My scalp prickled, and somewhere in my chest, a foreign sensation burned. In the beginning I dismissed it as my own irritation, but the longer Narza studied me, the more focused I grew on the slow-building tension.

A slight quiver inside shifted to something more potent.

I tilted my head, lips pinched. "Are you doing something to me?"

She narrowed her eyes. "Of course not. What is it?"

"I feel..." My hand pressed to my chest; breaths came in sharp, haggard rasps. My shoulders tightened, as though I were bracing against a force unseen. Sweat dampened my palms, and my pulse quickened to the point my head spun.

Fear was a weakness, one I fought to conceal, but this fear... it was detached. It didn't belong to me.

A sort of maddening power clung to me where an emotion separate from my own had taken hold as though I should be feeling it, but I wasn't afraid. The room grew musty, like damp soil burned my nose. I coughed on the grit of it in my throat. The musk of sweat followed. A hot breath of apple rum filled my lungs.

"Erik?" Narza studied me.

"How is this possible?" My head throbbed; I rubbed it away. "I feel *her*."

Narza's painted lips turned down into a frown. "Gods of the tides. You feel your pawn?"

My fists pressed into my skull as a flurry of moments flashed through my mind. Music, a slow, eerie tune. Need. Desire. All around me was laughter and slurred ale-heavy words. Then a face—a haunting face. I was terrified and captivated all at once as he played a panpipe. He whispered something. I couldn't make it out.

"What have you done, Erik?" Narza's countenance was one tangled in both heady concern, which dug into the smooth angles of her face, and anger, like I'd damned us all.

I startled back, but the moment my hand reached out for the latch, a heavy knock sent my blood to my head.

"Erik!" Larsson spilled into the room, Tait behind him. "Come quickly. There's trouble."

I yanked a knife from my boot, uncertain what was happening here, and pointed the tip at the sea witch. "Keep your word and remain at the Tower, and I will prove what I say about her magic. Until we meet again, Grandmother."

21

THE SONGBIRD

"KEEP YOUR HEAD up." Celine smacked the back of my shoulder. The woman was brisk, but I was starting to think it wasn't entirely because she hated me. More that she was on edge around all the cutthroats as much as I was.

Hair stood on my arms and my blood ran too hot. No. Fear would not take me now. I bit down on the inside of my lip to keep my breath steady.

Unfamiliar tunes were strummed over lyres. Savory hints of pungent herbs and sauces covered the reek of sweat and unwashed clothing. Loud barking laughter rattled from rafter to floorboard.

I took in the leaning doorframe, the dim flickers of tallow candles nearly burned down to the wick, the slap of paper cards from gaming tables in the corner. I picked out what was familiar and kept those in my focus. This was nothing more than an alehouse like the ones near the docks at the fort. Loud, pungent, and vulgar.

When the flutter in my veins subsided, I fell into step with Celine and Larsson.

Bloodsinger had abandoned us with Tait to some upper room. He'd hardly spared a glance at anyone in the rugged township beyond the confines of the sticky, boisterous tavern.

"This way." Celine swatted my arm and gestured toward a table in the corner. "We'll be out of the way. No one'll pay you much attention."

"What if they do?"

Larsson chuckled. "Hope they don't. The king would be forced to draw blood, and he's in his best coat."

They were mocking me, but I suspected they were also warning me. A bit of truth to their taunts. I was in a strange realm with different customs and laws.

Bloodsinger said he wanted to draw out my torment, but the man had hardly raised a hand to me, let alone a blade. I didn't know his game, but he put a great deal of thought into keeping me under watch by two of his crew. I wasn't entirely convinced Erik Bloodsinger wanted me dead as much as he insisted.

The clink of metal against wood sounded as Celine and Larsson adjusted their weapons and sat on ale-stained wooden chairs. Near the table, a hunched fae with a tattered cloak around his shoulders played a melancholy tune on a panpipe, occasionally humming along.

I smiled. The music, simple as it was, soothed a bit of my unease.

Through the dim light, I strained to catch any glimpse of Bloodsinger. No one lifted a gaze to us, no one even seemed to note a new crew had washed ashore. It was as if the patrons didn't even realize their king was nearby.

"Larsson Bonekeeper." A woman approached from behind and draped her plump arms around Larsson's shoulders. She pulled out a chain from inside his tunic. White polished beads—no, hollowed-out finger bones—were threaded on the silver.

Bonekeeper. He kept the bones from his kills.

The woman grinned sweetly as she fiddled with one of the bone beads. Her face was lovely but overpainted in reds and pinks. She had her hair in tight curls piled over her head, and slid her fingertips down the front of Larsson's tunic, groping his chest. "Been so long since you last came. Care for a visit?"

Larsson lifted the woman's palm and pressed a kiss to her fingertips. "Not today, Pesha."

She pouted her full lips. "All this way and not even a dance?"

"On the king's order, my girl." Larsson removed his leather hat and used one of the edges to point at me. "I'll be staying put for now."

Pesha narrowed her dark eyes at me and bared her teeth to reveal several serrated points. Oddly positioned, as though every other tooth grew like a dagger. She huffed, then sauntered through the crowd, seeking company elsewhere.

"She's part merfolk. Rare, since it's not often a sea fae rides a male with a fin." Celine snickered and filled a tin cup with crimson wine. She plopped the cup in front of Larsson. "Makes Pesha a favorite here, and Larsson is fortunate enough to be her favorite. Sorry, mate. Drink up, you've had quite a loss tonight."

He frowned but took a long gulp.

"Ah." I feigned a bit of sympathy. "Playing my captor ruined your plans with bedmates."

Larsson paused the cup at his lips. "Trust me, lady, if I want to take time to bed someone, I'll do it. And thoroughly."

A sudden ache for Jonas and his haughty bravado struck me like a molten bolt. I craved my friends. Hells, what a different sight this place would be if they were here. Instead of terrifying, drinking and laughing in an Ever alehouse would be a vibrant kind of adventure.

I faced the somber musician again. His tune was warm and comforting. He reminded me of the skalds back home with their poems and tales. He was a beautiful sort of bard.

Celine and Larsson spoke on the state of the Tower. They commented on the number of patrons and traders and unfamiliar fae. Sometimes they'd laugh at their fellow crewmen as they stumbled over their own drunken feet.

They ignored me. I didn't mind and kept focused on the delightful music. The bard lifted his eyes, as if sensing my study, and grinned. He gained a touch of energy from my attention and swayed his slender shoulders.

Now that I could make out his face, the musician wasn't as hardened on the outside as I thought. He was, in fact, terribly captivating. Strong features, a sharp jaw, a divot in the center of his radiant chin.

"You do not hail from these seas?" His voice was as gentle as a summer's night and as rich as an autumn afternoon.

"No." I couldn't recall a time I'd heard a sweeter voice than his. Every note flowed through my body, heating my blood, pooling deep in my belly until I . . . all hells, I had to clench my thighs together when a rush of unbidden need throbbed between my legs.

I sighed to keep from moaning.

"Beautiful." I applauded, silently pleading for more of the man's song.

"What's beaut—" Celine tracked to where my gaze lingered and shot up from her chair. "Shit!"

I cried out when her rough hands clamped over my ears. The musician rose to his feet, eyes on me, that pipe growing louder. I clawed at Celine's hands. How dare she try to block such a marvelous sound.

"You hear the call," the man sang.

He didn't speak it—no. Not even his spoken words could be so bland and tedious as normal conversation. Every sound was a melody. A sensual, delicious melody that had my chest heaving, my skin boiling in a desire I'd not felt since . . . since Bloodsinger had fooled me in my chamber.

"No, earth fae," Celine screeched. "Shut it out. Larsson, get the king. Get the king!"

I shoved Celine away and stood. Part of my mind was wholly aware patrons had paused their revelry to observe the struggle. I didn't care. How was it that the longer he played the more youthful he seemed? His skin was the color of tilled soil, his hair golden like sweet pears.

He smiled. I nearly stumbled when a rush of anguished want pulsed along my center.

"Let her go, you damn sea singer." Celine tossed one of the tin cups at my musician's head.

I might slit her throat should she harm his ability to sing and play.

The bard paused, studying Celine with a narrowed gaze, then flashed a cruel grin. "Lost your voice, little siren? Go ahead, try to sing me back, seductress."

Siren? Foolish of my lovely bard. Celine spoke to the tides, not the seduction of the heart.

"How about I cut out your tongue instead?" Celine said in a low snarl. "Release her."

"'Tis my right!" he shouted back. It only added to the harmony in my head. His eyes were a darker shade, and for a moment, his face twisted into something gaunt and sunken. "Claim a heart, my debt is paid, and I leave this pit."

"She belongs to your king, and—"

"She belongs to me."

I startled when the bard's face flashed in a horrible skeletal image. Sharp cheekbones, cracked skin, rotted teeth. In the next breath, when his lips touched the flutes of his pipe, his roguish delight returned.

My pulse slowed.

The surface of my body was overheated. Sweat gathered on my brow, and my breaths were more rasps than anything. I feared any moment I'd combust if the pressure across my body was not satisfied. Before I could stop, my hand slid over my belly, reaching beneath the waist of my trousers for the apex of my thighs. If my bard would not bring me relief, I would.

A hand slapped over my wrist, guiding my hand away from my belt.

"Erik?" His name rolled off my tongue like a reverent kind of praise. His name was beautiful. More lovely than even the song in my head. Something about the Ever King pulled me to him, drew a want greater than the man's haunting tune. Memories of Erik's body pressed against mine and—all gods—the way he'd kissed me in the sea.

A shudder danced down my spine. I might do anything for a taste of him again.

"Erik." I stroked my fingertips down the stubble of his jaw, my thumb lingering on the scar over his top lip.

Bloodsinger gripped my wrists and gently eased my palms away. He seethed at Celine and Larsson. "How long did you let her listen?"

"We hardly heard it," Celine said, a little desperately. "You know I'm numb to their songs, and Larsson favors women."

Heard it? Yes! My sweet bard.

I clutched Erik's hands and tugged him forward. "You must hear it. It's beautiful."

"Aye, love. I've heard it." He looked over my shoulder. "End it, sea singer. She's not yours to claim."

"Not even the king can keep her from me," the bard sang. "By right, I'm due the heart I capture. Was a vow of the debt."

Erik sighed. His shoulders slumped in defeat. "I've only just won her, now I must let her go." He faced the strange singer and held out one hand. "The Ever King will abide by your vow and set you free."

With a twisted sort of glee, the bard ceased his playing long enough to clasp the king's hand. It happened swiftly. The moment Erik had a hold on the musician, he slashed his first two fingers on the points of his teeth until a gush of blood slipped over his knuckles.

Without warning, the king shoved the bloodied tips into the ear of my bard. I might've screamed—I wasn't certain—most sound was drowned out by bone-splitting wails.

The bard clutched his ear and fell to his knees. His beautiful face twisted and split into something horrific. Pockets of skin on his cheeks were missing, and through fleshy tendons, his yellowed teeth were visible. His complexion was colorless, not even pale. It was nearly translucent.

The king took hold of my arm and pulled me against his side. "No vow of servitude outweighs the word of your king."

"Sing," the musician sobbed. "Sing, I beg of you."

He convulsed. What looked like sea-foam frothed from his ear. His horrid eyes rolled back in his skull. Jaw tight, the creature kept pleading through his teeth for the king to save him.

A crowd gathered. No one tried to help the dying heap of a sea singer. Most watched as though it were a delightsome part of the evening. A few gazes lifted to me, curious, maybe a bit unsettled. My body was still pressed against Bloodsinger's, and the feel of the hard planes of his form made the constant heat on my skin devolve into a maddening boil. I dug my fingernails into his arm, needing him closer.

Hells, I would fall to my knees and plead if only he'd put his clever hands on my skin again.

I arched against him, seeking pressure, any sort of relief from the ache pooling between my thighs.

Erik frowned and dragged me through the crowd, pausing at Larsson. He was handsome, with a strong jaw, and the right amount of beard. Without a thought, I stroked the curve of Larsson's arm. Gods, he was strong.

Bloodsinger let out a strange kind of hiss and pulled me back. "Get the draught, Larsson."

I never thought long on how much I liked his name. Larsson. Not as much as I enjoyed saying "Erik Bloodsinger," but close.

Larsson chuckled. "You may call me whatever you'd like, lady. I'll be Bloodsinger for an eve—"

"Go, or you lose an eye," Erik snarled.

Larsson paused when Erik looked ready to follow through on his threat and lifted his hands in surrender. "I'll find Poppy."

Hells, I said all that out loud.

"Aye, love."

"Quit making me talk." I pawed at my chest, unable to keep the burn of desire tamed. "These are . . . they're private thoughts."

"I assure you it isn't me making you speak." Bloodsinger led me into a back room already occupied by a naked man and woman, her body bent over a table, and his rocking hard enough the edge slammed against the wall. "Out!"

The couple screamed and scrambled for cover, never truly looking at the king. Within a few heartbeats they were fleeing, and Erik slammed the latch on the door into the locked position.

I tugged at my top. So bleeding hot. A fire must've burned in some inconspicuous place within the room. I gathered the skirt up my legs; if I did not rid myself of these suffocating clothes, I'd scream.

"Livia." Erik took my hands.

"Say it again." I pressed against his chest with enough strength that Erik was forced to catch me but lost his footing. His back slammed into the wall. "I love how you say my name."

Pressure from his thigh burned against my aching core. I moaned, eyes closed, and could not stop the need to seek more. Against his leg, I arched and writhed.

"Damn the hells," Erik muttered under his breath. He held his hands on my waist, letting me rock against him for a few breaths before shaking his head. "No, this ends now."

My body, from crown to foot, trembled in unforgiving need. He was refusing me, and I could not fathom it. The thought made me feel as though I'd retch any moment. Perhaps he didn't believe I wanted him. We'd been at odds; that must've been the cause of his reluctance.

I could show him—yes, I'd show the Ever King every seed of my desire belonged to him.

I stepped back and slid one arm out of my sleeve.

Erik's mouth tightened. His eyes went wide. "Livia. Stop."

"Don't you want me?" The shirt opened enough that cool air brushed over the slope of my breast. A little more and I'd be bared to the king. "We never did finish what we started—"

"Songbird." He took hold of my wrists again, breath heavy. Erik let his forehead fall to mine. "Sea singers have a lure to their voice. You've heard lore of a siren song—male sea singers use their pipes and lyres the way a siren uses her voice. For earth fae, it draws out lust, and you can't resist the song. I should've thought to look for one, but—"

I cut him off and slammed my lips to his. He needed to cease speaking. Erik was stiff but placed his hands on my hips, digging his fingernails into my skin. I slid my tongue against the seam of his bottom lip, and a deep groan rumbled in the back of his throat. The king tightened his hold on my body.

A new pulse of desire burned through me. This time it began at the scar on my arm, shooting to my heart in a single breath. I wanted him. Not the bard. Not handsome Larsson. I wanted Erik Bloodsinger.

With care, his palm slid up my spine. His fingers speared through my hair, gripping it at the roots, angling my mouth to his. I deepened the kiss eagerly. His tongue was warm and furious, and drew out an embarrassing whimper from my chest with demanding strokes.

He tasted like rain, fresh and clean, and an earthy smoke. I needed him everywhere. Even then, I was certain it wouldn't be enough.

I hooked a leg around his waist. His hips rocked against mine but stiffened straightaway, as though he were still battling his own need. I could see it in the fiery spark in his gaze, the way his chest rose in frantic breaths. He was as greedy as me.

My teeth dug into his lip. I bit down and scraped as I pulled back.

"Songbird." Erik moaned, breaking the kiss, and buried his face against my throat. "No blood."

Right. His blood meant death, a painful death. I panted in quick gasps. A death he'd proffered the seedy bard for taunting me with his song.

Erik killed for me. Never did I believe I'd embrace anyone's darkness in such a way, but the more I thought of how he tore me away, the more his eyes flashed in a possessive violence when he thought I'd belong to the sea singer. Gods, I wanted to tear my way inside him and never leave.

Frantic, my body pressed into his, wild and lost on a path I knew led to destruction, but there was nothing I cared to do to stop it. Poison blood and all.

Heat reached a breaking point inside me. I needed him. All of him. Before he could protest, I took hold of one of his wrists and guided his palm off my hip, up my ribs, until he cupped the underside of my breast.

Erik snapped back, breaking the connection, and returned his hands to my hips.

He tried to maneuver me a few paces from him, but I planted my feet and glowered. "I am freely yours. Isn't that what you wanted? I'm letting you take me."

A shadow passed over his features, something almost heartbreaking. His thumb traced the line of my bottom lip. "It's not real, love. I took you. I plan to slaughter your family. Remember all those gory details?"

"Stop it. Stop it." I shook my head, trapped in a delirious spin of unsatisfied sensual lust and the truth of his words, which dug deep into my chest like a rusted blade. I clutched the sides of my head. No. I wanted him. He was like a hidden piece of my heart. Yet I hated him. I should hate him.

"It'll be over soon." Erik's voice was distant, almost like he was speaking to me underwater.

Another person was there. My head was swimming, but I recognized Larsson. He spoke to the king, glanced at me, then left the room. In Erik's hand was a cup of something hot, the steam pungent with a tart, fishy scent.

Erik curled his hand around the back of my head. "Drink this."

I shook my head, pinching my lips.

He scoffed. "Not afraid of my blood in your mouth, but a tonic is where you draw the line?" He stroked my lips, easing them apart, and forced a few swallows onto my tongue.

A rancid flavor like old bread and sun-rotted fish caused me to gag and splutter. But soon, my eyes grew heavy, and the throbbing need eased. My pulse slowed. I was vaguely aware that Bloodsinger was guiding me back onto the bed. He scooped my legs in his arms and slid them beneath the mussed quilts.

He whispered something I didn't hear. Then I fell into syrupy black.

22

THE SONGBIRD

ALL THROUGH THE night, boots must've stomped over my skull. I could not understand why it screamed in hot agony.

Something cold dabbed my brow. I cracked one eye. A woman with a spot growing dark hairs on her chin pressed a cloth to my forehead. Her hair was the color of a pale sky, tied in a knot at the base of her neck, and her skin looked rough, like weathered leather.

"Ah, decided to wake?" She hummed a laugh and reached over a table topped with a mortar and pestle, herb jars, and a burning stalk of what looked like scorched grass. The woman crushed a few of her burning herbs into a wooden bowl and waved it under my nose. "Up you get."

I coughed, retching on the harsh burn of spiced herbs. Unappealing as it was, my lungs cleared, and the ache in my skull dulled to a mellow throb.

"What happened?" Haze wrapped around my memories. I recalled the Ice Fjords. Bloodsinger left us. A tavern and . . . sweet music.

I jolted upright. Music. Desire. The king.

With a groan, I buried my face in my palms. I'd clawed at Bloodsinger, shoved my tongue in his mouth. He could've done anything to me, and his touch would've sent me to a blissful euphoria.

"Hold your head up, dearie," said the woman, puffing out her lips. She patted my shoulder and handed me a cup of clear water. "Sea singers were once the brutalest of foes when land and sea met. Eggert had been bound to this old tavern for at least six centuries. Had a rather nasty debt to pay for stealing from a nobleman in the House of Tides."

"I was—" I sipped some of the water, wetting the dry patches in my throat. "I was his way to freedom?"

The woman nodded. "Only earth folk fall for a sea singer's tune. They want the hearts, you see. Something about eating one makes their youth return. Without it, they're nothing but rotting corpses with a voice. Hard to pay off his debt when your lot never steps into the Ever. I expect you made his last moments rather thrilling."

His last moments. I made his last moments filled with a feral need to survive, then I watched the creature die from poison and tried to bed his killer while everyone watched.

"No shame in what was done," she went on. "Sea singer lust is untamable. Not even the strongest of celibates could resist it. The illusion of pleasure is intoxicating, I suppose."

It was mortifying.

I'd need to face Bloodsinger again. I couldn't recall every detail of my lust trance, but I recalled him. His taste, the heat of his breath on my skin, his hands, his body. My pulse quickened; I had to close my eyes and repeat all his lies, his cruel words, and his threats to keep from tumbling down another spiral of disgusting, misplaced desire.

I didn't want him.

It was a trance.

Yet I couldn't keep my mind from spinning to the gentle way he'd returned me to the bed, the way he'd rushed me out of sight before anyone saw me unravel. The way he stopped.

A man who had utter control over me in a vulnerable moment had stopped it.

I let out a long breath. Bloodsinger didn't want me, simple as that. Except there were bits and pieces of moments where his eyes burned like fire behind his irises, and his fingers nearly bruised my skin from clinging to my body with such ferocity.

"Drink up, dearie." The woman pointed at the water. "Clears the system. Promised the king I'd send you to him once you woke, and he's not keen to wait around the fjords longer than needed."

Heavy disquiet settled like hot stones in my stomach.

"Oh, I brought you this." The woman set a sprig of some kind of herb with blue leaves on the table. "For the nerves."

"Nerves?" I blinked. "You saw me?"

"Don't know what I was supposed to have seen, but I know you've got wild nerves. Hard to breathe sometimes? Heart races? Thoughts spin?"

I nodded slowly. "How did you know?"

"Most boneweavers have a sense about these things."

"Boneweaver?" I grinned. "You're a healer."

"You earth fae and your odd terms." She pressed a hand to her heart. "Boneweavers have an affinity for breathing in the ailments of the folk they're weaving—healing, I suppose you'd say. Weaving sounds more intricate, don't you think? Anyway, once we get a taste, we can recommend proper remedies."

I studied the herbs. "I've had nightmares and . . . panicked thoughts since I was a girl."

The old woman nodded with a touch of sympathy. "The mind's a powerful thing, dearie. Don't you go feeling no shame, but don't you forget you own that mind of yours, it's not to own you. The serenleaf will help. Quite soothing after a few breaths."

She showed me how to rub the dust from the sprigs over my fingers so the scent would be with me most of the day. According to the boneweaver, some folk threaded the herb in their gowns or jewelry. Subtle, not to be noticed, but powerful enough it could help ease the sharp edges of the anxious nerves.

"I'm Livia," I whispered as she gathered her supplies.

With a kind smile, she nodded. "I know. Heard all about you from the king. He wasn't pleased with how long you were sleeping."

I frowned. If Bloodsinger hadn't wanted me to get locked in a twisted sexual trance, he shouldn't have left me alone in a tavern with a sea singer.

"About had to give him some serenleaf of his own to get the man to stop asking if you was breathing right."

My fingertips tingled. Erik pestered her over my well-being, not out of his own annoyance? That didn't fit.

The old woman chuckled and patted my shoulder. "Name's Blister Poppy. If ever you return to the Ice Fjords, you come say hello, you hear? Now, once you feel steady, there's some fresh clothes for you in the wardrobe. Next door down the hall, the king will be waiting."

I INHALED DEEPLY, drawing in the smooth scent of the serenleaf. The herb had a flavor like honey and milk and a sweet nectar.

I tucked the sprig into the deep pocket of the roughly spun wool skirt—a size too large—and smoothed out the billowy top. Almost positive I was adorned in a man's top, I didn't mind. Anything to rid myself of Bloodsinger's shirt. All I saw when I looked at it was the way I'd wanted to shred it to pieces and climb onto Erik's lap naked.

What had Poppy said? My mind lived within me, but I gave it too much control. Last night, horrible as it was, had been something beyond my control. It wasn't anything to be ashamed about.

I closed my eyes. Uncle Tor was always telling me to find a lesson in a struggle. I supposed next time I walked into a tavern in the

Ever Sea, I would be on high watch for sea singers. I laughed softly. No mistake, any strum of a lute or beat of a drum would likely send me bolting from the room from now on.

No matter how Erik mocked me, what happened taught me to always be on guard.

Shoulders back, I stepped into the room.

This wasn't a bedchamber. This room was meant for gathering or sitting. Woven rugs over the floor, a few plush chairs against a round table. A meal had been laid out, but my gaze found Bloodsinger straightaway.

Gods, he was horribly captivating. Rough and battered, but beautiful and villainous.

The scar cutting through his lip thickened the top peak. His skin had a rich bronze tint in the dawn, almost as though he might glisten in direct sunlight. I was accustomed to broad men, and Bloodsinger was strong, but strength wasn't all in his build. He was lithe too. A man who could lash out and cut through another before anyone could stop it.

Erik gestured to his feast. "Sit."

I did a quick scan of the wooden plates and goblets. Raw cuts of pink fish and steamed bitter greens and a tart-smelling jelly sauce were laid out over the top.

"I'm not hungry." I was ravenous.

"You lie so easily, Songbird. Getting caught in a sea singer's trance as you were will race the heart as if you're running great distances. Eat. You'll need your strength. And don't tell Sewell I said this, but you might as well enjoy the food here before we make the journey home."

"You've decided to return me to the fort?" I sat in one of the chairs with an arrogant grin. "A wise choice."

Erik took the seat across from me and picked at the fish without taking his gaze off mine. "You'll learn to call the royal city home soon enough."

For how long? I swallowed the question back and took a small pink berry off a plate. It tasted bitter until the juice dripped down my throat like a sugared glaze. "You always accuse me of lying, but you've told your fair share."

"I've told you two lies, and one was part of our game in your chamber. I am not careful with how I use my magic—that was the lie."

"I'm sure I can think of a few more from when you had your hand under my dress." All gods. I blinked, a little astonished at my own flyaway tongue.

"The same sweet lies you spoke last night when you choked me with your tongue." Bloodsinger's grin spread, wide, white, and menacing. Those sharpened canines were not wolfish like fangs but were vicious all the same. He tossed a piece of the fish into his mouth and slumped back in his chair.

Another glance at the meal and my insides twisted. My mouth grew so wet I had to swallow twice.

"Why do any of this? Feed me, clothe me, bring your boneweaver healer woman?"

"Poppy will curse your tongue for that one." Erik took a long drink from the goblet. "She's no one's boneweaver—a free soul, as she likes to tell everyone. Says it keeps those she weaves diverse and interesting."

I let out a sigh of irritation. "Still, you . . . you could've made me suffer last night, as you vowed. I was in such a state—" Gods-awful heat flooded my cheeks, but I forced myself to go on. "If you were to hand me to your crew, I would've been pliant and accommodating for anyone. You missed your true opportunity to make me suffer."

The gleam in his eyes transformed to a deep, heated rage. A shiver lanced down my back; I could practically taste the violence misting off him. "Maybe you're right. I should've."

His anger didn't come from a place of regret at missing a cruel opportunity. It was pointed at me. As though Bloodsinger was enraged I'd even suggest such a thing. He threatened me in one breath, then looked at me like he'd tear out the throat of anyone who came close.

I wasn't certain if it was the effects of the trance still peeling away, but my head spun, and I tired of it.

"What do you want with me?" The words spilled out like a plea. "You keep me safe yet tell me to anticipate death and suffering and pain. The way you took me, the way you tell me you plan such brutal things with me, makes little sense anymore."

"Tell me where the confusion lies so I might clarify."

I crossed my arms over my chest like a shield. Maybe more of a challenge. "If you cared about spilling our blood so much, I would be dead already, and you certainly wouldn't have thought twice about leaving my brother alive."

He swirled a finger around the edge of his goblet. "You want the truth, love?"

"Yes."

Erik's jaw pulsed once, then twice before he looked at me. "Your people deserve to suffer for what they've done time and again to people of the Ever. But you?" The king paused. "I might have different plans for you."

My stomach tightened. "And will I be . . . privy to these plans?"

"Yes. You asked for honesty, and I will give it to you. No matter how brutal."

I did ask for honesty. What was the point in sparing feelings? I'd rather be prepared. "Tell me."

"After the events of last night, I've come to realize the Ever is too foreign for land fae to be walking about freely."

Dammit. He planned to keep me truly caged, maybe bound or chained in his small chamber on the ship. I rubbed another sprig of serenleaf between my fingers. This wasn't a surprise, so it would do no good to wallow.

"I won't risk you getting your pretty neck carved up or taken from me prematurely." Erik took another drink from his goblet. "So I will claim you."

My brows pinched in the center. "Claim me? You have already taken me—"

"To claim a prize from a raid is more than simply declaring you belong to me. It's not done often, not unless a crewman feels a particular connection to a piece."

"A piece." I scoffed. "An object."

Bloodsinger tilted his head, grinning. "What would you like me to call you, Songbird? My pet?"

"Livia." My name sliced between my teeth, jagged and harsh. I clenched my fists. "I would have you call me Livia Ferus, daughter of Valen and Elise, blood of the Night Folk fae. Blood that is not yours to win like some treasure."

"Ah, but you might be my greatest treasure." Erik studied me, his fingers swirling around his goblet, his coy half grin never fading. "And what is wrong with it? The title you wish me to say is quite a mouthful."

"Bastard." I shook my head and looked away.

The king laced his long fingers together and leaned forward, propping his elbows on the table. "To be claimed, Livia, means it is punishable by death should anyone touch you."

"I've always dreamed of being an object for a tyrant. Tell me, Bloodsinger, how many women have you claimed before?"

"None," he said. "It is a risk. You will be mine, meaning you are in my possession. You're near me, in my palace, my chambers. We're not exactly seeing eye to eye, love."

"Think I'll stab you in the night?"

He hesitated. "No. You wouldn't be able to do it."

"Ah, this sick claiming ritual keeps you safe from me, then?"

"No." He slipped his hand inside his tunic and pulled out the silver swallow. "This does."

"That means nothing."

"It means something." Erik cracked his neck to one side before going on. "Out of all the earth fae, one girl came to see to the comforts of an enemy. I thought the first night I saw you that you would throw stones or rotten pomes at me. Imagine my surprise when, instead, you sat down and read to me."

I didn't want to talk about the past, didn't want to remember the war, the blood, the nightmares. I didn't want to remember that he still believed we had his gold disk hidden away. What would become of any of us when the king of the Ever learned I'd shattered it so long ago?

"This claiming, what exactly does it entail?"

"A public proclamation and brief binding spell." Erik picked at another piece of fish but never ate it. "I will arrange it once we reach the royal city. There is always a return feast when the *Ever Ship* arrives to port. We'll do it there." He leveled me in a sharp stare. "That means keep your head down for a few more sunrises, Songbird."

"And what does it make me, being your claimed possession? Your prisoner? Your whore?"

"It makes you mine." He glanced at the table. "It will demand the people give you respect. You will be untouchable, for you will be mine."

"I don't understand. Like your queen?"

Erik's face was unreadable. "There are no Ever queens. There are mates to breed heirs. No one sits on the throne but the king; it has always been this way."

It sounded miserable and lonely. He could say what he wished about my folk—perhaps they were his villains—but they loved fiercely and equally.

Bloodsinger sighed. "I do this not to rob you of more freedom."

"You've robbed me of all my freedom."

His jaw went taut. "I do this for your protection. You will be considered my property, and as such, you will not be harmed unless the one who attempts it wishes to suffer."

"Why does my protection even matter? When you first took me, you promised I'd suffer. You promised I'd watch my family burn. Now you want to protect me."

His eyes were distant. I wasn't even certain he'd heard me until he spoke in a low voice. "I was drawn through the Chasm, drawn to you, but there is something else keeping me drawn to you. Have you felt it? The burn at my touch?"

I shook my head at once—too swiftly—and the king grinned with a touch of venom.

"More sweet lies."

I let out a long breath. "What do you want from me, Bloodsinger? Yes, there is something that pulls me to you. It was what pulled me to you the night you ruined my life. I'd rather not think of it."

"Is it so horrid?"

"Gods, you're arrogant." I shook my head in irritation. "Yes, it's horrid. Do you think I'd revel in the idea of indulging some strange *attraction* to the man who speaks only of slaughtering people I love? To the man who had no thought for me, my life, or my future when he ripped me away into a world that despises me?"

"Attraction, you say?"

"Through all that, you only picked up that word?"

Erik chuckled softly and dragged his fingers through his hair. "You did not seem to mind all that much last night."

Wretched heat flooded my cheeks like a thousand pinpricks across my skin. "Mock me all you like for succumbing to a damn lust spell, I care little. Know this—in the daylight, I'd rather be doused in hot oil than let your mangled body touch mine."

Erik's grin faltered. If I'd not been so close, I would have missed it. "I suppose you wouldn't be the first."

The king stood, more distant than before, and a flare of shame clung to my chest. I shoved it down.

Erik went to the door. "Come with me, Songbird."

"Where are we going?"

Erik's jaw tightened. He scrutinized me for what felt like a thousand heartbeats, until he finally said, "To the purpose for our visit to the Tower. The truth of the Ever."

23

THE SONGBIRD

BLOODSINGER LEFT NO room for argument and led us to a boathouse near the back of the Tower. Tait, Larsson, and Celine were there. Larsson laughed at something Celine said, a smoke between his teeth as he wrapped ropes. Tait, somber and tense, adjusted a crimson scarf over his dark hair.

On our approach, their levity faded, and Tait's scowl deepened.

"You're certain she won't use all this against us?" Larsson asked.

"Tell me how she might use it against us. Do you suppose it is some great secret?"

How could I ever use anything in this kingdom against any of them?

Celine lifted a satchel to her shoulder, and I drifted beside her, a hazy memory of the night before pounding in my skull. "Celine," I said.

"Earth fae."

"I'm not certain if I imagined something." My gaze flicked to the scar on her throat. "But . . . did that sea singer call you a siren?"

I'd heard such talk of the power of a siren's song. A lure, a taunt, a power unmatched when sung. No man atop the water's surface could resist it. If she had such a voice, I'd never seen her use it.

Celine's mouth pinched in a tight line. "Maybe I was. Maybe I wasn't. Doesn't matter much for what we're about to do now, does it? All you need to know is I can sing a song that causes the water to drag you beneath the depths if I want. Better than lust, don't you think?"

She stepped around me, cutting off any more questions. I was curious enough to risk asking again but swallowed my words when Erik insisted we needed to load a boat.

A row of small skiffs and even longboats were tethered to narrow docks. I brushed my fingers over the stempost of one longboat, tracing the fangs of the great sea serpent, and longed for home.

Erik stopped in front of a different skiff, but watched as I practically caressed the serpent. He altered course and stepped into the longboat. "I assume you can row?"

"I can row."

I settled beside the king on a bench, the other three took places at our backs. I carved the heavy oar into the clear water of the lagoon, and nearly sobbed at the familiar burn in my shoulders.

"You are more adept with that oar than I thought," Erik said with a grunt and deep dig of his own.

"I fished with my father often." Long days spent under the sun, atop the water, with uncles or friends or just my daj and me were some of my most cherished memories. The burn of tears sprang behind my eyes. "Does it bother you when I remind you whose blood runs in my veins, Bloodsinger?"

He shook his head. "I'd never forget."

Willows and overreaching branches of towering trees shaded the passage. Beneath the water were black stones that glistened with crystal chips. We crossed the lagoon until the boat banked near stacked boulders with scars of white minerals crisscrossing over the surface.

The king held out a hand and waited for me to take it while the others secured the longboat. Trees were sparse, but sparkling streams spilled over the rocks in gentle falls, and pale waterfowl nested along the banks, chirping and cooing as we approached.

There was a beauty here that I'd never seen back home. Water was like glass or emeralds. Foliage seemed to glisten in the sunlight, and the songs of creatures were strangely melodic. When the magic of the Sea Folk lived in the voice, I suppose it was no wonder even the creatures called beautifully.

"This way." Erik tugged me up a muddy slope toward a cavern between two white stones.

I tried to keep my hold on his hand loose and uninterested, but the slick surfaces forced me to cling to his strength to keep from slipping over the edge.

Inside the cavern the air thickened and warmed unnaturally and held a rancid scent of scorched fetid wood. I covered my nose. Erik gave me a tormented look, as though he hated this place more than anyone.

Dammit. What if this was where he planned to end me? My breath came sharp and angry, and I tugged back against him. I thought I could face the Otherworld with bravery, with my head high, but now betrayal lanced through me, sharp and swift.

Erik pulled me closer as we walked, his lips brushing my ear. "Livia Ferus, blood of warriors, temptation of the Ever King, you have nothing to fear from me in here. I am the one who fears this place."

I blew out a quivering breath. How he knew the anguish of my thoughts, I didn't know, but he gave me a subtle dip of his chin and rounded a bend in the cave. I let out a small gasp. White stone was blackened and reeked of refuse, much the same as the scorched soil on Skondell.

The spread marred the crystal chips in the stone and devoured the beauty of it. Fury magic in my veins ached, yearning to heal the land, to hear its secrets. A heaviness lived here, like watching a slow death and being unable to look away.

"What is this?" I whispered.

Erik's jaw set. "We call it the darkening."

"This is what scorched that isle?"

With a nod, Erik released my hand. "It has been slowly eating away at the lands and destroying our resources. I've done all I can to find answers on how to stop it."

I hovered my hand over a stone. "How long has it been spreading?"

"It began a few turns ago."

My heart dropped to my stomach. I closed my eyes. "Do you think . . . the barriers caused it?"

"I don't know. Perhaps destroying the natural connection between our worlds played a part. Perhaps it is something else." His voice hardened. "What I know is you pulled it away. I've seen the power that comes from the mantle of the king, and it would have the ability to amplify healing this land. But here you are, with the mark of the House of Kings, and you healed the soil in Skondell. It cannot be coincidence."

Bleeding hells, no.

Erik took my arm with the rune mark. His thumb rubbed over my sleeve where he knew the scar dug into my skin.

"Erik," I whispered. "I don't know how to do this, I've never seen—"

"You did it already."

It was strange to hear a touch of pleading in the Ever King's tone. It shattered my heart. Turns he'd been trapped here, unable to protect his people, desperate to reach the realms of his enemies, desperate to take back what was his. He wanted the talisman he called his mantle, not simply to take revenge on my father but because he thought it would give him the full strength to save his damn world.

"You feel a draw to the Ever." His voice was soft, almost broken. "I've seen it in your eyes."

Panic choked in the back of my throat. "I don't know what this is and—"

"Songbird. I was pulled toward the Chasm. It was my last chance to find a way to defeat this, and I found you."

"You found me," I repeated, breathless, my head spinning.

"I *found* you." One half of his mouth curved. "What you did in Skondell gave me hope that until I have the full power of the Ever again, you might stay the disease, even a little longer."

I blinked and studied the rot over the stones. "The dark earth in Skondell, it . . . it had a magic to it. I sensed it."

Erik held my gaze. "And your magic pulled it away."

It was more. The darker side of my fury pulled it away. I didn't want to think what would happen should I truly dig deeper into this destruction.

I studied the scorched stones. Nothing was alive, nothing could live. Tendrils of inky black slithered across every stone like gangly fingers reaching for the flame to snuff it out. The Ever Kingdom was dying. Erik looked to some of the darkness overhead, tension written in every groove of his handsome face.

What burdens had he faced? He'd been desperate enough to dive through the Chasm, a last hope, into the realm of his enemies.

A sharp anger drove into my chest. My people often spoke of peace yet never tried to speak to the sea fae after the war. Almost like we feared any effort to do so might upend the hard-won comforts we enjoyed back home.

My fury magic laced through my fingers, a desire, a call to push back against whatever was happening here. To dig so deep might bring horrors to my mind, but wasn't it worth it to help the innocent?

I hovered my hand over a patch of darkness and closed my eyes. My skin prickled against the magic. Distant screams of pain echoed in my skull. I winced.

"What is it?" Erik whispered. "You fear this the same as us."

I clenched my jaw and held my hand steady. If I carved through the shadows, the pain, the screams of the agony that came from this darkness, I could see a shape. A figure, someone in the distance, like a shadow dancing beneath moonlight.

Blood. Flesh. Screams.

I snapped my hand back and opened my eyes.

"Bleeding gods, do you see that?" Celine's whisper drew me back.

A full arm's length of darkness was erased from the white stones.

My heart slowed when I blew out a long breath. There was sickness here, and I could heal it. Somewhere inside I knew, with time, with effort, I could reverse whatever had devoured the Ever Kingdom.

But it would mean using my fury in every way I feared.

Tait stared in disbelief at the pale stone that had been washed of the dark veins, the first expression other than hatred on his face. Larsson seemed suspicious and uneasy. Who could blame them? How long had they fretted alongside their king that soon their home would be devoured and their folk forced out or . . . lost entirely?

I clasped my hands in front of my body. "I will help."

Erik swallowed. A flash of heat glowed in his eyes as he dipped his chin.

"But," I hurried on, "you must vow you will not kill my father."

"Songbird."

"Serpent." I lifted a brow. "You still plan to challenge my father, to kill him. You think that will earn your power back, and I assure you, it won't. You've already destroyed my folk by taking me, so that is my offer. My magic for his life. You said yourself there could be risks with taking the mantle back."

"Yes, but the power inside it strengthens the Ever." Erik hovered a hand over a scorched place on the rock, then made a fist. "Its owner must be defeated by blood for it to be won. There is no other option."

I had to tell him. "There are things you should know about your mantle. It might be impossible to reach."

"No. It was there, I sensed it."

"And you were led to me," I insisted. "If you've been given a different way to heal your land, then take it, Erik."

He considered the words for a few breaths, then cupped a hand behind my head, both tender and as a threat. "Swear you will tell me what you know of my father's mantle, and I will stay my hand. Swear it."

I had no choice. He was vindictive, he'd been a fiend, but he was also fueled by more than revenge. He was a king leading a broken land and had acted in desperation. He deserved to know his mantle was never returning to the Ever.

With a slow nod, I whispered, "I swear."

"Good." Erik slipped his fingers into mine. "Then come with me."

24

THE SERPENT

LIVIA HATED ME. I should hate her, but there was a weak, pathetic piece of me that could not turn away from the woman. I couldn't rid my thoughts of her. To her, I might be hideous, but in spineless moments, I thought I might be content to kneel at her feet for the rest of my damn days if she healed the Ever.

When we returned to the Tower, I led her up the staircase to the highest rooms. My limp was more pronounced by making a second trip, and I caught Livia glancing at it more than once.

"You're to meet the Lady of the House of Mists," I said once we were outside the door. "Some know her as the lady of witches and the sirens."

Livia shuddered. "And sea singers?"

"Aye, love. The Lady of the House of Mists favors the spell casting side. She won't be luring you away."

"A true sea witch?" Her voice was strained. "They've always been more folklore than real."

"They are real, I assure you. Narza is a master at spell casting," I said, "and not even she has been able to clear the darkening as you did."

"Erik." Livia tugged on my hand. "You must know something about my fury—my magic."

"I know what you call your power," I said, quickening our step on the stairs. "Walk and tell me."

"When . . . when I dig deep enough, the land—" She let out a huff when her toe caught the edge of a stair. I held on to her until she righted again. "The land reveals moments to me."

"Moments?"

She nodded. Her hands trembled, each slender finger betraying the turmoil she tried to keep hidden. "Secrets are heard by the trees, the flowers, the earth. Blood and bone from death, be it battle or murder or the aged—it doesn't matter—the earth knows."

"You can see what has happened on the land?"

"Yes." Livia shifted. "Normally, I only see what has happened in that place. But with this darkening, it's different. Today I thought I saw someone in the shadows of my mind. I think they had some knowledge of the darkening, but I couldn't make them out. There was pain and I think a death. Erik, I don't know how it was caused, but I don't believe it to be something natural. It is a curse."

My body hummed in a sense of dread. I'd thought it was decay from the closed Chasm. What if it was darker? What if it had been caused with intention?

"Stay beside me," I warned, and continued our ascent to the Tower.

The high tower room kept a chill, and after stewing for a few nights, the space smelled of damp oakmoss and sweet smoked herbs.

"I expect you have much to tell me." Narza's voice came from one corner.

We shared blood through my mother, but that was the only similarity other than our proclivity to be vicious. Narza abandoned me after my mother's death. Perhaps she had every right, but I still burned in resentment for her disregard when I'd needed her most.

Livia stiffened at my side. I took her hand. "As promised, Lady Narza, I brought you the earth fae."

Narza narrowed her eyes. "I assume you still believe this girl has some power over what plagues us here."

With a tug, I drew Livia closer. It didn't take much prodding. She eyed Narza with a bit of wariness and pressed her soft curves against my side. "She chases away the darkening. I want to know why."

Narza circled Livia and me, a huntress to her prey. "Show me the mark."

With a touch of hesitation, Livia pulled up the sleeve. Narza tightened her painted lips and touched the raised skin of the rune. Livia cried out in surprise when my grandmother dug the point of her fingernail into one straight edge, drawing blood.

I stepped between them. "Do not draw her blood without warning again."

Narza chuckled. "Rather protective of your pawn, darling."

"I am 'King' to you."

"You are a boy whose nose I used to wipe clean."

"Is that so?" I tilted my head. "I recall my youngest turns much differently, Grandmother."

"Bleeding hells," Livia muttered under her breath. "She's your—"

"Grandmother? Oh, yes." I bared my teeth at Narza. "You have your drop; get on with it."

The sea witch watched the drop of Livia's blood slide off her fingernail onto her palm. She rubbed her hands together, humming a slow, breathless sort of tune. The blood ignited into a white flame in the center of Narza's hand.

My grandmother closed her eyes, humming, listening. The faint orb of light pulsed against the melody.

When Narza spoke again, her voice was dull, almost as though she spoke through a thick door. "You beautify the land, a lovely gift. Worthless during battle and survival, but how gentle, how sweet and precious you must be to your people."

Livia flushed and gritted her teeth. "That is not all I can do."

There was the fiercer side of my songbird.

"No, it isn't." Narza chuckled, eyes still closed. She rolled the glowing blood over her palm like a pebble. "Two healers now bear the mark of the House of Kings, both with their own darkness, but I sense if they were to unite as one, it might have wondrous consequences."

My ability was nothing like Livia's. I didn't see how we could unite as one power.

"You heal what is broken, an amplifier of the earth." For a moment, Narza paused, a furrow to her brow. "Strange."

"What's strange?"

Narza opened her eyes and stepped back. "Your magic flows from your heart, from desire."

Livia cast me a nervous glance. "Fury is in the blood, yes. What does that matter?"

"It means your heart must bond with the land. Naturally, the land of your birth is part of your heart, but the Ever?" Narza's lip twitched. "This is where your heart lies, or you would not be capable of accomplishing this healing. The land of your enemies holds value? I don't understand it."

All at once, the sea witch gripped Livia's arm above the rune mark. "When did this appear? What were you doing? Tell me."

I thought Livia might cry out, might tremble. She did nothing but yank her arm away and lift her chin. "It appeared after reading to a boy locked in a cell where his folk—the people who should've stood for him—were nowhere to be found."

Damn. No one spoke harshly to Narza but me. Should folk lash out at the Lady of Witches, they might soon find themselves with misplaced limbs or a tongue that no longer spoke.

I considered stealing Livia away to safety in one breath and tasting that mouth again in the next. Instead, I battled my own stun when Narza seemed more troubled than perturbed an enemy had called out her dismal presence during the war.

"You cared for him?"

Now Livia faltered. She cracked two knuckles at her sides. "I had compassion."

"Lie all you wish. It does not change that you do not even realize the danger you are in by giving your heart to the Ever. Tell me, did you come near the Chasm leading up to the return of the Ever King?"

Livia froze.

Narza cursed under her breath. "That is answer enough. You broke the walls between you." The witch leaned close to Livia's face, voice low. "He will discover the truth of what happened to give you that mark. Desperate as he is, do you think he will show you the same compassion when he does?"

Livia's breath grew sharp, haggard. It sounded damn near painful.

"I . . . I . . ." She turned to me for a moment, gasping, then reached for the door. "I must go."

Without a word, Livia abandoned the room. There was something off about all this. I felt as though it stood right before me, and I simply couldn't see it.

"What was that?" I shouted.

"Think hard, King Erik," Narza said, teeth bared. "The Chasm was closed to your blood until a woman who defied her people and comforted an enemy came near it. A woman who is drawn to the sea despite being of the earth clans with magic that thrives in your realm, thrives beside you.

"Fate smiled upon you, no mistake, for her gift is truly needed here, but to pull back such a fierce plague as this darkening, her power would need to bleed for the Ever. It does. I felt it, the draw, the desire, the sense of belonging. Think hard as to why, Grandson."

Livia told me often she despised my kingdom and everything in it, but there were moments when her eyes lit with the thrill of discovery, when she seemed at peace. She'd admitted to being near the Chasm when it opened, and after ten turns of being a prisoner in my own realm, I was led to her.

Ten turns. My heart stopped.

The same allotment of time that had to pass before I could challenge her father for Thorvald's mantle, the punishment and price for losing a sea witch's gift.

Narza kept her gaze on me as my mind reeled. The way I'd been pulled through the Chasm, the way I remained drawn to Livia. Each touch sparked in my veins. I thought I would find Thorvald's talisman when I returned, but I found her. She had the strength to heal my land exactly as I expected if ever I found . . .

No.

"Narza." My voice was low, lost. It was dangerous. "Your magic lived in the Ever King's mantle. Tell me if I've found the same power again."

"So I can witness another betrayal of a gift that ought to have been strengthened through love?" She looked away and lowered her voice. "Yes, you've been given that same chance, but you seek the approval of your sire too fiercely. Follow in his footsteps, and you will lose your mantle the same as him."

Narza moved to the window. Without a word, without a pause, she waved her hand, and a splash of dark water wrapped around her shoulders like a cloak, and she was gone.

Alone, a new coil of pressure knotted in my chest. *Shit.* I needed to find Livia.

Down in the corridor, Larsson and Tait stood on either side of the doorway, waiting.

"Where is she?" I quickened my pace until the cracks in my leg burned and protested under my skin.

"She came down upset," Larsson said. "Tidecaller went with her to your chamber."

I didn't look back at them until we made it to the black oak doors on the nobles' floor.

"Erik," Tait said under his breath, "what's going on?"

I spun on my cousin. "Stay out."

Tait's mouth tightened. I knew he wished to say a thousand things, probably pin me down, arm bent behind my back, and slug me in the shoulder until I pleaded for mercy the way he did when we were boys.

He wouldn't. Not in front of Larsson at least. Tait had too much respect—maybe fear—for the position of the king.

The front room of my chambers was dim; only the fire was aglow.

"I don't get what has you like this." Celine's voice came from my bedchamber. "Calm down a little."

Livia was leaning forward, breathing heavily, her elbows on her knees. She removed a serenleaf sprig from her skirt and held it to her nose. Celine awkwardly patted her head as though that might help.

"Tidecaller," I snapped.

She jumped and faced me. "I didn't do anything to her, she's just been like this since—"

"Leave."

Celine didn't argue. She knew me well enough to recognize when I needed to be on my own. With a bow to her chin, she slipped out of my room.

Tears stained Livia's cheeks as she rose from the edge of the bed. She wrung her hands in front of her body and tried to slow her breathing. Whatever this connection had become, I could sense where my heart ended and hers began. She was tumbling through unknowns, each one crushing her a little more, and soon they would choke the life from her.

I crossed the room and placed one palm on the side of her face, the other over the anguished beat of her heart.

The touch surged her pulse to her throat. Beneath my palms, the beat throbbed, but Livia didn't pull back from me. She even tilted her face to my palm, as though leaning into my touch.

"You are Livia Ferus," I whispered, "daughter of warriors, princess of earth magic, rebuker of the Ever King—"

She let out a snort. "Why does your voice help?"

I brushed a thumb over her cheekbone, wiping away a tear. "This fear takes your thoughts, and I won't tell you not to let it. Things are never so simple. But I will remind you of who you are, for you are a formidable foe."

She lifted her glassy eyes to mine. "My mother always told me to breathe deeply."

"Does that help?"

Livia hesitated. "Not the way you do, and I think I hate you for it. You should be horrid all the time."

"I'll try harder, Songbird."

Her smile was pinched, and her chin quivered. I didn't know what kind of magic or games of fate were at play here, but I would find out now.

"The mantle was a gift for my father from Narza," I said. "It was a gift to enhance the power of the Ever King. Should it be conquered or lost, the mantle could not be taken back for ten turns. All I could do was wait to challenge his killer.

"My uncle took particular care in preparing me to do so during the Great War, but . . ." I shook my head. She couldn't know what I'd done during the war. "There wasn't an opportunity before I was locked in a cell."

Livia placed her hands on my waist, almost like she wished to embrace me but thought better of it.

"When the Chasm opened, I thought it was fate granting me a

new opportunity, but I found you instead." I softened my tone. "Where is my father's mantle, Songbird?"

Her breath hitched. "Erik, I—"

"Where is it?" I already knew. Truth was written in the furrow of her brow, in the way she dropped her gaze to the floor.

"Please don't hurt them because of me." Her voice quivered.

"Where is it, love?"

Livia tightened her grip on my waist. "It's gone. That night, that last night when I showed it to you, I tripped on my way back and . . . it shattered."

I closed my eyes, throat tight, and let my forehead drop to hers. "What else?"

"The mark came right after," she said. "I never told anyone except my cousin that it appeared because I broke the talisman. I even replaced the original with a wrapped gold plate. A plate, and still no one noticed. No one even looked. Despite what you think, it is not a proud thing for my folk. It is a painful symbol of an unwanted war."

My father's mantle, his true power, was gone. Games of the fates were in full bloom, and something new had been shaped from it.

"I knew the Ever would heal if I found the power of the king again," I said softly. "I was right."

Livia's brows tugged together. "It's broken. I'm . . . I'm sorry, Erik."

"I thought it was my father's power calling me through, but *you* called to me. You are drawn to the sea; you're drawn to the Ever, to me."

Livia visibly paled. "What are you saying?"

I touched my thumb to her bottom lip, tracing the gentle lines. "I found *my* mantle, Songbird. It's you."

I paused for half a breath, then I kissed her.

25

THE SONGBIRD

I WAS PRESSED BETWEEN the wall and the hard planes of the Ever King's body, and I could not recall anywhere I'd wanted to be more. I ought to run, to claw at him, to curse him for stealing me away, but I leaned into him like reaching for a flame in the darkness.

An enemy to my people, and still I thought I might collapse if he removed his hands.

Erik speared his fingers through my hair, gripped the braids at the roots, and tilted my head. My lips parted, and his tongue slid against mine in slow, masterful strokes. He tasted like the cool sea air and a bite of smooth ale.

I shouldn't want him, but wanting him was the least of my worries—I craved him. When Erik left, I noticed. There was a missing piece of me, and I didn't understand it.

He pulled back, breath heavy and tangled with my own. "Because you're bonded with the Ever. You took the place of my mantle, and I took you. I won you. That is what you're feeling."

I blinked. "How . . . how did you know what I was thinking?"

His thumb ran over the rune on my arm. "You have it too, a pull to me, maybe even the ability to sense things about me. Open yourself to this connection, and I suspect you could feel my thoughts the way I feel yours. A dangerous bond for a king to have, love. You might learn exactly how to break me."

All gods. I'd absorbed the magic from the Ever King's talisman. I didn't understand it all, but the truth of it burned in my breast—I was his mantle, the amplified power of the Ever.

A groove of disappointment furrowed between his brows, and he took a step back. "That's what this is, Songbird. This pull is nothing but an unwitting bond."

He took another step from me. I glared at him, annoyed. Bond be damned, nothing felt so perfectly in place as his hands on me, and I should scream and curse the gods for such a twist of my fate. Every kiss, every touch, every moment of longing was a knife in the backs of my friends, my family.

Erik dragged his fingers through his thick hair. He was leaving. It turned my stomach with sick.

From the first moment I laid eyes on the boy king kneeling and defeated before the Sea Folk were locked away, I'd wanted to know him. Before the mantle. Before the rune mark. Before it all, I'd wanted to know *him*.

I was a traitor to my own people because I still wanted him. All of him. I reached for the king, curling a hand on the back of his neck.

A grin twisted the corner of his mouth. "Careful what lines you cross, Songbird."

"Those lines will change nothing."

"Still detest me, then?"

"Still plan to keep me captive?"

Erik slid his hands along the curve of my waist, and he dipped his face alongside my cheek. "I have many plans for you in my head right now."

"Then let me hate you *and* want you, and let us get back to it."

I kissed him with all I had. The lies from my tongue rolled onto his. I wanted him and tried to hate him. The differences were potent, but I demanded my mind cease its whirling. I wanted to do nothing but feel.

My hands gripped his tunic and drew him closer. The clack of teeth and frenzy of lips caused a moan to slide from my throat.

His leg spread my thighs, and the pressure of him against my core pooled heat between my legs. I groaned, unashamed. Erik pressed his hips against me. A short gasp slid from the back of my throat when the hardness of his length added friction to the ache.

It was as if his kiss unleashed a dormant creature inside me. I could not get close enough. I could not touch him enough.

Erik scraped his teeth down my throat; his tongue ran over the pulse point. One palm slid up the curve of my ribs. He touched each divot with his fingertips, almost as if giving me time to turn away.

My breath became heavy when his palm teased the underside of one breast. I arched my back, my nipples pebbling, desperate for his touch. Erik lifted his head for a moment, a gleam in his gaze I wanted to capture in my mind forever. The look of a man who wanted a woman, a man who'd do anything to have her.

He took my lips the same instant his hand covered my breast. I arched my back, arms around his neck, holding him closer. He tormented me as he pinched and flicked and kneaded my skin. His touch became a new obsession. Perhaps I was a traitor to my people, but in this moment, I didn't care. I wanted all of him.

Erik walked me back until my legs hit the soft edge of the bed. I fumbled into sitting without breaking the kiss. With a nudge to my shoulder, he urged my back onto the mattress. My feet were still planted on the ground as he reared over me, his palms flat beside my head.

I wrapped my legs around his waist, shuddering when his hand glided down the bare skin of my thigh.

He kissed me deeper, sucking my tongue into his mouth, as greedy for me as I was for him. Sharp desire to touch his body the way his clever fingers teased my sensitive flesh boiled in my brain. I tugged on the top of his belt and captured the heat of his moan on my tongue.

Erik pulled back, eyes dark, and slid his rough palms beneath the gown clinging to my thighs. Pain burdened one of his legs. I'd witnessed the way he grimaced, the limp, but he didn't wince when he lowered to his knees.

A startled huff broke from my throat when Erik slid my gown to my waist, baring my sex to him. "What . . . what are you doing?"

His sunset gaze held mine. "Have you never been touched, Songbird? Never been tasted?"

Heat flooded my veins in embarrassment but faded when his face moved lower so that his warm tongue dragged up the sensitive skin of my inner thigh. I shook my head.

"Tell me to stop, then." Erik's rough, calloused thumbs traced where he'd licked my legs.

My heart wouldn't slow, the beat rampaging through my skull. My insides twisted in desperate need. I bit my bottom lip. "I won't."

The same flash of hunger consuming me lived in Erik's eyes.

"Good" was all he said before a jolt of pleasure surged in my veins, like I'd leapt into a frozen lake in the dead of the frosts, when his tongue swiped over me between my legs.

Gods, his . . . his face was buried between my thighs, and I could not catch a breath.

He pulled back and swiped his tongue over his lips. "My perfect songbird. I imagined you tasted just as perfect."

Erik dipped his head and drove his tongue against the wet heat of my center again.

My breath would not calm, and I hardly cared. I propped onto my elbows, lost in a delirious stun as I watched the top of the king's head move with every flick of his tongue. A shudder of desire enflamed my skin in a blistering heat. His tongue and lips tasted all of me, his teeth nipped at sensitive flesh, and I couldn't imagine anything more . . . right.

I closed my eyes and hooked a leg around one of his shoulders, giving him space to drive me into madness.

"Erik . . . more." I let my head fall onto the soft quilts of his bed.

His hands cupped under my ass, bolstering me as he licked and kissed the arousal off my core with a ravenous frenzy.

"Say you hate me all you want, so long as all this is for me. Your cries, your taste, those ragged breaths. Those belong to me." He slung my other leg over his shoulder, deepening his angle.

I tangled my hand in his hair and tugged on the ends. He hummed, low and deep, against my entrance.

"Keep doing that," he rasped, "and I will forget to be gentle."

I let out a breathless laugh. "Who said that's what I wanted?"

Erik paused for a moment, then I thought I caught a whispered "Damn you" before his mouth claimed me again, only now he followed his tongue with a finger, then two. They dipped into my core, tormenting me until my body writhed beneath his cruel, perfect combination of tongue and fingers.

I choked on a sob when the rough callus of his thumb added friction and pressure to the tight apex. I rocked my hips against his face, unable to stop, as sensation built in the lower half of my belly. Something like a stream of heat rolled through me, from my toes, through my chest, to my skull. One wave after another left me locked in a bit of madness I didn't expect.

I whimpered and gasped and tried to mute the noises. Before the wave stopped, Erik reared over me and took my mouth with his again.

I tasted me on his tongue. Gods, I wanted to touch him the way he touched me. I wanted to experience the heat of his body the way he'd devoured mine.

My fingertips tugged on his belt. Erik's lips parted, and he widened his stance. Once I'd unlaced the top of the trousers, he guided my palm down his front until my thumb brushed through a sticky bead of arousal on the tip of his cock. To taste the musk of his smooth skin was a new experience I never anticipated I'd want more than I wished to breathe.

When my grip around the shaft tightened, a shudder rushed through the tension of his muscles, and short, breathless pants rolled from his throat.

A booming knock echoed through the room.

Pinpricks rippled up my skin, and Erik's eyes snapped open. We froze, my gown bunched over my thighs, pleasure still hot in my core, and my fingers down his trousers.

"King Erik!" Larsson's voice (I was positive he had a bit of a laugh in his tone) shouted from the corridor.

Never had I wanted to murder someone more than I did in this moment.

"What?" Erik snapped.

"Storms on the rise. Crew checks are in place. The tides are telling us the time to set sail is now."

"Damn the hells," Erik cursed under his breath, then lifted his gaze to me. "I must go. Tidecaller will come for you soon."

A frigid surge cooled the heat in my veins as he reeled back. There was a distinct absence without him near, and I hated it in a way I couldn't explain. A bond. We were unwittingly bonded, that was all.

But it wasn't. I'd never wanted a man the way I wanted Erik Bloodsinger, and I did not know what sort of woman that made me.

He refastened his belt. For a long moment, Erik hesitated, then he leaned over and bruised my lips with his kiss. When he pulled away, he whispered, "Still hate me?"

"Always," I said, desperate to either shove him back or pull him close. I gripped the quilts.

Erik's mouth turned up in a half grin, but his words were rife with something soft, something vulnerable. "Hate me all you want, but don't regret me. Promise me that."

Then I was left alone and wanting.

Don't regret me. If I were wise, that was exactly what I should do. I ought to regret letting my enemy put his mouth on my skin. I should retch at the idea he'd drawn out pleasure and sounds I didn't know I could make.

I should regret Erik Bloodsinger, but I didn't. I wasn't certain I ever would.

26

THE SERPENT

I'D LOST MY damn mind.

Long after the crew went to sleep belowdecks, I stood alone on the main deck and wiped my thumb over my lips. I could still imagine Livia's pleasure there and had to swallow the damn moan that wanted to slide free at the thought of her heat, her taste, her scent buried in my tongue.

I could spend the rest of my days with my mouth on her body, and I'd consider it a life well lived.

She'd never been touched, but I'd never done that to a woman.

Any females invited into my bed were kept turned away, never considered a lover, more a body to relieve the ache in my cock when I tired of my own hand.

A bond. Livia had taken on the power of the mantle, and unknowingly bonded to me as the king. It couldn't be more. Weaknesses were made when the heart opened its weeping sinews and let sweeter feelings inside.

A wretch named Hans Skulleater manned the helm tonight and in his deep timbre hummed the song. The moon was at its highest point and cast a cold light over the black laths of the deck.

I tore into a dry oat roll, leaned over the rail near the bow, and watched the dark water lap against the hull. How was I to manage the truth of my beautiful captive once we reached the royal city?

Not many of the crew had borne witness to Livia's bloom, and I wanted to keep it that way. Desperation had grown into the bones of Ever Folk. It would take one slash of a blade from some poor bastard who believed spilling her blood might heal it all.

I wouldn't be able to hide the truth of what Livia was from the house lords for long, but she needed to be claimed. She needed the respect and prestige of being the king's first.

The woman was prone to tumultuous thoughts and unease, but tonight it was me who could not calm the race of my pulse. I closed my eyes. Long ago, I dashed any limits of morality I would cross to save the Ever. It didn't matter who had to die, what twisted spells I needed to create, I'd do it.

The points of the swallow wings dug into my palms.

For the first time, I considered I might've reached a limit I couldn't cross. I could imagine killing her father, mother, even the pup. But now, the thought of watching light leave Livia's eyes because of my actions left a rancid burn in my stomach.

It was a good thing my father was dead, or he'd tear out my heart for being such a weak link in his long line of brutal kings.

"Dammit." A soft curse came at my back.

Livia rounded the mast dressed in a canvas coat too big for her body. The braids in her hair had been taken out, and wind blew the dark curls wild and free around her cheeks.

I couldn't look away, yet at the sight of me, she frowned and spun back the way she'd come.

"Songbird," I said, grinning. "What has you wandering about so late at night?"

"No reasons I'd tell you."

I did enjoy her bite.

"If you're looking for more of my mouth, I'm afraid I can't tonight. I'm watching the deck, you see." I opened an arm and gestured to the empty ship, taking too much pleasure from the rush of blood to her cheeks.

"I wasn't, I didn't . . . Gods, you're an arrogant sod. I couldn't sleep and needed some air. There were no thoughts of you."

I laughed and leaned my elbows on the rail again. "Not safe wandering on such a ship. Might stumble into the crew's chambers and I'd never know. I'd never hear you scream."

"Do you intentionally cause people to imagine the worst at all times?" Her shoulders rose and fell with sharper breaths. I studied her ritual, curious to learn more, and hating myself a little for it. When her pulse raced, Livia always clenched her fists or her jaw, or she'd close her eyes. I waited and . . . there it was. She drew in a long, quiet breath through her nose.

I cupped the back of her neck, drawing her face close to mine. "Breathe, Songbird. You're at no risk here. It's only me tonight."

"Yes," she whispered. "And you are the problem."

A thousand meanings laced her words. My gaze dropped to her soft lips. Thoughts of taking them again, tasting her, knotted in my gut. For a long, heated pause we attacked each other with our eyes, as if holding the stare the longest would peel back all the shields between us. When she grew too close to victory, I released her.

"Go sleep. We'll arrive by sunrise."

"I can't sleep," she admitted with a touch of reluctance. "Sewell has swallowed a boar. It is the only way to account for why the man sounds the way he does."

Before it could be stopped, a laugh rolled from my chest. "When his skull was broken, it wrecked his face. Something in his nose, I'm told."

Her lips quirked with a reluctant grin. I tried to see *him*, tried to see her as the enemy, but all I saw was her. The blue of her eyes under the sparse lantern light gleamed like a raw sapphire. Every flame brought out a warmer shade in the dark curls of her hair.

Livia hugged her middle and stepped back. "I'll just find somewhere else to sleep on this horrid ship."

"I believe you mean magnificent."

"This vessel"—she waved her hands about—"is the most hideous thing I've ever seen. What sort of ship has broken spikes everywhere, floorboards soft with rot, and those . . . fire weapons that will light the sails ablaze? A reckless choice, if I might say, for your prized monstrosity."

"The wood is not rotten. It's made from unique lumber in the royal city that is designed to give and bend to survive the Chasm. Quite expensive."

"Ah, I've always loved a man who tries to impress me with his purse." She arched a brow. "It's usually compensating for other lesser qualities."

Her eyes danced down to my damn trousers.

"Oh, you speak dangerous words." I leaned my face alongside hers, just enough to touch her cheek to mine. "But if you're curious about my ship, or possibly other things, you need only ask."

"I don't want to know anything about your ship and certainly have no interest in anything else."

"Ah." I pulled away and went to one of the ember spears and rested a hand on the sleek barrel. "So, you've no interest in how these work?"

She folded her arms over her chest, smug tension on her mouth. "A type of magic, I'm sure."

"Not at all. The ember spears are designed entirely from resources in this kingdom." She faltered. The barest glance of her eyes to the oil-glossed barrel gave her up. I opened the door where the cinders were loaded. "A lot of intricate mechanics, really. But I forgot, you're not interested."

Livia looked to the side, jaw tight, then huffed and stormed over to me. "Fine. Tell me. Better to know how something so dangerous works. I wouldn't want to blow off my hand before you have a chance to cut off my fingers."

"I take no joy in fingers," I said, flicking my brows. "I prefer softer tissues. Eyes, tongues, bellies."

"You're a wretch."

I merely shrugged. From a crate beneath the barrel, I removed a burlap pouch and showed her the contents. "The ember spears use these."

"What are those? Crystals?"

"No," I said, lifting one from the pouch. A soft, black sphere with red veins glowing as if flames were embedded within. "We call them cinder stones. Once used as a mere fire starter, but now we mine them for several uses. Hand me that bottle there."

Livia licked her lips but lifted the glass bottle beside the crate.

"Pour out a healthy dose right onto the cinder stone."

A gleam of excitement brightened her eyes. For the few breaths it took to pour the oil over the stone, she forgot to detest me.

Her mouth parted. "What happened to it?"

The cinder stone had hardened and enlarged now that the oil sopped into the porous outer layer. Instead of a pliable glowing stone, it was a dark shade and solid as iron. I tossed the pellet between my hands. "Scald leaf oil reacts to the elements of the cinder stone. It hardens the pores and cracks, swells, and becomes rather impenetrable."

"And these are what you fire?" She pointed at the barrel.

"Impressed?"

She ignored the question and hurried on. "But how does it fire? How does it travel the distance, being so heavy? With such a weight, the power of the blast must—"

"Be fierce," I interrupted. "It is. Here is what is called the touchhole." I patted the opening on the barrel. "We hold a flame to it, and when the heat mingles with the skald leaf oil, it bursts. The spear fires the blast forward. You won't blow off your hand unless you place it in front of the mouth."

Livia touched the iron. "And how far can they go?"

"Fifty paces. More with decent aim and fair wind."

She grinned, inspecting the curves, bolts, and details of the barrel. "All right, Ever King. These are, possibly, slightly intriguing."

I hated how her lax praise still felt like a brilliant victory.

"But," she went on, moving toward one of the sharp spines on the hull, "you'll never convince me these odious things are pleasant to look upon."

"Those odious things, Princess," I insisted, "are part of an array of history. Every spine represents an Ever King. With each new claim comes a new spine. This ship has seen many kings for thousands of turns. They never cease growing, love. They are the shield, the blade, the power of this ship, and they deserve your respect. Tell them they're beautiful."

Livia snickered and my chest tightened.

"Forgive me," she whispered to a long spine. "You're so ugly, you're almost lovely." She looked at me, rather pleased with her slight, then touched the shattered spine near her hand. "Not as impenetrable as the pellets, I see. What happened here? One of your endless enemies break it off?"

Tension snuck up behind and throttled me. A cutthroat reminder of the distance I should keep. "Yes."

The word was stacked in something harsh and cruel. Livia's smug grin faded.

"The spines crack when a king is defeated," I said, voice rough. "That was the spine that grew when my father was crowned as king. It broke at his death. You see, they fracture like a weak thing, for an Ever King should never be bested."

She took a step back and offered the broken spine a hesitant glance.

"Bloodsinger," she whispered, "I . . . I am sorry for—"

"Don't." In three strides I had her back pinned to the rail. She let out a shriek when my hand gripped her chin, holding her head beside the broken pieces of the spine. "Don't bring apologies. We're long past apologies."

I yanked my hand away, allowing the anger to gather like a hook to the chest, reeling me back to my purpose. The Ever was what mattered, not this unbidden desire for my enemy's daughter.

"Find somewhere to sleep," I said through my teeth.

She looked as though each word was a barbed lash, like I was nothing more than a beast backed into a corner.

I didn't wait for her to leave and made my way back to the helm.

"Move aside, Skulleater." I shoved the crewman away from the helm and took the handles.

"My King, you don't guide at night."

A muscle throbbed in my jaw. I let out a long breath through my nose, reached down to my belt, and flung the small straight blade before I had a full grip on the hilt.

Skulleater cried out when the knife plunged into the rail between his thighs, narrowly missing his leg.

"Hesitate with an order again," I snarled, "and my knife hits your throat."

"Aye . . . King Erik. Aye." Skulleater dipped his chin and hurried off the deck.

I watched him go and wished I hadn't. Mere paces from my chamber door, in the perfect vantage point to take in the helm, Livia stared up at me. Hells, I'd take her pitiful looks—the ones where I was nothing but a fiend in her eyes—over this. In this moment, she looked at me as if I'd taken her heart and torn it in two.

27

THE SONGBIRD

THE REALIZATION STRUCK before we left the ship. Erik Bloodsinger had a heart, one buried deep inside. One that felt a great deal, but one he despised. A beautiful black heart.

Last night created a crack in the rough surface of the king. He'd taunted me, but taught me about his weapons. He'd looked around his ship with a bit of pride, as though the vessel were deeply ingrained in his soul. A part of him.

How quickly it had all changed. Had I known any mention of Thorvald would emerge from innocent conversation, I never would have uttered a word.

Doubtless Erik didn't want to want me. The same way I didn't want to want him. He wanted to avenge his father; I wanted to save mine. We were the children of a war we didn't cause and were raised to despise each other, yet we couldn't seem to manage that one simple task.

He'd lashed out, but I couldn't determine if his fury had been aimed at me or himself. Last night, the king had seemed almost peaceful for a moment. He'd seemed to forget I was a tool, nothing more, and saw me as the girl who read tales to him.

I wanted to hate him, to guard up my heart against his brutality for the things he'd done and likely still planned to do, but with each damn sunrise, a bit of my shield against the Ever King slipped.

One side wanted to curse him, kill him, watch him suffer for the hurt he'd done to me. The other saw glimpses of the boy from the dark, lonely cell. The boy who said little but lit up just enough to let me know he looked forward to the nights I'd come and read my songbird fairy tale.

Last night, when he fought to hide a grin, when he seemed at peace describing how his contraptions were fired, the boy was there. Not lost.

Not yet. Perhaps my plan ought to change. Perhaps instead of finding a weakness in the king to exploit for my escape, I should find his heart.

"Glitter and gold, sing me home."

"What's that, Sewell?" Rolled furs from the Tower made a sleeping mat on the floor. I hadn't wanted to leave Sewell and had endured his roaring nose to ensure his healing wound didn't split during the night. I'd thought he might've visited Blister Poppy for healing, but after we returned to the ship, I learned the cook hadn't joined us ashore at the Tower.

I didn't know why.

Now he was ignoring me. He was still locked on whatever he saw outside. Steps pounded beyond the door followed by muffled calls for action. A horn blew overhead. "What's going on?"

With Sewell's attention turned away, I slid on a pair of trousers tossed near the door. They hadn't been there last night, and I suspected Celine had been forced to offer up more of her wardrobe. She'd only delivered the bottoms, of course. Why would I need a top?

I rolled my eyes and scoured through Bloodsinger's armoire until I found a pale top with fabric as soft as satin but as sturdy as wool.

It breathed deliciously of oakmoss and rain and a hint of smoke. It breathed of Erik.

Sewell was muttering gold and glitter again by the time I stepped onto the deck. Two men stood on either side of the door. The instant the sun kissed my cheeks, meaty palms gripped under each of my arms.

"What are you doing?" I tried to break free.

They said nothing and merely tightened their hold on me.

"No." I struggled. "Get your . . . don't touch me. I can walk alone, and—"

"Leave her be, boys." Tait leaned against the mainmast, sneering.

"The king had us keep watch," the man on my left grumbled. He was missing a tooth in the front, and the rest were painted black. Not rotted but made to look as such. "Didn't want her wanderin'."

"Where'd she be wanderin'?" Tait reached into his linen jerkin and removed what appeared to be a paper smoke like the ones we had back home; the difference was Tait stuffed his with herbs that looked poisonous and black. Tait dragged in a long breath before blowing out a plume of ashy smoke. "There's nowhere for her to go now."

The two guards laughed and left me alone.

"Welcome to the royal city, earth fae," Tait went on. "Glittering, isn't it? Pity folk like you rarely make it out alive."

His threat dissolved. Numb, almost without control, I gripped the rail, dumbstruck. The sunrise reflected over the smooth sea like a mirror, painting the water in soft pinks and gold. Sand, as white as bone, rolled over long beaches, and a wide cove seemed designed to welcome formidable vessels like the *Ever Ship*.

Iridescent fins sparkled in the sunlight as they dove in and out of the tide. From beneath the water, slender hands with four knuckles and long pointed fingernails took hold of the hull. A woman's face broke the surface. Horribly beautiful, with hair like a raven's wing and skin like the summer sky. Her eyes were as round as an owl's and her lips were full and dark.

Skin prickled on my neck when the woman parted her lips, revealed a row of jagged teeth, and cried out. Not a harsh sound, more like a sob.

The ship jolted and the bow shifted as more fins beat against the water, guiding us into the cove.

"Merfolk," Tait said.

The woman who'd made the cry lifted her orb eyes and grinned, a vicious kind of look, like she was starving. "My Lord."

Hells, her voice was a song in the breeze. Tantalizing and innocent.

Tait propped a boot on the rail and sneered down at the water. "Nixie."

"Do you not wish to swim, My Lord?"

"Ah, woman, do you never cease asking?"

"Not for a face as yours," Nixie said, reaching her spindly fingers up the hull. "I'd so love to see how it fares in my realm. What adventures we'd have."

Tait chuckled darkly. "Adventures with my bones, Nix? A man would be desperate to dive into the sea with you."

She pouted. "One kiss, that is all I ask."

"Not today."

My heart jumped when she snapped her gaze to me and flashed her teeth. "So lovely. Swim with me, My Lady."

Shouts of warning sounded in my head, yet a part of me wondered if diving deep alongside her might be one of the grandest adventures I would ever experience.

"Do your duty, Nix," Tait said, and shoved me aside. "Leave the king's prizes to the king, or you shall deal with him."

For the first time, the merwoman's face lost its pallor. She offered a quick nod, then disappeared beneath the tides, taking away the draw for adventures in the deep.

"If you want them to take the air from your lungs, swim with merfolk," Tait said sharply. "They will offer a kiss to see your thoughts. Be wise and never let them."

I swallowed. "I'll be sure to avoid it."

Tait scoffed but said nothing more on merfolk. Truth be told, it seemed he battled with whether to throw me overboard now that he'd admitted to their brutality.

Crowds gathered along a stone road that carved its way from the docks into a village. Homes with red slats over pale stone walls. Towering buildings for craftsmen and trade. A honeycomb of roads and archways, galleys and arcades, created a sprawling community, all surrounding an emerald hillside on which a fortress was built into the sides.

The palace was made of tall spires, sloped rooftops, bridges, and balconies. Gold edging flowed along parapet walls and watchtowers in front of two lofty doors. With the slope of the hill, the castle was staggered in partitions and connected by floating staircases or walkways. Through it all were several waterfalls spilling between the different levels.

"Gods, that's—"

"The palace." Tait leaned on one elbow, smoking and sneering. "Speak true, Princess. You thought we—what?—lived in sea caves and ate our fish raw, bones and all?"

Tait could be handsome if he'd cease the snarl. His face was made of sharp lines and edges. The dark stubble on his chin was dignified, not sloppy. The points of his ears were untouched by the hoops and rings of his fellow crewmen, but like his cousin, he kept simple rings in the lobes.

And he was trying to goad me. I wouldn't give him the satisfaction.

"You're wrong," I told him, grinning. "I didn't think you were quite civilized enough to live in caves. I suspected you simply dug holes in the sand."

A shadow deepened his eyes. With another puff of his herbs, he blew the smoke in my face. "Enjoy it while you can, Princess."

He stalked away as the ship settled against one of the docks. Dockmen secured thick ropes to the king's ship. Folk below lined up and cheered, ready to greet the crew.

It took time for the doors to open, for gangplanks to drop, and the crew to disembark. My fear of the ship didn't outweigh my fear of what would become of me once I stepped foot in this city. I hung near the king's chamber door as long as I could.

"Glittering and gold." Sewell hobbled to my side and took hold of my arm.

"I think I'll stay right here."

He gave his head a slight shake. "Come."

"No, really, I—"

"Found the earth fae." Larsson materialized around the post of the staircase. "Sewell, get on out there. You're to see old Murdock."

"Poor stitching, that one," Sewell said, frowning.

"Aye, but you know how he'll piss and moan if he doesn't get a look." Larsson clapped Sewell's shoulder. "The man is practically insisting. But Tilly's got her cherry rum for you already. It'll burn that skin right off your bones."

Sewell flicked his gaze to me. "Remember the dreary." His gaze fell to my arm, the spot with the mark of the House of Kings. Remember the dreary, meaning remember he'd warned me to hide certain truths.

I dipped my chin, fighting my churning stomach, as a few crewmen helped Sewell limp off the ship.

Larsson removed his hat and wiped his brow with the back of his hand. "You staying here? I promise you the dockmen who tidy the ship once we're off are rougher than the crew."

"I'm going to die, aren't I?"

"Oh, I expect you will someday, much like the rest of us." He chuckled.

I couldn't help myself—I smiled. Larsson had an easiness about him. He was loyal to his brutal king, no mistake, but he seemed a bit like Jonas. Playful, never taking life too seriously. He was a bit of home.

I followed him to the plank. Crowds had already swallowed up most of the crew. Wives swatted husbands on the cheek, shouting at them for being gone too long, then kissed them like it might be their last. Mothers found their sons and tried to clean off the sweat and blood they'd earned on the ship.

My heart hurt. It was so much like home, and now . . . I didn't know when I'd ever be swallowed into my mother's arms, or have my father pull me close and plant a kiss on my head.

I missed them.

I mourned them.

No matter what Bloodsinger told me about the early wars, I could never stop loving them.

I'd had lonely moments since being taken to think of what I knew of the final battle. There were holes in the history, secrets no one mentioned, including Aleksi. Whenever Bloodsinger was brought up, Alek changed the conversation, and I didn't know why.

My cousin was a little over eleven turns when the war ended. Like me, he was kept away, safe and hidden until the end. I could not recall a single interaction between Aleksi and Bloodsinger.

Stieg was another mystery. He knew the Ever King personally. Enough that my father's captain did not address Erik with titles; instead, he addressed him by his given name. He seemed to think he could reach Bloodsinger differently than others. Was it truly because he'd manipulated a frightened boy in a cell to trust him once?

"Time to disembark." Larsson's voice shook me from the daze.

He stood at the top of the gangplank and pointed at a line of wagons and a black coach at the bottom. Each was pulled by a trio of strange charges. A kind of stag bred with a mule. Stubbed horns topped their thick crowns, but every mane was thick and luscious, and the hooves weren't cloven.

"Horthane." Larsson made a lazy gesture at the creatures. "Your horses don't handle the air of the Ever well. But horthane are—what would you land folk say?—strong as an ox yet swim as well as an eel. Quite tame creatures for the most part, but do not approach without your hand outstretched. They must catch your scent first and determine if you're to be trusted."

"And if they don't?"

Larsson grinned, a divot puckering in his cheek, adding a bit more appeal to his face. "Well then, I hope you're not attached to your fingers."

I swallowed until I could stand with indifference again. In the back of the wagon line was a small cart with iron bars on the sides. Empty and ready for filling.

"Afraid you'll be taking the barred wagon."

There were bound to be bars eventually, no reason to be surprised. Still, I bit my cheek to hide the blur of tears. They'd try to break me, but I refused to let them. I'd fall into the Otherworld first.

Voices quieted once I stepped onto the dock. I kept my attention straight ahead while, all around, whispers followed me like a soft cloak. Words like "dark fae," "earth worker," even a few muttered shouts of "Bitch!" followed.

It wasn't until I stepped beside the barred cart that someone from the crowd hocked a glob of spit on my borrowed boots. Larsson shoved the man back into the crowd and unlocked the cage door.

That was what it was—a cage.

"Apologies, Princess," he said softly. "They're not on their best behavior."

"I doubt it upsets you all that much."

Larsson looked at the cobbles for a moment before he said, "I understand why my king must do what he has done, but whether you believe it or not, there are some of us who want peace. Not hatred."

Stun ate my words. I accepted Larsson's hand and stepped into the back of the cage. He locked the bars and gave me a final smile before striding away.

He'd been gone mere moments before folk pounded on the bars, before more spittle flew at my face. Angry words, threats, and curses were flung my way. More than one pebble, even a rotted pome splattered cloying juice on my cheeks after it struck one of the bars.

The people laughed, encouraging more, until silence, thick as death, fell over them.

I wiped the juice from my eyes as the back bars clanged open and a firm hand gripped my arm.

"Get out, love." Erik glared at me like he might throw me to his ravenous people.

Don't break. I gritted my teeth. "Plan to make me walk through all this, Bloodsinger? See if I arrive at my prison in one piece?"

"Your ability to conjure such brutal scenarios is, quite possibly, my favorite thing about you, but you won't be doing any of it. You'll be in the royal coach."

"Why?"

A wickedness, dark and a little mad, lived in his gaze. He used a thumb to wipe some of the sour juice off my cheek. "Because you are mine."

28

THE SONGBIRD

ERIK KEPT SATIN curtains drawn over the coach windows. I was glad for it. The less I had to see of the hatred in the eyes of his people, the easier I breathed.

"You'll be taken to my chambers first," he said, pushing aside one of the curtains and watching the procession for a moment. Bloodsinger slumped back on the padded bench and turned his attention back to me. "You're not to go anywhere else. Understood?"

"The king's chambers? Not a dungeon?"

"They're rather damp. I think you'll prefer the chambers." The corner of his mouth twitched.

"So everyone knows I'm your whore?"

Erik leaned over his knees. "Is that what you want, love?"

"Never yours. But perhaps you should ask Larsson if he'd be interested in taking me. He's rather handsome and doesn't make me think I'm going to die every moment I turn around."

Erik studied me for a long pause. Enough I could not puzzle if he battled with the thought of cutting out my tongue or . . . something else.

"Feel better getting that out?" he asked, and propped an elbow on the window's ledge, a fist against his cheek. "I am preparing to claim you as mine, so you should know that will be the last time another man's name is on your tongue."

"I might be your property, but you do not control what words come from my mouth."

Bloodsinger chuckled. "We'll see."

I stared at the curtains, refusing to look at him. The coach tilted up the hillside. Tension blistered like my skin might split open at every bend in the road.

Only once we reached the doors of the palace did Erik speak. "You will be untouched in my rooms. They are well guarded."

The door on the coach swung open, and Erik left me with a scathing look before he stepped outside.

All at once the coach became my haven. The moment I abandoned it, I would be isolated and forgotten from a world that only knew me for being the daughter of an enemy king.

Sweat beaded over my brow. The familiar, suffocating grip tightened around my lungs. All I desired was to draw a deep breath, to watch my chest expand as I took it in. Instead, breaths came in sharp, shallow puffs. Gods, I wished I had asked Blister Poppy for more of her calming leaf.

Breathe.

I smoothed my open palms over my knees, closed my eyes, and tried to hear the voices of those I loved.

Breathe.

Sometimes it was my mother's voice. Maybe Alek's. Other times it was the playful rumble of Jonas or the soothing tone of Malin, his mother. My father's voice was the one that replayed the most. Steadfast. Deep. Safe.

Be fierce, little love. I clung to it like a tether in the night, almost like Daj were seated right next to me.

I drew in a long breath through my nose. It filled my chest and unshackled the panic that held me captive. I clenched my fists for a count of three, then flexed my fingers until the tremble subsided, and stepped outside.

Air in the Ever was always heavy with water. We were not truly beneath the waves, but every gust of a breeze left a glisten of droplets over my skin. No mistake, it served the sea fae well with their need for water. Beside the palace, it was richer, like a warm rain fell against my flesh.

The front entrance of the royal house was formidable. Sun glared against the pale stones of the walls and two panels of dark glossy wood looked as if they were in a constant state of damp. There were no less than fifteen steps up to the doors, and all along the cobbled walk were men and women in simple blue dresses or tunic tops.

Hands crossed in front, they lifted their chins and looked to the heavens when Erik stepped into the center of the path.

A man approached the king. His trousers only struck his knees, and his boots seemed ill-fitted for his spindly limbs. With a whirl of his hand, he bowed. "Welcome back, My Lord. Your chambers have been prepared, and your guest has arrived for—"

"Alistair," Erik interjected. "I do not need to know what I already know."

Loose skin under the man's chin wobbled as he spoke. "As you say, My King. Now, regarding the return feast . . ."

Erik groaned, pointing his face to the sky. "What lies do I have left to use in order to escape it?"

"Afraid we've used the most common already. You've been ill too many times to be believable, and if I say you've fallen into a drunken stupor again, they'll replace your rum and wine with water," Alistair droned without a dip in his tone. "At this point we've reached kidnapping, poisoning, or lost at sea. Your return has quite clearly abolished the latter. And unless an assassin is lying in wait—"

"Always a possibility," Erik said.

"And I'm afraid there is little risk of a kidnapping taking place between the doors and your chamber." Alistair sniffed. "If I may, My King, the feast is tradition and, frankly, expected."

"Ah, but this journey was anything but expected." Bloodsinger reached for me, gripped my wrist, and pulled me against his hard body. One knuckle traced the bridge of my cheek.

I narrowed my eyes and stepped back, furious and repulsed. Not at Bloodsinger exactly—although he ought to shoulder a great deal of blame for being repugnant—but at the way my body trembled beneath his touch. The slice of his fierce gaze stilled my heart for two breaths every damn time.

"Quite," said Alistair. "Likely the reason your people are most anxious to meet you at the feast."

"Of course they are. Oh." Erik snapped his fingers at his steward. "Before the day is done, send a summons to House Skurk. Tell them their brother is dead, killed by the Ever Crew for treason. I'll expect their penance on behalf of his dishonor by the fortnight."

"Shall I request penance be made personally, or by offering?"

"What do you think, Alistair? Why would I want to see their wretched faces?"

The man dipped his chin. "I shall see to it the offering is here by the fortnight."

"See what you can find out about House Skurk using the lotus of Skondell for spell casts. Then remind them that should they disappoint me as their brother did, their bones will be hung over the coves to greet incoming ships." Erik turned to me. A cruel grin twisted the scar on his lip a little more as he held out a hand. "How is my wallowing in brutality, Songbird?"

"Horrid." Wildly, my mind beat against the notion of going near the man, but every eye turned to me. Some arched brows, others looked on in curiosity, but most glared with such violence I half expected someone to spring forward and ram a knife in my chest.

When the rest of the wagons rambled up the path and some of the higher-ranked crew appeared, half drunk on their pungent wines already, I had nowhere to turn.

To the crew that hated me, the people who despised me even more, or the king who'd sometimes touched me gently?

I placed my hand in Erik's.

For a mere heartbeat, heat irritated my palm. I winced, but promptly buried it with a frown as Erik lifted my knuckles to his lips.

"Such a well-behaved princess," he said, voice low.

I forced a grin. No doubt it looked more like a grimace. Erik kept a possessive hold on my hand; his body was stiff, rigid. The thrum of nerves pounded in my skull. He tried to hide it, but there was unease written in every sharp angle of his face.

If the Ever King was unsettled walking into his own palace, what horrors awaited me?

29

THE SONGBIRD

THE OUTER WALLS of the palace glittered with pale stones, but the inner corridors were ominous and dark. Black satin drapes were drawn over open windows, hiding away sunlight. The faintest glimmer of the dawn spread over the wood floors when the breeze caught the fabric. I slowed my step to look at one window. The satin rippled in a way reminiscent of a gentle sea. I thought it a coincidence until I breathed in the scent of the threads—wet sand and brine.

Erik pinched the fabric between his thumb and forefinger, stroking it gently. "Like your land gives to you, the sea gives to us."

"These come from the sea?"

"A vine found in the lagoons. Spun into threads that trap heat during the frosts and cool during the warmer months."

Without a chance to allow for more questions, the king dragged us forward. Rafters arched gently, and from each apex hung iron chandeliers with two dozen tallow candles. An occasional servant would pass us after stepping from one of the many rooms. The sight of Erik always drew a widened expression, one of fright, as though they could not wait until they were out of his presence.

We entered an expansive hall. On either side a new corridor branched off to some unseen place in the palace. Awaiting us in the center was a crowd of men in sharp gambesons or high-collared shirts and ladies in gowns frosted in jade or silver.

The king didn't bring fear to these people. He brought competition. All eyes turned to Erik and his procession. While they looked as if their hands had never touched a grain of dirt, the king was travel worn, tousled, and wild, like his Ever Seas.

Still, every man seemed to seek Bloodsinger's notice. Every lady whispered to the one at her side, snickering or flushing.

All but one. A woman, flanked on either side by two docile ladies with hair like seaweed, floated toward the king.

Her skin was the color of morning cream, and soft, golden curls flowed down her back to her slender waist. She was delicate and airy, like a thin piece of glass. The corner of her red painted lips tweaked into a coy grin as she lowered her chin in a nod. One to acknowledge her king's rank, but not one that would ever lower her own.

"Welcome back, My Lord."

Erik paused. He took half a step to one side, a step that placed him in front of me. "Fione."

Fione laced her fingers in front of her body, smiling sweetly. "You have been missed."

Someone snorted. I didn't look, but I took a guess that Celine had joined the procession.

Erik scoffed and drew closer to the woman. She didn't step back, letting her body press against his, and an unwelcome flash of annoyance lined my insides.

The king cocked his head, taking her in, tearing her apart with his scrutiny. Gods, were they lovers? The way she looked ready to devour him left me pleading with the cracks in the stone floor to widen and swallow me whole.

Memories of his tempting fingers sliding between my legs, the barest touch against my center, the way he'd tormented my breasts, his tongue—gods, it all had me aching in shame.

To add on the fact he might have a woman loyally awaiting his return brought bile to my throat.

Erik didn't kiss her; he didn't even touch her. After a tenuous gaze, he merely clicked his tongue and said, "Pleasure seeing you, Fione."

In two steps, Bloodsinger was back at my side, his grip on my arm. For the first time, the glass woman took note of the unfamiliar face in the room. Her pale eyes narrowed sharply on the place where Erik touched my skin, then on my face.

"Who is this, My King?"

"Mine" was all he said before he led us to the farthest corridor.

"Will we see you at the feast?" Fione called out.

Erik turned, the handsome curve of his mouth dimpling his cheek. "Unfortunately, I am told I must attend."

"Perhaps I might have the honor of sitting near His Highness."

"Perhaps." Erik didn't indulge the woman any longer before tugging me forward.

His focus remained locked ahead, his grip on my arm unyielding. The corridor came to an end at a large arched door with a brass knob, which opened to a winding staircase.

Erik kept a steady pace up the tower steps, but the slightest slump of his left shoulder gave up the limp he tried to hide.

When we were far enough up the steps to be alone, I pulled back. "Who was that woman?"

He seemed surprised at the sound of my voice for a few breaths. "Envious?"

"Not at all."

He chuckled. "Fione will tell you she is my mate, my woman—whatever you call such matches in your land."

"Mate?" My blood burned. "What a snake you are."

Again, the bastard chuckled. "Are mate matches so horrid to earth fae?"

"No, but"—I looked once over my shoulder, then lowered my voice—"but you touched me. You betrayed her."

One lithe motion and Bloodsinger had my back to the cold stone of the stairwell, his body pinned over mine, and his palm on my throat.

"I betrayed no one, love." His eyes dropped to my parted lips for one breath. "As I said, Fione will tell you we are mates based on an old agreement made before our births. Once I took the throne, I saw to it the agreement was dissolved."

"Does she know this?"

"Oh yes. It does not mean she does not try to get me to see her more appealing qualities." Erik flicked his brows.

"And have you? Do you play with women's hearts for your own twisted pleasure?"

"I can't figure out why you ask such things if you don't care."

"I'm sealing in my mind how horrid you are. Keep speaking," I said. "It only makes it simpler."

Bloodsinger's thumb stroked the center of my throat. "I've no interest in hearts, Songbird. Put your mind at ease; I always make my intent clear before any woman shares my bed. I'm sickeningly honorable."

I balked. "You are sickeningly something. 'Honorable' is not what I would call it."

Erik leaned his mouth against my ear. His breath was warm, his voice seductively low. "I did not hear your complaints when my tongue was slipping inside you."

I shoved against his chest, ashamed of the sting of tears behind my eyes. Such hopes for the night of the masque had turned into such a nightmare. The first night I'd allowed a man to touch me so intimately, and I'd started a new war.

I turned away, and the king had enough brains not to carry on. Erik took my hand and continued up the staircase.

Four flights up, two guards stood outside an inconspicuous door. Neither the king nor his men gave the slightest hint the other existed. Bloodsinger merely shoved through the door and slammed it behind him.

He released his hold on my arm. From the outside, I would not have anticipated such an ornate chamber in one of the towers. The sitting room was the size of the whole of my family's tower at the fort. Woven rugs with blue fish and jade waves covered the stone floors. An inglenook capable of fitting ten men inside was alight with a white-and-blue dancing flame.

Like a curious child, I reached my fingers for the fire, mesmerized.

Erik slapped his grip around my wrist again, coming from nowhere, and pulled me back. "Do they not teach folk on land to keep away from fire?"

Heat flooded my cheeks. I yanked my hand away and looked anywhere but at the king. "I've never seen fire like this, I thought..." I let my voice trail off. Nothing I could say would make me sound less like a fool.

"The air here breathes differently," he said briskly without looking at me. "Changes the shade of the flame. Still carries a bite that'll boil the skin."

The fire was beautiful, like molten sapphires. I readied to ask another question about the differences between the two realms, but words died off. Erik was gone.

I peeked through an arched doorway leading into a second room. The bedchamber. Two floor-length windows opened onto a balcony overlooking the sea. From here it glittered innocently. Everything seemed so bright, so peaceful.

The calm was deceptive and ensorcelled me into a false sense of security.

Full quilts and satin coverlets were smoothed over a plush mattress that looked as if it had never been used. A washroom branched off from the sleep area, and another open doorway led down a new staircase. I leaned my face against a narrow lancet to find where it let out.

My heart jumped. Below was a garden, untamed and made of dry wild brambles, but beneath the neglect could be something stunning.

Erik opened a wardrobe with edges carved like air bubbles floating to the surface of the sea. Unfazed by company, the king stripped his torso of the dingy white shirt from the journey and reached for something new.

I didn't intend to utter a sound. I fought to remain indifferent. I failed.

Across Erik's back, from the tops of his shoulders, around his ribs, to the lower curves of his hips were dozens of scars. Pink and gnarled. Some white and fading. Old wounds left behind from prolonged suffering.

By the hells, he must've been in horrid pain even now. Skin was left irritated, untreated. Movements would be uncomfortable. No doubt, they would burn constantly, pulling at the taut skin without proper cleansers and oils.

"They wouldn't do that to you." My voice was soft and small. Uncertain.

Erik slipped his head through a black tunic and faced me. "I know how disgusting it is for you to look upon such mangled skin." A shadow dulled the sunset red of his eyes. "So, believe what you wish, Princess, but I did not do it to myself."

Seeing the tormented flesh, my mind could not reconcile with the notion that it might be true. My family had humanity. They were just and fair. Loving.

The thought of them viewing an innocent as nothing more than a tool was nauseating.

"I will be gone for a time," Erik said as he ran his palms over his dark tousled hair. He paused at the doorway between his room and the sitting area. "You will remain here."

A sudden panic throttled my chest. I did not want him to leave. Not because he was tender and wonderful, but because Bloodsinger was clearly possessive. He wanted me and didn't, but his want seemed to win out more than his resentment. Odd as it was to admit, Erik felt like the safest person in the palace right now.

Sweat dripped down my neck. The room tilted, and I couldn't stop . . .

"Livia." Erik's voice shattered the panic. His eyes were narrowed. "Do not leave. I need to know you heard me."

I shook out my hands and peered through the lancet once more. "May I go to your garden? It's concealed."

"No." His jaw pulsed for a few breaths. "I say this for your own good."

"Right. A glittering cage."

Erik's gaze hardened. "You'll regret it should you choose not to listen."

The threat hovered like a dark omen in the room. Bloodsinger didn't wait for a retort, a plea, anything before he abandoned me to the emptiness of his unfamiliar space.

A shock jolted my heart when the door slammed, dislodging a golden framed mirror from the wall. Glass cracked. My reflection stood amidst the pieces, a true likeness to the deepening fissures in my heart.

I slid down the cold stones of the wall and hugged my knees to my chest. I was utterly alone.

30

THE SERPENT

"HIGHNESS, HE'S JUST arrived." Alistair materialized as though he'd misted into shape from a shadow. The man was portly, a size too large for his clothing, but he couldn't see what the rest did. His skin sagged around his mouth and eyes, and the tips of his tapered ears flopped over from age.

Bound to the palace until his final days, he'd served five Ever Kings. Next to Alistair, I was a bleeding infant.

Still, he blustered, as he'd always done under the watch of my father, and had the decency to treat me as the lord of this land the moment I stepped foot into the halls as a broken, limping boy.

We quickened the pace to the council room in silence until we reached the double doors at the end of a narrow corridor.

"What is your word on our guest?" Alistair asked.

"Send Celine to tend to her. Make certain she doesn't try to get bold and escape or slit her pretty neck out of desperation."

Alistair muttered a prayer to the god of the tides and kissed his center knuckle. Old rituals from Skondell he'd adopted over the turns. "She is from the earthen fae?"

"Play the fool if you'd like, Alistair." I scoffed. "You feast on gossip like you feast on air. The princess is to remain in my chambers, but send for a gown. She will be at the return feast."

"A gown? My King, perhaps you do not understand this, but ladies come in differing sizes. The needleworker needs time to shape and tailor cloth and—"

"Alistair, I may have been raised by cruel men, but I'm no stranger to the female form. The princess seems built like my mother, does she not?"

Alistair blinked. I did not speak of my mother—ever. I waited for his stun to pass, and his smug propriety to return. "Aye, My Lord. Their figures seem close. I will see what we have in the old chambers."

"Good." I turned away, anxious to conceal the new corded tension in my neck.

"You think it wise to bring the woman to the feast?"

"You don't?"

Alistair pinched his thin lips until they disappeared. "I think, My Lord, you have a fae from enemy lands. I think you have not claimed her as yours except for in your mind. I think there are many who seek vengeance for unjust wars."

"True," I agreed. "And I am the only one in this palace I trust."

"Yet you leave her to be alone with Tidecaller?"

"Celine is loyal to me out of oath. She won't touch her."

"You plan to claim the earth fae?" The old man locked his fingers in front of his plump belly, unruffled, always seeking direct commands no matter how eccentric.

"Make no mistake, Alistair," I said, grinning. "I claimed her long ago."

He bowed at the waist, then left me on the outside bridge leading to the main halls of the palace. I paused and glared at the sails on the new ship aligned with the back docks below.

Skulls with bloody eyes adorned the banner of Gavyn's vessel. White sea birch on the ship for the House of Bones was designed to be slender and sleek. Better for sailing through the narrow canyons in the isles where Gavyn ruled.

A turn older than me, Gavyn Seeker was the only face in the noble houses I could stomach, and it was a relief to see only his vessel.

Joron Seamaker from the House of Tides would've brought his eccentric ship with the dozens of angled sails painted with the skull likeness in a rogue wave of his banner. The deck bulged, and his helm was crafted in the center.

With no galley belowdecks, his crew survived by mastering their gifts to work the sea and its creatures. They fished with their songs, and if they failed, they starved.

Lord Hesh of the House of Blades was given his title of lord for reaching the uppermost rank of High Farer in the kingdom's fleet. The House of Mists did not associate with the House of Kings unless forced or enticed. Even then, Narza would likely find a way around it.

Gavyn had a purpose for being here, but the others could stay away for good for all I cared.

I didn't want Hesh or Joron to see Livia. Already, I wished my grandmother had not interacted with the princess.

She was my hope for defending the kingdom. With so many unknowns, anyone might try to take such a gift for themselves. But should I make it known she was mine, make her invaluable to the people, then they would stand for her the same as me.

That was the hope. That was what had to happen.

Certain no one was near, I turned from the council room and pulled back a panel in the wall. Hidden corridors sprawled through the walls of the palace like a web. I emerged into an alcove of one of the numerous studies.

Two women, dressed in the blue and gold of the servants, polished the silver edging across the hearth, unaware I'd arrived.

"I always thought earth fae had more fur," one woman muttered. "But you saw her? She's almost dainty-like."

The other woman snickered. "He arrives cold as ever, but all possessive over the earth woman. Talk says he's gonna claim her."

"She'll want to keep the lights doused," the first snorted through a laugh. "Think he's ever bedded anyone in the daylight with them scars?"

"Only the ones I kill right after I come." I stepped from the alcove, fists clenched.

A unified sob broke from both servants. The women fell to their knees. The first whimpered, "Highness, we . . . we didn't mean—"

"Get out of my sight."

They didn't question, didn't pause before scrambling to their feet and fleeing. I lifted my palms, studying the rough calluses, the scars along the meat of my thumbs, my wrists, and my forearms.

Mangled.

I wouldn't be foolish enough to think Livia would ever truly crave a touch from a man like me. There was a bond to consider. Any pull she felt toward me came from fate twisting our paths together beyond our control.

I glared at the door where the women had fled. I hated them, hated the way everyone here looked at me as though any moment in my presence would be their final breath.

It had been the same since I was a boy, when Harald barked his cruelty and drunken tirades through the hallways after the death of his brother. Once an uncle who laughed and allowed Tait to befriend me, all at once he transformed into the bastard intent on molding the fiercest, cruelest Ever King the seas had seen.

The men and women of this palace were witness to it all and did nothing.

Unfair of me, perhaps, to hold resentments against folk unable to step over the confines of their station. I did not pretend to be a fair man. Resentment festered, a gangrenous poison in my bones, until the sight of them brought nothing but disgust.

Another panel slid out of place on a far wall. Gavyn stepped through without a sound. Dressed in black, he tugged the scarf he used to hide his features in the royal city away from his mouth.

Brown skin, dark eyes, but hair with a touch of fire in the color, he always wore a grin like he knew every salacious secret in the kingdom.

In truth, he likely did.

Gavyn offered a lavish bow. "King Erik, you've been greatly missed. How we've bemoaned your absence and prayed to the gods, to the cruel creatures of the depths for your safe—"

"Sit down, you bastard." I yanked a chair from the table.

"I hear you have quite a tale to tell." Gavyn kicked out his legs, grinning. "What's this about Chasms and claims?"

"I should have known when I took on your damn family nothing would ever be private."

Gavyn's grin widened. "I assure you, My King, I'd find out all your scandalous secrets on my own." He winked with the arrogance he'd had since we were children and folded his fingers over his stomach. "Tell me about the earth fae and why we're not heading straight into a war."

"She bears the mark of the House of Kings." Trust did not come simple in the Ever, but Gavyn was one of the few I trusted almost implicitly.

"Aye, so I heard. Makes little sense to me. After you went through the Chasm, I studied deeper into the mantle given to Thorvald." He paused, drumming his fingers over the table. "From what I've learned, Thorvald's mantle was meant to be the full power of the Ever, but in truth, it never really took. More like it amplified his own command of the sea. Thoughts as to why?"

"No. You know better than anyone how little Thorvald spoke to me."

Gavyn scratched the side of his face and sighed. "It's led me to wonder if she's truly using the power of the Ever against the darkening."

"What else would it be?"

"Her own magic?"

"Possible, but why does she feel drawn to the Ever? Why does she say it feels different?"

"Therein lies the question, My King. A living talisman for the House of Kings has just . . . never been."

"You think I don't know? You think any of this makes sense? There is no other answer. I've felt the mark on her skin; I've witnessed the land heal beneath her touch."

"You know it puts you both at risk."

My fist curled over my knee. Across the kingdom were more Lucien Skurks. More cutthroats desperate for a bit of power.

"I plan to claim her at the feast."

"That'll help, I suppose," Gavyn said. "Fione will be devastated and likely force the whole House of Mists to curse you."

I smirked. "Fione wants my cock for no other reason than growing her own title. The same as all those women you say surround you."

He laughed and rocked back on two legs of his chair. "We'd be fools to think it meant anything more. Although, I'm not convinced it's the same for you and the earth fae. I had a moment to speak with Tait upon your return." Gavyn righted on his chair, and leaned over the table, a shadow in his gaze. "Enjoy your fight with the sea singer?"

My jaw pulsed. "Seems my cousin has a big mouth."

"Tait has the smallest mouth in the entire kingdom and would not speak of you unless he had concern or reason." Gavyn hesitated. "I ask if she is only a source of magic to you since you know as well as I do, a sea singer's trance will attract the victim to the true desire of the heart."

"Sea singers lure folk through lust."

"Erik. She would lust after anyone, but she desired you. Tait saw it." Gavyn studied his hands for a few breaths. "It can't be helped, and you know it. The song reveals the truth."

"What is the point of you saying this?"

"I speak as a friend." A rare admission. Men like us could not afford to have friends. "A new fate seems to be at play for the Ever with the mark, but perhaps there is more than one purpose the Chasm drew you to her."

Part of me wanted to agree; another wanted to stab Gavyn to get him to shut his damn mouth. Lust was physical, but a sea singer's voice amplified a heart's desire. I refused to see Livia's behavior as anything other than the physical draw for a warm body in hers.

In my silence, Gavyn let out a long breath. "It's not my place to offer conjectures, merely something to consider. Tell me what I am to do. It's been too long since you've utilized my more remarkable qualities, and I was beginning to think you'd forgotten me."

Needy bastard. "I will guard against threats here, but I need you to dull the threats on the other side of the Chasm."

Gavyn's brows arched. "A visit to the earth fae again?"

"A subtle one, and it must be done by you alone. Understand?"

"Ah. You wish violence upon me, I see." With a grin, Gavyn tried to shield the unease in his eyes, but there was hesitation there.

"Can you manage it?"

"I'll manage just fine."

I wasn't certain if he said it for my assurances or his own. "Bring the Night Folk clans word that their princess belongs to the Ever, she cannot be taken, then see to it they cannot find their own way through the barriers."

Gavyn tilted his head, bemused. "You think they'd risk so many lives by attempting to cross through?"

I lowered my voice. "I think her father would burn every bleeding world to the ground to get her back."

By taking Livia, I'd thrust a blade into the earth bender's heart—a deep, gaping wound. He'd owned my father's power for two decades. He'd fight to take my songbird back with even more ferocity.

Now that I had her as mine, I'd never allow it.

"As you say," Gavyn said. "I'll prepare to leave as soon as possible."

"You're certain you can do this without your ship?" I watched for any hint of deception or false bravado.

Gavyn's jaw flinched. "It will be taxing to attempt the Chasm after so many turns, but I've done it before, as you know. Hopefully, this time I'll do so with fewer shattered bones."

Gavyn last traipsed the Chasm during the war. An attempt that nearly cost him his life. Nearly cost us both our lives.

"If you cannot, then pull back," I said. "We'll find another way."

No one knew Gavyn's true ability. I called him by the name of Seeker, but to the kingdom he was known as Gavyn Bonerotter, thought to have an ability where he could crush bones with a touch. He couldn't, yet he served as the lord to the House of Bones. It was a ruse to keep him breathing. True sea seekers didn't live long before they were killed by blade or their own reckless magic.

A man like Gavyn didn't merely use the tides to carry his voice like Celine. He could become as mist and slip through any body of water in an instant to wherever he desired. Be it from one isle to another across the sea or from one pond to a pond in the private courtyard of another lord. Perhaps he might materialize in a washroom, knife in hand, ready to plunge it through a rival's throat.

Seekers, to most high-ranking nobles, were too great a risk to keep alive.

A journey through the Chasm without a ship was damn near fatal for anyone weaker than Gavyn.

"The earth bender king," Gavyn said after a long pause. "He'll truly fight for his daughter?"

I faced Gavyn. "I know he will."

His dark eyes burned in the hidden rage he kept locked beneath wit and charm and his title. "Does it not trouble you how rare that is here? So few fathers would raise armies for one daughter. Even for a son, I suppose it would depend on the rank."

True enough. When I was snatched by earth fae clans as a tiny boy during their small wars to be harvested for healing blood, there were a great many details I kept to myself about my father's attempts to retrieve me, both during and after. Had I not been a son, I would've been forgotten.

"The earth bender almost reminds me of my own father," Gavyn said.

"Don't get sentimental," I warned. "A great deal hinges on keeping protective fathers out of our kingdom."

"I suppose."

"Before you go," I said, voice low, "see to the other lords and find something for me to use to force their loyalty. They will not take the news of Livia well."

Lord Joron would try to study her, maybe even claim her power for himself. Lord Hesh would find it an abomination a woman bore the mark of the royal house and likely make a move to rid the Ever of such a stain.

"I'll leave straightaway," said Gavyn.

"Wait until after the return feast. No doubt your ship has been seen. Your face will be expected."

He smirked. "Debauchery in the royal city? With pleasure, My King."

"Gavyn." I didn't turn to look at him. "You also might want to get that injury you mentioned looked at by my boneweaver."

"I'm uninjured."

"This is too important to take the risk with injuries. No matter how small."

"Erik, I'm not injured—"

"I think you are." I turned to look over my shoulder. "Murdock won't be too occupied. Only one on my crew arrived with a wound and is being treated. My cook."

Gavyn visibly paled. "I see. And was he quite injured?"

"Thanks to the earth fae princess, not so much he lost his words."

"The princess?"

"Aye. She's bold at the strangest times and ran to help him during a damn attack from Lucien Skurk." I tilted my head. "As I said, there is no one but him there if you needed to get that scratch you were complaining about just now inspected."

Gavyn swallowed thickly, tugged a small knife from a sheath hidden in his boot, and dragged the tip over the meat of his palm. He gave me a sly grin once a small stream of blood dripped down his wrist. "Glad you noticed the scratch, My King. Probably best to have a look to be certain all goes well."

Gavyn pressed a hand to his chest, bowed, then tugged the black mask over his chin. I faced the window before he slipped out, part of the shadows of the corridors.

31

THE SONGBIRD

*B*REATHE. THE HEEL of my hand pressed over my heart, as if to keep it from cracking through my chest. I closed my eyes and drew a long breath in my nose, then out through parted lips. Twice. Three times.

There was no time left to sit and wallow.

The ceiling of Erik's room was high enough a single slip out the window would send me to the Otherworld. The door to the corridors was locked, but even if I escaped, where would I go?

No doubt, guards would send me straight back.

Trapped. I was trapped at the whim of Erik Bloodsinger. I turned about the sitting room once, soaking it all in. Satin draperies lined the windows, much the same as in the corridor. The sitting room was clean and orderly, a few crossed blades decorating the walls. Darker than my chambers back home but oddly normal.

There had to be something here to learn more about Erik Bloodsinger.

The only way to outwit a mark is to study it. Every weakness, every strength becomes a weapon. Lovers, vices—learn everything down to if they can piss straight or not. Victory lies in the brains, not the brawn.

The memory of Sander teaching me to be sly during a childish game of seek and find cracked through my heart. Sander may have been the studious twin, but he was truly the most devious. He took after Kase, the twins' father. The king of the Eastern realms taught his sons well the intricate dance of outwitting an enemy, even one physically stronger.

I rummaged through a stack of parchment on the table. Maps, dull missives from noblemen, a few charcoal drawings of new vessels.

My blood chilled at the sound of footsteps in the corridor. Five, ten, twenty breaths, I stood still, waiting. When no one came, I drifted into Erik's bedchamber, the place to find secrets of the Ever King. Then again, I doubted he would leave me unattended to riffle through his belongings if some grand secret was left here for me to find.

I dropped to my hands and knees to search beneath the bed first.

A thin layer of dust coated the threads of the rug. In the corners of the bedposts, a few silky webs from weavers strung over the wood. Strange such a simple thing could bring a sense of familiarity.

We knew so little of the undersea realms. I'd expected it to be buried in the waves or, at the very least, cold and damp. To see sunlight, smell blossoms, choke on dust and gangly weaver webs was oddly comforting.

Inside the wardrobe, I brushed my fingertips over Bloodsinger's coats and tunics and jerkins. More than once, I paused and let the scent of leather and oak settle into my lungs. My body warmed and my pulse quickened.

All hells. Even his damn scent was appealing. Thoughts of forced bonds made a grand attempt to convince me it was beyond my control, but somewhere deep in my chest, heat stirred at the thought of Erik's hands on my skin, his lips and tongue and teeth claiming me in the way he'd done at the Tower.

Liquid heat filled my lower belly. I let out a curse and tried to think of every horrid word he'd spoken, every show of violence, but even those reminded me of his intoxicating, beautiful black heart. It led me to wonder more about the secrets the Ever King kept deep inside the hardened thing in his chest.

Damn him. I let the soft fabric fall from my grasp and knelt, shoving aside boots to reach the back of the wardrobe.

Tucked away near the back was a woven basket with a thin paper tag on the top. My pulse quickened—the tag was labeled *Songbird*. I craned my neck to peek beyond the open wardrobe door to ensure I was still alone, then lifted the lid.

I'd readied myself to find severed tongues or a few shrunken sets of eyes; instead, I froze, stunned to the bone.

"You bastard." I bit the inside of my cheek as I touched the tips of each bristle, each corked vial filled with thin colors of dyes and paints. Watered down to a glaze. Paints not meant for parchment but for glass.

Bloodsinger supplied his palace with window paints.

I covered my mouth with one palm and dug through the vials with the other. Typical colors of blues and reds and yellows were in place, but there were more. Gold with flecks of shimmer powders, stone-dust gray, even a color like jade, but when the light struck the vial, it shimmered to rich violet.

How had he prepared this before we arrived? All I could think of was the moment Celine sent word somewhere through the tides. A mere morning after he'd taken me. Moments when he spoke as though he were readying to slit me from navel to nose.

He'd sent me window paints. A bit of home. A bit of comfort.

The same destructive turmoil clung to my heart. With each beat, it bled a little more for the loneliness, fear, and hate of a boy king who'd been tossed into a war and vengeance he'd likely been too young to truly comprehend.

With care, I took the basket from the wardrobe and placed it beneath one of the arched windows. An entire world existed beyond the panes, one I knew nothing about, yet I could not deny the desire to learn about it, from every peak to every cove.

"What are you doing?" Celine shoved her way into the chamber, a bunch of different fabrics in her arms. Behind her were three women, dressed all in blue, with their hair pulled back in tight knots, revealing the sharp points of their ears. Each woman carried something—linen cloths, a basket of dainty slippers, and a box with green sea pearl charms and silver hair chains.

Celine took note of the open wardrobe and basket of paints. "Ah, snooping. Good. He hoped you'd find them."

The women behind Celine twittered to each other in hushed words and looked at me like I'd sprouted a second head.

"Why did he do this?" I held up a vial of gloss.

Celine tossed the fabric on the bed and gave me a knowing glare. "You said you liked to paint, I suppose. I don't know, I wasn't in the room with you, thank the gods. The king told me to add a note to old Alistair to have glass dyes made. We don't have glass dyes here, so who knows if they'll even work."

My grip tightened around the vial and I held it to my heart. Either I hated Erik Bloodsinger for all his games, or the heat in my chest was something else entirely.

"Same as on the ship, I'm tasked with making you presentable," Celine went on. "All I'm saying is Hawke is the damn tailor for a purpose. The man knows more about bleeding attire than anyone in the royal province. But because of these"—she puffed up her breasts—"here I am."

"Or because the king trusts you."

Celine snapped her fingers at me. "I like that better. We'll keep that way of thinking."

"I can dress myself," I said.

"I should hope so. I'm not doing up your damn corset. I'm just here to assist. Whatever that means."

She jerked her chin toward me, and the three women shuffled forward.

Until the next clock bell chimed, I was prodded and stripped, my hair was brushed and braided, then smoothed again when it didn't sit right. More than once, I laughed. The three servants were flustered, and it was clear they'd never truly had a lady to dress in the palace.

By the end, I'd taken over my hair, leaving most of it down in waves, half braided into an intricate knot Mira's mother had taught me as a girl.

The stacks of fabric weren't only for me. Celine took the liberty of dressing herself in the king's room, and I hid my grin more than once as she muttered that it served him right to have her underthings strewn about since he kept demoting her to nursemaid for his captive.

When she emerged from the washroom, I didn't hide the smile. "You look beautiful, Celine."

Her mouth tugged into a grimace. "I'm not going. The crew'll never let me live this down."

"You're going." The iridescent skirt of the gown I'd been shoved inside rustled around my legs with each step across the room. It was a little big on the top, but a few pins kept it from spilling down my chest. "I always prepare for balls and feasts with my friend. She isn't here, but I am, and you are, and we breasts must stick together."

Her mouth parted and released a laugh that turned into a strange kind of chortle. "You're odd, earth fae, but not wrong. Soon enough, you'll learn that some of the upper nobles in the Ever see women as bodies meant for heirs, nothing else."

"Truly?"

"The House of Mists is where females hold the most power.

Witches and sirens. The men have voices of the sea, to be sure, but not as powerful as the women. Even still, voices are often overruled or stripped away." Celine smoothed the velvet of her full crimson skirt. "You see the claiming as a terrible thing, but in truth, to have the king's protection is likely the only way you will survive. An enemy female in the Ever?"

Celine didn't finish the thought, merely arched her brows and shook her head.

Voices in Erik's ear told him to be a wretch toward the women of his realm? I couldn't understand it. Queens had been fated to win the peace of my land, and they'd done it, kings by their sides, not at the lead.

The Ever King took a woman from her home. A cruel, vindictive act, yet he'd never put a hand on me. He'd never forced himself on me. Quite the opposite—he'd given me a sleeping draught when my lust was unbearable and had sent one of his boneweavers to tend to me. Erik had a woman on his crew, and not merely as a common crew member. Clearly, Celine was part of his inner circle.

I linked my arm through Celine's elbow. "Shall we go, then?"

"What are you doing?" As though my arm might reach out and strike, Celine waggled her fingers over the place we touched.

"Sticking together."

Like the three servants, she looked at me as though I'd grown a second head, but one that she liked.

32

THE SONGBIRD

I CLUNG TO CELINE'S arm like I'd clung to Mira. Truth be told, she held to me much the same. A wash of fright filled her bright eyes when we reached two wide doors.

The clatter of silver on fine platters, the roll of voices in low tones, and a few brisk laughs flowed into our corridor like an ebbing tide.

Celine swallowed with effort. "Don't you go anywhere without me or the king, understand?"

"What frightens you about your own people?"

Celine blinked, a shimmer of wet glass coating her eyes. "I've never . . . agreed to attend a return feast."

"Why?"

"Reasons." She blew out a long breath. "King asks me every time but lets me refuse. Aboard the ship is one thing. There, I'm a blade. I'm of use. Here, I'm a weak thing who slept her way into the king's good graces."

My stomach cinched. It didn't matter who Erik Bloodsinger bedded, but he was set to claim me. If Celine held a place for him in her heart, I did not wish this to hurt her. Against my best efforts, I liked her.

She glanced at me. "If you're thinking I bedded the king, I didn't.

I'm just saying that's what people say. I earned my high rank by proving I was of use."

The relief was potent, and I had no time—or desire—to unravel why. From a side door, Erik emerged, flanked by Larsson and Tait. The king was dressed in all black, from the coat over his shoulders to the boots on his feet. Where had he gone to prepare for the feast? Did he have another room? Did he go to that woman he insisted was not his mate?

I lifted my chin, refusing to care until my heart almost believed it.

The lack of contrast in his attire only brightened the tangle of red and cold in his eyes. On the ship Erik never had his head uncovered, but here the thick waves of his hair reminded me of damp soil after a rainstorm.

The absence of weapons and his hat emphasized how lithe and tall he was, how beautifully vicious he could be.

Erik's gaze roved over me, unashamed, as though he were soaking up every surface of my body. To be viewed in such a way was strangely intimate, and even more strange, I didn't despise it.

Men back home looked at me, but most saw me as Valen Ferus's daughter, a royal ambition to earn the eye of the earth bender king.

It was almost laughable how the man who robbed me from my home for a clear purpose of catching my father's attention for drearier reasons was the one who saw me as a woman. Like he saw every fissure of weakness, every strength and imperfection, and wanted them anyway. Not because I was my father's daughter. He wanted them because they were mine.

"Celine?" Larsson studied his shipmate and laughed. "By the gods, woman, I've never seen you not buried in oversized clothes. You've been hiding from us."

The trance locking my gaze with the king shattered. Celine

reached beneath her skirt and had a knife in hand, spinning it with a glare. "Taunt me, and it will be your last mistake."

Larsson took her hand and pressed a kiss to her knuckles. "No taunts, Tidecaller. Merely impressed you've managed to steal my heart in one night. How will I ever sail with you now?"

She elbowed him in the chest, drawing out a laugh, but accepted his outstretched hand. Tait was sullen and looked as though he'd swallowed something sour. There was an unease about the man, and I could not puzzle if he despised his king or was in a constant state of fearing for him.

Erik approached until our chests nearly touched. For a tense, drawn-out pause he studied me, then slowly took hold of my hand and kissed my knuckles the same as Larsson had with Celine.

"Songbird." His voice was as soft as an approaching storm.

"Serpent."

His eyes brightened. "This reminds me of another ball I attended not too long ago."

My lips pinched. "Well, I hope you're not expecting the same results. I assure you it will not be happening."

An empty threat. Erik Bloodsinger could do anything to me should he desire it, and no one here would ever stop him. I wasn't certain I'd stop him.

"I've no need to take you," he whispered. "You're already mine."

The king threaded my arm through his elbow. Despite his snide insinuations, I held to him as though he were the only thing keeping me upright.

Two guards opened the doors to the savory scents and riotous company of the feast. My stomach churned when Erik led us inside. Silence choked off the undertones of conversation, and all eyes seemed to dig into my flesh.

Blades adorned most belts, sometimes more than one. There

were more men than women, but it didn't matter. Everyone stared at me with confused rage. Sneers, glowers, sometimes muttered words under their breath followed me as Erik led us to the head table.

My blood chilled once I was seated. I dared lift my gaze only to be met with the same sharp stares, bemusement, and no doubt murderous intrigue.

The air grew hot, like falling sparks bit into my skin. Walls were too near, too tight, too confined. A heavy hand fell to my knee. I startled, unaware my leg had been bouncing enough the silver clinked against the plates.

"You are Livia Ferus," he whispered. The way his head tilted into me, no mistake, it would appear the king had his mouth all over my throat. I didn't move away; I soaked up his every word as he went on. "Daughter of warriors, blood of the Night Folk fae, painter of windows, challenger of the Ever King. These people can do nothing to you."

Our noses touched as he shifted away from me. A thousand words tumbled through my mind at what I could say, but none of them seemed right.

My heart rate slowed, and my breath grew even again. The way he looked at me wasn't rife with pity or annoyance that my skin grew flushed, or irrational fears attacked from behind too often. Erik gave me a subtle nod as if to tell me I was stronger than all that. I could suffer the attack but still rise the victor.

Without much thought, my palm covered his hand on my knee and squeezed.

The scar on his lip twitched when his expression turned smug. "Changed a few pieces of your impossibly long title, but I thought they suited."

He sat back, eyes forward, pulling away.

Dueling emotions collided in my chest. Erik was cruel—he slaughtered men and strung them up by their innards. The man didn't coddle—I wasn't certain he knew how—yet his simple reminder of who I was left me sitting straighter, more empowered than before.

Now he wouldn't look at me. He buried the moment of tenderness beneath smug grins and indifference.

The feast was uneventful. Most folk kept a healthy distance from the head table. Few came to wish Erik congratulations on the successful journey through the Chasm. They'd pause to sneer at me until the king shouted for them to keep moving.

I managed to eat a few bites of a strange gray fish with a sweet glaze that reminded me of heated honey. Celine peered around Larsson more than once, as if to ensure I hadn't trembled myself into a puddle of tears.

The twitch of concern on her face meant something. It meant a great deal.

At long last, Erik stood. The scrape of his chair over the polished stones on the floor silenced the hall. He studied his people with a narrowed look for a few breaths before he spoke. "For ten turns we've been locked away, prisoners in our own kingdom. Those days are at an end."

Cheers echoed through the hall. Folk raised their goblets and shouted Erik's name until he raised a hand.

"We have gone to the land of our enemies." He looked back at me, a dark gleam in his eyes. "And returned with a way to heal our kingdom."

I didn't waver under his stare. He wanted a challenge, and I wouldn't be the first to break.

"Fate is interesting in her games," Erik went on. "Livia of House Ferus is no mere prize. I have witnessed the use of her ability to heal poisoned soil." A few gasps followed. My pulse pounded in my skull. Erik silenced everyone once more. "Her worth to me and this kingdom is unmatched. She has become the mantle of the Ever King."

Voices rose in a bit of stun and chaos. Chatter echoed over the long tables, gasps and murmurs pummeled against us in a frenzy.

Erik allowed it for a dozen heartbeats before lifting a palm to draw back the silence. "It is for this reason I make a deeper claim beyond the power in her veins. Tonight, I claim her as mine."

I was spinning.

"Songbird."

I startled. Erik took my hand and tilted his head toward a wizened man with milky eyes and two black ribbons draped over his hands. Without a spare glance my way, the old man wrapped our clasped hands in the ribbon and hummed.

Sharp prickles of pain shot through the tips of my fingers, burning up my arm, until they reached my heart. I clenched my jaw to keep from doubling over. Erik's eyes looked nearly black, and a muscle twitched in his jaw.

For a fleeting moment, I felt as though the king pulled me into an embrace. His smoke and rain scent surrounded me. The heat of his skin kissed mine even though we hadn't moved any closer. As quickly as it began, the sensation faded.

The moment the ribbons were removed from our hands, Erik released me and hurried to put distance between us.

He faced his people again, a new grit to his voice. "The woman is not to be touched, threatened, or harmed in any way. Those who try will die. You will be known to me through the mark of the claim, and you will be granted no mercy. As the claimed and mantle of your king, she will have your respect. Nothing less."

Erik didn't say more before returning to his seat. For the first time since he tore me from my land, I didn't want to flee. I didn't care if a hundred eyes were locked on me, I wanted the king to face me. I wanted to understand why the unease in my heart didn't belong to me. The pressure, the burden of the unknowns, belonged wholly to him.

"CELINE WILL TAKE you back to my chambers," Erik said after the feast had transformed into dancing and celebration. Tunes that reminded me of falling rain flowed through the room, but at the king's movement, people came to a halt.

"You're leaving?"

"Upset I won't be beside you, love?"

I scoffed. "Not at all. I wondered how long I might be able to enjoy myself before I'm burdened by the sight of you again."

Erik's eyes brightened. "Afraid it won't be long. Whenever we return from the land realms, we record the interactions. I'll be aggravating you soon enough."

Then he was gone. Swallowed up in a crowd of sea fae who wanted to speak to the king.

"Hurry." Celine appeared at my side. "I've had all I can take of this damn dress."

I followed her back toward the corridors, but when we slipped through the doors, we ran into a broad man with dark hair slicked back.

"Lord Gavyn," Celine said, voice soft. The breathlessness of it was unnerving. The woman wore shaved teeth and attacked enemy ships. She was brisk and formidable, not meek and soft.

A lord. Younger than I'd expect. Dressed in a blue tunic threaded in gold and polished boots. He stood straight and proud like a noble. I clung tighter to Celine's arm. Erik hadn't wanted me to cross paths with any of the lords, but Gavyn wasn't looking at me. He was locked on Celine.

His brow furrowed. "Tidecaller. Why are you here?"

"I'm to watch the king's . . . mantle." She paused a moment before going on. "We breasts stick together."

Gavyn flicked his confusion to me, then back to Celine. "Keep your head down."

"And you, My Lord."

I watched him storm away without another word. Celine tugged on my arm, urging me forward.

"Who was that?" I asked, halfway down the opposite corridor.

"Lord Gavyn."

"Why did it look like you both were going to—wait, are you lovers?"

"I think I just vomited in my mouth." She glared at me, but less out of anger and more like she was trying to determine if I truly could be trustworthy.

"Celine, what is it?"

"Why should I tell you?"

"Well, the fact that you asked makes me think you might want to." Angry heat prickled up the back of my neck. "He hasn't hurt you, has he?"

"I don't understand you. You're supposed to be a bitch, and I should want to pull your hair out."

"Sorry to disappoint." The secrets she kept seemed ready to split Celine down the middle. Her body was tense, and it struck me—she had no one, the same as me. I took her hand. "You are the only person other than the king who really speaks to me. At the very least, just assure me Gavyn isn't hurting you."

After a moment, her shoulders slumped. "Gavyn is my brother."

"Your brother? But . . . he's one of the house lords and you're—"

"A nobody on the Ever King's ship?"

"The ranks do seem uneven."

"It's the way it needs to be."

The stun on Gavyn's face at the sight of her made a bit more sense. "He was uneasy about you being here, and you said yourself you never come to the feasts. Why?"

"Because no one knows what I am to him. It must be this way."

Her hand went to the scar on her neck, rubbing the puckered flesh. "If anyone discovered my true name, it could get both of us killed."

"Your true name?" My eyes widened. "You are a siren, aren't you? Why is it secret? Why do you claim the House of Tides when your voice is from the House of Mists?"

"Because it was cut out," Celine gritted through her teeth. In the next breath, she clapped a hand over her mouth, tears in her eyes. "Don't . . . don't say anything."

"Celine." I placed a hand on her shoulder. "I won't say a word, but how can your voice be cut out?"

Her chin quivered. "Not my voice, my song. The siren's call is kept here." She patted the scar. "It can be removed. Painfully."

Bleeding hells. "But you still have a song."

She lifted her eyes, a tear on her cheek. "Most Sea Folk have a connection to the water. I had help, but I practiced my call to the tides. Eventually they answered, but it is not my natural gift. I was renamed Tidecaller and forgot the past. Please, you cannot say anything. You don't understand how the mere breath in my lungs is treasonous."

"But why?"

"I told you, sometimes females are expendable in the Ever."

This was damn madness. Was Celine truly nearly killed, was she truly stripped of her voice all because she was a woman?

"Gavyn doesn't acknowledge you because—"

"Because I should not exist." Celine glanced over her shoulder. "Please, I can't tell you more. It isn't a matter of wanting, I truly can't for the sake of more than just me. But know this—you might detest what my king did to you, but Gavyn and I, we owe Erik Bloodsinger everything."

33

THE SONGBIRD

"DEEP BITES. LONG swipes." Sewell demonstrated a brutal strike with one of the cutlass blades used on the *Ever Ship*. I was more accustomed to knives and battle-axes, but I'd sweated from the early-morning hours to the lavender light of the dusk in the days since the claiming. I saw little of Erik, but he'd insisted on seeing to it I could hold my own with a blade.

I tightened my grip on the hilt of the sparring sword. Sewell struggled with his words, but his body moved like a warrior, one that knew how to strike from the shadows. Swift, deliberate, and unseen.

The edge of his blade came down on mine. My shoulders throbbed from the pressure, but I spun out, dislodging his blade. Sewell struck again. I parried. He jabbed. I sliced. When he ducked, I attempted to knock him off-balance. With his elbow, he slammed me between the shoulders, and I fell with a roll back to my feet as he'd shown me.

From the side of the hall, Celine shouted her opinions on my form, mostly criticisms, but occasionally she groaned at Sewell.

"Come on, you taught me better than that, old man." She shook her head.

Sewell pointed his blade at her, grinning. "Back your talk, Thunder Fish."

Celine blew out her lips. "I stand by my word that I could flatten you."

Sewell huffed and tossed Celine a blade. Forgotten, and given a moment's rest, I observed their fight for a few breaths before the cool steel of a blade leveled against my neck.

I froze.

"Don't let down your guard, love. Not in the Ever."

Erik lowered his blade but kept close to me. His fingers brushed over the back of my neck when he leaned his mouth against my ear. "Fight me."

Each word dripped through me like liquid fire. I swallowed and rammed my elbow into Erik's ribs. He didn't let out the slightest grunt, simply laughed and spun a gold-hilted cutlass in his grip.

I kept low, circling the king. Guards lined the hall. More courtiers gathered to watch. Even Celine and Sewell paused their match.

"Show me you can defend yourself," he said in a sharp tone, but beneath it all, there seemed to be a strange plea to his voice.

Doubtless, I imagined it.

Erik didn't wait for me to catch my breath before he lunged. Like Sewell, the king moved with a captivating finesse. His strikes came before I caught up to the previous move. I fought to gain the offensive, but kept backstepping, blocking every strike in a frenzy.

I managed to spin out and get behind him, but an off-center strike to his back ended with Erik finding the leverage to curl one of his legs around my ankle and knock my feet out from under me. I landed flat on my back with a grunt.

Erik made a cage with his arms and legs, pinning me to the ground. The red of his eyes was like a soft flame. Dark hair pinned to his brow from a thin layer of sweat. His body was hard and strong and too close to mine. The bastard only made it worse when he leaned his mouth over my lips.

"I think of you like this too often," he whispered. "The fire in your eyes, the sweat on your brow."

"It will only be in your head, Bloodsinger."

He chuckled. "Ah, but I've had a taste already, Songbird."

"I was feeling generous."

His lips brushed mine and I bit down on my tongue to keep in a moan. "You often rob me of words, but I want you to hear me when I say this." Erik pulled back, waiting until I looked at him before going on. "You have horrific footwork."

I rammed a fist into his shoulder. "Get off me."

He laughed and pulled away but held out a hand to help me up. I took it, almost on instinct, as if our dance kept us touching but also too uneasy—perhaps too reluctant—to cross those lines again.

The king didn't say anything before he turned away.

"Where are you going now?" Gods, I sounded like a child about to pout, but there was a growing side of me that didn't like watching the back of Bloodsinger's head walk away.

"Kingly business, love." Erik offered his horrid, beautiful grin. "Miss me often?"

"Never." I spun in the opposite direction, ignoring the way Sewell and Celine grinned like they knew something.

They knew nothing.

By the gods, I wasn't certain I knew how to explain what happened to me whenever the damn Ever King came near either.

THE KING SPOKE true. He was absent enough sometimes I thought I might miss him. A bond from the claiming, no doubt. There must've been some kind of magic that tethered me to Bloodsinger, and it was aggravating when he wasn't close.

Erik would slip into his chambers, take a moment to wash, dress, then leave again. For days he hardly said a word beyond a mere "Songbird" greeting.

I tried to ask Celine where the king spent his days. She'd tell me I shouldn't pester him about his time, and insist I was aggravating. But after the feast, she rarely left my side. I didn't think it was only on the order of the king.

Celine spent the days showing me the palace, introducing me to the wide-eyed servants, who rarely spoke with me, and testing me on the numerous stairwells that led to the uneven levels of the palace.

"Well?" I asked a week after Erik claimed me as his. "What do you think?"

Alistair, the old steward, tilted his head, full lips pouted as he squinted at the window. "What is it?"

I balked. "What is it?" The paintbrush was still in my fingers as I opened my arms wide to the glossy window. "It's Jörmungandr! The great sea serpent. Who else would it be?"

Alistair sniffed and took another breath to study the black body wrapped around wild blue waves. "I appreciate the artistic liberties; however, that is no Jörmungandr I've ever seen."

Celine snickered behind her hand. I puffed a strand of hair out of my face and glared at the steward as I packed the paint basket again. "Well, Alistair, I'm afraid I have terrible news."

"What is that, Lady Livia?"

"You have no damn taste in art."

Again, the man sniffed, but his folded skin lifted on his cheeks with a rare grin as he turned on his heel. "There are windows aplenty to practice upon, My Lady. Don't lose heart just yet."

TWO WEEKS AFTER the claiming, Erik slipped into his chamber when the moon was highest. I pretended to sleep, grateful he'd left me in peace all day—perhaps a little frustrated he seemed content to avoid me.

He rustled through his wardrobe. After I'd listened to the sounds of him shedding his clothes for clean ones, after I'd imagined the way his body looked with nothing on it, he stepped beside the bed.

My heart stilled when he gently eased the quilts higher on my shoulders, then the soft touch of his fingertips brushed away a lock of hair from my brow, a touch there and gone like the kiss of a breeze.

Then he left me alone.

Again.

"WE CALL IT the great hall," Celine said, grinning as she turned around the throne room, where the return feast had been served more than two weeks before. "It's what you call yours too, right?"

I'd started to take note of the subtle ways Celine tried to find similarities between our worlds. Styles of hair, the way soil grew vibrant plants, even the shape of our ears.

"Yes," I said. "We eat and revel in the great halls back home." I dragged my fingertips over the filigreed throne, made of black wood and engraved with crashing waves and sea plants across the back and armrests. I gave Celine a wink and started to sit. "Shall we see what it's like to be Bloodsinger?"

"No!" She wrenched my arm back with such force I nearly fell over. "No, only the king can sit atop the throne."

"Why?"

Celine licked her lips. "To sit on a throne would mean you are the equal of the king. There is no equal to an Ever King. It would lessen Erik's status and power."

"Gods, it's that symbolic, or is it some kind of spell?"

"It's the way of things. If the Ever King is powerless, then he has nothing."

I stared at the empty throne; a bite of sympathy took hold for Bloodsinger. He was forced to bear the weight of his kingdom alone and fight to keep his back from bending in the sight of others.

He was practically forbidden from having . . . anyone.

There are no Ever queens. I thought of my parents and how they confided in each other, depended on each other. They ruled together. When one bent under the weight of their crown, the other would take it for them both.

Erik could have bedmates, he could make another heir to pass on the burden of an entire world, but could he give his heart to anyone? His fears? His troubles? The more I learned of the treatment of the king, the more I hated it.

Celine kept me from the throne room after that and showed me the balconies, the numerous corridors, the unkempt gardens.

The gardens were terraced into four levels. Some levels were covered with bowers and blossoming nettles. Others with herbs and spiked fruits. The top level outside Erik's chamber was surrounded by stone walls, a single gate leading to the lower terraces, and filled with shrubs and strange willowlike trees with blue-veined leaves that seemed to glow beneath the moonlight.

I found particular comfort in the lowest garden near the king's private cove.

The slow, gentle roll of the waves called to me and added a touch of peace as I strolled through strange ferns that smelled of mint and between trees growing odd plums with yellow skin.

Celine walked nearly twenty paces in front of me before she realized I'd stopped and lowered to my knees in front of a wild bush with satin black leaves.

"You do like soil, don't you?" She chuckled.

"I thought everything in the Ever was underwater. It's always a surprise to see so much . . . land."

"My daj always explained the different fae realms to me as two sides of a coin. Either side can be flipped to the top."

Once I discovered the gardens, I spent most of my time there. My fury magic burned wild and desperate to connect to this new land, this new soil. Since the king was too busy to be seen, I didn't know how to ask his permission—and frankly, I didn't care to get it—before I began taming the grounds.

My blood heated as I cupped wilted blossoms until they burst into a flurry of colors and sweet, milky scents.

I conquered the sprawling, chaotic vines. My magic connected to the barest levels of the soil and plant life. My father could command the earth to break and bend; I commanded it to live. A sort of give-and-take of energy. I offered my magic, and the more vibrancy the earth returned, the longer I could use my own power.

On the days spent in the terraced gardens, Celine would sit with me, chatting about life on the *Ever Ship* while I worked. Soon, I laughed with her, like I did with Mira. I even told her about Aleksi as a new Rave officer, Sander's studious nature, and Jonas's proclivity to bed jealous women.

"One time a woman discovered he'd been with someone else," I said. "She broke into the other woman's bedchamber—not his—and cut her hair. Then she managed to use her familiarity with his side of his family's palace to slip into his chamber and leave it on his pillow. In the middle of the night. I've never seen the man so quiet and pale."

I snickered and touched a brittle vine with pink petals like a calm dawn.

Celine handed me a scoop of soil. "How was she executed?"

"Oh, she wasn't executed, simply banned from the palace. I think Jonas's mother and father laughed about it for two days. The poor girl whose hair was cut is what we call an elixist, a potion master in a way. She was able to craft a tonic to grow it back even more luscious than before."

Celine gave me a bemused look. "A woman terrorized a royal and lived?"

"She wasn't a threat, and Jonas did bring it on himself, but we don't go around slaughtering people, Celine." I paused to wipe sweat off my brow. "Is that what you're taught about us? That we kill everything?"

She considered me for a breath. "I was born into the rivalry between our worlds. When Lord Harald still lived, he never let us forget how the fae of the other lands slaughtered the Ever King and tortured the heir. We'd have what he called blood feasts every quarter moon, and he'd repeat the tale. He'd stir the hatred. He'd bring Erik out and—" Celine cut off her words and shook her head.

"What?" I brushed soil from my palms and squared to her. "What did he do?"

"He'd strip me down and force my people to look at my mangled skin, love."

I jumped as Celine flinched and closed her eyes. Ten paces off, Erik leaned against an arched bower, glaring.

I despised how my pulse raced, and not from the surprise. Erik had the scarf around his head, a black hoop in his ear, and his pressed top was unlaced, revealing too much of his broad chest.

At his side, Larsson gave me a wink. Tait kept his eyes pinned to the ground. His father was Harald, the bastard who'd truly been the one to bring the war to our shores. Erik might've been king at the time, but he'd been young, and from what it sounded like, he'd been trapped under the influence of a vindictive uncle.

Hells, I didn't know what to say and merely gaped like a fool, unable to grasp the cruelty of it all.

The king looked around the garden. Only half healed, but it was more orderly and healthier. Shrubs had aligned in neat rows, tangles of weeds and nettles were taken back and replaced with berms and lush, flowering bushes.

"You've done all this alone?" Erik asked.

"Celine has been here."

She raised her hands. "I haven't lifted a finger, My King."

"The gardens nearly look like they once did."

"Why do you neglect them?" I asked before I could swallow the words.

"They're not mine," Erik said, voice flat. "They were my mother's. Walk with me, love."

I offered a quick glance at Celine, but she'd already moved a distance away with Tait and Larsson.

We took a few languid strides through flowering shrubs, silent for a few breaths.

"You've avoided me," I said.

"Avoided? Not at all."

"Of course, how silly of me." I cracked three knuckles. "I haven't dined alone, slept alone, been alone but for Celine and Alistair, who, by the way, is quite fond of me."

"I don't doubt it."

"You're avoiding me."

"I thought you would appreciate knowing you have freedom to go about as you please without a king breathing down your neck." Erik stopped and leaned his face closer. "Unless you'd like me to."

I took a step back, irritated, a little overheated. "I'm managing fine."

Erik smirked. "Good. But I do have need to speak with you about something. Your magic, I want to understand it. Even those parts Narza said you're afraid to talk about."

"I'm . . . I'm not afraid."

He tapped the side of his head, a twist to his lips. "Bonded, love.

I know there are parts that frighten you, and I want to understand the darker parts." He looked at the vibrant garden. "Seems rather bright to me, but you did mention you see frightening things. I want to understand to better protect you."

Breath tightened in my chest like a tangle of knotted ribbons. "Protect me from what?"

"You were revealed as a powerful earth fae, a vein of power for the throne, and that power attracts all manner of crooked gazes. That bastard we killed in Skondell? There are more pirates like him out there. I've seen you fight—"

"And you mocked me."

"Sewell told me your footwork has improved, so I think what you mean is I assisted you." Erik's hand rested on my cheek. "I won't hide dangers from you, not when you deserve to hear them."

He didn't treat me like some fragile piece of glass; he told me to breathe and take the good with the bad. Erik let me shoulder it, let me know the truth to find a way to live with it instead of the fear.

It took a moment, but his steady gaze, the warmth of his palm kept me grounded and firm until the knot faded, and the thoughts of all the dreary unknowns slid back into the crags and crevices of my mind.

"People always keep darker truths from me," I whispered.

"That is something I can't afford. Not in the Ever. You are safer if you know what risks you face, Songbird. The same way it is safer if I know what you can do. I can't defend you if you keep things from me."

"I know." My palm covered his hand on my cheek. "I like that you tell me even if my mind conjures up a thousand drearier possibilities." I spoke lightly, but Erik didn't grin. His thumb brushed over my cheek. "I'm not weak because of it, but sometimes my thoughts—"

"Did I say you were weak?" he snapped. "You are not weak because of fears, but I will do what I can to help you wade between the fears that are plausible and the ones that are the mind trying to paralyze you."

My lips parted. No one spoke so directly about my proclivity to fret. I . . . I liked it. There was something about his firm tone, his logical words that helped chip away at what was true and what was a dark story my mind created.

"It started when I used my fury too fast and too deep once. I don't talk about this much." Truth be told, I never spoke of it, never opened that piece of me, afraid it might happen again. I didn't want to relive the nightmares in my head, didn't want to see the gory images that plagued a child's mind.

Erik didn't remove his hand; he didn't push or prod. He was simply there, as violently beautiful as the heavy tides.

"I told you my fury has another side to it. I can—if I'm open enough—I can feel the land. I didn't know I could even do that until the war," I said softly. "I would see the battles."

"You were near the fighting?" A bit of rage flushed his face.

"No. I took it into my mind's eye." I closed my eyes. "I wanted to make certain my parents were all right, so I dug deeper than I'd ever gone with my magic. I saw the blood, the pain, heard the screams. Every life lost clung to my soul. My parents had given me such a peaceful life, I never knew such horrors could exist. All the young royals knew how to hold a blade and fight if we needed to, but I had never seen death. Not like that.

"When I opened the connection, I didn't know how to control it and was devoured. It's not reliable, which makes me wonder if it is trustworthy with the darkening."

"Why do you think it's unreliable?"

"During one of the final battles, I saw my uncle die. I felt it, and I couldn't stop sobbing and couldn't tell anyone why. I'm glad I didn't, because when the battle ended, Tor was there to greet us. Bloodied but alive."

A muscle pulsed in Erik's jaw. He clenched his fists, then flexed his fingers as if unknotting an ache in his knuckles, but he said nothing.

I looked away. "Nightmares came after that; I still have them. I started to fear my fury, and nerves took hold. Now unknowns, possibilities of what could be, fester like poison in my head, and I let them consume me until I can't breathe."

The heat of embarrassment flooded my cheeks. I chuckled. "Telling you all this now sounds ridiculous since you were there. You fought. I merely heard them and had blurry images cast through my mind and can hardly think straight when the panic takes hold."

"Don't negate the pain of your experience." His tone was as sharp as broken glass. Angry, but not at me, more for me.

"I only mean, it must've been much worse to fight in those battles."

"I was there, true," he said, "but it was not the same for me. While that was your first experience with gruesome pain, I was born into brutality. My earliest memories are of blood and death."

A cinch tugged at my chest. "Even before your father died?"

Erik laughed, a dry, raw sound. "Thorvald was not what I would call a gentle father, I assure you, and his greatest fear was producing a gentle heir. He had his ways of seeing to it his fears were never realized."

I didn't know what his father had done to him as a child, but I hated King Thorvald for it. For the first time, I hoped my father had made him suffer. My fierce defensiveness and near bloodlust on behalf of the Ever King was startling, a little intriguing.

I didn't shove it away or fight the pull to stand between Erik and more pain. In truth, I wasn't certain I could.

"I could probably make tree roots stab someone, maybe a thornbush strangle someone too. I've never tried, but it's a thought I've had, a feeling that I could."

Erik looked at me as though he couldn't gauge if I was teasing. When I kept quiet, he chuckled. "Do that, Songbird. If ever it is a choice between your life or another's, strangle them with thorns."

My insides twisted. Such a dark thought, and I doubted I'd ever be able to truly stomach such a thing.

"This is helpful," he said. "I understand you a little better. Come on."

"Where are we going?"

Erik took my hand. "To heal the Ever."

34

THE SERPENT

HALF THE ROYAL city came out to follow us to one of the Glass Isles, a plot of land off the shores of the city that was covered in the darkening. Heads bowed as we made our way to the docks, but most peeked to catch a glimpse of the princess.

Livia wrung her hands in the folds of her skirt until I thought she might tear a hole in the fabric. I reached back and slipped my fingers through hers. "Pretend there is no one here but me, love."

Her cheek twitched. "Ah, but you are the problem, Bloodsinger."

She didn't release my hand until we reached the last dock, where a long sloop was readied with the banner of the Ever King whipping about in the wind.

Livia's expression brightened in an instant. "Sewell!"

She gathered her skirt in hand and hurried to the narrow gangplank.

"Glittering, this day." Sewell tugged on a rope, managing the black canvas sail. "Comin' aboard?"

Livia chuckled. "Seems that way."

Sewell winked and offered a quick glance toward Celine before I stepped onto the deck. "Going under, little eel?"

He was asking if we were sailing the way our ships were meant to sail.

"That we are, Sewell. Ready her to dive." I led Livia toward the helm. "I'll be taking us beneath the tides, Songbird. As we did through the Chasm, don't let go."

With a snide grin, she pressed her chest against mine and wrapped her arms around my neck. Nestled between my arms, she was positioned the same way she'd been the night I stole her away. The difference between now and then was the look in her eyes. A flash of something warm and almost greedy burned in the blue.

"Like this, Serpent?"

"Yes." Dammit. My voice was a rasp lined in grit and desire. The press of her curves rushed heat to the wrong places. I focused ahead. Once the skeleton crew was aboard, I whistled sharply and waved a hand. A gust of wind caught the sails, and the sloop turned away from the shore.

Livia's fingertips played with the ends of my hair behind my neck. She closed her eyes when the sea breeze kissed her cheeks. Gods, she looked made for the Ever.

"Take her down," I called out. More boats followed in our wake. The people were coming to witness the last thread of hope. My stomach lurched in unease. What if it was too much and we couldn't destroy it?

"We will," Livia whispered.

I froze, but she wasn't looking at me. I wasn't sure she realized she'd taken hold and absorbed my fear unknowingly. Little by little, this tether between us was growing. Little by little, I was handing over my scorched, rotted heart.

I couldn't stop.

A man he's not...

Low hums and chants rumbled over the deck as the crew worked the sails and readied to dive.

"Hold tight, Songbird," I whispered next to her ear.

Livia braced. Water spilled over the bow, the deck, until the sea swallowed us.

BOATS DOTTED THE shore. "They're here to watch?" Livia glanced over her shoulder as more folk arrived after us.

"I want them to see your power." I hesitated. "They need hope."

She gave a curt nod and faced the isle. Small knolls were once covered in lush ferns and tall grasses, trees with waxy, gilded leaves, and ponds with fish of all colors. Now the sand was left colorless, and the plants were withered and blackened.

"Erik." Livia tugged up her sleeves, eyes forward. "If I fail, what will become of your people?"

I crossed my arms over my chest. "If you fail, which you won't because you're too bleeding determined to prove yourself, I will do what I must to find them somewhere else to live."

"Where would you go?"

"Through the Chasm, Songbird. I would give myself to your people in exchange for the refuge of mine."

She closed her eyes, drew in a deep breath, then took a step forward as she whispered, "I'd better not fail, then. After all this, I'd wager my father doesn't like you much. He would make life quite unpleasant, I'm afraid."

"I'm sure he would." The instant resentment at the mention of the earth bender was missing. In truth, I could understand his anger toward me. Should he come to take her back, I'd likely be the same.

Celine gnawed on her thumbnail, Sewell flicked his fingers by his sides, while Tait and Larsson watched from the sloop.

I trudged up the slope beside Livia, until she came to a stop, far enough away from the others that no one would hear us. "Erik, I'm going to try my hardest. If it doesn't work, please know that. Despite how I was brought here, I don't want your people to suffer."

Guilt tore through my chest until I couldn't draw a deep breath. She wanted my people to live—her enemies—and all I'd done was threaten hers.

I should have recognized the dangers of getting too close to this damn woman at the first taste. Following her to that masquerade had begun my dangerous descent. From the first tug of the undeniable pull to the cautious chirp of her laughter to the cunning look in her eyes when she tried to intimidate me, I should've kept a distance. When I saw the sea singer dragging her away, the tight, noxious panic ought to have been a signal I'd crossed a line.

But here, when she feared the judgment and blades of my people, yet stepped onto an unfamiliar shore ready to dig into a magic she feared, all for their lives—I plummeted over a ledge for her, and I wasn't coming back.

My lungs only filled when Livia knelt and pressed her palms to the soil.

She winced. I ground my teeth to keep from shouting at her to stop. Slowly, her face softened. Five breaths passed, then ten more before the sooty plague broke into soft mists and rippled away from her touch.

Against the sea wind, the crash of the waves on the isle shore, the gasps and choked sobs rose. My pulse raced. Shadows fled from beneath Livia's hands. She stood, eyes clenched, and held her palms out to her sides.

"Stay with me, Erik," she whispered, and took a step forward. "I don't know why, but the nearer you are, the stronger my fury burns."

"Always." I kept her pace.

The ripple of retreating black grew under her hands, her steps. Like a great wind erupted from her body, darkness swept away and into the tides. Livia stumbled, gasping. I grabbed her arm.

"Gods." She drew in a sharp breath. "Keep your hands on me."

"Gladly, Songbird. Gladly."

"You're a wretch." She grinned, and I'd say countless wretched things if it kept that smile in place. "I was fatiguing, but your touch brought my strength back."

I was a fool. We were meant to take strength from each other.

My father always held his talisman when he commanded the seas to part or the waves to do his bidding.

To touch her as fury raged in her veins was strange. Like shards of it melted into mine, our magics spilled between us. Strong enough, I thought, connected like this, Livia's blood might be toxic. Perhaps, I might be able to summon the blooms as she did.

"You should try." Livia swiped at the drops of sweat on her brow.

"Do you realize I'm not speaking?"

She blinked. "I . . . I didn't. I'm *feeling* your thoughts."

"Disconcerting, isn't it?"

"Very." She rolled her shoulders back. "Still, it made a bit of sense that you might be taking some of my fury. Try to call the life back to the soil. I'm not sure I can do both without becoming exhausted too quickly."

"I don't know how." My magic killed things. It wasn't lovely and bright like hers.

"It's warm," she explained. "Almost like you call to it, and you'll feel it here." She pressed a hand over my heart. "Try."

Livia took up her pace again. I kept my hand on her shoulder but slowly unfurled one palm over the ground as we walked.

I didn't know how to call to the damn earth, so I closed my eyes and conjured up a memory of digging in soil, of placing dark seeds, then a blurry recollection of the elation when the tiny blooms broke the surface. The laughter and a woman's gentle embraces that followed.

"Erik, look!" Tait shouted. My cousin was distant, reserved, and always on his guard, but there was a touch of relief in his voice.

I opened my eyes slightly. Beneath my palm, moss-green clovers sprouted through the cracked soil. Livia paused, a little stunned, then beamed at me.

I lifted her knuckles to my lips. "You didn't fail, Songbird. As I said."

"Don't be an 'I told you so' kind of king."

"But I did."

Livia laughed. A true laugh, and I would kill anyone who tried to take such a sound from me.

Sobs from the people turned to cheers and praises and songs. We covered ground together, clearing away three knolls of the darkening before Livia lowered to her knees, and I fell back beside her, gasping, body aching.

"Larsson," I said, and weakly waved him over to me when he stepped onto the shore. A man of jests and taunts, he looked down at me with a somber expression. "Tell the people . . . tonight we revel in the hall."

He tipped the brim of his hat. "As you say, My King."

I closed my eyes and grinned. For the first time in turns, it felt as though I could take a damn breath.

"Livia," I said through a pant, "did you see anything? More thoughts when you connected to it?"

"Yes. The magic was potent today. I do believe this was caused by someone, not the earth. It was painful, as though it was a lash on the skin, an attack on the kingdom in a sense. But there was something else." Her brow furrowed in disquiet. "I don't know what to make of it."

"What did you see?"

"More what I felt." Livia dragged her bottom lip between her teeth. "Do you have a brother?"

Well, shit. "I don't."

She rubbed her forehead. "See, unreliable. There was this constant thought of the throne belonging to him. I don't know who he is, but . . . Erik, you must promise me you will be wary." Her eyes were round and pleading when she sat up. "I hate to say it, but what if someone caused a disaster like this all to take your crown?"

"Then they would not be the first." I stood, desperate to hide my unease. If it was true, then I had an invisible enemy with a damn blood claim to the Ever.

REVELS WITH THE common people weren't done beyond festivals, and we'd ceased with those after the darkening. There was nothing much to celebrate.

Unaccustomed to the flurry of drums, pipes, lyres, and laughter, part of me wanted to sink into the walls, but most of me was enraptured with the woman spinning about with Sewell in the center of the hall.

Livia's hair spilled around her shoulders in dark waves, and the shimmer of laughter lived in her eyes when Sewell dipped her back, nearly toppling them both. She was a beacon through the dark. A beautiful distraction from blood claims and curses and enemies.

I abandoned the side of the hall. Tait and Larsson both made moves to follow, but I held up a hand. A hundred gazes burned into me; I only looked at Livia.

"Sewell." I waited until he faced me. "Mind?"

For a pause, Sewell studied my open palm, then a sly kind of grin spread over his mouth. "Aye, little eel. Spin."

The moment I'd stepped into the hall, the musicians had slowed their playing as though waiting for me to rage or end the revel. With a gentle tug I pulled Livia against me, and the music began again. Louder, with more spirit than before.

"Songbird."

"Serpent." She slid one arm around my shoulders. "I was beginning to think you did not know how to revel and intended to stand surly and aloof all evening."

"I had planned exactly that." Slowly, I drifted my fingertips along the divots of her spine. "Until I saw that Sewell made you laugh, and I felt more violent than anything."

She chuckled. "Violent? I think you were jealous, Bloodsinger. As you should be. Sewell is my favorite."

I touched my lips to the subtle point of her ear. "Not the thing a man wants to hear when he's had his mouth on your body, dragging out those desperate sounds from your throat."

Livia let out a warm breath against my neck. "Erik, don't say those things."

"Why not?" I dragged my nose across her smooth cheek.

"Because." Livia dug her claws into my shoulders. "It makes me think . . . I'd like to make those sounds again."

"Good." My lips caressed the slope of her neck. "Because I've thought of nothing else other than your sweet legs wrapped around me, your naked body in my hands, and my name on your tongue right before you come apart."

Livia's lips parted against ragged pants. Her body went still in my hold.

With my thumb, I tugged on her bottom lip. "You want me as much as I want you, Songbird. Admit it."

On the surface, I was calm, snide, even arrogant. Inside, I was pleading, pathetic, and simpering. I never knew how desperately I wanted to hear the words from her, the words telling me she ached for me back.

I wouldn't get them.

One of the guards by the doors of the hall pounded on the wood and lifted his voice over the crowd. "Lady Narza of the House of Mists."

I froze.

Livia's hand pressed to my chest. "Why is she here?"

"Stay behind me." I stepped in front of her, using one hand to tuck Livia close against my back, then faced the entrance.

Crowds parted for a procession of several ladies of the House of Mists. Witches and sirens were both hauntingly beautiful. The difference was the women with siren blood had the darker eyes and ruby lips. The witches were more like a sea storm. Colorful hair and irises like smoke lived behind their pupils.

All powerful. All frightening.

Fione was amongst them, a smug grin on her painted lips when she singled me out in the crowd. Narza's guards surrounded the women with red-tipped spears made from toxic corals and shells found in the House of Mists' territory.

In her role as the lady, Narza carried herself as though she ruled from every corner of the Ever Seas. Half a head shorter than me, still she seemed as though she might crush me under her feet.

"Lady Narza." I gritted her name through my teeth, as sharp as jagged steel, and gave a nod of respect. "What a surprise to have you in the palace. I thought you vowed never to return."

"You've thought many things."

"Why are you here?"

"I've heard the strangest talk. Something about the king claiming his earth fae." Narza's painted blue lips twitched. "I wanted to see the truth of it for myself."

Blood pounded in my head; I tugged Livia against me.

Narza chuckled. "Rather protective of your bond with the woman. Is that the only reason?"

"She is the mantle of the Ever King, Lady. You will give her the honor of such a title."

"Still on about the mantle." Narza drifted around people, those too stunned by her presence to move, and came to stand in front of me. "Does that remain her only purpose?"

I tightened my hold on Livia's waist. "I owe you no answers, Lady Narza."

Her mouth twitched; no doubt the disdain she held for me was fighting to break through. "You do though. Since you believe it is the gift of my house that has bonded you both. You seem taken by her, but have you shown her your heart? Truly? Does she know you? To reveal the darkest pieces will only deepen the bond and only strengthen the ability to heal this land."

"I know exactly who he is." Livia took a step forward, nearly in front of me.

"Livia." I tried to pull her back. A woman who succumbed to nerves chose this as her bleeding moment of boldness? She didn't know Narza; she didn't know her power.

My damn songbird swatted me away. More than one whisper followed. No one struck at the king and lived.

Livia stopped a pace away from Narza. "I am willingly aiding the king. Perhaps it did not begin that way, but desires change. I know the beauty of his black heart; I've seen it. But I also know every bleeding step he has taken has been to save his people. I've seen that this curse in the Ever was caused by enemies amongst you."

A few gasps rippled through the hall.

"I also know the dark magic in the earth feels a great deal like a spell," Livia said, an arrogant grin twisted over her mouth. "What house is it again that casts spells?"

Narza had the decency to look surprised. "A spell cast, you say?"

"You know what my fury does," Livia said. "You know the earth reveals what was done to my heart and mind. That is the tale it told me."

Narza arched one brow. "If this is true, I make assurances that I will search for the traitor in my house without rest."

"See that you do." Livia folded her arms over her chest. "And you can also take your warnings of the king elsewhere. I have no need of them."

I didn't know what moves to make other than I was going to kiss the reckless woman in another breath if she kept fighting my battles.

"Hmm." Narza grinned a little viciously. "The last woman to hold such fire beside an Ever King was Thorvald's mate. I hope your flame is not doused prematurely as was hers."

Livia flicked her gaze to me. "Your mother?"

I didn't look at her. I only glared at Narza. "Tell her. That's why you brought it up, isn't it? Go on, tell her. Frighten her away."

"You think things, boy," Narza said, dark and low. No one gasped at her spitted title. Truth be told, I was certain most of my folk feared the sea witch more than me. "But I am merely looking out for the well-being of the innocent. If she claims you like you've claimed her, she deserves to know everything."

"Erik, what is she talking about?"

My fingernails dug into Livia's waist. "My mother was the chosen mate of the Ever King, but she was killed when it was believed her gentle demeanor might soften the heir."

Narza's eyes glistened. "That's enough talk of it."

"No." I scoffed and released Livia. She wouldn't want me touching her soon enough. "You brought it up, so finish it. Tell her what you think of me for what I did, *Grandmother*."

"Enough, Erik," Narza insisted.

"It will never be enough for you," I said, voice rough. I spun on Livia. "She wants you to know how my mother died so you can save yourself."

Livia's countenance shadowed. There was a shard of my heart that seemed to break away. It felt as though we'd shifted to something different. Now it would go back to scathing looks, to hatred and disgust.

"How did she die?" Livia spoke in a low whisper.

"Doesn't Narza's repulsion for me make it obvious?" I took a step for the door. "I killed her."

35

THE SONGBIRD

ERIK ABANDONED THE hall without another word. The heady quiet of the room crushed in on me, but more than uneasy, I was furious. This woman came into the king's hall, his revel, his hard-fought victory, and drew him back into the darkness that held him captive.

There was more to his parting words. In my soul, I felt there was more.

I took a step toward Lady Narza but paused when a rough palm wrapped around my arm. Sewell gave me a warning look. "Careful steps, little fox."

That was all he said before releasing me.

Lady Narza had young features, much the same as my own grandmother, but fae folk hardly aged once their bodies had matured. Seemed to be true for sea fae as well.

"I'm not some naive woman captivated by the title of king," I said. "I know who he is. I know what brought him through the Chasm. I've known since we were children in a war on opposing sides. What confuses me is how it seems his own blood doesn't know him at all."

I turned briskly to escape the hall but was stopped when a hand gripped my wrist and spun me around.

Narza's eyes burned with emotion. "There are dangers for you in this land. Dangers for him. If stronger magics are working to oust the king, you will only survive if your bond is sealed. You must see the whole of him if you are to let him in entirely. This was the downfall of my daughter—she chose not to see Thorvald's darkness."

"Yet you offered the bastard a spell in that talisman that only strengthened his power."

"Think me a fool if you wish, girl," Narza said. "Thorvald had the most cunning of tongues. Even I believed he wished to create a union that would only strengthen the Ever."

"And when it didn't go your way, you abandoned a tiny boy to the brutality of life." My blood boiled into my cheeks. It would have been wise to hold my tongue, but anger bled over. Countless thoughts of Erik suffering as a child, of his own father's rejection weighed heavy on my chest.

"Lord Harald would not allow me in the palace," Narza admitted softly. "He had wards put in place against me. Erik was twisted and used, and I was forced to watch as the last piece of my beloved daughter grew with a desire to become another Thorvald. He was always meant to be Erik Bloodsinger." She swallowed and stepped in front of me. "For the first time, I see him doing that because he found you."

"Because I became the new mantle—"

"There is no mantle." Narza's voice cracked. "There never was."

"What?" I held out my arm. "Then what is the mark?"

"A symbol of the heart bond I began for the House of Kings. A symbol that bonded you to my grandson because, even as young ones, your heart found itself in his.

"Kings across the histories have bartered with the ladies of my house for gifts of power, but all were made with weak bonds. More power, more brutality, more of everything. Thorvald wanted to be the most formidable Ever King. He was clever; he studied the past and lore of the sea witches."

She grimaced and stared at the floor. "He stole my daughter's love by promises he never intended to keep."

My head was spinning. "What was the gift of the mantle, then?"

"A bond of two hearts, girl. An old spell, but one that is nigh unbreakable when truly accepted. It would've given Thorvald the power of every sea, of every house, if he would've embraced and honored the power that comes from such a bond. My daughter loved Thorvald; she believed he loved her. How wrong we all were."

"What changed?"

Narza smiled sadly. "He got what he wanted, and his true intentions were made known."

He got his perfect heir. Another piece chipped off my heart for Erik.

I let out a rough breath. "You think Erik will be a new Thorvald, but you're wrong. His darkness pulls me closer the same as his light. I want all of him." I was falling in love with all of him. "I only wish his own people wanted the same."

Forget pride, forget what was wrong and right. I wanted Erik Bloodsinger, and I planned to have him for myself.

First, I needed to find him. I turned away from Lady Narza. She let me go, a new shadow in her eyes.

I'd find Erik. Not for answers to a dreary past but to quiet his anguish bleeding into my chest. Wherever he was, he was in the throes of despising himself.

I turned down a long corridor and cursed. Only guards strode the halls. Erik was gone.

Where would he go? I didn't know the palace well, but the urge to find him simmered to the brink of desperation.

"What a grand show." From an alcove window, Fione stepped into the flicker of lanterns. "Not only did you disgrace the most powerful woman in our realm, but your little tantrum has made our king look even weaker, like he needs his little pet to stand for him."

Hells, I tired of them all.

"You know, where I am from, women do not pit themselves against each other over a man and title."

Her eyes were dark, glazed with nothing but scorn. "Then you won't survive long here."

I clenched my fists. "You think him weak, but it is not a weakness to stumble. It is not a weakness to show you have a heart or . . . or to need others to hold you up at times."

"What a child you are. No one holds up an Ever King. They are born to be brutal, unfeeling, and your presence has revealed our king is not. Some think Thorvald would've been better off leaving Erik in your world when he was taken as a child, then creating a new heir."

"You say this, yet you want to be his mate?"

Fione chuckled. "It is inevitable. The lords will ensure the next heir is from the two most powerful houses. Not from some brittle earth fae. Mark me, I will claim a place alongside the king, and ours will be the fiercest bloodline. For I will never ruin my heir like Erik's mother ruined him by giving him too much heart."

I pressed my chest against her, heated anger in my veins. "I come from a land filled with strong kings, and I number Erik Bloodsinger amongst the strongest. He survived wars and torture only to return to his land again and again to fight for the trust and loyalty of his own damn people. He is stronger than you will ever be."

I shoved past her and turned down a corridor, not knowing where I was going, merely following the darkness.

"Livia."

I startled when Celine emerged from a damn wall. "How . . . where did you—"

"I heard you stand for him." Celine shifted on her feet, then all at once wrapped her arms around me. "He's never had someone stand for him. Wouldn't allow it, honestly, but I'm glad you did."

Stunned, a little uncertain, I gingerly patted her back. "Do you . . . do you know where I might find him?"

"Follow me."

36

THE SONGBIRD

COOL CRYSTAL WATER rippled over my bare toes. Celine had pointed me to the narrow cove at the base of the palace gardens. Here, the water appeared like green glass, and the sand was soft and light.

A solitary place, but one I found laden in peace. Opposite to the violent shores near the isles of the fort back home, this place was calm and soothing. Erik's scent of oakwood and clean rain was everywhere. Even the damn stone in the walls seemed to breathe of the king.

The sun bled beyond the horizon, and in the distance, cerulean fins splashed about. The merfolk dove in and out of the rising tides. Their hair was made of all colors—pale as the sand, raven's-wing dark, tree-moss green, even the deep blue of the lagoons.

Merfolk weren't as lovely as the walking sea fae, a touch frightening with their long fingers and orb-like eyes, but I could watch the graceful way they carved through waves all night.

At the water's edge, Erik was seated, knees bent, and in his grip was a green bottle. His hair was tousled, his sword removed and laid in the sand at his side. He'd stripped his boots and dug his bare feet into the wet sand.

Damn the hells, he was haunting and beautiful. Like a thorny rose in a tomb.

I quietly crossed the sand to him. Ten paces away, he tilted the bottle to his lips and took a long gulp. With a wince, the king tossed the bottle aside and let his head droop.

I shook out the sharp nerves from my hands. "Regretting me, Bloodsinger?"

His head shot up. "Songbird?"

"Serpent."

"What are you doing here? I thought you might have convinced Narza to send you home by now. I assure you, she'd find a way to do it."

"I'm not so sure." I sat beside him and hugged my knees against my chest. "I might've scolded her in front of the revel. I doubt she has much interest in helping me."

Erik studied me for a long breath, then his mouth parted in a white grin, and he laughed. "Bold at the strangest times." He faced the shore again. "Go enjoy the revel. It is for you, after all. My absence will soon be forgotten."

"True, I hardly noticed you'd left."

"Ah, I wish I could say the same of you. Unfortunately, I notice your absence as much as I notice your presence."

Bastard. His words caused my heart to beat against my ribs, bruising the edges.

Erik dragged his fingers in the sand. His position barred me from getting too close.

"Are you drunk?"

"Not nearly enough."

"Good. I want your head clear." My lungs burned from holding my breath and protested when I blew it out too swiftly. "Will you answer the question you know I want to ask?"

His jaw pulsed through his pause. My pulse raced, my body

heated, and for a moment I could nearly taste him searching the connection between us.

"You don't want to believe I'm a monster," he said softly. "You want to believe there is more to the story. There isn't, Livia. I'm not the broken hero you wish me to be. I'm the one who slits the hero's throat."

"A monster would not despise himself for taking a life if he did not care."

Erik glowered at the sky. "I'm starting to truly hate this bond."

"Strange. I'm beginning to enjoy it."

Erik's voice was soft when he spoke again. "I killed my mother because I loved her."

I rested my cheek on the tops of my knees. Erik wasn't accustomed to the pushing and prodding of someone caring over the toils of his heart. I wouldn't force it, but he'd left me wholly confused. "Have you ever told anyone about this?"

"Not details. All the kingdom knows is I killed my own mother."

Gods, the weight of it was tearing through his heart. I felt every bit of it.

My fingers trembled as I placed a hand on his arm. "Do you want to tell me?"

"Why do you want to know?"

"Because . . ." I hesitated. "Because I want to see you. All of you."

His eyes darkened, his brows tugged together as if he couldn't make sense of me. Then, slowly, his shoulders slouched, defeated. "It happened right before I was taken by your people for my blood."

"You were that small?"

He nodded. "I was four when the boneweavers theorized what my blood could do. My mother was a sea witch, but the House of Mists carries a great deal of siren blood amongst their people. It was rare to have a blood talent with an added gift of song.

"My father tested it on small fish, then sea birds. My mother hated that he kept forcing me to poison the creatures. She wasn't allowed to say much about my upbringing, of course. Those rules fell to my father. But because of her mother's influence, I was at least allowed to spend my days with her."

"Lady Narza is powerful enough to demand things of a king?" My insides tightened. Perhaps spouting off to the woman was not the wisest.

Erik chuckled. "Regrets?"

"I'll let you know if I end up dead in the morning."

"She won't kill you. No doubt she thinks that will be done at my hand."

I fiddled with the ends of my hair. "She's wrong though, isn't she?"

"She's wrong." Erik hung his head again, fingers drawing in the sand. "Narza gifted my father his mantle when my mother became his mate. She might've threatened to take it back if he denied her daughter the pleasure of having her child near."

I recalled Narza's insistence that the true mantle was a heart bond. If Thorvald had merely loved his mate, Narza would never have been able to strip him of his power.

"I don't know what she said to keep my father compliant," Erik went on, "and I don't care. It gave me my mother, at least."

"You were close with your mother."

"She was my whole damn world, and I hate it."

"Why?"

"Thorvald." Erik's knuckles turned white when his fists tightened. "He took note of how his pathetic heir cared more for the gardens than the sword. How his perfect prince cried whenever his blood killed the smallest fish. To love anyone is a crack in the armor of the king. A pawn to be used against you by enemies."

It was ridiculous and lonely and wretched. I could not imagine a life where my father viewed my mother as the body in which his heirs were born. He adored her. Cherished her. She was his entire world; my brother and I were beautiful additions to him because we were part of her.

"What did your father do about it, then?" I was almost afraid to ask.

"One morning, he took me to the gardens. He told me it was time to truly earn my name as Bloodsinger." Erik closed his eyes. "My mother was there with a guard holding a blade aimed at her ribs. My father took my blood and put it into two horns of wine. He forced her to drink it, then he drank it himself."

My stomach churned in acid. "They were both poisoned."

"I was told to choose who to save. So young, I didn't have the strength to sing for them both."

All gods. I pressed a hand to the ache in my heart. From me or Erik, I didn't know.

He stood with a wince and took a hard step away from me. "You don't need to hear this. It doesn't matter."

I rose and took hold of his arm. If he didn't want my touch, he never said, but he kept his gaze turned away. "It matters, Erik. You . . . you matter."

His eyes were a fiery sky when he looked at me. "I chose her. I chose her and . . . she wouldn't let me. She covered my damn mouth, Livia. My mother shoved me away, demanded I sing for my father, pleaded for me to choose the king.

"She didn't give me a choice. I tried to hurry. I thought . . . I thought I could do it and save them both, but—" Erik scrubbed his hands down his face and started to pace. He only stopped when I went to him, when I put my arms around his waist, when he dropped his brow to mine. "I couldn't finish healing my father's blood before she started . . . gasping and writhing."

Erik let out a rough breath. I tightened my hold on his waist.

"I was too late. I lost her and earned my father's hatred that day. He knew I would've let him die." Erik chuckled bitterly. "Gods, I tried to please him. I would've done anything to make up for it, to earn a bit of pride in his face.

"When I was taken away, I didn't think he'd come for me, but when I saw the ship, I thought he'd finally be proud for how hard I fought. Until he saw what had become of me. He was angry and said his perfect heir was ruined." Erik's palm came to rest on the side of my throat. "He lashed out."

"That's when he attacked?" I whispered.

"It happened so fast. All I really remember is screaming when I saw my father fall into the sea, an ax wound in his heart. He was gone, and all I had were his last words of disappointment."

"Erik." I winced. Unknowingly, Valen Ferus had robbed a heartbroken boy of what he saw as more chances to please a cruel father.

"After that, my uncle kept up Thorvald's attempts to harden the Ever's new king. Soon enough, I was convinced my mother was a weakness in my past and was determined to avenge my father and restore the power of his legacy."

The draw to defend Erik Bloodsinger grew more potent the longer I was near him. Calling it a bond didn't matter; it was real and burned through me like a flame catching wind.

"I know we lived different lives," I said, drawing my palms up his arms. "I know you believe love is a weakness, but it isn't."

"Because love brightens the heart, right? Chases away the darkness inside us all." He scoffed and tried to pull away, but I trapped his face in my palms.

"No." My thumb stroked the edge of his jaw. "Love can bring more darkness than we can imagine. I've seen the lengths my people have gone to protect the ones they love. They embrace darkness, they burn worlds, crumble empires, all to keep those they love breathing. That passion is what won peace in the land realms. Love can be the most violent, the most powerful of weapons, Bloodsinger. Power can be taken away, but that kind of love—that lives beyond the Otherworld."

His gaze blinked to mine. Deep in the gilded red of his eyes was a look filled with the same need, the same hesitation.

"Want one of my confessions?" I whispered.

His hands fell to my waist. "I live for your words, Songbird."

"I've felt calmer here than I have in many turns."

"I don't need to be coddled, love."

"I mean it." I shook my head. "I've felt like I'm going mad because I should hate every moment with you. I shouldn't sleep until I find a way to break free, but . . . I don't want to."

I ached for my family. Gods, I missed them, but somewhere since the night I'd been plunged into the sea, a shift had altered the desires in my traitorous heart. I couldn't imagine returning and being parted from the Ever King either.

"Livia—"

"No one catches you when you fall, Erik. Not even a king can hold such a weight alone." I didn't know what I truly wanted; all I knew was I didn't want him to leave. "What do you do to ease your burdens?"

He swallowed. The look was swift, but I caught how his gaze jumped toward the water. A grin cut across my mouth. He didn't need to say a word.

I slipped my fingers through his with one hand and, with the other, slid my sleeve off my shoulder. "Swim with me."

"You should return to the revel, before—"

"Stop talking, Bloodsinger." I took hold of his other hand and pulled us toward the water's edge. "I want to swim with you. Just you."

37

THE SONGBIRD

"THERE AREN'T ANY toothy creatures that will gnaw off my foot, right?"

Erik stared at me for a breath, bemused. "No, love. Those are in the cove around the bend."

I released his hand and reached for the clasp of my dress behind my neck. "Good. Then there's nothing stopping us."

With the next step, I let the simple dress fall off my body and bunch at my feet. Erik drew in a sharp breath with a curse on his tongue. I'd never been comfortable naked, but there wasn't much he hadn't already seen. The way Erik's eyes darkened to a polished ink whenever he came close, whenever his hands were on my body, had become a new addiction.

He was the first man I wanted to let see me. All of me. A man wrong for me, yet I couldn't stop wanting him. I couldn't find a reason to care that I did.

I stepped into the water until it reached my waist. Erik remained on the sand but stood straight and stiff. Moonlight kissed the slopes of my breasts. As cold as the water was, my body boiled under his scrutiny. His eyes roved from my face to the peaks of my nipples to the planes of my stomach.

"Coming in?" I asked sweetly. Erik shook out his hands and I chuckled. "Bloodsinger, do I make you nervous?"

"No," he insisted. "You unsettle me. There is a difference."

"You are a sea fae who commands the water. I want to see what you can do." I cupped the clear water in my palms and splashed it over my face, letting the rivulets glide over my bare skin. "Come in."

"I don't—" Erik looked over his shoulder for a breath. "I don't allow others to see me."

"I've seen you. You're rather bold at removing your shirt."

"No." He paused. "I've never let anyone see all of me."

I went still as though I'd been plunged headfirst into ice. *I know how disgusting it is for you to look upon such mangled skin.* Shame was potent and hot and grating down my spine. Erik's torture had been showcased in front of his people, used as a weakness, as fuel to inspire hate.

He hid himself away because of it, and I'd mocked him much the same.

I eased out of the water, naked and bared to him. His eyes pulsed when I leaned into his body and lifted my arm, showing off a pink scar.

"I fell on a jagged rock, and my friends made it into a snake by drawing a head on one end." I brushed my hair aside, revealing a scar behind my ear. "Sparring accident against my cousin. Alek told me it was my first battle scar left by a fearsome warrior. He was twelve and skinnier than me."

Four more scars, one on my ribs from stumbling down a rocky knoll while visiting Mira when I was nine. Another on my knee from skidding over rough soil. Two on my shoulders from willow switches Jonas, Sander, and I tried to use as swords until we realized they were more like whips.

Erik gripped my wrist before I could show him the bite mark

under my chin from one of my grandfather's hounds. "You are hardly mangled, love."

My shoulders slumped. "Erik, I said that out of anger. My intent was to hurt you when I didn't think anything could hurt you."

"I'm not hurt."

"Your scars bother you," I whispered, "but they do not bother me."

He scoffed. "Curse me, hate me, but don't lie to me. I know what I am. I know what people see when they look at me."

"What do they see?"

"Something weak," he said in a snarl. "I've spent my entire rule proving what was done to me does not lessen my strength as a king."

"Hmm." My pulse thudded in my skull when I gripped his wrist. "I was raised to see scars as a sign of strength—or, if you are me, a sign of clumsiness. Scars paint our stories; they give proof to the battles we've survived, the trials we've overcome. To me, what I see when I look at you, Erik Bloodsinger, is a king who has faced more than the kings before him."

His nostrils flared when I led his fingertips to my hip bones.

"Songbird," he said, rough and low.

"The more I look at you, the more I want."

"Don't," he warned. "I don't need false praise."

"I'm not saying sweet words to bolster your ego, Bloodsinger." I placed his hand to my thigh. He closed his eyes when I widened my stance. "I'm proving to you what I want."

Before I lost the sliver of courage, I slid his palm over my wet center. Pleasure at the barest touch rolled through me. Erik dropped his forehead to mine, breath sharp.

"Can't you feel how much I want you?" I drew my lips to the hinge of his jaw. "I shouldn't want you, but I do. When I look at you, I see the scars, I see your story written in every beautiful mark."

Erik's brow furrowed. I held to his wrist. Slowly, his fingers teased the heat of my slit. I gasped, arching into him. A low kind of growl slipped from his throat. He eased one finger inside my entrance, then another, exploring me in a way only he'd done, a way I'd only allowed him to do. As though I'd waited for his perfect hands, his perfect touch.

Then he broke away by stepping back.

"You promised you would get me in your grasp, then watch me bleed. You've succeeded in that, and I hate you for it, Songbird." A sharp crack carved through my chest, but before my heart fell out in shambles, Erik pulled my lips close to his. "I am in your hands, I am at your command, for you have made me love you, and you will be my destruction because of it."

My pulse fluttered when Erik reached a hand to the back neckline of his tunic and tugged, pulling it over his head.

Night shadowed most of him, but it was simple enough to make out that he was broad and carved from stone. A body made for sleek, swift battle. Starlight glinted over glossy scars along his ribs, belly, waist, and below his throat. I was certain more were there, but hidden by the dim light.

Sympathy didn't take me as I thought it might. Instead, fierce, possessive violence struck when I brushed my fingertips over the numerous gashes across his chest. This close I could see that Erik had inked most of the taut skin to look like black waves, but there were too many scars to cover.

How many gashes had been cut into a child to steal the blood pumping in his heart? It looked as though dozens of glass shards had cut through his body.

If my people did this, I thought I might hate them.

With a kiss to the center of his chest, I reached for the buckle on his belt and tugged until it unclasped, then dug my thumbs into the waistline of his trousers, pulling down, until the sharp lines of his hips showed more scars and more muscle.

Erik took a step for the water, hands on my hips, brow pressed to mine. When the ripple of tides lapped against my ankles, the king helped me ease his trousers down. I licked my lips when his cock sprang free, thick and velvet. My fingers danced, anxious to touch him as he touched me.

He tossed his trousers and sank into the cove with me. I gasped when the cold water hit my breasts and wrapped my arms around Erik's neck.

A sly grin spread his lips when he raised one hand overhead. Water rippled, then shot for the sky in cerulean walls. As though a dozen waterfalls flowed from invisible cliffs, we were surrounded by the gentle flow. I let out a gasp of delight when Erik swam to each one, me still in his arms, and touched the flow. Some water pulled out the verdant green of the sea, some a soft purple, and some a deep sapphire blue.

It was as though Erik summoned every shade of the tides in a collision of impossible colors.

I stretched my hands out to catch a bit of every shade, laughing as the spray dampened my cheeks.

When I looked back at Erik, his eyes burned in dark desire. His mouth was set in a tight line. I'd never been looked at in such a way, with such heated passion, like without me his world might shatter.

My heart lodged in my throat. I held his unblinking stare and slid the backs of my knuckles down his stubbled cheek. Words were pointless. Deep within my chest, I could feel his want, his possessiveness. It didn't need to be said.

Beneath the water, Erik slid his hands up my thighs. I trembled, and a sharp breath slipped from the back of my throat. He let out a rough growl, hooked my legs around his waist, and slipped a finger into the wet heat of my core again.

My body jumped. Erik tightened his hold around my waist and crushed his mouth to mine.

The kiss wasn't slow; it wasn't tender. It was consuming. All tongues and teeth, like we were desperate to devour each other. Erik drove his finger, then another, deeper inside me. He was cruel and gentle and wicked. Those vicious hands tormented me by dragging me to the edge only to pull back and start again.

Flashes of color brightened around us like a firestorm in the waves.

"Erik." My entire body trembled as I arched into him. He sucked in the hardened peak of one breast. The sharp edges of his canine teeth shocked my blood in a collision of pleasure and pain.

"It's been too long since my mouth has been on you," he rasped against my skin.

When he kissed his way to the other breast, my body writhed, overwhelmed, utterly lost in the rhythm of his mouth and fingers.

Water spun wildly, cascading over my hair, my face. I tilted my head back and arched against him, baring my throat to his tongue and mouth. He nipped and kissed his way over my neck, to my shoulders, back to my lips, as though he couldn't find his favorite place.

He pumped his fingers deeper, pooling heat low in my stomach.

"Gods," I said as my body shook. I matched his pace, rocking my hips against his hand. "Say it. Say you dreamed of me like I've dreamed of you."

"You've haunted me, love. Since the end of that war, I've never forgotten you." He burrowed his face in the soft space of my neck.

My whimpers of pleasure grew louder. Erik covered my mouth with his hand and chuckled with a touch of satisfaction when I bit his palm to keep from crying out. A tangle of emotions, desire and obsession, and . . . something fiercer coiled in my chest. From Erik or me, it didn't matter.

When he tipped me over the edge, I called out his name against his neck in a breathless gasp. Over and over, I called for him. Only him. I adjusted my hips, trying to find the tip of his length, but he shook his head.

Erik nipped at my bottom lip. "Not here."

"Why?" I kissed his throat. "You have me, all of me."

His fingers traced down my spine. "If you think I'm going to let the first time be ass deep in grit and sand, you underestimate me. I will take you, but it will be in my bed."

Damn the hells.

He cupped the back of my head, drawing me close, and spoke with a new sort of longing, dark and fierce. "Be sure before doing this, love. Do this, and I don't go back. You're mine."

A tremble ran up my arms. Buried in the dark timbre of his voice was a threat. A promise. I hesitated for a breath, then kissed him.

"I said I'm yours." I trapped his face in my palms. "I'm waiting for you to become mine."

38

THE SERPENT

I'D NEVER DRESSED so quickly. Even still, my shirt was disheveled, my trousers half laced, and Livia kept snickering at my back, trying to keep her dress from falling down those perfect breasts. This was dangerous, doubtless a horrible idea, but I'd damn us both for more of her.

When we reached the palace, I crushed Livia against me, put a hand on her face, and kissed her briefly. She kept her eyes closed when I pulled away. By the hells, I wanted to memorize every edge, every curve of her features with my mouth, my hands, everything.

"Serpent." Livia's breath heated my lips. "Is this as far as we're going? Because I'm not complaining, I—"

"No." I cupped her cheek and smiled. Unstrained, unburdened. "But we need to be quiet."

"A king sneaking into his own chambers?"

"My face gets seen, and all at once people decide they have need of me."

She slipped her fingers through mine, biting back a laugh as I eased one of the lower doors near the terraced gardens open and led us inside. In the distance, chatter echoed through the corridors from the revel.

Livia clung to my arm, kept pace with my stride, even accounted for the catch of my limp. The sound of heavy boots had us leaping into an alcove, bodies close, foreheads together, laughing softly as a pair of guards strode down the corridor on their patrols.

"Hurry." I tugged her up one flight of steps, taking them two at a time. Livia cursed and squeaked, trying to hold in a laugh when her damp gown caught under her feet.

"I am the one who has a crooked leg," I said, scooping her up under her arms. "Must I teach you to walk?"

She covered her mouth, face red. "Go back to sneers and cutting words, and I might stop laughing." She paused. "Never mind. You do this growl in your throat when you try to be rough, and—" Livia blew out a breath and locked a heated gaze on me. "Quicken your steps, Bloodsinger."

"Gods, woman, I'm not the one falling." I tightened my grip on her hand and finished the climb to the third level before I parted a hidden panel in the wall. "This way."

"I saw Celine use one of these. You never told me you had secret corridors."

"Livia." I drew her mouth close to mine. "I have secret corridors."

She kissed me. A burning kiss, one that bruised my lips, threatened to draw out poison blood. I'd sing her back to health until I drew my final breath if she kept kissing me this way.

The corridor led to my chamber, and the instant we emerged, Livia used her slight body and pinned my back to the wall. She roved her hands down my stomach, drawing out a guttural sound from my chest when her fingertips teased the top of my belt.

I wouldn't survive the night. No mistake, Livia Ferus was unraveling every thread of my being kiss by kiss.

A rough breath slid out of my throat when her sly fingers slid into my trousers and curled around my cock. In the gleam of her eye was something villainous, as though my captive knew that she'd gained all the control, that she was the one in command.

"Love." I gripped the roots of her hair and tried to find purchase to keep upright. "Shit, I'm going to come all over your hand."

"Then you've found out my plan." She purred and dragged her teeth over my neck. "I want to see you unravel the way you've destroyed me."

Livia tugged my trousers down a little more until she had a firm grip on my hard shaft. Her eyes widened with curiosity and heady want as she dragged her thumb over the smooth skin and explored from root to tip.

"Show me," she whispered. I barely heard; my head was too lost in a fog. "Show me how to do it."

Her fingers were silk. They'd brought me to the point of pain if I didn't release soon. Still, the innocent sincerity in her blue eyes brought my hand around hers. I squeezed until her palm added more pressure. I covered her hand as I guided her in slow, long strokes to the tip.

Her thumb brushed over the sensitive crown and I had to brace on the wall when my leg threatened to give out. "Dammit. There, right there. Gods!"

"If I cry your name," she whispered against my lips, "then you better shout mine, you bastard."

This woman.

I bit down on her shoulder. Livia sucked in a sharp breath when the point of my tooth snagged her skin. I licked away the droplet of blood and she repaid me by adding her other hand to create an endless stroke on my stiff cock.

"Livia." I let her name slide over my tongue like liquid gold. Heat gathered too low. "I'm . . . shit!"

Hot white ropes spilled onto her fingers when the release claimed me from the back of my skull to the pit of my gut. My head fell back against the wall as she stroked and pumped the last drops without a hint of shame.

The rich blue of her eyes was black when she pulled away, gaze locked on mine. The smallest curl of a grin played at her mouth. I couldn't catch a breath before Livia lifted her coated fingers to her mouth, then licked what was left of me off her skin.

My mouth parted. I knew she had little experience, but I'd never seen anything more intoxicating, more seductive.

I curled a palm behind her neck, pulling her close. "Get in my bed."

Livia grinned like she'd won some grand victory and backstepped toward the bedchamber.

A knock came at the door. "Highness, are you in there?"

"Leave," I barked.

"My King—"

I was going to murder whoever was outside my door. "Leave. Now."

"Forgive me, My King, but you've received a missive. We believe it to be from another house lord."

Dammit. It could be from Gavyn. He was readying to barricade Livia's people from ever finding her, and all I could think about was pressing her body against mine and having those beautiful legs wrapped around my waist. I was a bastard.

"Go." I pressed a kiss to her knuckles. "I'll get rid of them. I did warn you this happens the moment I enter the palace."

"Yes." She folded her arms over her chest. "And I told you I was willing to get sand up my ass."

Without a word, she spun around and closed the door to the bedchamber.

I knew little about love. Distant memories of a beautiful mother who told me she loved me each day, but everyone else looked at me with fear or disdain. I had a blackened heart, one driven by power and restoring a shattered kingdom, but in this moment, whatever jagged pieces I had to give, I wanted them to be Livia's.

Bring my destruction. Ruin the kingdom from my weakness. But perhaps this was the emotion Livia mentioned—where empires and worlds didn't matter so long as she lived. Preferably in my arms.

Mutely, I tucked my half-hard cock back into my trousers and practically ripped the door open. "What the hells do—"

A steel bolt skewered the air. I'd been trained well enough to be swift, always expecting someone to be preparing to slit my throat. Blade in hand in another instant, I rushed into the corridor as a man donned in black scrambled to escape through one of the windows.

My blade rammed through his shoulder in the next breath. He roared his pain as I tore back the black fabric shielding his face. Young, strong, with eyes like a violent storm.

"Not the cleverest attempt at assassination." I sneered, twisting the hilt of the dagger. He gritted his teeth and puffed out brisk air to keep from screaming. "I'll make this swift if you talk. Keep quiet, and I have countless ways to draw this out. Tell me what you're after."

The bastard laughed. "What will you be without your pet, Bloodsinger?"

It happened too quickly. He maneuvered a slender bit of steel from his sleeve, hand-shaved into a point, and rammed it into the side of his neck.

"Dammit." I covered the fountain of blood, but already, he coughed and spluttered. I readied to give him my own blood and sing him back to health when from behind the door of my bedchamber I heard Livia's distant screams.

39

THE SONGBIRD

DAMN ERIK BLOODSINGER. He'd ignited an insatiable fire in my blood, then left me to burn.

Rationally, I knew a king was often called away on a moment's notice, but the way my body still hummed in anticipation for his hands on my skin, for him to claim me in every way, was a new kind of torture.

I closed the door on him and paced the bedchamber.

Mere moments after the door closed, the latch from the garden door clicked. My heart stilled when three palace guards appeared.

"Lady?" A tall man with oddly dilated pupils spoke. "We were making rounds and saw the light but not the king. Are you well?"

The hair prickled on my neck. "The king insisted no one was welcome in his chambers without his permission."

The chill worsened when another man stepped closer. His eyes were a warm shade of yellow, but the inky pupil was slit like a snake's.

I didn't have time to command them to leave before the third guard, a fae with greasy hair braided behind his neck, rushed at me. Startled, I knocked my hip against the table in the room and fell back. I managed to roll to my side before the guard had his hands on me. Alek was the fighter in our family. Sure strikes, instincts clad in steel, but my moves were swift. Before I'd even finished standing, I had one of Erik's knives kept by the side of his bed in hand.

Blood pounded in my skull when I wheeled back and swung the point, nicking the greasy guard on the cheek.

"Bitch!" He doubled over, tapping his face gingerly.

Snake Eyes had me in his sights. He made his move. I tore a chair away from the table, letting it topple in front of him. He jumped over it but nearly lost his footing on the landing.

Think, dammit!

"You've nowhere to go, Princess," Snake Eyes said. "Nowhere!"

The door leading to the front chamber was on the other side of the guards, but they'd left the garden door wide open. I rushed through it and slammed it behind my back, bolting the lock in place.

Wood splintered when they crashed against it, cursing me with horrid threats.

I drew in a long breath. Think. Breathe. I rushed into the garden and ducked inside a lush shrub tall enough it would strike Erik's chest. Gods, where was Erik? I wasn't fool enough to think he'd been separated from me without intention. This was planned. They wanted the king gone.

I wrenched my thoughts free of the dreary scenarios. He would be fine. He had to be all right. Erik was a damn impressive survivor. Today would be no different. Breath burned in my lungs when the door to the gardens cracked against the side of the palace wall. They were here.

"I want his creature before she touches too much of the darkening," the man with the knife snapped. "Spread out."

I tucked my knees to my chest and gripped a branch until the hum of warm fury magic filled my veins. I needed the leaves thicker, denser. Little by little, the burn of my ability to craft the earth took hold, and the branches eased around me like a knotted cocoon.

Heavy boots shuffled down the stone steps into the garden. The whistle of blades against leaves and branches rattled me to my bones.

Rapid breaths slid through my nose, hardly filling my lungs. Fear and harsh nerves would leave me gutted and bloodied if I couldn't keep my wits while assassins prowled the garden. One look at the soil and a thought pressed against my skull, dancing a violent shudder down my spine.

Before I was born, my father had suffered beneath insatiable bloodlust once and fought every day since to keep the pull for bone and blood sated. Brutality, much the same, lived in me. I'd felt it before, and I'd been running from it for turns.

My fingers stopped trembling when I reached for the soil. Fury burned through my palms. Instead of blooms and sweet little buds on shrubs, I called for something else. I held my breath when the footsteps drew nearer. My palm hovered over the soil; the heat of my magic deepened to a bite. I winced. I didn't move, didn't breathe.

Nearby shrubs rustled. Dried leaves crackled.

A cruel laugh came from behind. "Lookit here. Found myself a little bird."

Anger collided with fear, and it was as if I shielded the softer parts of my heart only to release a different side—a darker piece I never showed to anyone. The corner of my mouth twisted. "I'm no one's bird except the king's."

If ever it is a choice between your life or another's, strangle them with thorns. When I flung my arms open, jagged roots burst through the soil. The points were splintered and sharp, and half a dozen new growths impaled through the man's boots, thighs, through his middle.

He choked and doubled over. With his body bent forward, the fleshy side of his throat hovered over the soil. I stood and gripped the back of his neck. His dilated pupils seemed to widen even more when I held out my free hand, wincing as fury fatigued my muscles.

From the soil, a shard of a root shot skyward, like a broken blade, and rammed through the center of his throat.

He gurgled on his own blood. The splatter of it dribbled down the dark wood, then in the next breath his body went limp, pierced and mutilated over the mutant roots.

I stumbled. Gentle fury could keep me energized for the better part of a day. This sort of violence, this amount of power drained my energy like a sieve, but I had to move. My fists gathered my bloodstained skirt, and I darted back for the door to the palace.

The two other men shouted ferociously across the garden when they caught sight of their brutalized companion.

I didn't look at them; I kept my gaze schooled on the door. A little more, a few more paces. A little—

I screamed when thick arms wrapped around my middle and dragged me down into the soil. A heavy body rolled over my back, and a knee jabbed between my shoulders, pinning me face down. I writhed and thrashed. I cursed and screamed.

Snake Eyes kicked me in the ribs. The harsh tang of blood soaked my tongue. I coughed and groaned, the blow dragging the air from my lungs. I was weakened enough, one guard rolled me onto my back and moved each knee on either side of my hips, straddling me.

Snake Eyes tossed back his dark hood, white teeth bared. Like most sea fae, he was hauntingly lovely, stocky, and built like a wall, with a thick neck and palms. His hair reminded me of rowan berries at the peak of ripeness.

The second assassin came up from behind and stood over me. A thinner man, but the blade in his hand was slim and swift, as I imagined he would be when he sliced up my innards. Snake Eyes reached for my throat. Somewhere in the mud of my brain, I found the strength to kick one foot into the soft point on his knee.

He roared and slapped my cheek.

The second guard yanked my wrists over my head, pinning me in place. Snake Eyes straddled me again. He wrapped one hand around my throat, then slowly lifted my skirt up my thighs.

Snake Eyes laughed. "No wonder the bastard claimed you. You're almost pretty." He spun a small knife in his hand. "At least for now."

The guard holding my wrists kneeled over my arms when I started to roll, giving Snake Eyes freedom to slash his blade across my leg. From inside his cloak, he retrieved a glass vial and pressed it against the trickle of blood.

"You're not going to heal this place for Bloodsinger," Snake Eyes said in a snarl. "You'll have a new master soon enough, pet."

All at once a new kind of rage took hold. Unlike my own, this was dark, vicious. I wanted to skin each guard alive. I knew just how to do it to cause the most pain. A brutal task I shouldn't know but did. They'd beg for death, and when I gave it to them, I'd serve their hearts to the hounds at the gates.

I didn't know hounds were at the gates, yet I saw them plainly in my head.

Air was fleeting. Black spots dotted the corners of my eyes, and I was out of time. I flung my body about as best I could, but the two men were too much.

I didn't see a way out, and I could accept it. Part of me was prepared for death. I would die fighting. I would die before they broke me. I would die with honor and enter the hall of the gods, where I'd raise endless drinking horns with those gone before me.

All I could do was watch as two blades aimed to carve me to shreds. I wouldn't look away. They'd damn well see me as they brutalized me. I stiffened, bracing, but Snake Eyes coughed. He choked.

A hand to his throat, he spluttered as water spilled over his lips. More and more water flowed from his mouth, down his tunic, and he could not take a breath in without gargling more water.

"K-kill her," Snake Eyes choked out. "Said to k-k-kill her if we got the b-blood."

The greasy assassin didn't hesitate. He lifted his blade, ready to slice at my body, but a sudden pressure leveled over my chest.

I tilted my head, afraid and curious to look in the same breath, and a muffled scream, scratchy and sore from my bruised throat, spilled out. Sprawled over my body, covering me like a shield, was Erik. He was heavy and slumped against me. When he shifted, his face contorted in a sharp wince.

I sat up, hands on his shoulders, and choked on my own breath at the sight of the blade pierced just above his hip.

"Erik!" My voice was rough, broken. It was little more than a rasp. I dug my fingernails into his shoulders. "Gods, you're . . . dammit."

"Not the words . . . one wants . . . to hear, Songbird," he said through rough breaths. With a groan, he rolled off me onto his uninjured side.

The assassin choking on the water gasped and staggered to his hands and knees. The second hesitated, as if stunned his blade had found the king. Snake Eyes had turned pallid and had gone silent.

They were going to run.

With the last glimmer of fury in my veins, I slammed my palms over the soil, and the same as the other assassin, barbed roots pierced through their boots, pinning them in place. Alive but screaming in agony as the bloody jagged roots tore through their toes and feet.

I slumped back, then forced my limbs to keep moving and crawled to the king.

The sword remained lodged in his back, and the soft bronze tint to his skin had gone pale. Blood soaked his tunic and the soil beneath him. Too much blood.

Erik let out a curse when he tried to shift. He'd taken a strike in my place. Teeth clenched, I leaned behind him and took hold of his shoulders. When I tried to lay him back, Bloodsinger leaned forward. "Don't."

"Stop shifting," I urged softly. "You'll cause more damage."

For a few moments he resisted, but soon enough, pain or exhaustion took hold, and he slumped onto his side, his head on my lap. Mindlessly, my fingers raked through his thick hair with one hand while my other kept a hand on the hilt of the blade, trying to keep it from sinking deeper.

"I mean what . . . I say, love." Erik lifted his dazed eyes to mine. "Shouldn't . . . touch me. Not with all the blood."

Three hells. I closed my eyes, desperate to steady my pulse. His blood was poison, and here I was practically bathing in it.

He coughed. "Don't get . . . any inside you."

I nodded briskly, shifting my legs to avoid the open wounds of my thighs touching him. He would fight me off if he knew there were gashes on my skin, and if he fought me off, he'd bleed out, no mistake.

"I'll do my best not to eat your blood, Bloodsinger."

Another cough, but it sounded more like the bark of a laugh. He winced. "I should've . . . filled your . . . ass with sand, love."

I placed a palm on his cheek and forced a smile. "You should've, you stupid fool."

"Erik!" Tait's rough voice came from the bedchamber.

"Out here!" I shouted.

Tait filled the garden doorframe, shirtless, and his dark hair wilder, as if he'd been sleeping. Perhaps not alone. Two guards had blades raised at his back, and behind them, Celine and Larsson tried to get a look.

"Get your hands off him." Tait's face twisted with rage.

Well, damn.

How it must look. Blood all over my hands, my grip around the blade stabbed into the king. One dead man, and two more impaled by roots.

In quick steps, Tait was at my side, and yanked my hair. I cried out against the burn, but kept a tight hold on Erik's shoulders.

"Release her, Cousin," Erik slurred. He tilted his chin toward the guards. "Look elsewhere for your king's killers."

You're not going to die. I repeated the thought over and over, afraid to speak it out loud.

"I might," he whispered, glassy eyes on me.

"No. I've seen worse wounds," I whispered. "It'd be a shame to die over this one, Bloodsinger."

"Right." He closed his eyes, a sly grin twisted in the corner of his mouth. "I . . . forgot you were the one . . . with a blade in your gut."

I snorted. My fingers stroked his hair swifter, as though the race of my pulse determined the speed of my touch. "It's not in your gut; it's lower. Quit making this worse than it is to get sympathy."

"Bring Murdock," Tait snapped at Celine and Larsson in the doorway.

"He's drunk," Larsson said. "I mean it. Bastard is passed out in the great hall with his hands on the bare breasts of Sheeva."

Larsson shuddered and grimaced.

"Then get him a damn tonic to clear his head," Tait snapped.

"No time." I tugged on Tait's arm and pointed to the blood pooling under Erik.

Tait's skin deepened to a heated red.

"We need to remove the blade," Larsson said. "It's too near the spine."

"He'll bleed too swiftly," Tait insisted. "Send for the boneweavers in the vales. We will tend to it until they—"

"I can help." I blinked, stunned to realize the words had come from me. But now that they were there, I lifted my chin in a show of determination. "I'm bonded with the king. He takes properties of my fury—wouldn't I take properties of his?"

"She knows he doesn't need a tree, doesn't she?" Celine muttered to Larsson.

My cheeks warmed. "Not earth fury, his . . . healing blood."

No one spoke for a moment, until Erik grunted. "No."

I ignored him and implored Tait. "I can help him."

"You do not have the voice of the sea, Lady," Larsson offered, but his head tilted with a bit of curiosity. "Perhaps your blood might poison him."

Ulterior motives, Songbird?

I pointed my glare at Erik. His brow was coated in sweat, and he tried to grin at his own tasteless sense of humor.

You die, then you take my heart to the Otherworld. Feel that, Serpent.

Erik's eyes darkened against the furrow to his brow. When I tightened my hold around his shoulders, one of his hands gripped my wrist, squeezing gently.

"He can help me," I whispered. "He cannot heal himself, but what if my blood could if he sang?"

"We're running short on time, then." Larsson shoved his hands in his pockets. "I say give the woman a chance. Might be the only way to deal with the king."

"No." Tait shook his head. "There's too much risk."

"Fine, if it doesn't work, then I'll use my earth fury," I said.

"Again, the king needs a boneweaver, not a shrub," Celine insisted.

"My magic connects to the properties of each plant," I said. "Are your boneweaving herbs not plants? I might be able to sense those that can heal him."

"Erik's blood is different, earth fae," Tait snapped. "His blood is not only poisonous, it thins too quickly. Bleeds too much."

"Tell her all my weak . . . weaknesses, Cousin."

Damn fool. I glared at Erik. I hoped he sensed that thought. If his smirk was any clue, I guess he did.

"And he's bleeding too much now." Larsson removed his hat and scratched his sweaty head. "Let her try."

"You're mad." Tait scoffed. "You think I'd let her put hands on my king under the guise that she's healing him?"

I gestured to Bloodsinger's wound. "Do you have a choice?"

"No," Erik warned. "It's too . . . great a risk."

Tait ignored him and glared at me. In the next breath, he had one palm covering my face. I let out a muffled shout but broke it off soon enough. Tait wasn't attacking; he was . . . doing something else.

A slow, gentle hum rolled over his tongue. Tait had a beautiful voice, and the more he sang, the more warmth coated his palm and bled into my skin, and in the next breath it was over.

Tait wrenched his hand away. He flicked his gaze to Erik, then to the guards. "Bring her whatever stores of medicinal herbs we have, and get the king into the room."

40

THE SONGBIRD

LARSSON AND TAIT led him into the bedchamber while Bloodsinger flung curses and promises they'd lose all manner of limbs and parts. Tait was not the king, but he was of the royal line, and with Erik wounded, he fell into his role with ease.

He kept his voice steady, offering direction and commands until Erik was positioned on the bed in a way the blade wouldn't dig deeper.

Celine kept close to the garden door, an occasional twitch to her cheek. I stood a pace away and scrubbed my palms free of soil and blood in a basin near the window.

"What did Tait do to me?" I asked, voice low.

Celine shifted on her feet and kept her eyes forward. "Heartwalker. He read the desires of your heart." She clasped her hands behind her back. "It is the only reason he trusts you enough to be here. Your truest desire must've been to help the king."

I scrubbed my fingernails with more fervor. Tait could actually read the desire of my heart? My desire *was* Bloodsinger. All of him, every scar, every glimpse of his beautiful black heart, I wanted for myself.

I cast his cousin a narrowed look. Tait held my stare for a few breaths, as if trying to break through any lies, any tricks I might've played on his ability.

I didn't look away as I sat on the bed and took Erik's hand possessively. A challenge. A promise. After succumbing to the pull toward the king, I would like to see Tait Heartwalker tear me from him in this moment.

The king was pale, but his face was stone—hard and unmoved. No doubt he hid a great deal of pain but would refuse to reveal it with such an audience. The sight of him tightened my chest, heat fluttering through my insides.

Once three wide baskets filled with vials, pouches, and dried roots were brought to the king's room by three guards, Tait barked, "Everyone out."

The guards abandoned the chamber at once. Larsson opened the door to the garden. "We'll keep watch on those bastards."

Celine followed outside as if she couldn't escape fast enough.

"You realize if your blood can take on his ability, you might end up killing him?" Tait glared at me.

I let out a long breath. Was it worth the risk? Erik was fading. His blood seemed to flow endlessly. My hand touched his clammy skin. He curled his fingers weakly around mine, and the warm hum of power coated my skin. A connection I had with him alone.

"I need to try." I kneeled over the bed and rested a palm on Erik's cheek until he blinked his glassy eyes open. "Erik, I think I need your voice. Will you try?"

He didn't speak but dipped his chin in a nod.

I didn't waste another moment and used one of Tait's knives to slice my palm. One hand on Erik's shoulder, I waited until the same connection that came when we worked together to heal the darkening took hold.

Then, slowly, I placed my bloodied palm against the wound on his side.

A few breaths and his body shuddered. "Gods."

His face contorted in pain.

"Erik." I grappled for him. "Sing. I need your voice. Sing, please."

Tears fell from my cheeks onto his as a gentle, distant hum came from his throat. Soft, dark, beautifully haunting, Erik's voice was a force I absorbed to the very marrow of my bones.

"Blood is slowing," Tait said, a new enthusiasm in his voice. "Erik, keep awake. Keep going."

The wound slowed the weeping of blood, but Erik let out a rough gasp and his head fell back. His breath was shallow.

"Dammit." Tait reached for the baskets. "That's all the help we'll have. You say your earth magic can help, then do it."

My hands trembled as I dug through the baskets of healing herbs. Every few breaths, I'd look at Erik. He wasn't moving. He looked half in the Otherworld. A sigh of relief burned my throat when I found a small leather-bound book with drawings and dosages based on height, male or female, grown or a child.

It seemed boneweavers did like to leave traces of common healing practices despite the ability to heal being embedded in their magic.

The trouble was I did not understand the dosages. The book was written in symbols and languages foreign to me.

"Tait." I held out the book. "I can't read this. See if you understand anything."

He frowned but snatched the book from me. "Murdock wrote his own symbols—probably a symbol for each herb—like his own damn codex. I can read the measurements."

I nodded and removed several vials of powder, running them beneath my nose, drawing them into my lungs.

The burn of every scent sparked the heat of my magic, but it was difficult to focus on the properties with my fatigue. My mind seemed to wander. It questioned and second-guessed.

Royal blood on land, in most cases, birthed powerful fury. Jonas and Sander were horrifying when they truly struck with their nightmares. Mira's magic could cast uncanny illusions. One might think they were trekking up a hillside when, really, they were falling headfirst over a cliff.

Fear of being monstrous as I'd been today had created a rift in my magic. I lacked trust in what I could do.

The slide of steel and leather drew my gaze from rummaging. My heart skipped as Tait held a knife over Erik.

"What are you—"

Tait sliced through the king's tunic, cutting it away. Erik was silent but adjusted enough for his cousin to ease the top off. Only once his skin was bare did Bloodsinger open his eyes to look at me.

In the brighter light of the room, I saw clearly the cruelty written on his skin.

Deep, jagged grooves were carved on all sides of his heart. Sideways, up and down, slanted gashes raised in puckered scars. His belly looked as though claws had scraped back and forth over his insides. Round scars in every divot of his ribs.

Blood still flowed down his side, his legs. Already the coverlets of his bed were soaked in it.

"Earth fae." Tait's sharp voice brought me back to focus. "Tell me the names of the herbs you select, and I will see if I can find any hint of them in the codex."

Nerves wanted to muddy my brain. I fought against the spin of the room, the tremble of my hands. The pain etched on Erik's skin—my jaw tightened—proved he'd endured enough blood loss in one lifetime.

Focus. I straightened my shoulders. I was no healer, but I knew how to find the herbs that could.

"Give me one moment." I opened the vial containing feverroot and placed a sliver of a black leaf in my mouth.

A sharp, earthy flavor sank into my tongue. When I drew my

mind to a still, when I held tight to the risks facing the only man who could both keep me safe and kill me, all the uses for such an herb grew clearer.

Feverroot could be used as a simple seasoning to counteract sweetness or as a blood thickener.

"Feverroot. It can help clot the blood."

Tait flipped through pages of the mender's book, a grimace on his face. He tilted his head to one side. "There is an old language symbol for head heat right here, but the direct translation is close to the word 'feverish.'"

I dipped my chin and measured out the dosages for a man Erik's size and prayed we were right and didn't poison the king.

One by one, I went through the vials. Most were odd names of plants we did not have at home. Fury connected to them, broke them apart, revealed in my mind what uses I might find in each plant. White oak bark for pain and swelling. Hells Mouth Nettles for infection.

Some were useless to us. Herbs to heal an ache in the tooth or blurred vision. I set aside only herbs that had uses for wound care. After I spouted off the properties, Tait would offer any thoughts about old translations.

Erik's breath grew shallower. Tait lifted his eyes off the page of the codex. "We're out of time."

Across the bed were measured powders and liquids. I shook out my hands and took up a damp towel from the washbasin and stood beside Tait's shoulder.

"Be ready," he snarled at me. "There will be a lot of blood."

Some moments I could hardly tell if Tait cared about Erik, the way he sneered and snapped. But now his face was locked in fierce concentration. A bead of sweat dripped over his brow, and it seemed as if it might take a thousand men to peel him back from the king.

Without another word, Tait pulled out the blade.

"Damn you." The king jolted upright.

Tait held him back down. "Now, woman!"

Fury burned in my veins. I couldn't heal bodies through magic, true, but I could add potency to herbs, I could enhance their natural healing properties. "I need the feverroot."

Tait took the measured powder with care and handed it to me. We began a strange dance of adding herbs, stopping the blood, then pressing the remedies into the wound. Tait would push against Erik's skin while I fought not to retch as I filled the wound with herb after herb.

His blood never seemed to cease flowing, and I didn't know how Erik was still breathing.

My body was flushed, strands of hair stuck to my forehead by the time a ghastly-looking mound of herbs was packed into the gash. Like a stone bandage. But the blood had stopped, and the king's skin had a bit more color to it.

I slumped onto the bed, one hand absently falling to Bloodsinger's leg. "I think . . . I think we might've done it."

Tait appeared to be as pale as his cousin. Mutely, he gathered the herbs and filed them back into the basket. "That should hold for now. Go. You look like you've been vomited out of a sickly whale. I'll watch him."

"No." I stood, body trembling, but I took a protective stance in front of the king.

Tait's lips curled enough that I could see the jagged points of his canines. "No?"

"Those men came to kill the king and take me for my magic. I'm not leaving him, since I am the only person in this room who I know does not want him or me dead."

"You think I'd betray my cousin?"

"Oh, I think many things of you." Again, an unnerving desire to defend Erik Bloodsinger took hold. I didn't understand it, but felt a great deal like a rabid pup about to lash out and bite should anyone come too close. "You're the next in the bloodline who can take the throne, right?"

Tait looked ready to finish the job of the assassins. "You don't understand how our world works, earth fae. You don't understand anything about me."

"Nor do you know anything about me." I placed a hand on the bed, positioning my body between Tait and Erik's sleeping form. "There is a debt to be repaid here. Bloodsinger saved my life. Where I am from, that means I owe him. That means I'm not leaving him with anyone I don't trust. And I don't trust you."

For what seemed a thousand heartbeats, we glared at each other. I prayed he couldn't see how desperate my body was to collapse, how much blood I was losing from the gashes on my legs.

At long last, Tait scoffed, a wicked kind of grin on his face. He lifted the basket of herbs and backed toward the door. "All right. You desire to protect him. So do I. I'll guard the outer doors. No one comes into his chambers without me knowing."

"No one touches him without going through me."

Tait chuckled darkly. "And what a fearsome thing you are."

He could mock me all he wanted. I knew I looked as though the Chasm had spat me out; I knew the only reason he was truly leaving was he'd done his trick of reading my heart. It didn't matter. I slumped on the bed in relief when Tait left with a final word that I was to inform the king if he woke that the assassins would be taken to the prisons beneath the palace.

My head spun as though locked in a fog. I checked the bandage on Erik's waist once. My fingertips brushed the top of a thick, puckered scar on his hip bone that trailed beneath his trousers.

While he slept, Erik was softer, almost peaceful. I brushed a bit of dark hair off his brow.

"Don't die, Serpent," I whispered. "I'm not finished with you."

41

THE SERPENT

CLUMSY HANDS PRODDED at the wound in my side, drawing vomit to my throat from the pain, and I wanted nothing more than to cut them off.

A looming form hovered over me in the dark, and loud nasally breaths blew against my face.

"Murdock," I said, voice rough. "Touch me again, and you lose your fingers."

The boneweaver smelled of sweet ale, but his eyes were clear when he glared at me. "Your flesh is packed with more linens than your bedding, Sire."

No wonder it felt as though my ribs were made of stone. Still, I swatted him away. "That stuffing kept me breathing, no thanks to you."

Murdock's bulbous cheeks flushed in a deep rouge. His hair was shorn to his scalp, and his head seemed too small for the plumpness of his body. If the bastard hadn't built up an immunity to my blood, I'd send him to the far seas to heal spiked silverfish for the rest of his days.

"Next time, do try to avoid getting stabbed on the first true revel in turns."

"An excuse you made up in your own head." I propped myself

onto one elbow, wincing at the tug of skin beneath the bandages. "You are boneweaver to the king. There are no excuses."

Murdock rolled his eyes and pointed to a tray beside the bed filled with varying vials of powders and tonics. He went through each one, describing how it would help with the healing, the pain, even the potency of my blood until the wound sealed.

"Then, of course, here is a serenleaf tonic should the nightmares continue."

I narrowed my eyes. "You're losing your touch, and I'm rethinking my decision to keep you in the employ of the palace. No mare demons have touched my head."

"Ah, My King." Murdock chuckled and stuffed his leather satchel with the supplies he didn't plan to leave. "I'll remain in your employ not only because you trust me with your life, but because I am the greatest boneweaver in the royal city. Perhaps the whole of the Ever."

I balked. "Tell that to Poppy."

"The old hag—"

"Your aunt."

Murdock ruffled. I took a great deal of pleasure drawing out the unspoken rivalry between my boneweaver and Poppy.

The man cleared his throat, mouth tight, and held up the vial again. "As I was saying, for the nightmares. Not yours, my arrogant King. For your claimed." He waved toward the door leading to my mother's tattered gardens. "The girl hasn't slept in the two nights you've been healing."

Two nights. I sat up too abruptly and cursed when fire bit along the edges of the wound. In all my muddled thoughts, Livia had slipped through the cracks. She'd stayed with me; she'd bleeding saved me.

"Where is she?"

"Wandering." Murdock tucked his satchel beneath his thick

arm with a sigh. "Well, it has been another pleasant visit. Follow my instructions, and I shall look in on the wound in the morning."

I wasn't listening. I kicked my legs off the edge of the bed and yanked my boots on. The wound ached, but I was no stranger to pain and buried it until all that remained was a dull jab in my side. Outside, the top tier of the garden was empty but for the blood and bits of flesh still mangled on jagged roots in the soil.

Shit, I'd forgotten. Livia impaled one of the bastards before trapping the others, nearly lost her life for it.

One hand on my side, I spun around, an unease that was not my own growing heavy in my stomach. Where was she?

On the shore of the cove, a dim lantern flickered and cast ghostly shadows over the curves of a woman. I quickened my steps down the staircases, carving through each garden tier until my boots sank into the damp sand of the beach.

Livia paced, eyes on the sea. She was wearing a pale dress with the bodice laces loose and open over her chest. I'd never been truly struck silent before, as in words couldn't form. I was too absorbed in the smooth curves of her legs, her wild dark hair whipping around her cheeks.

Much the same as I'd been struck when I caught sight of my songbird buying ribbons for her masquerade, I was lost to her now.

"Erik." Livia startled when she turned to pace in the opposite direction. Her blue eyes narrowed on my bandages. "You shouldn't be up. You'll split the skin open."

"I've dealt with flesh wounds before," I said lightly, but there was a harsh truth to it. "Why are you wandering about after more than one blade nearly took your head?"

A furrow of worry gathered between her brows. "Celine assured me your private gardens and cove were well guarded. At least, she told me they were ridiculously guarded, and if you never want another person to enter, your guards will make it impossible for folk to do so."

Her words rambled and quivered, and the longer she spoke, the tighter her grip wrenched on the lantern's handle.

I limped toward her, unashamed of my wince. She saw the damage; there'd be no point hiding it. Livia didn't back away. She held my gaze, unblinking, and her chin quivered just enough to be seen when I curled a hand around her wrist.

"Why are you out here, love?" I asked again, softer than before.

She sniffed. "I killed a man."

"And he doesn't deserve your tears."

"He was still a someone. I . . . I . . . I've never killed anyone, and I thought . . . I suppose I thought I should feel some great remorse, but it hasn't come, and I keep thinking what sort of woman does that make me? I could've snared him like the others, but I chose to kill him. My fury can be dark and dangerous, and I knew it. I wanted to kill him. Because I knew they'd come to kill you. I've never felt so . . . so violent."

She'd bloodied her hands to save me. Beautiful, reckless woman. If I was not cautious, Livia Ferus would unravel my every dark, wretched belief of what I was to become as king. Of what I deserved.

I placed my hand on her cheek, my thumb tracing the gentle line of her lip. "I know the feeling."

Livia let out a sigh and rested her forehead against mine. "Every time I try to sleep, I replay it over and over, as if my mind is trying to find some shred of humanity, some proof I'd exhausted all my options. But I keep realizing I killed because I could. Because I wanted to and—"

"Livia." I clasped her face between my palms, silencing her breathless words. She hiccupped and drew in a few more sharp gusts of air through her nose. My thumbs stroked the ridges of her cheeks until her shoulders slumped. "You killed a man who tried to kill you."

She shook her head, ready to argue the point.

"Yes." I wrapped an arm around her waist, palm open on her back. The movement—hells, even standing—was beginning to unravel the healing skin on my side. I hardly cared. "Taking a life is no small thing, but doing so to save your own does not make you a monster."

A tear fell onto her cheek. She let her head drop until her brow pressed against my chest. "What if I am?"

For a moment, I hesitated, then placed a hand on the back of her head and held her against me. "Then you are the most beautiful monster I've ever seen."

Livia's fingers curled around my shirt. Her cheeks lifted into a hidden smile.

"We all have darkness in us." I closed my eyes, recalling the words my mother spoke to me before she died. "But there is beauty in the darker pieces as much as there is in the light. We find it by how we use our darkness. What were you thinking when you killed him?"

Livia lifted her head. She used the back of her hand to wipe a trail of tears away. "I was thinking he'd kill me, then . . . he'd kill you. They wanted to use my fury to steal your throne. They wanted credit for saving the Ever. But . . . mostly I knew they would hurt you."

"You protected folk from a dangerous ruse," I said, guiding her out of the scenario. "That is darkness well spent."

Her eyes were red from fatigue and tears. Her body trembled slightly. She needed to sleep. The gentle roll of water over the sand was soothing, and Livia seemed drawn to it.

I tilted my head to the stars. With a bit of reluctance, I released her and lowered myself to the sand. My leg throbbed. My side burned. No mistake, I probably moved like I'd met my thousandth turn, but once I was seated, I sprawled my legs out and lay back.

"What are you doing?"

"Lie with me," I said, opening one arm to the side. "Let the worries rest for a moment."

She paused for a few breaths, then slowly lowered to her knees, then her side, and curled against my body.

"I kicked you at the fort," Livia whispered. "Does your leg still hurt terribly after all this time?"

I cradled her head against my chest, chuckling. "Ah, don't sound so hopeful, love."

I jolted when she bleeding pinched me, then snickered into my shirt. "I wasn't hopeful, you bastard. I was starting to get slightly concerned—hardly worth noting, it is such a finite amount."

No doubt, she'd unravel all of me.

"You kicked—a rather sloppy kick at that—an old injury," I admitted. "When I was taken captive for my blood, I tried to run, but didn't realize how high the room was from the ground. Snapped the bones of my leg straight through the skin. Never healed right."

The truth was the bones were never allowed to heal right. I'd been left to become a symbol of the brutality of our enemies in the hope our people would fight for Harald's revenge and win him the power of the lands on either side of the Chasm.

Livia nestled closer. "I hate what was done to you."

"Yes, well." I was desperate to talk of other things. "There's nothing to be done about it now."

Livia gingerly fiddled with the laces of my shirt. "I'm sorry. No one from my clan has likely ever said it to you, but I'm sorry for what my people did."

Gods, I was a bastard for truths I kept unsaid.

I cleared my throat and raised a hand, pointing at the sky. "Do you see that star, the flickering one, right over the horizon?" Livia tilted her head and nodded. "Good. Follow it to the star on the northern point, then across, and down. Do you see the line of three?"

I lifted her hand in mine, extended her finger, and together we traced the stars.

"What is it?"

"His name is Voidwalker." The corner of my mouth twisted. "A fearsome warrior who can cross worlds. See his head, then his steady arrow he holds?"

Livia squinted. "Bit of a stretch, but I suppose it might look like a man with an arrow."

"Watch what you say about his likeness, or he may never lead you straight and you'll be lost to the tides." The corner of my mouth curved. "When we sail the Ever Seas, Voidwalker leads us. That point of his arrow remains throughout the seasons, steady and sure. It is the only star that follows us through the Chasm and connects to your sky, Songbird."

I lifted her hand again. "Follow that string of five. See how they tilt and curve as though spilling over a ledge?"

"I see it."

"She is named Starfall. A lesser goddess who was shunned from her mother, the maker of sea storms. Her mother is a wretched woman who uses the skies to devour sailors and their vessels. Now, to be a constant thorn in her mother's side, Starfall fades on nights before the sky turns violent, giving ships the chance to make berth or tie back sails."

Livia snickered. "Sounds like a terror for her mother."

"I rather like her tantrums. Saved my ass a time or two." Once more, I raised her hand to a trio of stars straight overhead. The center star gleamed brightest while the two on the sides seemed to flicker dimly, then bright. "But Nightfire, he is who I wanted you to meet. Cursed to remain in the sky for his acts against the gods."

"What did he do?"

"Saved his love from the clutches of arranged vows. He slaughtered the whole of the marital feast and hid his lover away, deep in the skies. For his crime, he was chained in the sky, and the only way he might get free is if his love finds her way back to him by using the stars of his blade as her guide. The trouble is they never stay as bright as the center star. See that? She can't find her way."

"That's a sad tale, Bloodsinger."

"It's not finished." I eased her pointed finger across the heavens to a star nearest the pale moon. It blazed in a cold blue glow. "She improvised and made a barter with the goddess of hearts. She would give up her life on the lands and become a beacon for her love to find his way to her instead. She loved him for his darkness, you see. Even after the blood he'd spilled, she wanted to live out her days with him. To her, he was a beautiful monster."

Livia yawned, voice soft and slurred. "Did he find her?"

I looked down. She'd closed her eyes and draped one arm over my stomach. I tightened my hold on Livia's shoulders. "I think he did."

42

THE SERPENT

"ERIK." CELINE SLAPPED my shoulder, voice rough. "Get up."

If one more person woke me by striking me or prodding my gaping wounds, I would use their bones to strengthen the hull of my damn ship.

"Tidecaller, if—"

"Gavyn's back." Celine's voice cracked. "You must hurry. Something's happened."

Livia sighed in her sleep, head against my chest. We'd remained outside near the water. I'd counted the constellations of the Ever until her soft breaths lulled me back into a dreamless sleep. My arm tingled in numbness from keeping it wrapped around her all night, but I'd hold the woman every night if it chased away the dark dreams.

Now I was torn. When I'd last rushed off to leave her, she ended up pinned in the garden, and I added a new scar to my collection.

"I'll stay with her," Celine said, as if she could read my thoughts. "I swear to you, I won't let anything happen to her. This . . . this involves her too, and you're running short on time."

"Where is he?" I asked, gently easing away from Livia. Her face pinched, and she tucked her knees closer to her chest against the chill once my body was gone.

"In my bedchamber."

Celine would never betray me. She'd lose too much if I were ousted as king. "I vowed she'd be safe," I told Celine. "Do not break my promise."

She gave me a nod, and for the first time I saw the tears in her eyes. Something had gone horribly wrong. I pressed a kiss to Livia's forehead and hurried to the lower levels of the palace.

By the time I arrived, the ache in my side was hot and irritating. No doubt, the wound in my side wanted to split open and bleed out. I'd deal with Murdock's complaints later. Celine's chambers were spacious for one person, but with the bodies in the room, it was cramped.

"What the hells happened?" I held my side and hurried to the window.

Gavyn was seated, sweat on his brow, teeth gritted, and face pale. "I might . . . say the same to you." He tried to grin, but it ended in a wince.

Gashes lined Gavyn's bare shoulder, like he'd been slashed by a dozen knives, and Sewell was on his knees, splinting Gavyn's crooked wrist. "Bad tides, little eel."

"The Chasm did this?"

"Not exactly, it—godsdammit!" Gavyn glared at Sewell as the cook tightened the knot keeping the splint in place.

All Sewell did was give Gavyn's cheek a hard pat, then Tait emerged from the washroom holding a basin and clean linens.

"Why is Tait here?" I glared at Gavyn. "Sharing our plans with everyone?"

"Good thing he did, or I wouldn't have been waiting for him and he would've bled out," Tait snapped.

"Always one for overexaggerating, Heartwalker." Gavyn started to chuckle but cursed when Sewell tapped his cheek again when he moved too much.

"Gavyn will heal," Tait said, "but right now, we have bigger problems."

Bleeding across Celine's narrow mattress was another man. A damn earth fae. His breath was shallow and broken. His skin was battered and covered in open gashes, much like Gavyn's shoulder.

"I made it through, but before I could shield the Chasm or even deliver your claim on . . . on the woman," Gavyn started, pausing every few words through his own pain, "he was there . . . like he was waiting for me. I tried to turn back, but . . . he held on and . . . you see what became of him. It crushed him."

"Peeled you good and deep too. Lies on your tongue, boy." Sewell narrowed his gaze at Gavyn and finished securing the splint on his wrist.

Gavyn blanched. "I didn't lie. I was trying to take care and was safe until I wasn't! Can't exactly fade into the tides completely with a damn leech on my back."

I studied the bloodied face of the man. I knew him. The day the sea fae were banished from the earth fae realms, he'd been there. A boy like me, tucked between his battle-worn fathers, but he looked at me like he knew the truth. Like he knew the secret we all were keeping.

"He's dying, Erik," Tait said softly. "What are you going to do?"

My jaw pulsed. Do this, and he might find a way to take her from me. Perhaps she'd see him and realize there were ways to leave the Ever. I could let him die. Cut off her world for good. Keep her here always.

She wouldn't know if I let him die.

But I would.

With a harsh sigh, I peeled back the bandage from my waist and dipped my fingers into the trickle of blood seeping through the herbs and thin stitching Murdock had placed. When the tips were coated, I approached the bed. "Hold him still."

Tait hesitated for a moment but complied. He tipped back the fae's head, exposing a wide gash on his throat, and I dragged my fingers through the blood.

The door crashed open.

"Tried to stop her!" Celine called over Livia's shoulder.

Anger burned in my throat. "Then why didn't you?"

My songbird filled the doorway, eyes wide with panic. "Aleksi!" She looked from my bloodied fingers to the man on the bed. "Erik, no, don't do this. Please."

"She said she felt you and took off!" Celine insisted.

Damn bonds. She knew I could heal, but it was as if my own unease and her panic had set her off in a frenzy.

"Hold her," I shouted when Livia tried to rush at me.

"Bloodsinger." She struggled against Celine's grip. Tait went to aid her. Tears dropped on her cheeks when I swiped my bloodied fingers across her cousin's throat.

Livia thrashed and screamed. "Erik, stop. Gods, stop!"

I held her glassy eyes, then leaned my face alongside his. Livia stopped the fight, eyes red, and watched in stun as I started to hum. Low, deep, haunting.

A sharp burn gathered in my chest as it always did with the healing. To poison with my blood was simple. To use it to heal was deeper, more challenging, as though it took bits of my own strength and gave it to the one stepping into the Otherworld.

With a wound in my side, the song was agonizing. Livia drew in a sharp breath when the tune strengthened. I closed my eyes, gripping the edge of the bed. Her cousin coughed. His chest heaved, and it was as if he were gasping for air.

"Stop! You're killing him."

"Hush," Tait snapped, and pulled her back. "Let it be."

"Erik!"

I clenched my jaw, body trembling. "Take her out of here."

Poison or healing, it wasn't pleasant. I couldn't lose the song, or he would die.

Livia's face was bloodless when Tait pulled her back into the corridor. Even Sewell abandoned Gavyn's side to help drag Livia away. She screamed and cursed and promised violent things that cut off when Celine closed the door.

I blew out a breath, painful fatigue taking hold. I lowered to my knees and placed my palms on the sides of her cousin's face.

"You better live, you bastard. If you die and she despises me again, I will take back what I did for you during the war." I closed my eyes and sang.

43

THE SONGBIRD

BETRAYAL STUNG DEEP in my bones. A molten blade to my heart. More so when Sewell was the one who added a touch of serenleaf onto my tongue when I couldn't seem to get my bearings.

Why was Alek here? He'd—gods—he'd looked as though a dozen blades had cut at him, then two dozen boots had stomped over his bones. Erik offered my cousin blood. Poisoned blood. Maybe in his mind, he thought he'd put Alek out of his misery—until he'd started to sing, more distinct than I had ever heard before. Smooth as satin, haunting as shadows, a sound that dug and clawed beneath the skin until it was etched into the bones.

More than the sea singer, Erik's song hooked me by the heart and pulled me forward to anywhere Bloodsinger might be.

Then he banished me.

"Sewell." I crossed the small study where they'd dragged me away. "Take me back. Now."

The cook looked to Tait, who then looked down at the odd clock he kept in his pocket.

With a nod, Tait tucked the clock back into his trousers. "Danger's gone."

Celine took my hand with a bit of hesitation. "We had to take you away. You were straining his song."

Questions and anger and fear—all of it tangled into silence instead. They led me through the corridor back to the chamber. I didn't know what to ask first. When Erik sang, it healed, but could it heal such damage? Why was Alek here to begin with?

Gavyn had something to do with it. In my frenzy, I'd noticed the lord was bloodied and bandaged. I wanted to know everything. I couldn't ask any of it.

The hot tang of blood still soaked the floorboards. Gavyn was absent, and all that was left were two men seated as far as possible from the other.

Erik's sunset eyes were glazed, and he slumped onto his elbows over his knees. At the sight of me, his lips twitched like he might want to smile but couldn't find the strength.

"Livie." Alek's soft, broken rasp snapped relief through my heart. Upright, seated on the edge of the bed, he was still coated in blood but was breathing.

"Alek." I rushed to him and flung my arms around his neck. "What . . . what are you doing here?" My hands padded over his shoulders, the bandages, the shreds of his Rave tunic. "What happened?"

He dropped his head to my shoulder and hugged my waist. "We've been trying to get through since you were taken. So many ships have been swallowed up, so many Rave lost. Your daj . . . he tried to bend a damn canyon through the sea. We couldn't get through."

I held his face in my hands. His gilded eyes, which Jonas always told him looked like a goat's, were red with tears. "You swam through?"

He shook his head. "Rave watched the Chasm night after night. I took every bleeding shift, then it opened again. This fae materialized like he'd been sea mist, then shaped into a man. I didn't hesitate, and—" Alek glanced at Erik. "I glamoured him."

Alek's magic was different than mine. Adopted from the bloodlines of Southern realms into the Night Folk clans, he held trickier magic than earth fury. Any beating heart within my cousin's sights, if Alek wanted them in his command or grasp, could be summoned to his side as though he caught them in a snare.

"The instant I touched him, he turned back into mist again," Alek said, "but it dragged me through."

Gavyn. I didn't know what Celine's brother could do with his voice, but he had to be the fae who'd turned to mist. He'd been sliced from the rage of the Chasm along with Alek.

"Did you send the House of Bones through the Chasm?" I looked over my shoulder.

Sewell stood beside Erik, forcing the king to finish a drink made of something that smelled of pine and salt. More color tinted his face, and his eyes were the familiar intoxicating burn of red. He rose without a wince.

"Yes. To avoid this, Songbird." He gestured at Aleksi. "I wasn't giving you back, and I didn't want all your damn people killing themselves trying to get through for nothing."

My heart battered my ribs. "I wonder why you care, Bloodsinger. Didn't you want them all to die?"

"I don't think you need to wonder, love." Erik leaned casually against the wall, that irritating perfect smirk on his lips. "You know why."

I didn't know if I wanted to slap the man or kiss him. Likely a little of both.

"Bloodsinger." Alek stood, movements slow and achy, but he kept the straight stance of a Rave warrior and faced Erik. "Release my cousin. I'll gladly take her place to repay the debt owed—"

"Do not speak another word," Erik warned and shoved off the wall.

Alek didn't listen and barreled on. "You saved my father; the penance owed should fall to my house, not Livia's."

My stomach plummeted to the soles of my feet. Erik trembled with a desperate kind of rage and gripped Alek's tunic, slamming his back to the wall.

"Erik!" I gripped his arm, trying to pull him back, but froze when he spoke.

Face close to Alek, he hissed each word through gritted teeth. "Speak again and you damn us both."

"You know there is a debt to be paid," Alek said, voice low and dark.

"I cleared our debts that day."

Alek scoffed weakly. "I will always be in your debt."

"What are you talking about?" My fingernails dug deeper into Erik's arm, but my attention was locked on my cousin.

Erik released Aleksi and backed away. "Nothing."

"Don't lie." I snatched hold of the king's wrist. "Curse me, hate me, but don't lie to me."

Erik glowered. I didn't shrink beneath the heat of his stare. It was more proof of the secrets he kept.

"She should know." Alek's eyes darkened. "To explain to our people why I stayed."

"You are not staying." Erik jabbed his finger in Alek's face. "And she is not leaving."

"Let her go." Aleksi was close to pleading. "Do whatever you want to me. Torture me, make me the whore, just stop hurting her. Let her be free."

His eyes took in the bruises on my neck, my cheeks. Oh, the things he misunderstood.

"He's not hurting me, Alek," I whispered. "But one or both of you will tell me what you're talking about."

The door closed. Tait stood against it, hands in front of his body, but the others were gone. "No one can hear now."

"I'm going to murder you," Erik growled.

Tait simply shrugged.

Alek wheeled on me, barring Bloodsinger from us, and took hold of my shoulders. "I've never told you. No one even knows that I saw the truth. Daj"—he closed his eyes—"Tor, he was struck during a battle. A blade to the heart, Liv. He died."

I shook my head. The horrors I felt when my fury had shown me a bloody death and the anguished pain of my uncle Sol for the death of Tor flashed through my mind.

"Stop," Erik said through gritted teeth. He stared at the floor, fists clenched.

Alek tightened his hold on my shoulders. "I saw it."

"H-how?"

"You remember what it was like being cooped up in that fort, not knowing. I wanted to fight alongside my fathers. I wanted to be there, so I snuck out. I saw . . . I saw my daj on the ground, everyone huddled around his body."

"He wasn't dead; his heart still had a slight beat." Erik made a move for Alek, but stopped when I held up a hand.

"Then he was a damn breath away from the Otherworld," Alek snapped and turned back to me. "Bloodsinger was in a tree speaking with Stieg, then I watched him use his blood to heal Daj. Bloodsinger brought him back like he'd never been wounded."

My heart stopped. A fog clouded my mind, but I managed to school my gaze on Erik. He didn't look away. He didn't deny any of it. The Ever King hardened as he once did, as though any word from me might cut worse than the assassin's blade.

"I told you I felt him die." Perhaps my uncle hadn't been in the

Otherworld, but if my fury had felt his body fading, he'd been moments from death. My voice steadied. "Again, I wonder why you would heal an enemy. Not just any enemy—the people you told me tortured you."

"That's what you told her?" Alek scoffed. "Our folk didn't torture him, Livia. They saved him and brought him to his father."

My breath caught. It didn't make sense. Why would he despise them if they were the ones who saved him?

It isn't so simple. Erik's voice filled my heart.

He looked nowhere but me. I blinked through a sting in my eyes. *You let me hate them for you. You let me think horrid things of my own family.*

"Stieg told me the truth after you were taken," Alek went on. "I couldn't grasp the random moves of the Ever King, so he explained the history."

All I've had is hate, Songbird. Hate and a drive to avenge the last Ever King. You hate long enough, you shadow the truth, all to keep away anything that makes you feel.

I studied him for a long pause. *You have more than hate now.*

"That's why my daj was near enough to kill your father," I said softly. "He was bringing you back. You told me yourself Thorvald lashed out after seeing the torture. But it wasn't from my family, was it?" I pressed a hand to my head when my thoughts swam, when my pulse grew to a frenzy.

"I need you to breathe, Songbird."

I snapped my gaze back to his. "They fought smaller wars before facing the sea. You were a captive of their enemies in our realms, weren't you?"

It never made sense to me why Thorvald came to the shores so long ago and attacked a woman. The sea hadn't been fighting my people—not yet at least—but it was the catalyst that caused a rift between our people. A step toward the final war.

"How do you know Stieg, Erik?"

He shook his head and turned his back on us, hands in his hair. Tait's mouth tightened, but he dipped his chin, as if telling me to keep going, keep pressing.

"You saved my uncle." I curled a lock of hair around my finger, pacing. "You tried to close the Chasm to keep my people from losing their lives by trying to cross through."

"Don't ask me more."

"Why? Is the answer going to reveal you have a heart you're so afraid of showing?

I'm not your broken hero, love.

I nodded, hardly recognizing that the words were felt, not heard. "You're not my hero, Bloodsinger. You're my beautiful monster."

He flinched as though I'd struck him. Alek arched a brow and bounced his gaze back and forth between me and Erik.

"You saved my cousin when it does nothing to benefit you."

"No one said I wouldn't use this to my benefit."

I folded my arms over my chest and stepped close enough that our noses nearly touched. "How do you know Stieg, Erik?"

He frowned. "It doesn't matter. None of this changes anything. We are still here, you are still mine, and there is still no peace between our people."

I'd learned enough about the Ever King to recognize that when he was pressed to reveal a heart beneath the hate, he lashed out.

In this moment, Erik was the man back on the ship throwing knives at crewmen.

Instead of turning away, I leaned into him. My palms slid up the sides of his arms. He stiffened. I raked my fingers through his hair at the back of his head and tilted his brow to mine.

"Everything has changed, Serpent." I brought my lips close to his ear so only he could hear. "You don't need to hate for him anymore, Erik. You don't need to please him; you've always pleased me."

His hands gripped my waist. "I took you away. Hate me, Songbird, or you will be my undoing."

"You took me," I whispered. "I should hate you for it, but you showed me your darkness. Turns out I'd cross the skies—or seas, in our case—searching for your kind of darkness, Bloodsinger."

He let out a sharp breath and closed his eyes.

I needed answers, but more than that, I needed him. "Come with me."

Before he could grumble or protest, I took his hand and tugged him toward the door. Erik glanced back at Aleksi, whose brow furrowed in confusion. In the corridor, Sewell and Celine still stood guard at the door.

"Will you keep watch over my cousin for me?" I asked.

"More damn foxes." Sewell sighed but patted my cheek. "Safe and sound."

That was all I needed before I pulled the king toward the stairs leading to his chambers.

44

THE SONGBIRD

NO GUARDS STOOD outside his doors. Erik no longer trusted anyone close to me, and instead, three bulky men from the Ever Crew kept a distance from the doors, blades in sight.

They grunted a greeting when we reached the door. Blood pacts kept the Ever Crew loyal. They were brisk and had no propriety, but they'd fight for their king like they'd fight for anyone on their crew.

When the lock clicked, I wheeled on him. "You've saved more of my people than you've killed."

"I wouldn't say that. I did plenty of killing during the war."

"You're infuriating," I said, pressing my chest to his. "Why did you lie to me about what happened to you?"

"I never lied," he said. "I told you land fae drained me for their use. They did."

"You let me think my family—my parents—were the ones responsible."

Erik hesitated. "An omission that wasn't supposed to matter. *You* were never supposed to matter, but you do. You ruined everything, and I don't care. Ruin me. Destroy me. As long as I have you."

Wretched, beautiful man.

I kissed him. Hard. Erik groaned and wrapped me in his arms, crushing me to his chest. His muscles relaxed, as if my touch were a surge of peace that could finally bring his anger, his pain to rest.

With me still in his arms, Erik walked me backward until my back struck the wall.

My palms slid down the planes of his stomach and reached his belt. He released me and flattened his palms on the wall beside my head. "Songbird."

"Serpent." My voice was rough, like I'd swallowed sand, as I freed the buckle on his belt.

"Don't do this because you feel a debt from what you heard today."

Vulnerability on the Ever King was a new cracked edge in his hardened shell. I wanted to slip through and never leave. There was meaning in his words. Hesitation, hope, and fear. He thought I wanted him out of obligation. He thought I was giving myself to him because he'd saved my uncle.

I flattened his palm over my heart. "This has always been yours. Before any bond, you pulled me to you in that cell, and you never stopped. Don't doubt me, for I tried to do this at the cove and you went and got stabbed."

He chuckled, then dropped his head to my shoulder. "My warning still stands. Do this and I'll never give you back."

I cupped one side of his face. "Be sure before you do this, Serpent. Do this, and I claim you."

His eyes flared in a dangerous kind of desire. One heartbeat, and Erik had his mouth on mine again. Desperate, heated, and lined in a touch of anger for pushing him so far, the king claimed my mouth as though it might be the last time.

His tongue slid against mine. He gripped my hair and pressed all his weight on my body. Trapped against the wall, unable to flee, I'd never felt so safe.

Erik's mouth abandoned my lips and roved down the slope of my throat. The scrape of his teeth, the nip beneath my ear, drew out a soft moan. He bit harder and a collision of pain and desire flooded my veins. My core throbbed when I arched against him, searching, needing more.

He grinned against my skin, then with one hand gripped my wrists and pinned them over my head. Heated kisses down my neck, over my chest, sent shock waves pulsing through my body. His teeth and tongue marked me. They bleeding claimed me all over again.

Erik lifted his head for a heated breath, then scooped me under my thighs and hooked my legs around his waist. He carried me toward the bedchamber. If the limp to his step caused him any pain, he didn't show it, only dug his fingertips deeper into my skin when I kissed him.

I sucked his tongue. He moaned and quickened his pace.

A shriek of surprise sliced through the kiss when Erik flopped me onto my back on the bed. He reared over the top of me, propped up on his elbows, careful not to crush me into the bed, but I didn't want careful. This moment—hells—it felt like I'd been waiting for this, for him, all my life.

I clawed at his shirt until it was stripped off his shoulders. His scars were bare and open, but Erik didn't flinch, didn't shy away. The wound on his side was bandaged and stitched, but it could split. With his palm against my face, Erik guided my gaze back to his. He shook his head, mutely telling me to focus elsewhere, then gingerly started unthreading the laces of my bodice until my mind could hardly conjure up a thought.

"Bloodsinger," I said. "I've seen your hands draw a blade much, much faster than this."

He pressed a kiss to the hinge of my jaw and grinned. "Patience, Songbird."

"Patience was spent at the cove. Hurry your hand, or I will do it myself."

A low growl rumbled from his chest. Erik reached into his boot and removed a knife. A knife!

The bastard grinned with a twisted pleasure when my eyes widened in surprise. "Careful what challenges you level against me."

Without another word, Erik sliced the tip through the bodice, cutting it off my body. He levered to his knees, straddling me, and worked the knife through the whole of my dress. The blade landed on the floor with a clatter, and the king pulled the shredded dress off my shoulders.

"Damn you." He devoured me with his eyes until his gaze reached my legs. Rage soaked his features as he took in the gashes left by the assassin. His voice went dark. "Which one of those bastards did this?"

I swallowed past a knot and stayed quiet.

Erik cupped the back of my neck and drew our faces close. "Doesn't matter which one. They're dead. Their blood will spill at your feet."

The harrowing way his voice tilted to something dark sent an unnerving thrill through my blood. Erik had his darkness, but I was learning mine. I kissed him for a long moment before he pulled away again and rid the bed of the remnants of my dress.

I always imagined being exposed in such a way might cause me to curl away, to hide and recount all the physical flaws I found on my body. With the Ever King, the way he looked at me like I was something precious, something so stunning he might get on the ground and worship me, I embraced every searing glance.

"Touch me," I said, bringing his palm to the skin of my stomach.

Erik dragged his fingertips over my ribs, caressing the side of my breast. "You are my destruction. Do you know that? I will never have enough of you."

For a few breaths, Erik studied me as though he were searching for a storm, for a glimpse of hesitation. When he didn't find it, he palmed one breast.

His touch was chaos. Beautiful, intoxicating chaos. Gentle and rough, fast and tender. I might've been his destruction, but he was my ruin. I would break into a thousand pieces if it meant Erik was the one to piece them back together with his touch.

He ran his thumbs across my nipples. The cool air combined with his touch pebbled them into hard peaks. I gasped. He moaned again and pressed his hips into mine, the strain of his length clear in his trousers.

My head fell back as he pinched and flicked, drawing me toward a delirious madness. Erik dropped his head. I was captivated by his touch, but I didn't expect the shock of pleasure when the heat of his tongue wrapped around the soft skin and sucked.

"Erik." I cupped the back of his head, holding his mouth against me, unable to catch a deep enough breath. My head was swimming, but I wanted to fall into Erik's touch, his kiss, his body.

I wanted to make him feel the same and slid my fingertips down the front of his trousers until I found the tip of his hard length. One brush of my thumb over the head, and Erik shuddered.

"Gods, woman," he rasped. "You can kill a man."

Dark heat sparked in his eyes. One corner of his jaw pulsed in tension as he pulled back, standing at the foot of the bed. A ferocious tangle of need and want and reverence burned in his gaze, and the slightest tremble in his fingers was clear when he hooked his thumbs into the waistband of his trousers. With a quick tug, his cock sprang out, so strained and taut it looked damn near painful.

I raked my gaze over the planes of his chest, the healing wound on his side, the carved angles of his hips.

"I will never get my fill of you either, Serpent," I said, voice hoarse.

Erik tossed his pants aside and came back to the bed, his body hovering over the top of me.

I brought his head down and kissed him for all the turns I'd thought of my serpent beneath the waves. I kissed him for the turns I wanted to spend in the safety of his embrace. Every divot, every scar earned my attention. A soft caress as I memorized the body of my captor, of the man who'd stolen his way into my heart.

Erik roamed one hand between my thighs. Gaze on me, he slid one finger inside my core. "Gods, you're so ready for me, aren't you, love?"

Any reply dried up on my tongue. My hips bucked through the slickness pooling between us. He pumped his hand slowly at first, then with each heartbeat added more friction.

"Erik." I moaned and bit the edge of his bottom lip.

"Blood, love. No blood."

By the hells, I almost didn't care. His hand, his lips, all of it had me writhing as ruthless shocks of heat pooled in my stomach. "Don't . . . don't stop."

Erik added a second finger. I let my knees fall to the sides and shuddered when he reached a new depth, stretching me gently. He curled his fingers. His lips kissed my throat.

I whimpered, desperate for release. "Erik, oh gods . . ."

"Say you're mine, Songbird," he growled against my neck. "Say it."

"Yours. I'm yours."

His fingers quickened in pace and pressure until I could not conjure a clear thought. I dug my fingernails into his skin as I stiffened, reveling in the delirious wave of heat dancing through my blood. My head fell back, baring my throat, and I let out a rough, quivering gasp as Erik's touch slowed enough to bring me back from the beautiful haze.

When I opened my eyes, the king was gazing at me with a tenderness strong enough to knot emotion in the back of my throat.

He settled his hips between my thighs, gripped his length, and aligned it with my center. When he paused, I hooked my legs around his waist and held his face in my hands. "Don't you dare ask if I'm sure."

"I don't want to hurt you," he whispered. "You'll take me slow, but you'll take all of me."

There was something indescribably safe and beautiful about the way Erik looked at me. His hands held my legs, gently positioning me in a way that was comfortable. He kneaded my skin, caressed over the flutter of my pulse, and held his gaze steady as he pushed inside, just the tip.

I touched the bottom curve of Erik's lip. He was not without sharp edges, but to my soul, I knew Erik Bloodsinger was a light in my darkness. He was the beautiful monster I would always want, would always love.

Truth be told, I'd been falling for the Ever King since I saw his sunset eyes in the dim light of that barred cell.

We both watched as Erik slowly slid deeper inside me. He paused and kissed me tenderly when I winced from a bite of pain. I drew in a few slow breaths and relaxed. Erik dropped his forehead, breathing heavily, and held my gaze as he went deeper.

My fingernails dug into his hips. Pain was there, but it dulled once he filled every part of me. When he was seated inside to the hilt, Erik paused. For a dozen heartbeats we were still, lips parted, swallowing each other's breath.

Erik threaded one hand with mine; the other he kept pressed on the bed, holding his body up just enough so he didn't bury me into the mattress. He kissed the swell of my breast again, his tongue swirling around the peak as he started to move.

The burn of an ember ignited between my legs. A slow, steady warmth unfurled like spilled liquid fire. Each slow thrust rolled against the sensitive bundle of nerves until my body was alight in heat and pressure.

I gripped his hair, gasping. His eyes closed as a soft moan slid from his throat from the mounting pleasure.

"You feel so good wrapped around me," Erik gritted out between thrusts. "You were made for me, Livia."

I rolled my hips, unable to stop reaching for more, like I wanted Erik to crack me in half. He set a rhythm that had me writhing and whimpering. Not too fierce that I'd be in constant pain, but not too slow that I didn't feel every plunge of his hips.

Heat gathered between our bodies; sweat dripped off his cheek onto my chest. I breathed all of it in, the sweet hint of leather and sea in his hair, the oakwood soap on his skin, the lingering blood from healing Alek.

There were answers I still needed—to understand him, nothing more. Whatever darkness remained to discover, I wanted it all. I wanted to greedily take it.

I locked my ankles around Erik's back. The red in his eyes flared. His breath shifted into jagged pants. Tension flooded my insides, drawing me back to the torturous edge I'd never cease craving after this moment.

Erik's thrusts grew deeper and more frantic. Coiled pressure melted into silky pleasure. From my head to my drenched core. When it burst, I sobbed his name as my body clenched around his. He held me steady, his face buried against my neck. Pants and curses fired off his tongue as he drove deeper through the beautiful anguish of my release until he found his own.

His cock twitched inside as hot streams of his release filled every piece of me. The feel of him marking me from the inside out was a rush of pleasure, of affection, of love, of which I'd never tire.

For a long pause we didn't move, simply held each other, breathing heavily. Erik didn't lift his gaze, but tightened his arms around me, keeping us bound as one. Tender strokes of his hands over my skin struck me with the notion that, perhaps, the Ever King needed safety within the intimacy of my arms as much as I needed the solace of his.

After a moment, he pulled away and gathered a soft linen. A deep frown curved his face when he drew back, and a bit of blood coated the cloth and bedding.

"Are you all right?" he asked, almost angry. Not directed at me, it seemed he was frustrated at himself.

I touched his lips. "I'm indescribably all right."

Erik's tension faded. He finished caring for me, then slowly brought one hand to my face and brushed some of my wild hair from my eyes. "Don't regret me, Songbird."

I stroked his cheek and grinned. "I never will, Serpent."

45

THE SERPENT

LIVIA'S FINGER WISTFULLY twisted a lock of my hair. She kept her cheek on my chest, her naked body curled around mine.

I couldn't recall a time when I'd been so . . . calm. The constant simmer of rage against a man for slaughtering my father had always been there.

Fueled by others, anger and hate created the unwavering belief that the earth bender's death would seal my father's acceptance from wherever he was in the Otherworld. If I earned my father's acceptance, I'd earn the people's. I'd stop being seen as the broken heir, given a crown only because his capture got the true king killed.

"Erik," she whispered.

"Hmm?" My arm tightened around her body on instinct, as if my skin realized there was a wider gap between us and that wouldn't do.

"How do you know Stieg?"

I knew the questions would come. There wasn't sense avoiding them any longer. She was mine.

"Your warrior was a captive," I said. "Taken during one of your fae wars and locked away with me. He protected me."

"I didn't know Stieg was captured." Livia rose and propped her head up with her fist. She didn't look at me with anger at the truth. Nothing but a desire to know more lived in those eyes.

"I was young, so some memories are hazy," I admitted. "But I remember him. I remember how he fought the guards when they came to carve into my heart. I trusted him after that."

"Alek said my . . . my people rescued you. How?"

"I don't know exactly, but the warrior always told me his people would come for us. They did. Stieg was injured, and I couldn't walk well, so I remember a woman carried me out. She had hair that looked like blood to me."

Livia drew in a sharp breath. "Queen Malin. She's the mother of my friends Jonas and Sander."

I vaguely recalled Stieg addressing the woman as a queen, but most of it was a blur. "I saw your father. He looked ready to attack us, which I still don't understand, since your mother was there. She stopped him." I narrowed my eyes. "I've never seen such violence in someone's eyes. Has he ever hurt you?"

"No. He'd never." A sad smile crossed her face. "Did you know my father survived a fate curse?"

I shook my head.

"A curse of bloodlust. One of the queens back home still calls him the Cursed King sometimes."

Curses abounded in the Ever. Lady Narza knew how to cast them, and I had few doubts her power was what kept my father compliant to her demands. It was why my father made me my mother's killer instead of him. Narza wouldn't hesitate to destroy Thorvald, but the child her daughter loved? She stayed her hand.

"It might explain why my father was quick to call upon his axes if the urge was still in his blood," she whispered.

The draw to bloodlust was no stranger to me. To be lost in a curse of blood and gore . . . I almost let a drop of shame fill my chest for harboring such hate against a man who'd aided in my rescue.

"I've tried to convince myself something he said wasn't real." I trained my gaze on the rafters overhead, unable to look at her. "When my father spewed his disdain for what had become of me, your father . . . stood for me."

"What?"

Maybe I was a monster. For so long I'd buried the small details beneath anger and the need to restore my own father's brutality on the throne. "He said I'd shown more bravery than warriors for surviving torture, and they'd keep me if I was unwanted by my own people."

"Then he meant it, Erik." Her voice cracked. "My father does not deal in weak threats, not when it comes to littles."

I scrubbed my hands down my face. "I know, because he offered it again." Shame was potent, sour, and hot on my tongue. "At the end of the Great War. He told me after what I'd done for your uncle, I could have a place with your Night Folk."

"He's never mentioned that. Neither have my uncles."

"Because I made certain to become a threat to him." I pulled myself up and leaned against the headboard. At once, Livia tucked against me and draped an arm around my waist. "I vowed to return and kill him. I healed your uncle to repay Stieg, but I told your father there would always be a debt between us for Thorvald."

"I don't understand why. There was a chance for peace."

"My uncle Harald had a poisonous tongue, love. Understand, I was truly convinced the only way to be a chosen king of the Ever was to gain favor from the previous king. I knew Thorvald cared nothing for me when he lived, so in his death was my only chance.

"Truth be told, if my father hadn't died, I'm certain he would've killed me." I scoffed bitterly. "Your question about another heir unnerved me, for there was already some talk he had a bastard—his spare."

"Do you think it's true?"

"I have no doubt Thorvald wanted a different son, but if there was another heir, he'd have challenged me by now." It wouldn't make sense to wait. If a blood claim was to be made, it should've been made when I was weaker, younger, and less violent.

Livia traced a scar across my chest. "Did you want to stay? With my people, I mean."

"For you." I tilted her chin up. "You intrigued me. I knew you were the earth bender's heir, and I wanted to be nearer . . . to you. But Harald was dead, our armies were weakened, and I couldn't abandon the Ever. There were too many dependent on promises I'd made."

We were silent for a long pause until she said, "Thank you for healing Aleksi. He is more brother than cousin to me. I am curious about Gavyn though."

"I'm going to need to kill him, then."

She snickered and pinched my ribs. "Not like that, you jealous fiend. What is his ability?"

My jaw tightened. "Livia, if I tell you this, you cannot speak a word to anyone. Gavyn's voice could get him executed by the house lords."

Her eyes widened. "I swear, I won't say a word."

I hurriedly explained how he could alter his form, and why it was considered too risky of an ability. Why it made him a spy and potential assassin.

"Celine told me they owe you everything," Livia said. "She . . . she told me she was born with siren blood."

"Celine has a damn big mouth," I grumbled. My fingers threaded through her hair. "But they were part of those who were dependent on my promises. Their father was the lord over the House of Bones. He committed several crimes against the crown. One being he kept Gavyn's voice a secret. After Gavyn was born, Thorvald commanded their father to kill his mate, a powerful siren."

Revealing these truths of my father made me hate him more and hate for him a little less. "Thorvald had his son slaughter his mate, after all. He wanted the other lords to show the same devotion to the Ever.

"The difference was Gavyn's father loved his mother," I said. "He hid her away, but never severed their bond. After Thorvald's death, my uncle discovered the mate was not only alive but had borne a second child for the House of Bones. A siren daughter.

"Harald executed the mate and cut out Celine's song." I let out a long breath. "My uncle planned to force Gavyn's father to finish his daughter's torture, but I ordered something different. I was a young king, but still king."

"You intervened for Celine's life?"

"Harald never allowed me friends, even took Tait from me. Believe it or not, we were once close like you and your cousin. Gavyn was as close to a friend as I had because he could slip in and out of the palace grounds with his ability. We got to know each other as heirs with secrets. I knew what it was like to have a mother taken away, and I didn't want him to lose his father and sister, so I told my uncle I wanted Celine as practice for my poison."

She pressed a kiss over my heart and hooked a leg over my hips.

"I hid Celine amongst the servants. Harald never noticed them. After the war, I kept her on my ship and showed her how I call to the sea. Her siren blood helped develop a new, unique voice for the tides. We gave her a new name, and no one knows she's Gavyn's sister. Gavyn made me promise to keep her identity hidden, or she could be used against him or lose her life if anyone who believes as Harald and Thorvald do discovers her bloodline."

Livia sighed. "I still think it's ridiculous how folk believe that loving anyone beyond themselves is a weakness."

I studied the soft shape of her face. Livia was my weakness. Use her against me, and I would unravel. Yet in some ways she was my ultimate strength. The notion of her being harmed again drew out the fiercest desire to fight and kill in her damn name.

I didn't start wars for Gavyn or Celine or their father. Even if I knew deep down I cared for them a great deal. But for Livia, I'd burn the kingdom and start any war if it meant she was safe.

"What happened to their father?" she asked.

"Harald tortured him," I said. "Planned to do it for days, but after the first night, somehow he disappeared from his cell. No one found him again."

"Gavyn?"

I shrugged, avoiding her gaze again. "He likely had something to do with it."

She didn't press for more and was quiet for a few moments.

Livia stole my breath when she maneuvered over my body, straddling my hips. Her eyes burned. "You, Erik Bloodsinger, are the kind of darkness I would follow across the skies and seas."

My head cracked against the headboard when Livia reached between us and took hold of my cock.

"Woman..." I gripped the bed linens as she stroked and circled her thumb over the sensitive tip.

Livia aligned my length with her dripping center and gave me a vicious grin. "Say you're mine. Say it."

My breath slid out in a short rasp when she slid over me, tip to root. I held her waist like a ballast against the rage of a storm on the sea.

"I'm yours." I buried my face against the slope of her neck. "Gods, I'm yours."

I LEFT LIVIA asleep in my bed. Sewell, Celine, and Larsson were added to the defenses at the door. The Ever Crew wouldn't betray me. They'd die if they did. Blood ties made it so, should they go against their crew. Deeper, almost, than the ties to the houses of their voice. Gavyn's crew would be the same, even the poor bastards who sailed beneath Lord Joron and Lord Hesh.

When I entered the dining hall, Aleksi was hunched over a bowl of syrupy gruel and honey. Tait was silent and somber against the back wall, keeping watch on him.

I pulled out a chair and sat.

Aleksi narrowed his gaze. "What are you doing with my cousin?"

I chuckled. "You don't want to know."

His jaw pulsed as he stirred the honey deeper into his bowl. "She willing?"

"I'm no rapist." I slumped in the chair and kicked out my legs. "I'm assuming you've been told the importance your cousin has for the Ever."

"Your man there explained about your dying lands, yes. He told me Livia's fury has been healing it. He also told me you believe she's somehow bonded to your title as king, which I find ridiculous."

"I don't care." I didn't. The unwitting bond forged between us meant nothing to me. It was not what fueled my actions or rushed my heart when it came to Livia Ferus. She owned me by her own doing. She could be powerless, and after the way she kissed me, fought for me, after watching her body ride me until I could not think straight, I'd go to the hells and back for the woman.

"You should care. My uncle will never let you keep her."

"Not his choice."

"Oh? Is it hers?" Aleksi lifted his brow. "You'd let her go home if she truly wanted?"

I looked down. In a way, I still held her hostage. I wanted her for myself, but could she ever be entirely mine if she felt forced to be here?

I shook the thought away and glared at her cousin. "I came here to explain that those marks you saw on her skin were not from me. Your cousin was a damn warrior when assassins came for me and to take her magic for their own uses."

His eyes went black with rage. "These assassins are dead, right?"

"There's the brutality of the 'peaceful' earth fae." I grinned and helped myself to a bite of his meager meal. "One is dead, by her hand. There are two more rotting in my cells. It's impressive, the risks you took to save her, so I thought you might want to help me question them. I need to know who sent them, if you'd like to help me seal their fate."

I knew little about the boy I saw clinging to his fathers after a war ended. But what I saw now was a man with hidden viciousness under his skin of honor.

The corner of his mouth curved. "It'd be a pleasure, Bloodsinger."

46

THE SONGBIRD

CROWDS GATHERED IN the great hall. Celine and Larsson woke me after dawn. I'd been disappointed to wake alone, the king nowhere to be found. I'd been told to dress and follow them to the hall. My body ached in beautiful ways, and I wanted to crawl back into Erik's bed and memorize every scar on his skin all over again.

At the entrance to the hall, Aleksi stood beside Tait. All hells, I was a distracted fool and, for a moment, forgot my cousin nearly lost his life searching for me.

A tear slid from the corner of my eye when I gave him a tight embrace. "I'm not being harmed" were the first words I rambled out.

"I know that now. Bloodsinger and I spoke before the dawn."

A prickle of heat rushed to my cheeks. After we'd . . . Erik went to my cousin. "Oh. I'm sure that was interesting."

"That's one word for it." Aleksi pulled back, a soft smile on his face. "We will need to speak, Liv. Soon. I want to hear the story from your mouth."

I gripped his arm and nodded. "I'll tell you everything, and you must tell me of home, of my parents."

Alek's face fell. "I've never seen Uncle Valen as the beast they once called him, but I think I've seen glimpses now."

My heart snapped. I couldn't leave them like this, wondering if I was being brutalized every day. Now with Alek gone, we had to get word to them.

"I'll speak with the king," I whispered. "We can find a way to stop the fighting."

Alek offered a smile, but I wasn't certain he believed me.

Celine and Larsson joined us; I briefly introduced them to Alek. Skepticism lined Celine's features, but she gave Alek a nod of hello. Larsson was more amiable and asked Alek questions about the journey through the Chasm, then called him Bloodsummoner, a way to show he accepted him into the Ever culture, by the time we reached the center of the hall.

"I'll be back, Livie." Alek squeezed my arm. "The king has need of me."

"Need of you, what—?" But he was already gone.

I strained my neck and looked over the heads of the people when the heavy doors opened. Erik appeared all in black, and atop his head was a gold circlet with hints of crimson. I'd never seen the king's crown before. Made of sharp edges like jagged waves, it added a bit of vicious power to his appearance.

"Blood flows through the gold," Celine said under her breath after I remarked on the beauty of it. "And a spell was cast over the crown, so only a true heir can wear it without it burning the skin. Today he wants it known that he *is* the Ever King."

"Why? What's he doing?"

She didn't need to respond. I saw for myself.

With the help of Tait and—hells—Alek, Erik dragged the greasy assassin and Snake Eyes into the hall. Ropes were slung around their throats; they were naked, bruised, and already bleeding.

Erik released them in the center of the crowd. People drifted away from the prisoners, forming a circle around them. Through the heads of his people, Erik found me. His eyes burned with violence, but the grin on his face said more. It said all the things our bodies spoke last night.

"It is one thing for a king to be attacked," Erik said. "It is not the first time, nor do I think it will be the last."

My stomach cinched. To have him brought so close to the Otherworld again was a new fear that ran rampant with all the possibilities.

I blew out a long breath. Erik was looking at me. He grinned, and my heart swelled with his voice. *You are Livia Ferus, blood of warriors, body of a goddess, destroyer of the king's cock...*

I snorted a laugh, bit my bottom lip, and looked away. Bastard.

Erik's face shadowed when he faced his people again. "But to attack her."

My heart stopped when Erik pointed at me, and every head seemed to swivel at once. *Don't bend, don't falter.* Erik was facing his people and demanding they look upon him as the king he'd always wanted to be. I was his. I needed to straighten my spine and be his.

"To try to rob us of the hope she has brought to the Ever," Erik went on, voice dark and cruel, "that is a slight I cannot forgive with a quick death. It is made worse since these traitors refuse to give up who sent them."

Murmurs scattered through the crowd. Erik went to Tait and took a bronze dagger from his hand. "I promised blood would spill at your feet," he said to me, as though no one else watched. "I keep my promises."

"The king values an enemy more than the Ever!" Snake Eyes shouted.

My fingertips went numb when a gasp filtered through the hall.

The second assassin's voice was rough and dry, but he followed with, "He was willing to sacrifice himself for the whore, willing to leave you defenseless."

"The king is no king!" Snake Eyes shouted as the crowd slipped into a tense silence. "He vowed to slaughter our enemies, now he lets them live, brings them to our courts, all to have his bitch suck his cock."

A few cries of surprise bounced off the walls and voices rose with more vitriol. Panic seized me from behind when more than a few heated glares locked on me, and Celine stepped forward like my own personal shield.

Damn the hells. If she was reaching for the blade, they were going to attack.

Until silence choked off the whispers when Erik shoved his way through the crowd, and in less than five strides had his arms around my waist. I cried out when he lifted me half over his shoulder and stormed to the front of the hall.

I didn't have time to ask what he was doing before I was tossed back into a wide wooden seat.

I blinked, pulse racing, and glanced at the finely carved wood under my palms. My lips parted. Erik's shoulders heaved in rough breaths as he backed away, eyes burning.

He'd tossed me onto his throne.

He'd . . . made me his equal.

"Thorvald is dead!" Erik roared, wheeling on his people. "For twenty turns you have placed me in the shadow of my father's crown, the same way you have blamed me for ten turns over the outcome of a war I never wanted. A war brought to the earth fae through my uncle." He turned slowly, taking in every gaze. "I am Erik Bloodsinger, and I will no longer bow to the words and legacies of others.

"I wear the crown of the Ever, I sail the *Ever Ship*, I bear the mark of this kingdom. I. Am. Your. King. And she"—he pointed behind him—"she is mine. She is the Ever Queen."

My fingernails dug into the wood of his throne. I gaped at the faces looking up at me—confused, uncertain, some with glowers of suspicion. There were pieces of me that hated them for their mistreatment of the king and wanted to scream at them for their lack of trust.

Erik had done everything within his power to defend his kingdom. He'd given up a chance to be accepted amongst people who'd honor him, all to lead his resentful people through sorrows after a war.

"The first Ever Queen," he said, a little breathless, and turned back to me. "If it is what she desires. I will not force you to stay, Songbird. The choice is yours."

Emotion knotted in my throat. He was setting me free.

I scanned the faces and found Celine. Her eyes were wide, her mouth open, but she grinned. Alek looked at me with a bit of stun much the same. I loved him, I loved everyone I left behind. I missed my family, my land, I missed lazy days with my friends. Even Rorik's antics, I missed desperately.

I swallowed and found the king's gaze again. But the way I would miss Erik Bloodsinger would destroy every thread of my heart. I'd wanted passion and chaos and a love that caused a delirious kind of need.

I'd found it in my enemy.

"Crown or no crown," I said softly, "I will always belong to you."

Erik let out a sharp breath. His lips curved into a villainous grin.

"To attack the king is one thing," he repeated, a new darkness to his tone. With the blade in hand, he went to Snake Eyes and gripped the rope around his neck, wrenching the man's head back. Erik dragged his face alongside the assassin's. "But to attack his queen will send you to the Otherworld in pieces."

Erik rammed the dagger through Snake Eyes's ribs, and the great hall filled with anguished cries.

I sat straighter on the throne, crossed one leg, and placed a hand on either armrest, watching. I didn't look away as Erik slaughtered them—as promised—at my feet. He was wonderfully brutal. The king killed with a finesse I never knew I'd find captivating, but I couldn't look away.

Erik poisoned them, then sang them back to health, only to poison them again. He took fingers, ears. He blinded each assassin, then when they had little life left inside, he rammed the dagger through the backs of their throats.

When he was finished, he was soaked in blood. Bone and flesh littered the great hall. People were silent, but after a long-drawn pause, one by one his court lowered to their knees.

Erik stood above them, sunset eyes on me.

I took in the carnage at my feet. Flecks of blood had stained the hem of my dress. Perhaps I should be afraid of the look in Bloodsinger's eyes. Possessive, unhinged, and wild. I wasn't. I was lost to him.

My mouth twisted into a small grin. *You're my beautiful monster.*

47

THE SERPENT

DAYS AFTER I'D placed Livia on my throne, the palace was still locked in a frenzy as servants and courtiers and common folk adjusted to a woman in power. I wouldn't take it back. There was a rightness in my chest, like this was the path I should've taken all along.

Carpenters were half finished with a twin throne in the great hall. Carved in foxes and ivy and a swallow in the center of the back. The royal smith set to work fashioning her a circlet in the shape of oak leaves and would present it at an official coronation at the next full moon.

Of course, if I'd known there'd be such a need from the house lords to discuss my lunacy, I would've killed them all—save for Gavyn, who found it wholly entertaining—and been done with them.

"Lord Hesh," I said, desperate to sound bored. The man was made of more stone than flesh. The only small piece of his towering form were his teeth, ground down from the constant tension in his damn jaw. "As I told you, if I cared for your opinions on the royal court, I would have consulted you. Alas, I care little."

"My King," Joron interjected. He was as slender as a sickly tree, with knobby limbs to go with it. "We seek not to tell you how to rule your court, but what you have done . . . it is a weakness against us. You've given the earth fae—"

"What?" I snapped. "What have I given them? A union? A call to peace? You recall the days the Ever Folk went to their realms, when trade was once prominent between our people, when the lands thrived together."

Joron spluttered. "Those were different times, My Lord."

"And they will be again." I faced the far end of the table, one fist curled over my leg. "Lady Narza, what do you say? Think a queen is a weakness for the Ever?"

"What else will a woman say?" Hesh grumbled.

"I don't believe I was speaking to you." I gave the lord a warning glare and took pleasure in the way he pinched his lips. "What say you, Grandmother?"

Narza had been silent, but to the surprise of every house, she'd arrived after Joron summoned a council to discuss the blasphemy of an Ever Queen. My grandmother had had little to do with me after the death of my mother. I'd always resented her for it, always wanted her to steal me away to her house to escape the cruelty of my father.

She never came.

Oddly enough, in this moment she looked at me without indifference. More like she did not recognize me.

"I say," she began, "our king has been burdened by a broken kingdom for a great many turns. At times to heal, it requires vast change. I am optimistic your act to change the way of things will only benefit our people."

Not praise exactly, but it meant more than I expected to have her approval. Hesh and Joron muttered until Gavyn flamboyantly expressed his enthusiasm for a new queen.

"Already the king *and* queen," he said, "have cleared away the darkening on the far isles in the House of Bones. They are stronger together, and I for one like the king a great deal more when the earth queen is near."

I narrowed my eyes and fought the urge to kick his damn shin under the table.

Slowly, I rose from my seat. I'd been kept long enough from Livia, and I tired of their blustering. "The truth is, I do not need your approval. Any of you. In fact, Lord Joron, I would think hard on your support of your king and queen. Or the palace might take note of the lotus trade you've begun with the privateers in the far seas."

Joron's eyes widened, and the blustering fool startled in his seat when I slammed my palm on the table.

"In fact," I went on, "your involvement in the Skondell lotus trade makes me wonder if you might be the one financing House Skurk to betray your king."

"No." Joron shook his head vigorously. "No, Highness. I . . . would never involve myself with such a house. We've used the lotus for study, that is all. To find new uses. I swear to you."

I pulled my hand back before the cretin could kiss my damn rings, and gave Gavyn a quick glance. He'd done his duty and found more than one wretched secret.

"And Hesh." I drummed my fingers over the table. "You'll return to your province to find the sirens you've been holding beneath your manor are no longer yours for whatever twisted reason you were keeping them."

Narza's eyes burned in a swift unforgiving rage. "What is this? You've imprisoned blood of my house?"

Hesh saw females as tools to expand a bloodline, but beneath the surface, he feared Narza. "Trespassers. I am within my rights to detain them."

"Liar!" She seethed. "You want their voices, is that it? Want to lure folk to your province? Or is it you merely want to use their bodies in the hope you secure an heir with a unique gift, like our king?"

I slammed my hand on the table again. "Let this be a warning—I do not care for your opinions on the queen, and I will be watching to see that your support is given to her with unwavering fealty. In fact, I suggest you each look within your own houses and consider how much stronger you might be if you did the same."

Without another word, I abandoned the council room.

Alistair was waiting in the corridor; I glared my annoyance and tried to hurry past him.

"You cannot avoid me forever, My King."

"I can and I will."

Alistair snorted. "There are matters in need of your attention unless you would like me to defer to our new queen. She has a much softer tone and does not fling blades."

I fought a grin. "No, I don't want you to defer to the queen, since I am going to see her, and that would take her from me. The same reason I do not want you to defer to me."

Alistair's breath puffed through his thin nose as he tried to keep my pace. "I am trying to feel pity for you, My Lord, truly I am. But you live in a glittering palace, have the power of the kingdom, a beautiful mate—"

"Gods, old man, what is it you need from me?" I stopped in the middle of the corridor and faced him.

"Peace talks." Alistair smoothed his too-tight gambeson. "Do you still wish to attempt a truce between the earth fae in time for the coronation? If so, it would be to the benefit of us all to not anger the house lords."

If anything about this made me uneasy, it was the thought of bartering a truce with the man who'd offered me peace more than once only to have me steal away his heart, leaving him to wonder what horrors she was facing day after day.

Odds were he'd take her back and ram one of his axes in my skull.

"Lord Hesh and Lord Joron can sink to the depths of the Ever Seas for all I care," I said. "If they cannot accept there is no healing the Ever alone and a woman is their savior, that is their risk to take."

Stand against my Songbird, and they would meet their end much the same as the assassins.

"Livia is preparing a missive to send to her folk for a neutral meet. With the earth prince and princess speaking for us, peace is attainable. The lords will need to accept it."

"I'll see to it the palace is accommodating for a swell of earth fae." Alistair snapped his fingers. "Oh, one final matter." From inside his gambeson, the man removed a pouch. "As you requested. They're ready."

I grinned when I looked inside. "Perfect."

Servants and palace staff still avoided me, but their eyes weren't filled with as much fear as I strode past, more like they were curious if I'd slipped into madness or truly had a sliver of a heart.

"King."

Halfway up the staircase to my chambers, I startled. "Narza? I thought we had finished our conversation in the council room."

Disguised as the blind hag, my grandmother stepped from a deep alcove window. "You've given your heart? Last time such a claim was made, it nearly destroyed the bloodline of the House of Kings."

I leaned close. "Then let it burn."

Narza tilted her head, a wildness in her eyes.

"I'll burn the Ever," I repeated, voice low, "and start anew if I must. There is no world where she does not own me."

"Then guard your bond, Erik. We still do not know who is behind the spell cast of the darkening." Narza hummed. "Dangers are amongst us."

"And I face them with my queen."

"I hope you do, Grandson. I suppose we shall see." A sly smirk painted her illusioned haggish features, but she said nothing more as she backed into the alcove.

By the time I reached my chamber door, my temper was shorter, and I thought if anyone else kept me from seeing her, I would do as Alistair said and begin flinging knives.

"Why are so many damn people in my room?"

Livia snapped her gaze up from the table near the fire nook, as did Alek, Tait, and Celine.

"I wanted opinions on the missive," Livia said, grinning. "I'm trying to keep your head, Bloodsinger. So are they. Perhaps a bit of gratitude."

"Ah, I see." I opened the door to the corridor. "You all have my appreciation for getting your asses out of our room."

Celine gestured to Alek and Livia. "I think you two better speak to your folk, not the king. He'll get us all killed the moment he opens his mouth." She glared at me as she strode past. "Last time I help you, *Highness*."

"Doubtful."

Tait followed. He'd been sullen since we were boys, but there was a touch of something lighter in his features. Still, he hardly acknowledged me. I hardly acknowledged him. Alek hesitated as he approached.

"You most of all," I grumbled. "Why are you still here? Go home."

"A debt must be repaid, Bloodsinger." The corner of his mouth curved. "Trust me, you'll want more than Livia's voice standing for you against my uncle."

He gave Livia a bemused look, then followed the others out of the room.

I had my arms around her waist in the next breath, my lips on her throat. "I see you painted more windows." My eyes lifted over her shoulder to the scene of a trapped monster waiting to be reunited with his lover in the skies.

Nightfire had always been my favorite myth. I liked that it was becoming Livia's.

"You were gone last night. Nightmares crept in, so I painted this to chase them away."

I tightened my hold around her waist. "I don't like that. If you can't sleep, I don't care if I'm across the damn sea, call to me and I'll come."

"I'm not calling you for every horrid dream. I've handled the mare demons for turns on my own. I'll be fine."

I lifted my head. "But you don't have to be alone anymore."

Livia held my stare for a long pause, then kissed me slowly for a breath before she swatted my shoulder. "By the way, you have horrid manners."

"I do." I pressed a kiss to her throat, then opened the pouch from Alistair. "I have something for you."

Livia's eyes brightened when she removed the pale necklace. Runes etched and painted in liquid gold lined the slender piece, along with a matching pair of filigreed earrings. "Erik, they're beautiful."

"For a queen." I fastened the clasp of the necklace behind her, my fingers lingering on the warmth of her skin. "No one will forget what will happen should they touch you now."

A groove formed between her brows as she inspected the earrings. "These are made of bone."

"They are." I touched one of the gold runes on her necklace.

"Bone from . . . ?"

I gripped her chin, drawing her lips close to mine. "Anyone touches you, then you wear them around your neck."

"Gods, these are . . ." She blinked at the necklace. "The assassins?"

Her stun left me wondering if I'd gone too far, shown too much of the darker pieces, but after a moment, Livia crushed her mouth to mine. She dug her fingernails into the back of my neck, drawing me closer, as though she couldn't stand a sliver of space between us.

She broke away and whispered, "I would follow your darkness across the skies and seas."

I went to kiss her again, but she pressed a finger to my lips. "Although, you should know, everyone you just tossed out of here was here to help you for when we go to my father, and—"

"Songbird." I trapped her face in my palms. "I have been pulled from you for the better part of two days. My patience is spent. Do you wish me to go after them and praise their efforts, or do you want me inside you?"

Livia swallowed. I tracked the movement down the slender curve of her throat. She didn't hesitate before her hands were clawing at my belt. I tore away her dress and bodice with as much frantic need.

I didn't have time to move us to the bed before Livia yanked my hips, pulling me off-balance, only to land with her back to the wall. One palm flattened next to her head, the other dragged along the length of her thigh, up the divots of her ribs, to the swell of her breast.

Livia jerked when I pressed my thumb against the hardened peak. My teeth scraped across her neck. She moaned and reached her hand between us and curled her slender fingers around my shaft. Blood abandoned my head. Couldn't be helped. With every touch, this woman had my body raging for more, like a boy who couldn't control his own damn cock.

After a few slow strokes, Livia bit her lip nervously and shoved me back.

"Too much?"

She shook her head and stopped my heart when she turned me around, so my back was to the wall, then lowered to her knees.

My blood overheated, sweat prickled over my brow, and she'd done nothing yet. Merely looked up at me, a sly smirk on her lips. "Do you like this?"

A deep moan slid from my throat. I threaded my fingers through her hair. "All I need is you. That is what I like. All of you."

In truth, no one had done this. Worshiped *me*.

Trysts were done with lanterns doused, faces turned, and emotions deadened. To see Livia, hands across every scar, her body heating for more of me, it was another blow to the shields I tried to keep between us.

Livia's tongue swiped out and teased my tip before wrapping me with her soft full lips. Heat blazed over my face. I fought to keep my bleeding senses as she swiped her tongue back and forth.

My body grew rigid and trembled from the pent-up pleasure as Livia dragged her hands up and down my legs. One soft palm curled around my length, stroking me in time with her hot mouth. The bones in my weak leg threatened to give out, forcing me to use the wall as a sort of crutch.

A hum vibrated from her throat and I was undone. "Livia, you feel so damn good."

What a sight—those full lips wrapped around me, her mouth taking me in like the taste of me was her deepest desire. Unbidden, I rocked my hips. She gagged and a tear slid from the corner of her eye.

"Shit, sorry," I said through a rough breath, and tried to give her distance.

Livia let out a muffled kind of hiss and wrapped her arm around my hips, pulling me back.

"There, love. Gods, right there." I winced when the burn of release grew closer. Blood boiled in my skull. I wanted her body clenched tightly around me. I wanted to spill into her. With an agonized growl, I tugged on her hair and eased her mouth away.

Her face was flushed, lips glistening, and she looked at me like she'd done something wrong.

"Perfect, Songbird. You're too perfect." Each word slid out in a pant when I heaved her off her knees and spun her around so that once more her back was to the wall. No time to stumble to the bed, I gripped beneath Livia's thigh and hooked it around my waist. I teased the tip of my length against her entrance. "Together."

Livia nodded frantically and dug into my shoulders, whimpering and nipping at the lobe of my ear. There was something feral, almost primal, about the way she crushed me to her. After everything, it meant she wanted me. She was here because she wanted *me*; she wanted the Ever.

I was not a good man, but I was a man who kept his word. Should she wish to return home, to leave me, I would be nothing but an unfeeling wretch, but I would honor my word. She hadn't asked yet. I'd live in a way that she never needed to.

I aligned my crown and nudged just beyond the opening of her seam. Livia arched and bucked her hips, pulling me against her, until I slid deep inside. We groaned in unison. Her eyes fluttered. I forced mine to remain open, consumed by her gentle features, her pleasure, the little smile in the corner of her mouth.

My hips rocked at a punishing pace. The slap of our skin echoed through the room and created a furious collision of our bodies. My fingers pinched the peak of her breast, and I licked the other. Livia bit her bottom lip. She tugged at my hair.

Deep, long thrusts had my pulse like fire in my head. A maddening spin that left me feeling out of control and in control all at once. Then I pulled out.

Livia cried out in protest, but promptly swallowed it down when I took her other leg and lifted her in my arms.

She locked her ankles around my waist, arms around my neck. "Erik, I'm close. So close."

"With me, love. You come with me." I slammed back inside.

Livia drew in sharp moans, as though she couldn't breathe, but when I tried to slow the pace, she cursed and rocked against me like she wanted to bruise me for being so foolish.

With my name ripped from her throat, a violent shudder ran through her body. Her walls clenched around me; Livia whimpered as her body writhed through the violence of her release. I followed a heartbeat after, going still as I spilled into her. I held her legs around my waist, head back, the final pulses of release throbbing between us.

Livia's chest rose in heavy breaths. "Serpent."

"Songbird." I kissed her pulse point, breathing her in.

"I love you. Every dark, beautiful piece."

Like a fist wrapped around it, my throat tightened. Words failed me, so I kissed her. I kissed her until she understood I would crush worlds for her. I would cross the skies and seas to chase her light.

I'd never stop.

48

THE SONGBIRD

"UNCLE VALEN WILL want his head," Alek said. He sat in one of the chairs in the front room, a boot propped against the edge of the table.

"I know." I stared out the window with the painted image of Nightfire and his star lover in the night sky. My fingertips traced the distance between them. Sometimes the myth of the lovers in the sky felt too much like my existence. As though the passion, the love I felt for Erik Bloodsinger was doomed to separate us.

"You're certain this is what you want, Liv? You have a choice, you know. There is no need to feel like you must stay the way I do."

I smiled over my shoulder. "Alek, I've loved the sea king since I was a girl on the opposite side of a war. We're bonded."

"Yes." Aleksi scoffed. "His mantle. That is what causes me to worry. You both think it must be this way, when perhaps it can just be a means to broker peace."

"He is my desire, Alek." I fingered the bone necklace around my throat. My beautiful monster. "He's my *hjärta*. Bond or not."

Aleksi's face softened. A *hjärta* meant one had found a love so deep it was the other beat of your heart, a true harmony between two souls.

"I think you don't want me to stay because if I am at Erik's side, I am not by yours." I arched a brow in a playful challenge.

"Neither you nor Bloodsinger can be rid of me. I meant what I said and will serve him during this time of his kingdom's need."

"You know he views saving Uncle Tor as a payment to Stieg for protecting him as a young boy, right? You're the one keeping a debt between you."

"I know." Alek waved me away. "But the truth of what he did for Daj has weighed on me since that day. It's why I wanted to be a Rave. I wanted to catch the Ever King when he came through again, because I knew he would—gods, I knew he would. I was going to expose the truth, force peace talks, and receive a lot of grandeur, hero's banquets, and honor for my future littles for being the brave warrior to soften the heart of the Ever King." He leaned back in his chair and propped both boots up on the table. "Thank you, Cousin, for robbing me of my heroic fantasy."

I chuckled and faced the window again. It was still surreal to have my cousin with me, but I was glad. Alek had stepped into the Ever as a balance between worlds. Where I was the daughter of Thorvald's killer, Aleksi was the son of Erik's saved.

He'd drawn the interest of many courtiers and had already settled in with Sewell, who called him the golden fox. I assumed because of Alek's eyes. Even Tait smirked when Alek managed to make Celine and Larsson laugh.

He'd joined us as we sailed to the isles about the kingdom, pushing back the darkening. Day by day, Alek was coming to realize the Ever was not the enemy we thought. They were fae folk, the same as us. They fought for their realm; they protected their families the way we did.

In the weeks since Erik had given me the title of Ever Queen, I'd spent more than one night talking to my cousin into the early-morning hours. Sometimes, Erik would join us in the conversations. A dark, silky presence who only uttered a few words. In vulnerable moments, he'd admit how the anticipation of the fairy tales I read had kept him hopeful in the cells all those turns ago.

Most often he was silent, or he'd leave Alek and me to talk alone.

In somber moments, Alek recounted the pain of our friends at my capture. Mira had nearly killed one of her own guards when they'd taken her away, trying to fight her way to me. Sander had spent every waking hour beside Mira's father, who had a proclivity for maps and cartography, trying to find a way into the Ever.

Jonas—playful, carefree Jonas—Aleksi said he'd uttered perhaps two words and his eyes had been the inky black of his dreary nightmarish magic since I disappeared.

I needed to put my parents' hearts at ease. I needed to see my friends.

We were nearing the time when I'd return home and I would meet them. Not as Livia, heir to the Night Folk throne. I would be the Ever Queen. I'd be there to speak for the Sea Folk. I'd face my father as a queen of his enemy.

Strange to be afraid. My father loved me fiercely, and I'd never doubted it. Perhaps that was the trouble. He loved me enough to kill the man who'd taken me from him. He loved me enough to think Erik had cast some sort of spell on me, and the only way to be free of it was by Erik's blood.

A thousand scenarios rampaged in my head. Sweat gathered between my fingers, and the familiar flurry of my pulse started to rise.

I closed my eyes. *I am Livia Ferus, daughter of warriors, healer of lands, Queen of the Ever.*

Nerves still prickled up my arms, but I pictured Erik adding his own touch of vulgarity to the saying, something like *the delicacy of the king's tongue.* He tried to make each one more tantalizing.

"You're at peace here, Liv." Alek came to my side and studied the painting. "You don't seem so . . . burdened."

"I love our people, Alek. I love our family. But when I came here, it felt as though I came home." I met his stare. "I can't explain it. Even when I tried to hate Erik for taking me, there was a sense of being right where I needed to be."

Aleksi hesitated for a long pause before he took hold of my hand. "Then I will stand with you until our people finally make peace with the Ever. Now, I better be off. Celine insists on my input over the final design of your crown, Queen."

My stomach swirled in delightful heat. Queen of the Ever. Queen of Erik Bloodsinger. I could hardly believe it, and every morning it took at least five long kisses from the man before my mind relented to the truth.

This was my life.

Someone knocked on the door. Without invitation, Larsson stuck his head into the room. "Livia—I mean Queen." He winked. "Some of the darkening has spread rather aggressively over the ridge near the Black Isles. The king is returning from the province of the House of Bones and will meet us on the way."

The Black Isles were near the hidden coves of Lady Narza and her sea witches. Difficult waters to navigate, according to Erik, and in the center of treacherous seas. It must've meant the darkening was critical for Erik to attempt it so late in the day with high tides approaching.

"Right. I'll leave a missive for Alek and Celine to let them know."

I hurried to change into a simple linen dress and followed Larsson toward the docks. The Ever Crew sailed under Erik's command, but all were skilled sailors, and whenever they returned to the royal city, they often used their own vessels for short journeys to the various isles.

Larsson's skiff was made of white laths like ivory and boasted large black sails.

"You did not wish to go to the House of Bones?" I asked, stepping over a broken board on the switchback steps leading to the docks.

"You know the king keeps his trusted few near his queen." Larsson flashed his white teeth and took my hand, helping me over a lip and onto the final staircase.

The wind whipped my hair around my face. I took in the abandoned sloops and skiffs around the docks. "Oddly empty today."

"I think the people are uneasy about peace talks," Larsson said. "They feel their world is about to change. I wouldn't say they're wrong."

The Chasm would remain open. Our people would build new peace. Those were the things I hoped we saw in the coming days.

"Wait! Larsson." Tait emerged from the upper steps, waving.

"We'll be back soon enough, Heartwalker," Larsson returned.

"Wait." Tait took the steps two at a time with ease, lithe like his cousin. "Where are you going?"

"There's a return of the darkening in the Black Isles," I said. "We're to meet the king there."

Tait's eyes narrowed. "Yes, I saw the missive. Tidecaller reached out to the king to ask if we were to meet him or remain at the palace. Trouble is the king had no idea what she was talking about."

When Larsson's grip tightened on my arm, my heart dropped.

"I wish you hadn't done that, Heartwalker," Larsson said, voice low. "I actually liked you."

It happened in a single breath.

Larsson drew a blade. Tait reached for his but was a heartbeat too slow. Larsson rammed his knife deep into Tait's belly. I screamed, but from the shadows of the docks, two men lunged from behind and encircled my waist, dragging me toward the skiff.

Larsson ripped his knife from Tait's stomach, watched him fall back, then wiped the blood over Tait's dark hair.

"Sorry, mate," Larsson said snidely. "Had to be done. I wouldn't go around your father in the Otherworld. I think he might've figured out you knew Bloodsinger was going to kill him."

Blood coated Tait's chin. My pulse raged in my skull, muffling sound, but I knew I screamed his name. I pleaded with him to keep breathing. I screamed for Erik three times before one of the meaty brutes at my back stuffed my mouth with a dirty cloth.

I thrashed and kicked and fought, but one of them was the same as three of me. My feet didn't even touch the ground.

The man who held my waist tossed me onto the deck. I landed on a ridge on my hip. A shock of pain lanced up my side, but I scrambled away, spitting out the rancid cloth. Larsson shouted for the ship to set sail, then crossed the deck in three strides.

Before I could throw myself over the rail, he gripped my hair and yanked me back on deck.

"Bastard." I clawed at his wrist, drawing blood.

He slapped me hard enough it felt like my jaw unhinged. After a pause, Larsson wiped the blood off his wrist and took hold of my hair again.

The carefree, kind man was gone, replaced by a sinister grin and dark eyes filled with hate.

"The power of the Ever." He laughed with a new kind of viciousness and stroked my cheek. "Time for you to be of use to the true king, not my pathetic brother."

My heart stopped. The same rage I'd felt from the emotions of the creator of the darkening bled in Larsson's eyes now.

"Although, I should give Bloodsinger some credit. He's damn hard to kill." Larsson's mouth tightened. "And you, what a vicious little thing you are. Slaughtering a trained killer with roots. I thought I'd seen it all until that day."

The assassins. It was a cruel strike to my chest to realize that Larsson had sent the assassins to take me.

He was a trickster, a liar, and we'd all been duped.

"You did all this," I said, voice low. "You started the darkening."

"An unfortunate experiment that got a bit out of hand. But now we have you, not worthless scum like Lucien Skurk, to help us find a way to control the blight."

Damn bastard. I narrowed my gaze. "I'll never help you."

"We'll see, *Queen*." Larsson glowered and snapped his fingers. "Take her."

His two grunts dragged me back to my feet, leading me toward a narrow nook near the stern of the ship with iron chains and manacles awaiting my limbs.

Before they released me, another person stepped into view.

My eyes went wide for half a breath, stunned as theories and questions and rage reeled in my skull.

In the end, my lip curled, and all I could get out before another dirty cloth was stuffed in my mouth was "He's going to slaughter all of you."

49

THE SERPENT

THE BOW OF the ship carved through the surface. Water slapped against the hull and spilled over the deck. My first glance at the palace, and I turned the helm over to Skulleater and ran for the rail. I'd been an isle over, one bleeding isle away, when Celine called to me.

There was no report of darkening on the Black Isles. Narza would've sounded an alarm. There was no need for Livia to be sailing anywhere.

I'd never experienced such fierce panic. My chest felt as though it had caved in. I couldn't catch a deep enough breath and instantly abandoned the iron-filled isles in Gavyn's province. The royal smith resided there and had prepared blades for the Chasm journey, but also gifts of the Ever for the earth fae.

None of it mattered now. I'd left it all in a frenzied rush to return home.

"Erik. Straight ahead." Gavyn pointed for the cove. He'd not hesitated before following me onto the *Ever Ship*. "On the docks."

A man was sprawled over the stairs, making a pathetic attempt to pull himself up the long journey back to the palace.

"Shit!" I went over the rail before the ship docked. The tides drew me in, then with a rough wave of my hand, tossed me back onto the shore. I sprinted to the staircase until fire spread through my leg. "Tait, you bastard."

Tait coughed, blood on his chin. He clutched his middle and had the nerve to grin. "Took you long enough. I came straight . . . straightaway when you . . . got stabbed."

I levered his head onto my lap, pulse racing. Tait was bleeding out. I dragged the meat of my palm over my teeth until blood bubbled out and pressed it against Tait's open wound.

He closed his eyes. With his head against my chest, I sang. A low melody, the same as I'd done when Alek arrived broken. Tait's insides were pooling with blood. I called it back. The wound sliced through his innards; I demanded it to close. He hissed against the discomfort when his outer flesh threaded at the sinews and started to pull back into place.

"Enough." He elbowed my ribs. "I can walk now."

"It's not sealed."

"Then I'll get a damn bandage. He took her, Erik."

Panic danced through my chest, pulling my thoughts down a narrow ledge between madness and destruction. Tait staggered to his feet and gripped my arm.

"Erik." With a smack to my face, he drew me to look at him. "Keep your head."

"Too late, Cousin," I said, a chill to my voice. "He took it when he took her. Thoughts of his head in my hands are all I have now."

"Good enough."

I took the stairs to the main doors of the palace three at a time. "How did Larsson get around the blood bond of the crew?"

"I don't know," Tait said, breathless, but he kept a steady pace behind me.

"There are spells to break such things," Gavyn insisted. "Might have had the help of sea witches."

I let out a hiss of frustration and imagined every way I'd take bits of Larsson's bone from every damn limb once I found him again.

The pain of it was crushing, almost suffocating. For nearly ten damn turns, Larsson had sailed at my side. He'd been loyal. Now to do this. To hate me so fiercely in such a way he'd risk his own kingdom—it was a betrayal that lashed to the deepest sinews of my scabrous heart.

We didn't make it through the doors to the palace before being bombarded by Celine, Sewell, and Aleksi.

"Why are you covered in blood?" Celine paled at the sight of Tait.

"Not important." He swatted her hands away from his middle.

"Where is she?" Alek shoved through the others.

"Gone" was all I said before storming into the great hall.

"Erik," Tait said, "you need to know Larsson has a desire for the crown. I took hold for a few moments before he was gone. He believes the crown is his."

"He's a lunatic," Celine snapped.

"Two eels," Sewell said. "Winds whisper tales of two eels."

My jaw tightened. "Winds" meant rumors to Sewell. Two eels. Two of me. "A bastard of Thorvald?"

"Once thought it true," Sewell said, clear and direct. He pounded a fist to his chest. "Saw whispers in the daylight."

I paused. "You saw Thorvald with another child?"

Sewell shook his head, frustration on his face when he tried to find the words. "Saw him and a . . . fox."

Sewell had known Thorvald more than anyone still living. He'd sailed alongside the *Ever Ship* before the Chasm was sealed off by the earth fae. Before I'd been taken as a child, Ever Folk often surfaced to the fae of the earth realms. Trade, barter of magics, seedy deals—it was all done with a healthy trepidation between the different fae.

It had changed when they summoned my father and stole his heir. But before the betrayal, was it possible my father had bedded an earth fae? Possible he'd fathered a bastard between worlds?

"Anything's possible," Tait grumbled when I mumbled my thoughts under my breath. "Our fathers were the same when it came to bedmates, you know that. There was no loyalty."

"Might explain Larsson's ability to avoid a blood bond," Gavyn added. "Blood of the king or the lord doesn't need to bond to his own damn ship, now does he?"

If he shared Thorvald's blood, it could be a possibility the *Ever Ship* would bow to him. I was dangling over a damn precipice of madness and bloodlust. Either would do, so long as it brought me Livia.

"But to be an heir of the Ever, a chosen mate must bear the child," Celine said. "A bastard wouldn't be able to wear the crown."

"We've all heard the rumors of Thorvald's bastard," Tait said. "Even if Larsson has the blood of the Ever King, he'll never have the same power, not since Erik and Livia restored a united throne. Their heart bond is unmatched."

"Unless Larsson has a heart bond too," Gavyn muttered.

Tait paled. "You think Larsson has a woman at his side?"

"I think he has whatever damn sea witch helped cast the darkening."

"Why destroy the Ever if he wants to overtake it?" Celine asked.

"It doesn't matter!" I spun on them. "He has Livia. She is what matters. I will find her, then tear the answers from his damn mouth when I have my hands on him."

I was done speculating. Every breath took Livia farther from me. I kept a hand on my leg, wished someone might cut it off to stop the pain, and gave into the significant limp until I reached my chambers. Once inside, the others immediately dug into a hidden panel in the wall and removed knives, cutlasses, daggers, even barbed arrows.

I secured a black scarf over my head, my blade to my waist, and shouted down the corridor to Alistair to signal the bells of the Ever, a signal to sound an emergency departure for the Ever Crew.

"Dammit!" All at once, my heart stilled. "I can't feel her. I can't feel Livia."

She should be calling to me. I should hear her in my damn heart. Bile burned my throat. It couldn't mean she was gone. If he hurt her, I'd tear Larsson's body apart piece by piece.

"Then I'm beginning the hunt." Gavyn said, gripping my shoulder. "I will scour the kingdom, Erik. The smallest body of water, I will search it until I find her."

Words I wanted to say, that politeness and gratitude Livia wanted from me, tightened in the back of my throat. I said nothing, merely nodded and clapped my palm on the side of his neck.

Gavyn turned to Celine and pressed a kiss to her forehead. "Look after the king, Tidecaller."

"Larsson will know of you." Tears glistened over her long lashes. "Don't you dare die, you arrogant lord."

Gavyn pulled her close, but his gaze lifted over her head to Sewell. The ship's cook shoved his hands in his trouser pockets and pointed his gaze to the floor, avoiding Gavyn's eyes.

"Daj." Gavyn released Celine but kept his arm around her shoulders and wrapped the other around Sewell's neck. "I'll be all right. You watch your own back. Watch Cel's."

Sewell cradled Celine's head to his shoulder when she hugged his waist.

When Livia asked me if Gavyn had freed his father from the prisons after that first day of torture, I'd offered vague truths. I'd kept the secret for so many turns, it was instinct. Since I was a boy, I'd known Gavyn broke into the cell and released his father by using his seeker song and a small bit of water. After all, it was me who'd left a bucket of rainwater in the corner of the cell.

For too many turns we'd tried to hide Sewell's face from the house lords, hidden him in plain sight on the *Ever Ship* where he could embrace the sea but be safe. Where the truth that his daughter still lived could vanish into the sagas and histories of the sea.

Where all three would be left alone at long last.

His mind was sharp, his body strong, his love for his children unchanged. Harald's brutal torture merely confused a few words.

"I have no more time," I said. "We need to find Larsson."

"Erik, if he has the blood of Thorvald, if he uses Livia to clear the darkening, then he could turn the houses against you," Gavyn said.

"Makes sense," Tait replied bitterly. "You've caused enough turmoil." He held up his hands in surrender when I glared at him. "I didn't say it wasn't good turmoil. I'm simply saying we know Joron and Hesh did not approve of a queen."

"You need more blades at your back to bury him," Gavyn said.

Aleksi gripped my shoulder, a feral gleam in his gaze. "You need the aid of those who would fight for your queen with the same ferocity as you."

My body tensed, but I understood exactly what he meant. For Livia I'd do anything. I only hoped this move didn't get my head removed before I found her.

CROUCHED IN FRONT of a full flowering shrub, I cupped one bloom and stroked the velvet petals between my fingers. Leaves and vines were remnants of Livia. One fist curled around the silver swallow dangling from my neck.

She'd be here again, taming the wild branches and flowers. I wouldn't stop until she was back. Until I heard the playful way she called me Serpent. Until her skin was pressed against mine.

The bells rang out over the city.

"Erik." Tait stepped around a bower. "The crew is gathering."

I rose and offered a final look at Livia's gardens. She'd brought life back to the Ever. To me.

Sleepy and disheveled, the Ever Crew gathered on the docks, bidding their wives, their littles, their rum farewell. At the sight of me, most tried to bow their heads, but I carved through the crowds too swiftly to care.

"Erik," Tait said at my back. "Before we do this, be certain this is the move to make."

"What am I to think through, Cousin?" I snapped. "She is gone. There is no risk I will not take to get her back."

Tait gripped my shoulder and forced me to turn around. "They could kill you, and I—" His jaw pulsed. "Erik, you were my brother once. You are all I have."

I hesitated for half a breath before patting his face. "I'm not greeting the Otherworld until she is back. Help me get her back."

He shook my shoulder twice. "To the end."

I gave him a nod.

"I know you killed him," he whispered as we approached the gangplank. "You had my loyalty already, but after you killed Harald, it was sealed in blood that day."

I kept silent, not admitting anything, but I didn't deny it either.

Behind closed doors, Harald beat and brutalized Tait to the gates of the Otherworld often. He'd forced distance between us as boys, but the bond of brotherhood still had a glimmer of light left. I'd never told anyone that I'd slipped into Harald's war tent when the battle drew closer to its end, poisoned him, then slit his throat to make it look like an assassination.

I always suspected Tait knew by the way he'd studied me across the camp when they took Harald's body to the sea.

We stormed onto the deck. Already much of the crew was in place, humming their eerie shanties and setting to work beneath a high moon.

Celine stood near the steps of the quarterdeck and handed me my tricorn.

I swallowed back the unease and slowly placed it on my head. "He left?"

She nodded. "Gavyn will be hunting the seas. House of Bones stands with the true Ever King."

I climbed the steps to the helm. Aleksi leaned over the rail. Shadows coated his eyes when he looked at me. He would be needed to speak—and to speak quickly. But there was always the chance the earth bender's rage would overpower even his nephew's voice when we stepped foot on land.

I gripped the handles of the helm, offered a last look at the moonlit glitter of the royal city, then waved a palm. Wind snapped the crimson sails. The ship lurched. Eyes narrowed, I took in the bustle of the crew. "Make ready to dive, you wretches."

Shouts and commands spilled across the deck. I kept my sights on the stars in the sky. The gleam of Nightfire and his lover. *I'd cross the skies, Songbird.*

The bow tilted forward, carving through the black surface. Songs of the crew were haunting as the water boiled around us, taking us below the waves mouthful by mouthful.

> *A man he's not, we work we rot,*
> *No sleep until it's through.*
> *A sailor's grave is all we crave.*
> *We are the Ever King's crew.*

ALEKSI WAS PALE when the ship surfaced through the Chasm. His knuckles had gone white from clenching the rail.

Tait clapped him on the shoulder. "All right, earth fae? I thought you were supposed to be a warrior."

Aleksi shoved him off. "It's disorienting."

"Better than coming through without a ship though."

"I'll take a ship over being crushed." He came to my side. "Keep a distance. Rave don't come too near the Chasm line. The ship will be safe here."

I peeled my grip off the handles.

"Tidecaller." I crossed the deck to her side. "Man the helm. The ship is yours until I return."

"I should come with you," she whispered so only I could hear.

"You must remain here. Guard the ship." I removed my tricorn and handed it to her. "I need you to be here so you will know if Gavyn finds her."

Celine swallowed with effort but placed the tricorn on her head. "Aye, My King."

The Ever Crew would remain behind. Only Tait and Aleksi joined me in the small boat. Alek guided us to the darker side of the jagged isles. Rough tides made it impossible for their longships to sail this route.

With the Ever King, the seas soothed soon enough.

"Shore patrols should be here," Alek said once we pulled the boat onto the rocky beach. He tugged a dagger from a sheath on his leg, his gaze on the empty paths leading toward the fort. "Stay low. They might be at the point of striking first and asking questions over graves later."

Meaning they might kill their own prince before we ever got a word in for our defense.

We kept low up the hillside, Alek and Tait three paces in front of me. Every few steps, I'd run my fingers through the long grass. Livia's fury magic lived in this soil, and it brought a sense of nearness to her.

"They're not here," Tait muttered, and took out his own blade. "Something's off."

"Agreed." Aleksi spun the dagger in his grip and stepped over the crest of the ridge.

In the next breath, shadows seemed to fall upon us.

"Illusions!" Alek shouted.

Dammit. Some fae clans had wretched magic that tormented the mind with illusions and tricks of the eye.

Roars of warriors broke the darkness. It sounded as though they came from all sides—overhead, underfoot, from the flanks. I reached for my blade, but the moment my hand curled around the hilt, Aleksi and Tait were gone.

I shouted their names and made a run for where the ground fell out from beneath them. A hidden pit dug into the top of the knoll swallowed them up. Beneath a plume of dust, a net released from its snare and snapped over the top of the pit.

Shadows faded and cloaked warriors erupted from the tall grass.

Dammit! Aleksi's shouts were muffled over the roar of the guards. Without a moment's pause they surrounded me. I didn't fight. I didn't pull back. Hands took hold of me and shoved my face down in the soil.

I held steady when a cold blade leveled at my throat. A laugh, cruel and raw, followed. "Bloodsinger himself. Some balls you have to show your face."

A man peered down at me. His hair was braided off his face and runes were inked along his throat and chest. Kohl painted his chin and satin-black eyes. An unnatural darkness, like the whites were blotted out. His face was stubbled, and there was a madness to his grin. "My name is Jonas of House Eriksson. I hoped I'd be the one to catch you."

Jonas. I knew the name. Livia mentioned it when . . . all hells, he was her friend. Another royal of the earth fae. He'd need no reason to cut us down.

"Nothing to say?" Jonas landed a kick to my ribs. I grunted but kept my jaw locked. He lowered into a crouch. "You took them from me. From us all. I ought to slit you open right here."

Pain was speaking. No doubt he thought I'd slaughtered both Livia and Aleksi. I gave him the honor of holding his stare but didn't speak. What was the point? He wouldn't believe a word, not without Alek.

Slowly, he sheathed his blade and stood. "Gather the sea fae caught in the trap." He sneered back at me. "I'll be taking Bloodsinger to Valen. Remember my face, sea king. For I will not look away, not for a moment, as the Night Folk king tears you apart."

ACKNOWLEDGMENTS

I'm a little choked up as I write this. I will never be able to thank my readers enough for loving these worlds. First, with the Broken Kingdoms. You loved those earth fae enough that it expanded into the brutal, mysterious world of the Ever Kingdom. What a ride it has been. Thank you, from the bottom of my heart, thank you.

I am so grateful for my family for putting up with my early-morning rock-Viking music and late-night writing sessions to build these characters. Derek and kiddos, I love you so much. Across the skies and seas, you all have my heart.

Thank you to Sara Sorensen for catching all my plot holes. You have to find those plot holes across worlds now, and you will always have my gratitude for thinking of things literally no one else would ever think about. Thank you to Megan Mitchell for your skill at finding typos missed even after I've read the book no less than a thousand times. Thank you to my other editor, Jennifer Murgia. Trust me, without you all these books would be rough.

Thank you to the Wicked Darlings: You brighten my days with your theories and questions and GIFs. IYKYK.

Thank you to my father in heaven for leading me on this journey. It has been life-changing. Here's to more wickedly romantic tales.

LJ

Enjoy this exclusive bonus content, which reveals the events that forced Sewell and his family into hiding long before the Serpent and Songbird ever met.

1

THE FLESHRIPPER

*T*HEY'D FOUND HER.

Panic, as sharp as a burning blade, dug into my chest. I crashed through the heavy door of the lord's chambers. Lamps were lit along the corridor. The flickers of blue and green flames collided with the pale stone walls of the keep at the House of Bones.

Servants shouted. Shutters over the arched windows slammed shut. I bellowed orders to seal the doors and passageways below the keep. Others raced to the narrow canals and rivers that carved across our shores.

A boom rattled every pane of glass and drew me to a halt in front of one window still left open.

"Damn the gods of the tides." Beyond the shores was the *Ever Ship*.

It was monstrous and glorious. Black laths made of bone and wood, crimson sails with the seal of the House of Kings, and jagged, sharp spines for every Ever King in the bloodline since the gods churned the seas of the Ever.

I'd learned to sail on that ship.

I'd learned to be ruthless, to be devoted to my king and land.

Now it came for my blood.

Ember spears fired another blast of flame and heat. The heavy cinder stones pummeled the gates of the shore.

There was no more time.

With a firm grip, I tugged one of the kitchen stewards—an elder to me but a man who followed my every word with fealty—and drew him close. "Prepare a skiff on the black tides."

"M-m-my Lord, no." His voice was breathless, desperate.

"Do not question me, Pucey." Teeth bared, I gripped the back of his neck. "We fall tonight; accept it. Make ready for me to sail. Not a word of our whereabouts or I'll find you. I'll shred every layer of flesh from your bones."

For a moment there was a flash of annoyance in his eyes. Pucey Eyeeater had served the House of Bones for as long as I could recall. To be accused of disloyalty would set a flame to his blood.

He shirked my grip. "Consider it done, My Lord."

Without another word, without a chance he might catch a glimpse of the agony spreading through my chest, I barreled through a doorway, taking the steps to the upper rooms two at a time.

At the end of the corridor was a narrow door; painted images of sea vines and fatted whales lined the edges. On the first try, the door didn't budge.

Wise boy.

I pounded a fist on the door. "Son, open the door. Hurry!"

I heard the scuffle of small boots across the floorboards. Next, a frantic jiggle to the lock. Finally, the door swung open. My heart cracked.

Thick tears coated Gavyn's brown cheeks. His dark hair belonged to his mother and fell in messy waves around the sharp points of his ears. No mistake, he'd been fitful in here, knowing it could all go wrong, likely blaming himself.

Even at nine turns, the boy knew the dangers of his voice. He knew what would become of us if the truth of our lies were ever found out.

"Daj." His voice cracked.

To Harald, to the dead Ever King, house lords were to shape their heirs with a firm hand, brutality, and indifference.

I never fit in with the house lords.

I could not look on my son with disregard or without affection. The moment my mate told me he would come, I spent nights pressed against her warm skin, whispering all the tales of the Ever Seas he would ever learn.

That had never changed.

Time was short, but I could pause for a breath and wrap my boy in my damn arms.

I crushed Gavyn to my chest, pressing a kiss to the top of his messy hair. "We've known this day could come. It's time to go."

Gavyn nodded. "Blood . . . Bloodsinger won't rat us out, Daj. Maybe he . . . can help."

I shook my head. "Not with this, Son. Not with this. He's too young. Harald holds too much power and listens too much to the powers of dark fae."

The most dangerous soul in the Ever had discovered our secret not more than three turns before.

At first, I thought our boy king might rush to his cruel uncle and give us up. I'd braced for this day to come long ago, but Erik Bloodsinger—a turn younger than my own son—had never uttered a word.

Truth be told, he made certain Gavyn could disappear to visit his maj in peace, always offering reasons the heir to the House of Bones was not at his father's side during meets at the palace.

Harald was never meant to learn that Yulla, my lover, my mate, was still alive. After all, I was supposed to have slaughtered her four turns ago.

King Thorvald had forced his son to do the same to his own mate.

I hoped the dead Ever King was rotting in the seas of the Otherworld for what he had done to Bloodsinger's soul that day.

In truth, I'd wondered if Thorvald had broken his boy to the point that Erik would be as vicious and cruel as his sire. His silence on my treason was proof enough the boy king had a great deal more of his mother than his father filling his blood.

Another boom shuddered through the walls of the keep. With a tug, I urged Gavyn from his room. "Stay close to me. We're going to the grotto, then to the far seas. Understand? We don't return here."

Gavyn's chin quivered. "I understand, Daj. I . . . I don't care, if Maj and Cel are safe."

I patted his cheek gently, offered what I hoped was a soft enough smile, then hurried with my son to the back of the keep. As we went, a few servants dipped their chins, tearful and resigned to the fate of the House of Bones.

They were loyal from the moment I did not bend to Thorvald's command. Most suspected Yulla was alive and hidden.

None knew of the daughter of the House of Bones. Trust my folk as I did, I would never give up Celine. She would be killed swifter than her mother if Harald ever knew.

Truth be told, Gavyn had never even said anything to Bloodsinger. The boy king knew my son's mother was alive, but not that he had a sister.

Outside, the moon hung low in the velvet sky.

The House of Bones was wet with heavy mists that tangled around ferns and streams and honey blossoms.

"My Lord." Pucey, hooded and crouched, emerged from a thick shrub, gesturing for us to follow. "It be ready."

I handed Gavyn into the small skiff tethered to a post on the bank of the Black Tide River. It would take us to the open waters where our grotto was hidden near the shores of the House of Mists.

Lady Narza held no love for Thorvald, not after what he had done to her daughter—the king's mother. As the lady over the sea witches in the House of Mists, I had to hope if she learned the truth of what I'd done, she would say nothing.

Yulla was a siren from the House of Mists. Surely there was loyalty there.

If Narza knew I'd hidden half my family near her shores, the Lady of Witches had never said.

While Gavyn settled on the bench of the small vessel, I turned to Pucey and whispered, "You know what to do if it goes wrong."

Pucey swallowed. "Aye, My Lord. They'll know nothing of him. We'll guide him to follow your steps. Swear to you."

I gave a swift nod. If plans were foiled, I promised Yulla our littles would live to the sunrise. I would do all I could to save them both. But Gavyn was the only one who had the ability to truly disappear.

Pucey held out one arm. I hesitated, then slowly clasped his forearm.

My steward dipped his chin. "I am honored to be part of the House of Bones and to serve you, My Lord. No matter if we never meet again, it has been my honor."

My throat tightened. I nodded, then stepped into the skiff.

Gavyn kept close to my side, eyes toward the darkness of the horizon. With a final glance over my shoulder, I watched the fiery blasts of the *Ever Ship* ignite the keep in brilliant gold and red.

A glance at my home, my folk, my place in the Ever. I knew it would be my last.

2

THE FLESHRIPPER

STARS GLITTERED OVERHEAD. The folktale of the Nightfire constellation had never struck me so fiercely. His three stars flickered and brightened in different hues, but I looked to the brilliant star near the moon, said to be his lover beckoning him home to her.

I felt the same.

White-tipped waves thrashed the nearer we sailed toward the rocky shore. Islands and vacant lands were speckled across the Ever Seas.

We'd selected one with more foliage and a freshwater spring near the top. Covered in mists without many decent docking shores, the island had served us well these four turns. No one had bothered Yulla or Celine.

Not a chime into our journey, and the steady rock of the sea had lulled Gavyn to sleep on the bench.

Gently, I nudged his shoulder. "Wake up. We're here."

He rubbed his eyes with his fists, but a slow, cautious smile split over his face when he saw the mouth of the cave. My pulse quickened. Almost there. Soon we'd be free. I'd sleep beside Yulla again every damn night. Hells, I'd never let her out of my arms again.

I'd be there more often for all of Celine's firsts. I was sly enough, I'd snuck away to know my girl these turns. But I did not see her often enough. I had not had the honor of teaching her how to swim in rough tides or to hoist a banner. I'd not taught her to throw a blade.

I could not hold her every night, sing to her until she slept. I could not tell her every morning how she was one of my favorite faces to see with the sunrise.

All the things she deserved from a father.

Now we could have them. Far from here.

"Leave us."

Gavyn's stomping foot drew my attention.

I frowned and let out a hiss of annoyance when the bulbous eyes of a mermaid peered over the rail of the skiff. "Be gone. We've no desire to swim today."

"Lord of Bones. Stop."

My blood chilled. She spoke in a warning voice. In the next breath, water spilled over the side of my small boat. In mists and foam, Narza took shape.

The sea witch was tall and formidable. Her hair was braided in bright cerulean plaits, and her eyes were wide with warning.

At once, my hand went to the hilt of my blade. I did not care who she was, what power she held, I would not let a soul stop me from reaching my family.

"Sewell." Narza held up a hand. "Do not take him in there."

Her broken gaze drifted to Gavyn.

Gods, no.

I looked back to the witch. "You sold us out."

Narza's brow furrowed. "Never. I did not know what you hid here, it was not my place to know, but I suspected. You know Thorvald's command would never hold favor with me. Not after . . ."

Not after the Ever King had killed her daughter.

Slowly, I let my hand release my blade and looked toward the grotto, a harsh jagged ache splitting my chest. "Are they gone?"

"No," Narza whispered. "But they've been found out."

"How?"

"Merfolk overheard Harald torturing one of your servants until they gave up where you sail to every seventh night." She stepped closer, keeping her voice low so Gavyn would not be able to hear much. "They don't know the boy knows, Sewell. This is his chance to live."

A promise. They would live. I would do everything to make certain my littles lived.

I held Narza's piercing gaze for a breath, another, then nodded. "Will you take him, My Lady? He will not leave me."

She winced. "Aye. For what you have tried to do here, you are honorable, My Lord. He will always be watched by the House of Mists. I swear it."

Deftly, Narza handed me a pouch. She tilted her head. "It will make him sleep. I'll return him to the House of Bones, where they will find him sleeping, unaware of any treason. I will speak for him."

An ache built behind my eyes. I would miss my boy. I'd miss watching the man he'd grow into. With the heel of my hand, I wiped my eyes. "Tell him he was loved, won't you?"

Narza was a stern woman. Grandmother of the Ever King, lady of all sirens and witches. She had her own secrets, her own treasonous thoughts toward the House of Kings, no mistake.

Still, when I asked the question, she gripped my hand. "He will never doubt it."

I cleared my throat and turned to Gavyn. My son kept himself tucked near the bow and looked at me with fear in his eyes. I lowered to a crouch and opened my arms, beckoning him forward. Gavyn did not hesitate.

He flung his arms around my neck. "Did they hurt my maj? Cel?"

I forced a smile. "Our secret's up, Son, but we'll be all right. We're the House of Bones; we don't quit, do we?"

Gavyn shook his head. "Never, Daj."

"I'm going to sneak in and see if I can get our girls, yes? But they're closing in, so I want you to stay with the Lady Narza. She is on our side. You understand why?"

Gavyn offered Narza a befuddled look. He didn't trust the sea witch. Doubtless because the woman had nothing to do with Erik Bloodsinger. To Gavyn, she'd abandoned her grandson to Harald.

I did not understand her absence either, but knew there had to be a good reason Narza left her daughter's son to the cruel hands of Thorvald's brother.

"She will look after you." With slow motions, I pinched the crushed herbs Narza had packed into the pouch—a common sleeping spell—and sprinkled it over Gavyn's head without him realizing. It took moments for his eyes to flutter. I caught him before he toppled backward. Jaw tight, I held him close, breathing him in once more. "I love you. Until the Otherworld."

Two men from the House of Mists had clambered onto the skiff at Narza's signal. One was young with similar eyes to the Lady of Witches. He took hold of Gavyn's limp form, then offered a final look to me.

In the next breath, my son was pulled beneath the tides.

"Narza," I said, voice rough. "Gavyn's voice—"

"Does not need to be spoken of to anyone," she interjected.

Narza's voice allowed her to read the abilities of other magics. She knew Gavyn could turn into the very mist of the sea, disappearing and reappearing in the smallest hint of water.

Seekers were considered deadly, too impossible to control.

If Lord Hesh or Lord Joron or bleeding Harald ever learned of my son's true voice, he would be killed faster than any of us.

I pounded a fist over my chest, a signal to the sea witch she had my eternal gratitude. Without another word, I dove into the sea.

The grotto had a lower entrance that filled with the high tides. I swam through the narrow opening and surfaced in a natural pool inside. Lanterns we'd fashioned to offer my mate and daughter light during the nights and days were vibrant and made the damp on the rocky walls shimmer.

Each move I took was with care—silent and slow.

Until a vicious scream carved through the cavern and dug into my bones.

Yulla.

I kept low and leaned behind a large boulder, where I could keep peering into the main cavern unseen.

Damn the gods.

Three burly men held Yulla's arms. She was battered and bleeding. Her long dark hair was matted in sweat and blood. Her gown was torn halfway down her chest. A dangerous sort of rage heated my blood. If they touched her, they'd suffer.

Their screams would lull me into the Otherworld.

"Don't touch her," Yulla hissed.

She thrashed and tried to bite and strike at the two men holding her back.

My gaze snapped to the third. He stalked toward a pair of jagged stones. Huddled, sobbing, was my little tideling.

Celine had only reached her fourth turn but had the sweetest siren's call, just like her maj. She had Yulla's long willowy hair but with a few brilliant shades of silver, like stars in the dark silk. One ear had been misshapen at her birth, and she tugged on the rolled flesh where it was missing. A nervous habit we'd been trying to break.

She loved to splash in the tides, loved to sleep against my shoulder, she loved sneaking too many sour currants with me when Yulla wasn't looking.

My world would be shattered without her as much as Gavyn, as much as their mother.

"Come on out, girl." The man laughed, slapping a dagger against his open palm. "I've been looking for a good target to prac—"

His voice cut off. His breath caught. A look of horror crossed his features when he pawed at his throat. My house dagger pierced through the front. A direct shot from the back of his neck through the front.

I wasted no time, taking the stun of his two companions to draw my blade and rush into the cavern. Yulla cried out and took one of the sods at her side while I took the other. She had no blade but clawed like each fingernail was made of jagged iron.

"Take Celine, Sewell!" she cried.

I slashed my sword against the blade of the second brute. "I'll take you both."

"Bone Lord." The man I fought flashed his teeth. "You betray the Ever. You'll burn here. But I'll make you watch me take your mate first. Then maybe you can watch your little bitch get eaten by the eels before we kill you."

My lip curled. Our blades locked, drawing our faces close enough that I could make out every pockmark on his rough, scaly cheeks. I snapped my teeth. "Best of luck."

I kicked his knee, drawing him forward with a hiss. He made ready his blade, but not fast enough. When he stumbled over a ledge in the stones, I rammed my blade through the underside of his chin until the point of my cutlass burst through his brow.

"Don't move, Lord Sewell." Across the cavern the last man had Yulla pinned to his chest, his knife against her throat. "Drop your blade, or you watch her die."

I yanked my sword free of the dead fae's skull, then wiped blood from my lip with the back of my hand, never taking my gaze off the last bastard I had left to kill.

"Take her, Sewell. You promised. I'll await you in the seas of—" Yulla winced when the knife drew blood, digging deeper into her flesh.

My hand tightened around the hilt of my sword. At my back, my little daughter sobbed. At my front, my lover, my mate, begged me to let her die and flee.

I could never.

I had to have them both.

I had to have my whole family.

"Let her go," I said, voice steady. "Let her go, and I won't sing."

A flash of fear filled the brute's eyes. He knew what my voice could do, how it could slaughter with ease.

"We'll disappear and you live another day," I went on, rolling my sword in my grip. "Your choice."

For a moment, he hesitated. Even lowered the blade slightly. For a moment my hopes soared. Until it all ended.

Celine screamed.

I wheeled around and faced the cruel sneer of Harald. He had my girl by her hair. Gods, she was so small next to him.

"Oh, you won't be singing." Harald Songtaker stood near the mouth of the grotto with a handful of the crewmen from the *Ever Ship*. "Figured you'd try to flee if we distracted you with the ship. Traitors are so predictable."

A low hum rumbled around the cavern. Damn the gods. A hand went to my chest when the sharp bite of icy power froze my own voice. It was Harald's gift—to take the ability of other sea fae to call upon their magic.

The only ones who seemed immune were the earth fae we'd encountered over the turns and the tiny Ever King. More proof Harald was never accepted as the true leader of the Ever and Erik Bloodsinger had the true power of the land, even if the boy did not understand it all yet.

What did it matter? I could not sing.

My greatest weapon, the ruthlessness of my voice, was taken from me.

Harald's dark hair was tied off his brow with a blue scarf. His eyes were hardened and burned like angry fire. Like most of the bloodline in the royal house, his canines were sharper, more elongated.

Thorvald had been broad with a sea tint to his skin. Harald was shorter, sturdier, and once a decent man. Until the earth fae slaughtered his brother.

Until he met dark fae from their realms and chilled any goodness he'd held in his chest.

Harald stroked the tears on my daughter's cheeks, a knife to her little heart. He laughed and jerked his head to the crewmen at his back. "Bring my bastard. Let him watch. See if we can break some of that weakness from his bones."

The men behind Harald were all part of the Ever Crew. Most honorable, most brutal. Still, they were blood-bound to follow orders. Until King Erik reached at least thirteen, they would follow Harald's command by proxy.

The Ever King was still in his tutelage, after all.

With more care than Harald likely wanted, two men from the crew walked forward with another boy between them. Young Tait Heartwalker was smaller than Gavyn, had a blackened, swollen jaw, two fingers that were bent at odd angles, and two red-gold eyes that looked heavy with more pain than such a young boy should ever know.

One of the Ever Crew stayed by the boy and kept him away from his ruthless father.

"Watch, bastard," Harald said. I could not recall the last time he actually spoke his son's name. "This is how you lead." He looked back to me. "When we got the truth from your servant that you'd defied the order to rid the Ever of your mate, I did not anticipate we'd find this little sweet."

Celine whimpered when Harald tugged on her hair again.

I wanted her to look at me, wanted her to know I'd be with her. Yulla sobbed behind me. I'd failed them both.

"They have nothing to do with my choices, Harald," I snapped. Gods, I hated the indifferent tone of my voice when I barreled on. "And you make assumptions about their importance to me."

Harald scoffed. "You hid the bitch"—he jerked his chin at Yulla—"when she ought to have been slaughtered turns ago. Had a forbidden little with her. Don't try to disregard their importance, Sewell."

"Can any man blame me for wanting to keep a bedmate? She's wild, satisfying. She is my plunder, and our laws allow me to keep what I've earned. Not even the king could take it. Thorvald desired a dead mate, well, fine for the dead king. I prefer a mate where she belongs—in my bed."

Harald narrowed his dull eyes as though he considered I might speak true.

It was enough of a distraction, no one took note of the blade I slowly slid from my sleeve, creeping nearer to my palm.

Harald shook his head. "So, if you're to be believed, we could use the mate. If that's all she's good for, that is."

Rage, hot and wretched, burned in my blood. Any man to put a hand on my Yulla would be torn into such slight pieces, not even the Otherworld would recognize them as a whole soul.

"Ah, I don't share what is mine, Songtaker. You should know that."

"Hmm. What I know is the rest of us proved our loyalty and rid the Ever of useless mates after our heirs were born." He cast a withering glare at his boy. "Although, I've considered taking another to try again for something better. The point is, Lord Sewell, you didn't. You hid her, bedded her, kept a rare daughter from the crown. Now you expect us to think they mean nothing?"

The blade was cool against my palm. Another breath, another heartbeat, and I would have a clean aim for Harald's heart. I might not survive the attack from the crew after he died, but at least the Ever would be free of his wretchedness.

The heir to the throne, I had all the faith, would bring the Ever Kingdom to a new glory.

Harald shrugged. "If they mean so little to you . . ."

Leather hit my palm when the blade slid out. Time seemed to slow. I raised my hand to throw the knife in the same moment Harald signaled to the man holding my Yulla at my back. Panic sliced through my heart.

The knife flew, but my distraction caused the blade to go off its mark enough that Harald sidestepped, laughing.

By the time I reeled around, the bastard had a firmer grip on the knife against Yulla's throat.

"No!" I bellowed and raced for her.

He wrenched it over her slender neck. I saw nothing but blood, heard nothing but the splutter of her words.

I fell to my knees, catching her as she fell. "Yulla, no, no, no." My palm pressed over the gushing wound, tears scorched over my eyes.

She looked to me, convulsing, but . . . she smiled.

For a small moment, a single breath, my mate, the only woman I'd ever loved, smiled. She reached a trembling hand, her fingers brushing over my lips.

Then she was gone.

The spell surrounding me shattered, and the cries and commands that had been muffled came back into focus.

My daughter screamed. Harald had her hoisted over the shoulder of one of the crewmen. I made a move to chase after her, but a heavy blow struck the side of my head, and every wretched truth of the grotto faded into black.

3

THE SEA SEEKER

IT WENT BAD.

The whole plan went bad. I knew it. Felt it. When one of those tricky witches from the House of Mists was there in my room, looking all sad and wretched, I knew it went bad.

Got him to talk though. Took a bit of nudging, but Tavish from the House of Mists looked like he might understand something about losing folk. I didn't know his story, but he admitted my daj had gone for the grotto.

Admitted Harald found out about little Cel. He said some merfolk saw prisoners being tugged away to the House of Kings. That meant I had a bleeding face to talk to.

Or kill.

I gripped a hand around one of Daj's old dull knives he gave me on my seventh turn. The ponds of the royal gardens were covered by unmanaged thorns and briars, but it was the closest I could get to the door where he slept.

In a low crouch, I staggered up the stone steps until I reached the arched doorway. Using a whalebone and the point of my knife, I waited until the lock clicked, then slipped through the crack in the door.

Stupid boy. I told him he ought to start blocking his damn door.

I crept over the woven rug toward the oversized bed fit for a hundred men—at least it seemed like it.

Knife in hand, I levered onto the edge of the royal bed.

"Lookin' to kill a king, Seeker?"

My heart felt like it jumped to my damn brain. I stumbled over the furs and coverlets of Bloodsinger's too-huge bed. There he was, leaning against the door to the washroom.

Shorter than me, messy dark brown hair with touches of sun red buried in there. He was battered. Then again, the young Ever King had been tortured. Daj told me all about it. Trapped in the earth fae realms (I never thought they were real before) when he was barely older than Cel.

He left the Ever without scars on his skin, without a limp, then he came back different. Harsher, with deep scars across his body.

Erik Bloodsinger snapped at everyone, like a sharp-toothed fish snapping his jaws. But with me . . . I don't know, somehow we almost seemed like friends. Two boys carrying secrets. I learned the truth about his maj, how he was forced to send her to the Otherworld. He learned I could turn into sea mist.

But if he was with Harald now . . . I'd kill him.

"Did you order 'em to be taken?" I held the knife out, ashamed how my voice trembled like a stupid babe.

Erik tilted his head. "Who?"

Gods, I couldn't stop the tears, and I didn't try. The Ever King looked almost frightened when he watched me break, like he didn't know what to do, what to say.

He probably didn't. No one showed emotion in this bleeding palace, and I couldn't stop.

"They found her." My voice broke and I used my sleeve to wipe away the wet seeping from my eyes and nose. "Harald. Daj went after them, and . . . and I don't know where they are. Did you . . . did you rat us out?"

"Shut it, Seeker," Bloodsinger hissed. His voice was higher than mine, but in the moment it was sharp as a blade. "Made a vow I wouldn't, didn't I?" The Ever King limped into the great sitting room connected to his bedchamber. He pressed a small hand to his bad leg and locked the door, then wheeled on me. "Tell me what happened."

I let it spill. The attack of the *Ever Ship*—Bloodsinger didn't know his wretched uncle had taken the ship without him. I told him how Narza showed up. The king ruffled at that. How the House of Mists said they saw some prisoners.

When I finished, I was slumped into one of the padded chairs, voice raw and dry.

Erik's face was pale, a horrified expression dug into it. There were days I forgot he was the king of the Ever. He looked too small, too much like me. Still, the weight of a kingdom rested on his shoulders, but his expression slowly shifted, like he might burn it all after hearing the news.

"Harald is listening to dark earth fae. He's not the king!" Erik shouted.

"We gotta find them," I said. "My daj, my maj, and my . . ." My voice trailed off before I mentioned Celine.

I should've known the king would catch it. Yes, he was a boy, but so was I.

Us boys of the Ever weren't stupid sods.

"And who?" Erik's red eyes burned like the flames in the lanterns. "You keeping things from me, Seeker? Thought we said that was pointless long ago."

True enough. Three turns back, I'd disobeyed my daj, practiced my seeking, and landed myself in the pond of the king's gardens. Being only six turns at the time, I hadn't meant to be so stupid.

Erik was there. I hadn't seen the young king since he'd been rescued from the earth fae realms. Thorvald had been dead for a mere turn, and I half expected to find his heir—like the rumors said—chopped up and missing eyes and limbs.

He wasn't chopped up but had more than a few gashes.

I'd gotten on my knees as Daj always said we ought to do to a king, and pleaded he wouldn't rat my voice out.

All the young king asked was if my daj knew.

With a bit of reluctance, I admitted he did. Something about the confession that my daj knew I held forbidden magic that often led to an execution and still had not given me up intrigued Erik Bloodsinger.

For weeks, we kept meeting. Sometimes to have mock battles with wooden swords, sometimes to try some of the stolen sweets he'd taken from the royal cooking rooms.

Soon enough, he told me about his maj. It was the only time the Ever King seemed close to tears.

I made my confession—my maj was alive.

We vowed to keep the other's secrets, so long as we always told the truth to each other.

I lifted my gaze to Erik's. "I kept one secret. I've a little sister, Bloodsinger. They'll kill her. She's not yet five turns."

Erik's eyes flashed with a touch of surprise, but he didn't shout at me or complain I'd not kept my end of the bargain. All the boy king did was stare at the blue flames of the fire in the inglenook. "I'll find where he's taken them. Get gone, Seeker. Don't let them trap you too. I'll send word when I know."

The thought of leaving the royal city dug deep into my belly until I thought I might vomit.

When I hesitated too long, the Ever King rolled his eyes. "Fine. Stay here, then."

Without a protest, I hurried to the bedchamber and curled

under the furs, more terrified than I wanted to let on. Even if Erik was the king, I was still bleeding older, and it wouldn't do if I started blubbering again.

The door clicked, and Bloodsinger was gone.

All I could do now was wait.

4

THE FLESHRIPPER

BLOOD DRIPPED INTO my eyes.

All night, I'd remained locked in the dark with only thoughts of my Yulla and fears for my littles to haunt my mind.

Now two more brutes dragged me through the palace faster than my bruised and battered body cared to move. What was the point?

Part of me believed they'd take me to see the heads of my family piked on a fence. I steeled myself against the anguish, preparing to see them all dead.

Another part imagined they would kill me in front of my tidelings, then sell off Gavyn and Celine to a life of misery.

"Get up." One of the guards grunted and heaved under my arm, forcing me upright.

The second shoved against the doors of the great hall and let me stumble inside. A crowd had gathered. Folk of the Ever, some nobles from all the houses, courtiers of the palace, all looked at me with a wary contempt.

From the dais where the Ever King's throne was placed, a slow applause built. Harald rose from the king's seat, sneering. Behind him stood the dark earth fae who stole strength from our sea witches, spoke of nothing but revenge against the earth fae who'd killed Thorvald and corrupted our lands.

He would take the Ever to war against the earth realm, no doubt. And Harald would allow it.

He'd destroy our lands.

"Lord Sewell. How was your night?"

Laughter rippled through the great hall. One of the guards struck me on the back of my skull. I cared little and glanced around, desperate to find my littles.

Harald crouched in front of me, his eyes like an empty storm. "Your pretty mate was sent to the tides. I bet we'll be finding pieces of her for weeks. No burial, no ceremony, no funeral pyre. She will be forgotten, as will you."

My jaw pulsed with unmanaged fury.

Harald clicked his tongue and stood. "You were a good house lord, Sewell. Which is the only reason I now offer you a chance at a swift death. Your son was found, unaware of his father's treachery. He has the House of Mists at his side." Harald seemed perturbed at the notion of it.

From the corner of my eye, I found where Narza and several witches and sirens from the House of Mists stood. Somber, dressed in dark silks. I took their stoicism to mean they mourned the loss of one of their own.

Yulla. Her voice, her sweet siren's call would not be heard in these waters again.

I returned my glare to Harald. "My son is innocent."

"And he will stay that way if you do as I say." Harald snapped his fingers and a palace guard shoved me forward.

"No." The word slid over my tongue. My girl was dragged forward, her tiny wrists bound in rough rope. Tears had stained the soft brown of her skin, and her brilliant blue eyes sparkled with more. Bruises marred her face, and a bloody bandage covered her throat. My heart stalled. Gods, no. They'd cut out her damn siren call.

Bastards. I wanted nothing more than to see them all torn to pieces for touching my daughter.

Harald took hold of the rope, tugging Celine against his leg. She cried and whimpered but lifted her gaze to me.

I smiled. Forced, no doubt, but she was terrified. I'd die before I looked away.

"You hid a child from the crown, Sewell. A rare daughter for a lord. Might be rather powerful for all we know." Harald patted Celine's head, laughing when she flinched. "Here is where you must make a choice—your heir and bloodline living on in the House of Bones, or your girl."

"Speak plainly, Harald." I would never choose between my children. I'd die first.

"The girl will not live." Harald flashed his teeth. "I assure you, we will see to it she dies slowly and painfully. Then you will follow. Your boy will watch."

"You bastard. She is a child."

"What does that matter? She will not always be one." Harald knelt beside Celine and pressed a kiss to her cheek, laughing when my girl let out a choked sob.

"Tideling," I whispered. "Look at me. Only me."

Gods, she was so sweet, so small, but she lifted her chin and held my stare.

"You can spare her a violent death," Harald said. "If you are the one to kill her."

All gods.

I did not see a way out. I did not know how to best Harald here. Not when he blocked my voice, not when he had blades pointed at my daughter, not when Gavyn was alone and vulnerable.

Celine trembled. I wasn't certain how much she understood, but she knew there was danger here. How could I do it? How could I put my hands on her and watch the light leave her precious eyes?

"Make your choice," Harald hissed.

"He has no choice."

Murmurs filtered across the great hall. My heart stuttered in my chest. Flanked by two young crewmen, the boy king stepped into the hall.

Erik Bloodsinger was skinny and scarred, hardly formidable. One ear had recently been pierced when he reached the age of eight, but the other would not come until he reached ten. His voice was high and pitchy and he walked unsteadily on his crooked leg.

Still, the boy had a fire in his eyes, a hatred and power that urged grown fae to give him a wide berth.

He met my gaze for half a breath and smirked. Slippery as a little eel, that was the boy Ever King.

Erik faced his uncle. Harald returned the look with disdain. Once he doted on the future king, but that all changed with Thorvald's death and the dark fae. Harald wanted the crown, but the blood crown would never choose him.

"Erik," Harald snapped, "this isn't for you."

"I thought I was king. Isn't everything for me? That's what you always tell me, Uncle." The boy looked around. "All this is mine. I ought to learn to protect it."

"Aye, but this—"

"I want the girl." Erik sneered at Celine. "I need somethin' to test my blood. Never know how much to use to cause damage and all that. Call it practice."

"No." I tugged on the hands holding me bound.

"Well thought, Nephew." Harald's face brightened. He barked a laugh and handed the end of Celine's rope to the crewman next to the young king.

Celine cried out for me, reaching her bound hands. I struggled, desperate to reach her. The boy king was just like Thorvald, brutal, murderous, and now—

I hesitated. Erik met my gaze before he turned to follow the crewman and my sobbing daughter. He . . . winked.

"Execute him in the morning, says I," Erik said, trying to keep his small voice demanding despite his youth. "Let him think about her screams."

"And that is a glimpse at the Ever King who will take us to our revenge one day!" Harald bellowed, drawing a few cheers from the crowd. They applauded Erik Bloodsinger. They cared nothing for the tears of my girl.

They were the last things I heard before I was pulled away and tossed back into the dark cell.

"MY NEPHEW SHOWED promise today." Harald's dark voice cut through the room. He held with him heavy mallets, chains, and blades, all rolled in sealskin. "I've been told your girl has done nothing but scream as he poisons her and sings her back to health."

Harald dropped his weapons.

I said nothing, watching his every move.

"I know the king wished to see you slaughtered on the morrow, but I thought we could have a bit of fun first."

I closed my eyes.

Soon, Yulla. I shall be with you soon.

I didn't fight when Harald bound my wrists and stretched me against the wall. I bit down on my roars of pain when he slashed into my skin, when he beat my bones. I felt my mind grow hazy with each club to my skull.

Thoughts, words, time—they all melded together into a cloud of unease as he beat me. Tortured me.

Soon. I would be with her soon.

5

THE SEA SEEKER

"IT'S BAD, GAVYN," Erik said in a hushed rasp. He held the pail of rainwater he'd collected through a night storm.

I swallowed through emotion. "He dead?"

Maj was gone. Bloodsinger hadn't wanted to tell me, but I could see it. The way he looked at me when I asked about her, I knew. It was the same look he had whenever I brought up his dead mother.

Gone.

I didn't know how to live in a world without her. She wouldn't sing to me again, wouldn't tease me about my wild morning hair anymore. My maj wouldn't wink at me anymore right before we played a trick on Daj.

I blinked through broken memories. No. I had to think about what to do now. Maj needed me to save the rest of us.

She'd want me to look out for Cel; she'd want me to protect Daj.

Erik grunted when he lifted the pail a little more and made a move for the door. "Saw him breathing last I checked. But Harald got to him real bad."

"I gotta get him out, Bloodsinger." I glanced to the place beneath the king's bed where we'd fashioned a bed for Celine. She hugged her skinny knees to her chest, asleep, but still whimpering through nightmares. "He's not gonna make it if I don't."

"What the hells do you think I'm doin'?" Erik held up the pail. "Wait at least a chime before slipping into the cell, the fifth one from the back wall. Window's small but not blocked."

Gods, he was placing water in the cell of my daj, giving me a shot to free him.

"A chime," Erik whispered, then hooded his head and slipped into the dark corridor off his room.

I BLEW OUT a breath. I'd cried enough these last days to bring shame to the whole of the seas of the Otherworld, where ancestors swam.

The window had a few jagged pieces of old iron. Bloodsinger was younger, but he was proving to be a bit wiser. It was both comforting and annoying.

I shouldn't let a younger little outsmart me, but tonight I was glad he knew a bit more. Beside my daj's cell was a small stream that led to one of the inlets. The window was left unguarded, no doubt because it would take my daj breaking his shoulders or something to slip through.

Too small for him but perfect for me.

I shook out my hands and slipped inside. The cells below the palace reeked of stagnate water, piss, and rot. I coughed against the stench of it and carefully maneuvered down the cobbled wall until my feet found damp ground.

My breath choked in the back of my throat.

"Daj." The word croaked. I hurried to the corner of the cell where my father was rolled against the wall, bloodied and still.

My fingers shook when I touched his shoulder. He flinched with a groan.

Damn the gods. Harald had him balancing near the Otherworld. He'd taken out his rage on my father's head and chest. Like he wanted to crush his skull and heart. One more strike, and he'd meet Maj, no mistake.

I glanced over my shoulder and saw the pail of rainwater, disguised to look like a chamber pot. With hurried, quiet steps, I pulled the bucket to us and took hold of my father's arm. I'd done this with toys, blades, and books. If I was holding tightly to them in one hand, and touching the water with my other, my voice would evaporate whatever I was holding along with me.

I'd never tried it on another sea fae.

There wasn't a choice left to make. Daj needed out, and we couldn't leave a trace that Bloodsinger and I had anything to do with it. Sewell of the House of Bones needed to disappear.

"Hang on, Daj," I mumbled, and placed my free hand in the rainwater.

A low hum like the wind on the tides broke the silence of the cell. The shift to sea mist was calm, gentle, a little disconcerting. My skin rippled like a rolling tide, then little prickles of damp coated my skin. It always felt as though I'd walked into the first moments of a rainstorm, right before the torrent began.

My song peeled me through the small bucket. With focus and intent, I led us to the nearby stream. Slowly, the misty sensation on my flesh strengthened to something as slick as eel skin until I found my feet again.

I gasped when my head emerged from the splash of a rogue wave in the stream.

Gods, he was heavy. My father was iridescent while my song wore off but as strong as the ships we sailed.

Still damp and slick, I winced as I pulled him onto the banks of the stream. Once he was sprawled on the grass, I rushed to his side, checking to see if I'd torn him to shreds even more or if his heart still beat.

I pressed an ear to his chest and grinned in relief when the slightest thud pounded against my cheek.

We weren't in the clear yet.

Before I'd entered the cell, I knew I'd have to carry Daj to the shore where we could sail to a small cave, so I hid a cart fishmongers used in the royal city. It took more time to lever him onto the back, and truth be told, his legs dangled off the edge the entire journey to the shore, but I managed to heave him onto the rowboat and sail far from the palace and Harald's cruel hands.

6

THE FLESHRIPPER

SLIVERS OF LIGHT scorched through my skull when I tried to crack my eyes. The pain of Harald's torture hadn't faded.

"He's talkin'," a low whisper broke through the haze. A boy's voice, one I knew too well. Gavyn sniffed somewhere nearby. "But every time he does, it doesn't make much sense."

Damn the gods. Lucid moments were there. Over the days, I'd tried to speak. Words, full phrases, all of it was there in my mind, but I could not get my bleeding mouth to work.

Garbled sounds and thoughts were spoken instead, as though my mind were trying to make up new expressions for the simplest words—even my own son's name, I'd not been able to speak.

"He got pounded in the skull over and over."

My blood cooled. I lifted my chin and caught sight of the boy king.

Unbridled rage was misplaced against the boy. He'd taken my girl, likely poisoned her, likely listened to her screams. Yet he was a child as much as her. Harald was to blame. Still, I wanted to snap Erik Bloodsinger's neck for what he'd done.

"Daj." Gavyn's big eyes fell in front of my face, blocking the sight of the young Ever King. "You're all right, Daj. We've got Blister Poppy workin' on you. She won't be talking to anyone. Then we've got a plan. A big one."

"Let him rest, boy. Strikes to the head leave a mind disoriented." Blister Poppy, a boneweaver without loyalty to any house, stepped in front of me, grinning. "Let's take a look at those wounds."

The woman adjusted bandages on my head. I clenched my fists, wanting to speak, but was unable to get my tongue to move with any more than grunts and desperate words that became trapped.

I needed Gavyn to get away from Erik Bloodsinger.

I needed my boy to know what he'd done to his sister.

With a trembling finger, I pointed at the boy king, then slid the same finger over my throat, again and again until Gavyn saw.

"What's he sayin'?" Gavyn leaned over me again, a single tear on his cheek. His voice was smaller when he spoke again. "Daj, are you . . . are you talkin' about Maj?"

An ache, fierce and harsh, slashed through my chest. Yulla. Gods, she was gone.

My eyes clenched, but I shook my head and gestured the idea of someone smaller, younger. Then I pointed at the Ever King again and drew my finger across my throat.

"The little," Erik said, bloodred eyes narrowed. He folded his skinny arms. "He's meanin' your sister."

Did Gavyn know?

"Oh." My son faced me, a cautious smile on his face. "You saw Bloodsinger take her, that's what you're saying?"

I nodded.

"Daj, Cel's all right." Gavyn looked back at the boy king. "She's hidden. Erik didn't touch her. He saved her from Harald. We're gonna hide her right in plain sight."

Blister Poppy rested a hand on my shoulder. "There are those, Lord Sewell, who do not stand for what noble houses do to their mates. You have allies here, and one is a growing king."

I couldn't speak, but I pinned Erik Bloodsinger with my gaze.

The boy looked away, staring at a small dagger he spun in his hands. I knocked my knuckles against the bedpost until he looked back.

Erik glared at me, no doubt unused to seeing affection; no doubt he would wither should I embrace him in gratitude.

All I did was press a fist to my chest, a gesture of loyalty to the king of the Ever.

Erik frowned but nodded.

"We're gonna hide you both," Gavyn whispered. "Everyone thinks you're dead. No one knows that I know. I'll keep the House of Bones, Daj. Celine will live; so will you."

I winced. They'd live, but as long as there were beliefs that matched Harald Songtaker's, my young ones were at risk. We could not be the same bonded family as we once were. It would mean secret grins whenever I saw my son as a house lord. It would mean that I might not even see my little tideling much at all.

I closed my eyes, broken, filled with rage, filled with gratitude they still lived.

"It's not perfect, Sewell," Poppy whispered, "but they will live. You will live under the banner of the Ever King." She leaned closer so only I could hear. "Guide him away from Harald's word. You know as well as I there is more to the boy than they are making him to be. He has your son, your girl, and you to show him what it means to lead. To give everything for those he loves. Teach him love is no weakness."

I swallowed thickly. It was a grand task she was asking of me. Harald polluted his nephew with hatred toward the earth fae for slaughtering Thorvald. Doubtless there would be war one day. I peered to the place Gavyn stood near Erik.

Two boys forced to face too much. Two boys already stronger than their fathers.

I wanted to offer Blister Poppy a simple yes, a vow to agree, but

I could not do more than mumble. With a nod, I made the same gesture to her—a fist over my heart.

Whatever happened from here, Erik Bloodsinger had the House of Bones. He'd saved my girl, and I suspect he had something to do with Gavyn taking me out of that cell. No matter what the tides brought, the Ever King would always have us.

Keep reading for a sneak peek of the next book
in the Ever Seas series:

THE EVER QUEEN

PROLOGUE

That Day

HIS ENDING WASN'T going to change.

In truth, the boy had always known this was how his story would go—such was the way of landing on the losing side of a war.

Gentle water lapped on the shore at the boy's back. Warriors stood between him and home. Damp sand dug into the dirty trousers covering his bruised knees, but there was a bit of relief in the chill of the sea that allowed him to breathe again.

Nights spent cramped within the cruel stone walls of the cell were at an end. Now he'd face his fate.

At his side, another boy awaited punishment much the same. A boy the young king was meant to hate. But the king could not entirely despise the other young sea fae. Another failure he ought to add to the list of ways he had yet to be the king his father would've wanted.

The second boy, battered and dirty, was the only one from home who'd remained.

Others from their realm had already fled in their garish ships of bone and soft wood, of black and blue sails. The moment the fighting ended, they faded beneath the violent tides.

The boy king feared the folk on the shore, feared the blades on their belts, the blood beneath their fingernails. But he still held a bit of power—pulses in their jaws, avoidance in their stances, the way they stared at the boy king like he might lash out in the next heartbeat. He feared them, but no mistake, the fae of the earth also feared the king of the sea.

As he listened to the punishment leveled against the second sea fae by kings and queens of enemy realms, the young king curled his bruised fingers around his new small charm. The girl had tried to make it more valuable than it was—"silver" was a grand term; the small swallow was more like soft tin.

Still, from the moment his little songbird sped away through the tall grass, the young king clung to her parting gift. Hate boiled like the poison in his blood, yet . . . he could not shake his thoughts of the little bird who'd told him grand tales in the darkest night.

One look. One final glance. He could steal one more from the girl before he was locked beneath the waves. Instead, when the boy raised his eyes, he was met with an enemy, war battered but deadly, and clad all in black.

The dark eyes of a fae king who could bend the bedrock took him in like the night drinking the sun. Perhaps the boy's ending would not be banishment. Perhaps the earth bender king would stain the sand in poisonous blood without a thought.

"You did not challenge me, boy," said the enemy king.

The challenge. The entire purpose for the sea king's arrival to the earth realms. Like a fool, he'd shamed his kingdom. One soft moment of the heart, one healing song given to a dying enemy, and the boy forfeited his chance to reclaim the power he lost for his father all those turns ago.

"The opportunity was taken by other things" was all the young king said.

Fear was there, but he wouldn't show it. Weakness was not meant to live within Ever Kings, so the boy lifted his chin, waiting for the blow of the same dark, deadly ax that had carved his father's heart.

Excerpt from THE EVER QUEEN

Unease slithered down his spine when the earth bender lowered to one knee, when he placed himself nose-to-nose with the boy.

Why would a victorious king descend to the same level as his defeated foe?

The earth bender king could snap the boy's neck, yet he spoke the next words in a soft voice, almost kind.

"You could stay here. You'd be welcome amongst our folk and still lead your people if you wanted. There are kings and queens here to guide you."

Stay? The father of his songbird, an enemy, a man he'd come to kill wanted him to . . . stay?

Swifter than a star falling in the night sky, the boy glimpsed her over the enemy king's shoulder. She stood beside her pale-as-frost mother. The girl was dressed in a pretty green gown, and a gold chain draped over dainty, dark curls. Different from the simple nightdresses hidden beneath her oversized fur cloaks she'd worn when she snuck out to his cell.

Sapphire eyes caught his, and the boy felt a shift. Something sturdy took hold somewhere deep in his chest, a feeling he'd never known before.

Stay. He could stay and hear more of her tales while . . . kings controlled him. That was all this was, another chance for a new version of Harald or Thorvald to shape him into a handcrafted king of their liking.

With a curl to his lip, the boy turned back to the enemy.

"I know what the guidance of kings means, Earth Bender," the boy said in a low snarl.

"I am not your uncle, boy. Nor am I your father."

Gods, could he read minds? The boy held his breath, uncertain what moves to make when his enemy, a man who should slit the boy's throat this moment, lowered his voice again.

He spoke even softer, even kinder, as though the earth king

knew the secret and sensed the pull to the little bird standing beside her mother. As though the earth bender didn't mind if a sea serpent befriended a songbird.

"Stay, Erik Bloodsinger," he said. "There are folk here who would be better for it if you did."

Once more, the boy looked to the girl. *Better for it.* Would she be better if he remained in her world? Doubtful. Still, the boy wanted to agree. More fiercely than anything, the boy wanted to forget the disdain of his father, forget the hatred, and remain with the little bird and her stories.

But hatred was a fickle thing. The blur of want and desire could be blotted out when loathing and fear held fast.

The boy chose his ending. He chose not to remain where songbirds sing their haunting songs. He vowed blood where the enemy offered peace. The boy saw to it the earth bender had no choice but to lock him away.

While the tides spilled over the head of the young Ever King, as violent currents swallowed him and dragged him home, he thought of her.

He thought of how one day he might find a way to finish the tale he began on the land of his enemies. He could rid her of the enemy king since, as he'd already come to realize, she wasn't theirs.

She was always going to be his.

1

THE SERPENT

*F*OR LIVIA.

Her name kept rushing through my head with every kick, every strike from the earth fae warriors.

I needed to live for her. I needed to return to the *Ever Ship* and find her. All I needed to do was survive long enough for Aleksi to speak for me.

Jonas, a prince from one of the earth fae realms, sneered at me as his men shoved a dirty scrap of leather into my mouth. I swallowed against the musty taste of it, as though it had been tucked down sweat-soaked trousers and baked beneath a hot sun.

Jonas gripped my arms and forced me up. Fire lit in my thigh, as though a flame were devouring the bone.

"Send a signal to the shore watch," Jonas commanded. "There could be more of these sods in the tides."

A little longer. Survive a little longer.

Two warriors were trudging toward the trap in which both Alek and Tait had fallen. Soon enough, they'd realize their error. I would face the earth bender—on my damn knees if needed—and we would bleeding sail back to the Ever and find my queen.

I didn't fight when Jonas commanded two warriors to bind my wrists. I didn't fight when they tugged me forward to where a row of earth stallions awaited their riders. The charges were strange-looking. I'd seen them before, but unlike the horthane of the Ever, these beasts hardly seemed capable of swimming in the tides. Dull teeth, rounded hooves, and swishing tails that looked like fae hair.

"Henrik." Jonas nodded at a warrior. "On second thought, let the other sea fae rot for a bit. I want the focus on the king."

The warrior dipped his chin and halted ten paces from the sinkhole in the knoll. *Shit.* They were leaving Aleksi.

From here, the muffled shouts of Alek's and Tait's voices were there, but wholly unintelligible. Perhaps it was a spell, a curse of fate, but they sounded like nothing more than men shouting through a door far away. Alek's own people did not realize they'd ensnared a prince. A prince whose voice and support I desperately needed.

A rush of panic tightened in my chest. Through the rancid gag in my mouth, I grunted and protested. Jonas merely freed a chuckle laced in venom, mounted his charge, and yanked on the tether around my wrists. I stumbled at the pull.

Jonas leaned over his leg, eyes narrowed. "Keep up, Bloodsinger."

I was dead.

The prince tugged on the rope again, and I limped forward, the weight of suffocating failure pressing on my spine with each shuffled step.

What would happen to Livia if I did not reach her? Would Gavyn find her? Perhaps he could bring her home, get her free of the troubles of the Ever. She could . . . return to the peace I'd shattered.

My face tilted toward the sky. The stars were different here. Only Voidwalker would be recognizable, but he was at my back, hovering over the sea.

When I was gone, I hoped . . . I hoped the gods might let me live in both skies like Voidwalker. That way, I could always see her.

The warriors kept a steady pace. There were times I stumbled, and the earth prince didn't slow, merely told me to get up and

Excerpt from THE EVER QUEEN

quicken my steps. By the time we reached the ominous gates of the main fortress, sweat coated my brow, and my leg had long ago shifted from burning pain to sharp, numbing pricks, like stitching needles dug into every pore.

From one of the watchtowers, a warrior blew a curved horn. The procession halted for a bit at the gates, giving me time to catch my breath through the lump of sweaty leather.

Iron chains clanked; thick rope stretched and groaned as a heavy portcullis broke free of its resting place, allowing the warriors entry.

Eyes studied us, every damn move, as we made our way inside. Murmurs followed like shadows when the folk within the gates recognized me.

At the wide, arched doorway that would lead into the main hall, we stopped.

Jonas kicked a leg over the furs atop the back of his steed and dropped to the dirt. He leaned into a guard at the door. "Where is King Valen?"

"The tower, My Lord."

"Fetch him. Now!"

The guard seemed startled at the briskness of the prince's tone. It didn't take much to guess he did not speak in such a way often. No doubt most of the earth fae folk behaved differently since I'd robbed them of their princess.

Not so long ago, the windows had been draped in festive ribbons and shades. Stacks of sticky breads and sugared sweets had lined the table for their masque. Now, inside the hall, sweets had been replaced with pungent ale, swords, and scrolls of poorly drawn maps of what I guessed was their version of the Ever.

They were drawn wrong. They'd never find Livia by guessing, and they'd never get through the Chasm with their slender ships that looked more like sea serpents than vessels.

I couldn't die here, or she would die.

I knew Larsson could kill, and ruthlessly. I'd seen enough to give him the damn name of Bonekeeper.

Chatter ceased when Jonas pulled on the rope. "We have Bloodsinger!"

A few gasps followed. Blades were pulled off the table. With a great shove, Jonas knocked me down onto my knees. The leather fell from my mouth, and laughter rose against the rafters overhead.

Two boots, scuffed and coated in mud, stepped in front of me.

"Pick him up, Stieg," someone shouted from behind.

The man knelt. Slowly, I lifted my gaze to meet the warrior.

Stieg still had scars on his jaw that crept out from beneath his braided beard. One scar cut through his eyebrow, given to him while trapped in that room with me as a prisoner all those turns ago.

If anyone would listen, it would be the warrior.

"I didn't harm her," I rushed out in a quick breath. "I didn't harm either of them. You must listen—"

"I warned you," Stieg said, a touch of sadness in his tone. "I cannot protect you now, Ever King."

"Listen to me," I gritted out. "Your prince is trapped in the knoll, Stieg."

The use of his name furrowed his brow. Stieg rose, lifting me back to my feet. He kept his hold on my arm, spun me to face the hall, but flicked a hand at two men beside a narrow doorway.

When the men abandoned the hall, I dared hope.

Two paces away, Jonas still wore a vicious kind of grin, and now stood beside a man who shared his face. A brother. Livia had mentioned there were twin princes.

Black like the thickest ink spilled through the whites of their eyes with their dark magic.

Around the princes were warriors gripping blades until their knuckles whitened. Men, women, all of them studied me as if they hoped their eyes would peel the flesh off my bones. Close to Jonas was the woman who'd been beside Livia the night I took her.

She tapped a dagger against her dainty palm. Runes were inked down her forehead, chin, and throat. She, perhaps, looked the most ferocious of them all.

Doors to the side of me slammed against the walls, knocking two shields from their hooks, and the hall silenced like a wave leaving the shore.

There in the doorway, the earth bender king stood, axes in his hands, shoulders lifting and falling in heavy, angry breaths. Eyes that once held pity for a boy at the end of the war now burned in malice I could taste.

Stay, Erik Bloodsinger.

The man standing across the hall was not looking for peace. He wanted blood.

Red lined his black eyes with a touch of bloodlust. Dark hair spilled over his brow, unkempt and wild. A king of might and dignity during the war, now he seemed more beast than man.

I didn't have time to take in much of anything before Valen Ferus, killer of my father, spun one of his blacksteel battle-axes in his grip. Long, Night Folk fae legs had him across the hall in less than ten strides.

Stieg abandoned me in the same moment my back slammed against the stone wall. Air fled my lungs from the blow, then was blocked from returning when Valen used the handle of one ax to crush my throat.

"Where is she?" he roared in my face.

His words from so long ago filtered through my mind—*Stay.*

I was certain the earth bender king would see to it I would always remain. He'd make it so my bones littered this land until they turned to dust.

Keep reading for a preview of

BROKEN SOULS AND BONES

the first in a brand-new romantic fantasy series
from LJ Andrews, available now!

PROLOGUE

THE FERAL BAY of the king's hounds stirred her from the nothing. Mists tangled around knobby branches and the sting of lingering heat from the flames still burned in her eyes.

"Keep those closed." Leather-wrapped fingers brushed over her lashes. "Don't let anyone see the silver in those eyes, girl. Hear me?"

The voice was hoarse and rough, older than hers but not as deep as her pap's.

"We get snatched, then we're dead. Maybe we shouldn't have done it." A new voice, a boy's that was young enough it cracked and squeaked, uncertain if it was yet a man's tone or still a child's.

"Quiet. We're here now, and we're seeing it through," snapped the first. "Get yourself into the damn shadows and stay down. Go. *Go.*"

A petulant protest from the second followed, but in the end the scrape of boots faded into the briars of the wood and was lost in the mists. The girl shifted and whimpered, muscles aching from running. Her mother had told her to run—screamed at her to do it—and not look back.

Ropes held her tightly when she shifted, trying to break free, all at once desperate to find her family.

Through the haze in her mind she recalled the cruel sound of the door cracking against the wall, the iron and bronze blades cutting through the air, seeking flesh to split. She recalled the screams and blood.

So much blood.

"Stop fidgeting, godsdammit."

She froze. Those ropes keeping her bound were arms. And her cheek was pressed to cold leather that reeked of ash and sweat and the bite of forest mist.

Buried beneath a dark cowl she could make out a stubbled chin. Not bearded in long double braids and bone beads like her pap's, but a ghost of a beard was there.

She wanted to cry out, to plead with the man to let her be. There were straps of leather for knives and weapons over his shoulders, much the same as the raiders who burned her village. Fear choked off her pleas into nothing but jagged whimpers.

"Not a word, girl," he whispered, and she felt her weak body lower to the chilled forest floor. Brambles and little pebbles jabbed into her ribs. She tried to shift, but those leather-wrapped fingers curled around her chin, tilting her head back. "This'll sting, but it won't last long. Don't make a sound."

A hiss slid through the girl's teeth when a sharp bite of pain lanced across her throat. Through hooded lashes, she watched the faceless man pull back a knife. He mumbled strange words and brushed his fingers through something wet and hot on her neck.

She trembled, keeping still, terrified he might use the edge of his blade to finish her off.

In the next breath, her eyes fluttered, heavy with fatigue, and his sturdy arms scooped her up once again.

The fear burning in her veins faded to something gentler, something calm. Enough that the girl thought she might fall into a deep sleep.

Until her body shifted and she was handed over to new arms, thicker and smellier.

"She going to talk?" A smoke-burned rasp of a new voice broke the darkness.

"I've made certain she won't recall much of anything about this night. See that she's forgotten from others' memories."

"With what you be payin', I'll bury her in the realm of souls if you want. Won't be found, this one. You've my word."

Her pulse raced, her mind grew frantic, but her body kept still when heavy steps thudded across wood, and somewhere beneath it all was the lap of the tides and the smell of brine and rotting scales.

With a grunt and a breath of smoking spices in her face, the man nestled the girl beside rigging and damp linens.

"Blessed little barnon, you are." The man spoke in common tongue, a dialect known throughout the three kingdoms and over the Night Ledges where feral folk claimed no king. Doubtless he was a tide wanderer, a soul without a land to call his own. "They coulda torn out your skinny little throat."

His thumping steps plodded away over wooden boards—a longship. She was on a boat.

No, she couldn't leave. There were people she was leaving behind. But . . . who?

As though the thick mists of the wood dug into her skull, the girl could not recall the fading faces in her mind. It was merely a feeling, a sense there was something—someone—she was forgetting.

Before the weight of exhaustion drew her into a murky sleep, the girl saw a darkly clad figure on the water's edge, a glow of flames at his back.

Across the breast of his leather jerkin was a double-headed raven. The emblem of Dravenmoor—the enemy kingdom. The land behind the raiders.

By the gods, they'd found her, and the curse in her eyes had finally destroyed her entire world.

1

ROARK

THE BOY'S DEATH was my fault.

Uther was found face down in the river near the stone walls of the royal fortress before dawn. A new Stav Guard in the unit assigned to my watch, a mere boy of eighteen. The body was rent down the middle, chest flayed, ribs torn apart like a cracked goose egg.

He was sent to the hall of the gods in Salur too soon.

The flat cart holding the young guard's corpse rolled past a line of stoic Stav. The palace healer attempted to cover his pulpy face, tinted blue from a night in the water, but when the wheel struck a stone in the path, the linen pulled back.

My fists curled, digging into the callused flesh of my palms.

Uther's pale eyes were left open, too stiff to close, staring lifelessly at the noon sun in a wash of fright. Splatters of blood coated his neck, his lips, his shredded black tunic of the Stav.

"Dravens," a lanky Stav Guard murmured to another. "Had to be. Uther was a bone crafter."

I closed my eyes, despising the truth of it.

Tales of the different crafts of magic were written in the sagas of the first king, the Wanderer, who rescued a daughter of the gods. As a reward, the Wanderer was given pieces of the three mediums of the gods' power—bone, blood, and soul—to strengthen his fledgling kingdom.

Most within the realms of Stìgandr believed the tales were mere fables, but magical craft was real enough.

Bone craft manipulated bone into blades that were nigh unbreakable. It crafted healing tonics from bone powders, and poisons from boiled marrow. Blood craft used blood for spell casts and rune work. Soul craft took power from the dead, and was the common gift of Dravenmoor, the kingdom across the ravines.

Dravens despised King Damir of House Oleg, the king of Jorvandal, insisting he used craft to strengthen his warriors and armories through corrupt and forbidden ways.

I would not say they were wrong, but it did not lessen the rage in my blood that a boy was slaughtered for merely doing his duty.

"If I could, I'd burn every damn Draven on a pike," the guard went on.

His fellow Stav hissed at him to be silent, his gaze finding me—their superior and a Draven.

My blood belonged to the enemy kingdom, but fealty belonged to Jorvandal after being left for dead at the gates of the fortress a dozen winters ago.

But to some, even my own men, I would always be their enemy.

The heel of my boot cracked over the pebbles when I spun into the arched doorway of the Stav quarters, a longhouse built to fit dozens of men.

In the great hall, flames in the inglenook were dying to embers, and drinking horns of thin honey mead were toppled from recent nights of debauchery. Stav trainees had spent the cold months at Stonegate, but after the revelry, they were all now returned to their families and villages across the kingdom to await orders from the king.

A few younger Stav staggered to their feet, readying to greet me.

I could reprimand them for not standing by for their fallen brother, but at the sight of the green tinge to their faces, the red in their eyes, perhaps they simply couldn't bear it.

I ignored their murmured salutes and strode into the larger chambers meant for Stav officers. My chamber was more a wing than anything. A library and study, a bedchamber, and a washroom. I bolted the door behind me and crossed the woven rug to the washroom in ten long strides.

Along the jagged scar that carved across my chest, throat, to the hinge of my jaw was a roaring ache, like I'd swallowed the howling rage of the sea.

Bile rose in my chest, and a harrowing sort of shadow coated my gaze.

I gripped the clay washbasin, breaths sharp and deep.

Violence was no stranger to me, but it grew harder to keep the lust for blood tamed. I was the Sentry of Stonegate, and the Sentry was meant to be the stoic measure of restraint.

In this moment, I wanted to be more of a monster than those who'd slaughtered Uther.

Heat slowly faded as the storm in my head lessened. I cupped the frigid water in the basin and splashed it over my face, then returned to the bedchamber.

"You, my friend, have the most pitiful stomach. The sight of death and blood has you spewing? Honestly, what sort of royal guardian have I shackled upon myself?"

Startled as I was that another voice was in my chamber, I did not show it.

Sprawled out on my bed, ankles crossed, Prince Thane the Bold smirked back at me, likely aware I'd been berating myself. In my haste to reach the washroom, I'd foolishly left my chamber unchecked.

I frowned and it only widened his grin.

You are an ass and belong in one of the hells. My fingers moved swiftly in response, but Thane could follow even my most frenzied gestures since he'd found me outside the keep, bloodied and broken, my voice carved out the same as my place in my own clan.

"Really?" The prince chuckled. "Which one, the molten or frosted?"

Both. What if I'd had a knife in my hand?

"Roark, my oldest, dearest, most frightening friend, the better question is, Why *didn't* you have your knife in your hand? Growing careless, Sentry."

I shook my head and went to a personal cart topped with a wide ewer of aged wine and a horn. I filled only one horn when Thane waved a palm, refusing my offer.

"Jests aside," Thane said, kicking his legs over the edge of the bed, "you're taking this death too hard."

He was my charge.

"Roark." Thane sighed. "Don't blame yourself for the actions of those bastards. It is not your fault."

It was. In so many ways the death of the young Stav was entirely my fault.

We don't know why he was killed, I told him.

"We'll find out, and when we do, whoever is responsible will pay."

I used one hand to respond. *Why are you here? Isn't your mother forcing you to plan your own wedding?*

"There likely won't be a wedding if Stav Guard are getting slaughtered." Thane winced. "Apologies, I'm careless with my words in your state of distress. Allow me to try again. Yes, I've managed to slip my mother, flee the palace like a frightened child, and come to see you instead."

I let out a breath of air, a soft laugh.

Thane was a warrior prince from the golden ridge of hair braided down the center of his head to the bones pierced in his ear. He stood just taller than me, and I was no small man. But bony Queen Ingir and her endless revelry was enough to frighten away any man lest he be tossed into the madness of imported satins, silks, and different flavors of fillings for iced cakes.

"I've come for a purpose." Thane reached into the pocket of his trousers and removed a tattered, folded parchment. "You have heard of Jarl Jakobson, yes?"

The jarl obsessed with finding favor from the king?

Thane jabbed the folded parchment in the air between us. "The very one. He's made quite an interesting discovery."

The prince handed me the missive. I read it through once, then once more. Thane was no longer smiling.

My fingers gestured swiftly. *Jakobson is certain of this?*

"Seems my father's blood casts have finally worked."

King Damir couldn't claim the blood-tracking spells as his since the queen was the blood crafter in the fortress. Not that it mattered.

Seasons ago, King Damir took spilled blood from the house of the lost crafter. If any soul from the same bloodline came near, blood crafters would know it. The king's spells forced every village to have a royally decreed blood crafter within the borders.

All of it was done to find the child who'd disappeared. A child whose magical craft had brought three kingdoms against a small village in the knolls.

There was nothing left of it now.

"But there's trouble." Thane interrupted my thoughts, pacing in front of my doorway. "Jarl Jakobson's blood crafter has sold the woman out to Draven Dark Watch scouts."

So the missives speak of a woman? The child who escaped was said to be a girl, more reason for greed and bloodlust from kings and queens to seek her out. *Any house sigil?*

It was common in the kingdoms to ink a brand below the left ear of a child by their first summer, a mark of bloodlines and heraldry for houses and clans.

One of Thane's brows arched. "Said to be manipulated. Some of the runes were added later to make a brand of the nameless. Curious, don't you think?"

If one wanted to hide rare craft, adding ink to a house sigil until it looked like a waif-and-wanderer symbol—folk without clans or house bloodlines—would be the wisest action to take.

"The jarl found the correspondence between the blood crafter and the scout," Thane explained. "Of course, Jakobson now wants some sort of reward for being the township to unearth the lost craft."

The prince went to the tall arched window, looking out at the distant wood over the walls. "My father always suspected the reported death of the girl was a ruse. You know that's why he forced each jarldom to have a blood crafter casting their spells. After all this time, he was right. A melder has been hidden from the king. A woman." Thane shook his head. "The first in five hundred winters, Roark. You know what this'll bring."

War, was all I gave in a one-handed reply.

If this report was even true, there would be new battles from the Red Ravines of Dravenmoor to the small seas of the kingdom of Myrda.

Damir would not allow anyone to take his prize again, and the queen of Dravenmoor would return for retribution for what she lost during those raids so long ago.

A melder's craft was only found perhaps once a generation, and rarely in a woman's blood. It was a collision of all three crafts—dangerous, coveted, and owned by Jorvan kings through treaties made long ago.

"War is certainly a risk. Which is why you're to go to this Skalfirth village." Thane chuckled when my mouth tightened. "The king has already arranged for Baldur to go with you. What a fortunate bastard you are."

A soft groan breathed from my throat. Baldur the Fox was as cunning as his name, brutal but a damn skilled Stav.

We'd trained together since boyhood, but when I surpassed him in skill with the blade, he built up resentment toward me. My rank in the Stav Guard as Thane's Sentry made me the prince's blade, his protection; it required me to do anything to keep the royal blood in his veins from spilling, even becoming a killer in the shadows.

The Sentry was not a true leader in the king's Stav, more assassin and brute when needed. Still, my position kept me under Thane's word and not the king's.

Baldur spent the night after my ranking by drunkenly mocking me, as though I ought to be disappointed.

As though I had not been placed exactly where I wanted to be.

"I wish I could be there," Thane said. "But with the attacks, I doubt I will ever be permitted to leave Stonegate again. Not unless my father sires another son, but alas, my mother would need to allow her husband into her bed for that to happen."

As soon as the words were out of his mouth, the prince paused and shuddered.

What does the king wish us to do if it is confirmed the lost melder is alive? I gestured the question slowly, already anticipating the reply.

"Deal with the traitor who sold her out first, then use your methods to bring the melder home. Roark." Thane's voice lowered. "I know you don't always care for the craft of melders, but you must admit it has its uses to keep our people safer."

Debatable. My jaw pulsed.

Thane chuckled and rested a hand on my shoulder. "The king plans to increase patrols and move his ceremonies to more private locations. In fact, that is the other piece of this. Only select Stav will join you, guards who are sworn to secrecy. They will not speak of what you find in this village."

It wouldn't matter how the king tried to keep craft hidden behind the walls of the fortress. Blood and death always found melders.

The magic that ran in the veins of a melder crafted abominations that left souls and bodies corrupted, altered, and vicious.

Last harvest, the king's personal melder had been slaughtered. I felt nothing but relief with Melder Fadey's death. I thought, for once, there might be peace if melding craft were not here.

Gods, I'd almost allowed myself to forget the past wars, to forget lives had been lost trying to reach a small girl with silver in her eyes. Perhaps, I hoped, the Norns of fate had already cut her threads of life and sent her to Salur.

Maybe to one of the two hells to burn or freeze.

No mistake, now blood would spill again.

"We do this discreetly for as long as we can. We don't want another raid," Thane said, soft and low.

I closed my eyes against memories of distant screams, of smoke and burning flesh.

No kingdom escaped without loss. Thane lost his uncles. The smaller kingdom of Myrda lost its loyal seneschal and the queen's nephews.

Me—I lost my homeland and voice.

"You're to leave at first light," Thane said, clapping a hand on my shoulder. "Be careful, my friend. This woman will not be Fadey. I'd hate for her to bespell that dark heart of yours."

I scoffed. *I'd slit her throat if she tried. I have no love for melders, and that will never change.*